I0760461

Sun & Blood

Sun & Blood

Summary: Daughter of the alpha, Violet Draven discovers why she's different from the other wolven and must find ways to fend off a bully from another clan.

For information contact :
http://frostcrystal.com

Cover and Interior by Crystal Frost
Hardcover ISBN: 978-1-957051-01-7
Softcover ISBN: 978-1-957051-02-4

First Edition: March 2022

10 9 8 7 6 5 4 3 2 1

For my love, Richard,
Come what may.
Thank you for choosing me, beating the odds, and loving me every day since. Thank you for being the logic to my heart and the anchor to my wings. Thank you for deep throaty laughter and forehead kisses. Thank you for your undying support and encouragement of my stories – even if you think the sheer amount of them is insane, haha. One done, hundreds to go!

Sentinel Rising • Book 1

Crystal Frost

Chapter 1

Violet

THE CRACK OF BONE ECHOED ACROSS THE FIELD. *Spectators on both sides flinched as the pain-filled scream shattered the stunned silence.*

Violet's breath turned white in the cold January night air. A wave of nerves crashed over her while she, and everyone else in the bleachers, waited to learn who had been hurt.

Large, hay-bale walls surrounded the outer edges of the hundred-yard AstroTurf oval, making it impossible to see where the medics went after they found an opening and disappeared through it. Home teams had the privilege to place the hay walls wherever they wanted, but only Stanislaus Clan would stoop so low as to purposefully block the visiting spectators.

Even without the hay walls, Violet wasn't sure she would've been able to tell who was hurt anyway. Her vision wasn't as sharp as it should be and she struggled with dim lighting.

Surrounded by forest, with the moon barely starting to wane, the stadium lights at each end of the oval field were only half-lit. The Clan Games helped exercise teen wolven abilities, which included their night vision. As long as there was even a small source of light, wolven could see in the dark as if it were only nautical twilight—the second twilight phase where both the horizon and brighter stars are visible.

"I'm sure Jax is fine," whispered the cute brunette beside her.

Confusion pulled Violet's attention to Mya. Even in the dim light, she could see her friend anxiously wrapping her explosion of chestnut coils around her fingers.

It took longer than Violet would ever admit, to realize what her friend had said. Jax... Right... Mya thought Violet was worried about her twin. Which would make sense.

Guilt crashed over Violet. She tucked a long, dark chocolate strand of hair behind her ear and nodded, not trusting herself to speak. Jax should have been her first thought.

Closing her eyes, she focused on opening her mind and reached for her twin brother. Wolven connected to their clan alpha, luna, beta, and family through the clan link as soon as their wolf spirit emerged—usually around puberty. So, naturally, everyone around her had the ability to speak with someone directly through their mind. Everyone, that is, except Violet. Jax was the only clan member she'd ever been able to connect with.

Once Violet felt her brother's presence, she imagined herself poking at him as she asked, *"Are you okay?"*

"I'm fine." Jax's quick, grumpy voice floated through her mind. *"It was Aiden."*

A sharp yelp caused her eyes to shoot open and a collective gasp to fill the stands.

"The bone is set. They're bringing him out." Jax's next words were heavy with command, urging her to obey, *"Make sure he rests."*

Frustration poured through Violet and she pushed the emotion through their connection. *"No need to be bossy. I would have done it anyway."*

Jax had been giving her a lot of orders lately. In fact, she couldn't remember the last time he'd said please, or thank you, for anything.

"He's so aggravating," she grumbled.

"Who?" Mya stretched her neck to try and get a better view.

"*Your* future alpha." Sarcasm and annoyance dripped from each word as Violet turned toward her friend. The concern on Mya's face, however, made her settle. "Jax is fine. Don't look so worried."

Mya nodded, but her green eyes remained fixed on the wall of hay they couldn't see around. "Jax isn't the one I'm worried about." Her slow, airy voice exposed how preoccupied her mind was, "You shouldn't be so cynical about his future position. It's wonderful he is part of the alpha bloodline, and don't forget he's your future alpha too."

A sly smirk tugged at the corner of Violet's lips. "I suppose that's why your reprimand sounds so sincere."

Rosy pink flared across Mya's cheeks, amplifying the line of freckles across her cheekbones. "Sorry. I'm distracted."

"That part is obvious."

"I'm glad Jax is okay."

"I guess I am too," Violet teased, shoulder bumping her friend which made Mya grin before they both looked toward the field. "They should be coming off the field any second now with Aiden. It took a little longer because they needed to set a bone."

Mya's caramel skin had shifted to a sickly ash color when Violet turned back to her.

Realizing her mistake, Violet held up her hands. "He's okay. They set the bone. You'll see any second no—"

The crowd erupted with applause as the medics appeared between a small opening in the hay walls, Aiden centered between them. He raised his non-injured arm and waved to the crowd.

Relief sank Mya's shoulders, crumbling her spine. "Thank goodness," she whispered.

"You know..." Violet nibbled on her lip and wondered if she could play a bit of matchmaker. Her friend had been showing a lot of interest in Aiden lately but hadn't made a move. Maybe this could push them closer. "Jax told me to make sure Aiden rests. Why don't you go invite him to sit with us?"

Mya's face flushed once more and she twisted her hair around her finger. "I don't know."

"If you don't go talk to him, I will. Jax would kill me if I didn't follow his orders."

Her friend blinked at her, then coiled another curl around her finger and looked back at the sandy-haired Aiden with a thoughtful expression.

A grin tugged at Violet's lips.

Mya had been eighteen for three months now. She'd already gone through the trials, shifted into wolf form, and everything. The sudden interest in Aiden—someone she'd never really paid much attention to before—had Violet suspicious, especially since wolven were able to find their mates once they turned eighteen.

The moment he and the medics stepped off the field, a whistle blew from high above, and the game continued. Aiden waved the medics away and stood in front of the small opening he'd come from, shifting his weight back and forth, like he couldn't wait to get back out there.

"Okay. I'll just go talk to him." Mya nodded a second later as if she had to convince herself. "If I don't, he'll probably try to run back out there."

Violet chuckled and tossed one leg over the other as her friend hurriedly made her way down the bleachers.

The Blood Zone activated, drawing Violet's attention to a wolven seated atop one of the hay mountains with a paintball gun in his hands. Red paintballs flew through the air in rapid-fire, drawing the crowd to the edge of their seats… even though there wasn't much they could see.

If the field were visible, spectators might have been able to see the large red rectangle stretching from the home side to the visitor's side. Snipers from both teams sat atop hay mountains inside something resembling a crow's nest on a ship, watching for members of the opposing team. If hit, the player was sent to the opposing goal, and game points ceased for their team until that player was rescued by another team member.

Violet tipped her head back to cast a curious glance up at the nearest referee, seated twenty feet in the air, and watched him track something through the Blood Zone.

She followed the ref's gaze and not a second later, a Patrick-shaped blur sped past one of the openings before disappearing behind another wall of hay. Patrick was a scout. He was tasked with locating the opposing team's flag and rallying together the knights to retrieve it. He was one of the best, too. A lot of scouts were hit in the Blood Zone, but Patrick had never walked off the field with paint on his jersey.

"This setup has got to be the worst in the history of the Clan Games," said a familiar male voice from Mya's old spot.

Disappointed and unable to see anything else, Violet sighed and glanced at the guy who'd filled Mya's spot. "Hey, Tucker."

A grin spread across his well-formed mouth before he bumped her shoulder with his arm. "Enjoying the game?"

"Trying to." She tossed her long, high-ponytail over her shoulder and sighed. "But you said it, this setup sucks."

Amusement lit up Tucker's blue eyes, which stood out more than usual with the blue and white jersey he wore. "You know, it's completely open on the other side."

"What? Really?" Violet's back straightened. "Those jerks purposefully blocked the visiting team?"

"Yup. I only know that because we get to walk the field before the games. Do you really expect anything different from Stanislaus Clan, though?" Tucker tipped his head toward her, making his jaw-length, dark blond hair fall into his face. "They've always had problems with us."

Violet nodded her head in agreement.

Clan territories were set and adjusted by the lycan kings and queens. Wars were no longer an issue unless sanctioned by said kings and queens, which very rarely happened. The biggest threats were rogues and the Blood Moon pack, which Violet had only heard rumors about. They weren't considered a clan because they didn't have their own territory, never stayed in the same place, did not follow Lycan Law, and were notorious for bloodshed.

That being said, it didn't stop clans from having rivalries.

Violet chewed her bottom lip for a second then launched to her feet. "Wanna sneak over to the other side with me?"

Mischief swirled through Tucker's eyes for a second before he cleared his throat and thrust his chin toward the field. "As much as I admire your reckless behavior, I'm swapping out with Patrick in just a minute."

Unlike human sports where team members had to stay with their team and coach at all times—inactive wolven team members were allowed to wander as long as they stayed nearby. Games had no time limit and could potentially continue for days if an opposing team's flag was never found. Time outs only happened if someone was in need of medical care, and penalties were extremely rare. Swapping out team members was done informally, so as not to interrupt play or distract the other players. Everything done during the Clan Games was meant to help teach; including building responsibility to find and swap out with your teammate efficiently.

"Well, there goes my plan of watching you play."

Tucker tilted his head to the side, expressing his curiosity.

Folding her arms, Violet kicked her hip out to the side. "Patrick's my brother's personal bodyguard for me, remember? There's no way he'll let me go over to the dark side."

His grin spread at her *Star Wars* reference. "Don't tell him I suggested it, but you could go now before I'm called out there."

Violet's gaze zeroed in on Aiden and Mya, who were shamelessly flirting right outside the field boundary lines. At least he wouldn't be trying to join the game anytime soon.

"You know." Violet grinned. "I think I'm going to take you up on that suggestion."

Tucker's brows lifted and his lips curled into a full-blown smile, softening the harder lines of his jaw and cheekbones. He stood and offered her a hand to help her down the bleachers, which was ridiculous, but also very sweet.

"Don't get caught," he whispered once they were both standing on the ground.

She leaned into him a little. "Me? Get caught?" She pulled her fingers from his grasp and practically purred, "Never."

Silver enveloped the blue in Tucker's eyes when she dragged her bottom lip through her teeth for the "v" sound.

Oops.

Wolven's eyes changed color when their emotions were heightened, which meant she'd pushed her flirting a little too far. Needing to distance herself, she turned to leave, but he caught her elbow and spun her around to face him.

"You're trouble. You know that?"

Violet lifted her chin, craning her neck a little to look up at him. Tucker stood at about six-one, maybe six-two, which was average-ish height for a wolven male. She barely pushed five-four, average for a human, not a wolven female.

"You're only in trouble if you get caught," Violet whispered.

A sly smile slowly spread over Tucker's face, then he drew in a quick breath as he leaned down—

"Violet!" snarled an angry male voice behind her.

She groaned and dropped her head forward. "I'm in trouble."

Tucker snickered. "Your bodyguard has arrived." He took a step back and nodded toward the guy now boring holes into the back of her skull.

Warmth traveled up Violet's chilled spine as Patrick stopped inches from her.

"Tucker," he spoke over Violet's head. "I've searched along the home side and the Blood Zone. Make sure you get in and out of there as fast as you can. They have a pretty accurate sniper. He almost got me."

Shocked, Violet turned her head and saw Patrick tugging his jersey to the side. A few tiny flecks of red paint were splattered across the blue and white fabric near his hip.

"With how Stanislaus laid things out, it makes sense that their flag would be closer to the visitor's side. It would be easier to conceal."

"Unless they're cheating," Tucker growled. "I wouldn't put it past them."

"I guess you've got your work cut out for you, then."

Tucker dipped his head in a nod. He tossed a small smile in her direction and walked away.

Stepping around the mountainous Patrick, Violet watched Tucker throw one last look in her direction.

He winked, then disappeared behind the hay.

"Jax is not going to be happy about this."

Violet continued staring at the hay wall before her as she innocently asked, "Happy about what?"

"You flirting with Tucker," Patrick grunted.

"Tucker's a nice guy."

"Not nice enough," he growled, making the hair at the top of her head stir with his breath.

Annoyance zipped through Violet's veins. She whirled on her twin brother's best friend and lifted her chin so she could glare at him. Craning her neck back for Tucker was easy compared to Patrick, who stood six and a half feet tall and was currently standing toe to toe with her. Dark loose curls, kept short on the sides with a few inches on top, fell over his forehead when he lowered his chin to meet her stare. His gorgeous golden-flecked hazel eyes were filled with a heat Violet didn't understand.

"You don't get to tell me who I can and can't date, Patrick." She'd meant it to sound authoritative, but her words came out a whisper. Why did he have to stand so close?

He searched her eyes as if looking for the lost piece of a puzzle. After a deep breath through his nose, he took a step back, putting some much-needed distance between them. "I'm only telling you what Jax will think."

"If it were up to Jax, Violet would never date," Mya interrupted and smiled broadly at Patrick. "Speaking of dating, where is your current girlfriend?"

A loud groan rolled out of him. "She's not my girlfriend and thankfully she had to work tonight."

Violet scoffed. "Seriously, if she's not your girlfriend, why do you tolerate her?"

He shrugged a shoulder. "Free scones."

Mya shook her head. "Wow. That answer was just about as bad as she is."

"Mya!" Violet rounded on her friend, surprised by her attitude. Usually, she was determined to be nice to people.

"What?" Mya looked at her with wide eyes. "She is horrible to everyone. She's only nice during her shifts at the cafe and that's only because she wants more tips. Besides." A mischievous glint lit her green eyes. "You could do so much better, Patrick."

Violet bunched her lips together and shot her friend a warning glare. "Well, if his track record is anything to go off of, she'll be gone within the week. Isn't that right?" She patted Patrick's arm.

He didn't answer.

He just watched her.

Violet's hand slowly slid off his arm as the sorrow in his eyes seeped through her. The emotion was gone a second later, replaced by his meticulously crafted mask of calm.

"Anyway, at least Violet has good taste in guys and there are plenty of options," Mya interrupted, and the tendon in Patrick's jaw twitched.

Violet smirked at her bestie and raised a brow. "Like Aiden?"

Dipping her chin, Mya tried to hide the blush that consumed her face. "I'm calling dibs."

Violet chuckled. "He's not really my type, don't worry."

"No, your type is tall, blond, and gorgeous blue eyes."

A low growl rolled out of Patrick, making both girls look at him with wide eyes... but his attention had been pulled toward the field.

Violet returned her attention to Mya. "You do realize that Tucker is pretty average height for the clan, right?"

"Most males are six foot. He is six-two. He's tall." Mya gave her a pointed look. "Especially to you."

Violet snorted. "Just because you're as tall as Wonder Woman doesn't mean you can dis my height."

It was true. Mya stood at five-ten, the exact height of Wonder Woman, and a pretty average height for female wolven.

"What height?" Patrick mumbled, proving he was listening even though he was staring out at the field... or rather the hay walls.

Violet elbowed him in the stomach and he grunted. "No need to be rude."

The corner of his mouth ticked up in a smirk and he cast a playful side-eye in her direction. "Fine. You're not short. You're fun-sized."

Her eyes narrowed. "Like a freakin' candy bar?"

"Why not?" He shrugged. "You never stop eating them. Maybe they stunted your growth."

The teasing glint in Patrick's normally hard eyes made it impossible to fight the smile pulling at the corners of her mouth. She shook her head and was rewarded with a twitch of Patrick's lips.

People often gave Violet nicknames based on her height, but Patrick had so many, and more than half of them referred to food; "short stack", "chipmunk", "half-pint", "pint-sized", "nugget", "small fry", "short stuff", "munchkin", "shorty". "Fun-sized" could now be added to the food side of the list. One of the first nicknames he'd ever given her struck the wrong way and "kitten" was never used again. It was the first time she had stood up to Patrick and he had looked equal parts terrified and amazed.

"Maaaaybe I was wrong," Mya thought out loud. "Maybe your type is really tall, dark, and hazel."

That snapped her out of it. Violet lurched back, returning to an acceptable distance from Patrick. If Jax had seen that, it would have been a lot worse than anything Tucker-related.

"I don't have a type," Violet grumbled, dropping her gaze to the ground. That was both a lie and a truth. The truth was, there had only ever been one guy Violet really liked... the lie... well, there was only one guy, so he was her type.

The one guy she'd given her word to never date.

She stole a glance at Patrick only to find him watching her, again. Heat flooded her face. She opened her mouth to try to dig herself out of the situation, but the Blood Zone exploded with rapid-fire, drowning out her words.

Which was probably a good thing because knowing her track record, she would have just made it worse.

Jax's voice rang over the chaos, "Man, we are getting creamed out there!" His sweaty dark hair flopped a bit as he jogged over to them carrying a lacrosse stick. "I'm getting worried we're not gonna win, even if we do find their flag."

"What's the score?" Violet asked, while subtly taking another step away from Patrick and toward her twin. "We can't see anything from over here."

"Not good, that's what it is. They keep sending our clan mates to the cage, including Tucker, who's only been in for about a minute, so we can't score anything." Jax propped his stick on the ground and his gaze quickly swam over her—a common practice he started developing when it became obvious she was weaker and he felt the need to protect her. His violet eyes were a near-perfect reflection of her own, but his were often hard, missed almost nothing, and had a habit of swirling liquid gold—the color of an alpha.

Hers were just purple.

"Doesn't help that they're playing dirty." Patrick stepped up beside Violet—making her take a step to the side to keep a respectable distance—and crossed his arms.

"What do you mean?" Violet asked.

"They broke Aiden's arm," Patrick growled. "That should have cost them all of their points, but the refs acted like it was an accident."

She looked up at the nearest referee. "Maybe they've been paid off."

"There isn't any other explanation."

Aiden's slightly higher tone interrupted their ramblings, "I'll be fine." He wiggled the fingers sticking out of his sling as he came up beside Mya and threw his good arm casually around her shoulders.

Mya looked like she wanted to melt on the spot.

"It doesn't hurt at all anymore," Aiden continued. "A few more hours and it'll be as good as new."

"They snapped your forearm, Aiden!" Jax yelled, drawing a lot of attention. "Both bones!"

"Why don't we take this conversation away from the stands?" Violet hissed the suggestion and pulled on Jax's arm until he followed her, which made the rest of them follow, as well. She rounded the field, placing them in neutral territory where all the concessions were, before releasing her twin's arm.

"What is wrong with you?" she growled, turning on her brother with narrowed eyes. "Do you want to start a fight?"

Crossing his arms, Jax snorted. "I would love to go after a few of those Stanislaus pri—"

"And if you did, you would send our entire clan over there!" She back-handed his arm. "Let go of your emotions, and get your head on straight."

Usually, Jax was the one leading the way. He was the future alpha after all, but lately, he'd been increasingly hot-headed. It felt weird to be scolding *him* for a change.

Jax glared at her. "Are you trying to tell me what to do?"

"Easy," warned Patrick, who stood to Jax's right.

The pressure of Jax's aura was staggering. They wouldn't be eighteen for a couple of months, but his authority already made most of the clan submit to him.

Mya shifted her weight, staring at the ground. Aiden kept his amber-brown eyes lowered, but moved so he was slightly in front of Mya. Patrick lowered his chin, but his attention switched between Jax and Violet.

Annoyance flared within Violet. She felt his power, but she didn't feel the need to cower.

"I'm not *trying*, Jax." She crossed her arms, mimicking his stance. "You want to settle this? Then find a way to beat them fair and square. You start trying to pull what they're doing and the refs will call it. You go after their team and you'll disqualify us."

Liquid gold swirled into Jax's purple eyes. His mouth opened, but a low laugh from behind her stopped whatever he was about to say. The gold overtook the purple and a growl rumbled through his chest at the same time a shiver rolled up her spine.

"You're gonna let a little snack like her tell you what to do, Draven?"

The gravelly voice of Vikter Stravek made Violet clench her teeth as she spun around. If looks could kill, Vikter would have been reduced to ash—starting with his perfectly styled, short, blond hair and designer clothing.

Although the haughty future alpha of Stanislaus Clan had never really bothered her before, Jax and Vikter had a rough history. The two had been paired as opponents in last year's Clan Duels, where sparring tournaments took place. Jax had broken Vikter's nose and things only got worse between them. That was enough for her to go on the defensive, especially since she was now standing between the two of them.

"Snack?" Violet growled, scrunching one side of her nose.

Vikter's golden eyes lazily drifted over her. "It's a reference to your height. As in, I could eat you up in one bite." He snapped his teeth together and a couple different growls sounded off behind her.

"What is up with everyone comparing me to food today?" Feeling her aggression shift to annoyance, Violet leaned her weight to one side. "And what does that make you? The big bad wolf?"

His dark chuckle sent a wave of unease over her. "Something like that."

"Take your huffing and puffing somewhere else. We're busy." She sneered at him, but instead of moving away, Vikter took a step closer.

Jax gripped Violet's shoulder hard enough to make her flinch, but he didn't seem to notice as he moved in front of her. "Get out of here, Stravek."

Vikter held up his hands. "Whoa, easy there, Draven. I'm just saying hello."

It was always weird to Violet how the two of them called each other by their last names. Like they had to make the point that they weren't friends so badly that they couldn't even be on a first-name basis.

"Fine, you said it. Now leave."

"I'm not done talking to my snack."

"Stop referring to me as food!" Violet snapped.

"Only I can do that," Patrick muttered under his breath and Violet may have laughed if she wasn't so surprised to see him nearly shoulder to shoulder with her... well... shoulder to elbow. Man, she really was short.

Sighing, she turned back to Vikter who was smirking at Jax. "I have no interest in talking to you, so we're done."

Her nails dug into Jax's bicep when she tried to pull him away, but he didn't budge this time.

"Afraid of a little confrontation, Draven?" Vikter taunted.

Violet's head tipped back as she groaned. That was not helpful.

Jax snorted. "You wish."

"Jax, let's go." Aiden walked around her and clamped his free hand on her twin's shoulder. "You're needed back on the field soon."

Mya twisted her curls around her finger as she stepped beside Aiden. "He's right. You need to get some water and sit down for a bit before heading out there again."

Tension slowly eased out of Jax's shoulders and Violet just about hug-attacked Mya.

"Yeah, all right," Jax muttered as he backed up, not taking his golden eyes off Vikter until he was a good twenty feet away.

"Hey buffer-boy," Vikter called.

Violet urged Jax to keep moving, pulling on his arm once more and grabbing his shirt, but his feet had slowed the moment Vikter called out to Aiden.

"I suggest you learn how to block." Vikter snickered. "That or... I dunno... make sure your arm isn't pinned when someone stomps on it."

Her hands were empty.

Violet spun in time to see Jax leap off the ground and drive his fist into Vikter's face when gravity reclaimed him.

"Jax!"

If their sudden brawl hadn't drawn attention, her shriek did. A wide circle spread away from them as she raced forward, yelling at her twin to stop.

"This isn't worth it!" she yelled when she reached his back, mimicking his movements as Vikter attacked again. Her nails dug into his sides, desperately trying to break his concentration on the perceived threat. "You'll get Sentinel Clan disqualified!"

"You better listen to her, Draven." Vikter's fist collided with Jax's shoulder, knocking him into her. "Unless you think you can win."

He threw a combination of punches and Jax moved so fast that Violet was briefly left unprotected. Thankfully, she was far enough away that Vikter's knuckles missed her by a couple inches, but she felt the wind on her face.

"You've never beaten me in the duels, don't start thinking you can now," her twin warned, and his fist connected with Vikter's stomach.

Violet took his moment of pain to jab Jax in the side. "Jax, we need to go!"

Vikter's head knocked to the side when Jax's left hook caught him unawares and he stumbled back a few steps. Jax'd been proud of that move since he mastered it a month ago. With the majority of people being right-handed, it wasn't often someone threw a hook with their left. Typically, people threw a hook with their stronger arm. He'd even surprised their father.

Black spots darkened her vision before Violet could comprehend what had happened. Her head snapped back and her butt hit the ground. Years of training moved her muscles automatically, rolling her through the impact so she rolled over her shoulder and landed in a crouched position. The world spun and she lowered one knee. Her eye watered and her cheek stung.

Jax had hit her. Not intentionally of course, but his elbow had knocked her backward.

A thunderous roar ended all other sounds and a shadow leapt over her.

Mya dropped to her knees in front of her then took Violet's face gently in her hands. "Are you okay?"

The slightly blurry form of Aiden appeared and he sucked in a sharp breath between his teeth. "We need to get her home. She doesn't heal as fast as we do. I'll grab some napkins."

Flustered by the attention, Violet waved them off. "I'm fine."

"You're going to have a nasty black eye; it's already swelling." Mya held her chin firmly, looking over Violet's face.

Huh. That would explain why it was hard to open her eye.

"He hit you hard enough to break the skin. I'm sure you'll be able to cover most of it with concealer."

"I don't wear concealer," Violet grumbled as her head throbbed. She tenderly felt her cheekbone and pulled her hand back to find blood smeared across her fingertips.

Aiden had barely made it back and handed the napkins to Mya when he yelled, "Patrick!"

Violet whipped her head around and moved to follow him as he darted toward the others, but then the world tipped over.

"Woah!" Mya grabbed her shoulders, keeping her from falling over. "Maybe don't move that quickly."

She drew in deep breaths until the world stopped moving and Mya held the wad of napkins against her face.

Taking the napkins from Mya, Violet slowly began looking around. Vikter was a good thirty feet away, crumpled on his side, with a nasty head wound that was bleeding a fair amount.

A couple of people were crouched around him, but none of them seemed very concerned. With his alpha status, he would heal in a few minutes.

The more shocking image was Patrick holding Jax against a tree, his feet dangling a good foot off the ground.

"Patrick!" Violet yelled, and regretted it instantly. She smashed the heel of her free hand against her head and winced.

"Stay out of this. He's just mad that I hit you." Jax's voice ricocheted off her skull and the pain nearly made her throw up.

When her stomach stopped threatening to leave her, she held her hand out toward Mya. "Help me up, please?"

With widened eyes, Mya shook her head, making her curls bounce. "I don't think that's such a good idea."

"Please?"

Bunching her lips together, Mya nodded.

It took a couple seconds to get her feet under her, but once they were, she handed her bloodied napkins to Mya and told her friend to stay back as she staggered toward Patrick and Jax.

"Put me down, Patrick," Jax's order was clear. Many nearby wolven bowed their heads or flat out left the area.

Patrick didn't move.

Aiden stepped closer to help, but Jax shook his head, and the currently still injured wolven stepped away.

She was almost within arms reach when Jax's voice infiltrated her head once again. "*I told you to stay out of this!*"

The pressure on her head was too intense. She sank to her knees as a small cry escaped her lips. With her hands over her head, she missed Patrick dropping Jax and both young men rushing to her. They called out to her, but their words weren't clear.

Something that smelled of chocolate peppermint with a hint of cedar dropped over her, lending her comfort and warmth. After an impossibly long minute, her head started to clear. Patrick's jacket was resting over her while he and Jax bickered in whispers a few feet away.

"Patrick?" She practically whispered his name, but he was there in an instant, down on one knee and holding her hand. "Can you take me home?"

Playing on the protective bodyguard within him had been her plan all along. If Jax hadn't tried to explode her brain, she was sure she could have deescalated the situation with ease. Patrick had always protected her—always made sure she had what she needed and felt safe.

A shaky sigh filled the pounding silence around her as he closed his eyes briefly, then sighed. "Yeah," Patrick answered softly in a voice that was low and rough. "I can do that."

"Are you sure you're okay to drive?" Jax asked.

"She's safe with me," Patrick's growl was low and threatening.

Jax nodded and patted his best friend's shoulder as if he hadn't just been pinned to a tree. "I know. But, are you okay to drive?"

Patrick nodded.

Sighing, Jax squeezed Patrick's shoulder. "I'll let Coach know you had to leave." He began walking away when he stopped to look over his shoulder. "I'm sorry, Violet. I didn't mean to lose control."

If she thought she could answer without throwing up, she would have, but the nausea was too much. She'd see him later anyway.

People gawked when Jax walked away. No reprimand. No challenge. Nothing.

But they didn't know the relationship that Jax and Patrick had. As long as things went according to plan, Jax would be alpha one day, and Patrick would be his beta. That didn't explain moments like this, when it appeared Patrick had the upper hand, but it was Jax's ability to remain calm that really set him apart. Where most alphas would lay into their betas, Jax met Patrick with understanding and compassion.

She hoped he would run the clan that way someday, but then there were moments when his thick skull got in the way... like with Vikter.

Mya tentatively approached, returning the napkins to Violet as she eyed Patrick. "Are you sure you'll be okay? If you want, I can take you home instead."

Softly squeezing Patrick's hand, Violet looked up at Mya. "I don't want to take you away from Aiden. Go have fun. Patrick won't let anything happen to me."

A tentative smile slipped over Mya's face before she nodded. "I know." She tossed a look behind her at Jax and Aiden's retreating backs, gave Violet a little wave, then hurried off to join the other boys while she called over her shoulder, "I'll check in on you later."

Vikter began to stir and a growl rumbled out of Patrick. He helped Violet to her feet, then held her steady while she found her footing.

They'd made it about halfway to Stanislaus Clan's visitors parking lot when his arm wrapped around her waist, "Come here." His gentle tone pulled her toward him, just as much as his arm did.

There, surrounded by nothing but trees, Violet allowed herself to melt into Patrick's hold. She pressed her non-throbbing cheek against his chest so she could keep the napkins against her cut and closed her eyes, listening to his rapid heartbeat.

"I'm okay," she whispered, knowing he would hear her.

The racing of his heart began to slow and he pulled back to gaze down at her. Sadness pooled behind his beautiful hazel eyes, making her suck in a shuddery breath. He'd never looked at her that way before.

Ever so gently, he pulled her hand and the napkins away from her face. His palm cupped her jaw as his thumb traced just below her cheekbone where it stung. "I'm sorry. This shouldn't have happened."

"I stepped into the fight."

"I should have stepped in sooner, so it never got to that point."

"All that would have done is turn the fight into two on one, and then more people would have joined Vikter, and it would have kept growing from there." Violet shrugged a shoulder. "My cheek will heal, and at least I don't feel like I'm going to throw up anymore."

"You're probably right." He nodded. "I'm not a doctor, but I don't think you need stitches. I'm more worried about infection and concussion."

She scrunched her brows together. "I'm wolven, remember? It's incredibly rare for us to get infections. The concussion part, though..." She put the napkins back on her face. "Yeah. I'd be surprised if I didn't have one."

Patrick released her with a grim look on his face. "Let's get you to the real doctor, so she can diagnose you herself."

Chapter 2

Violet

***THE RIDE HOME TO SENTINEL CLAN** was pleasantly uneventful.*

Patrick kept a mostly one-sided, quiet conversation going the whole ride. He wasn't really talking about anything, but it was enough to keep Violet engaged and awake.

By the time the wrought-iron front gate came into view, the sting in Violet's face had turned to a throb and her head was still pounding. Two wolven males in black tactical pants and Under Armour long sleeve shirts materialized from the shadows and approached Patrick's truck. One went around the back, checking under the vehicle and inside the truck bed with something that resembled a large mirror on a stick—not that there had been a bombing or a stowaway in years, since the kings and queens stopped clan wars, but it was still better to be safe than sorry. The other guy came to the driver's side window and casually rested his forearms where the window usually was... wait... When had Patrick rolled down the window?

"You're back early from the game." He nodded to Violet, then turned back to Patrick. "How'd it go?"

"It wasn't going well when I left," grumbled Patrick as he drummed his fingers along the wheel. "We're pretty sure Stanislaus is cheating."

Shaking his head, the guard sighed, "Let the alphas work it out."

"Jax already tried." Violet piped up, gesturing to her face. "The jerk's got a stick up his—"

"Jax did that to you?"

A quiet growl filled the truck and Violet eyed Patrick as he explained what happened.

"Good on you for trying to stop them, but next time, let Patrick or someone else handle it." The guard patted the truck as he stood, missing Violet's glare. "All clear!"

On his command, the gates began their slow process of opening, and Patrick rolled his window up. Patrick's truck was old, but he took great care of it and it purred like it was still young. The truck didn't have powered windows like all cars nowadays, which meant he had to circle his arm about repeatedly to get the window to move.

"I'm not helpless," Violet grumbled once his window was completely closed and they'd passed the front gate.

Patrick's sigh made her cross her arms. "He didn't say you were."

"He told me to let someone else handle it. Doesn't that kind of imply anyone *but* me?"

"You're looking at that the wrong way. He doesn't want you to get hurt. No one does."

"I dodged all of Vikter's attacks, Patrick."

His jaw pulsed. "There was one that would've hit you."

The breeze that had brushed her face as Vikter's punch fell short had shown just how close she'd come to getting knocked out. "I was out of range anyway."

"You wouldn't have been if he was fighting you instead of Jax. You're not as fast as the rest of us."

"You think I don't know that?" Violet slapped her hands onto her thighs to keep from hitting him. "I'm reminded of that fact every day!" She groaned when her raised voice increased the pressure in her head.

They both stayed quiet as the truck rolled over a large wood and steel bridge. A wide river rushed beneath, cold and fast. During the summer you could catch the more daring wolven tubing down the water, but Violet had never been a fan of the river.

Patrick broke the silence as he nearly whispered, "We'll add some more speed work to your training."

Sighing, Violet turned to stare out the window. He didn't understand.

How could he? Everyone knew he was stronger and faster than Jax. Some even wondered if he was stronger than Alpha Draven. More than a few felt he should be the future alpha, not beta. He had no idea what it felt like to be slower and weaker.

A mile separated the front gate from the inner one and neither of them spoke again until they neared the second gate. Two giant wolves with luminescent bronze eyes fell in step with the truck—the black one winked at her and Patrick revved the engine, making the wolf pin his ears to his head and snarl. The tawny one wisely stayed back and did his job, sniffing around the truck.

Violet clutched the door and her seatbelt when the truck jumped, making Patrick swear, and the front end nearly lifted off the ground.

Rolling down his window as fast as possible, Patrick yelled, "Justin! Get off my truck!"

A large tongue swept across the back window and the black wolf shook with laughter as he pranced in the truck bed, rocking the truck from side to side.

"Justin!" Patrick yelled again and although the volume of it caused a spike of pain across Violet's head, she laughed at the playful antics.

A pale-blond woman stepped forward from the gate, snapping at Justin to get back to work. The black wolf whimpered before leaping from the truck bed and bounding into the trees with the tawny wolf close on his heels.

"Stupid mutt," grumbled the woman that Violet couldn't remember the name of. She threw her long braid over her shoulder as she stared after the two wolves. "You're clear, Patrick. Good to see you, Violet." She lowered her chin in respect and submission before stepping back to allow Patrick to drive through.

The community parking lot was inside the gate to the left. Unless someone bought a car specifically for themselves or, like Patrick, showed up with one, cars were shared with other members of the clan. With Sentinel Clan's member count somewhere between five hundred to a thousand, they didn't have the parking space for everyone to have their own vehicle, anyway. Cars were only ever used if you left the base, so it was easier to have one large parking lot than it was to build a driveway or garage for everyone. Some wolven hadn't ever left the compound, which was something Violet couldn't understand. There were times when the fences around their wolven community, even though their land was vast, were stifling to her.

Within ten minutes, Patrick had walked her to Dr. Penmann's tiny clinic, never taking his hand off the small of her back. It was what he had fallen back on when she wouldn't let him hold her arm to support her. Wolven of all ages, both in human and wolf forms, moved out of their way as they walked up the dirt street to the small doctor's office where a single, small lantern swayed in the breeze above the door.

The receptionist smiled and directed them back to one of the two patient rooms. No questions. No paperwork to fill out. Unfortunately, Violet was a regular here. Plus, wolven couldn't exactly keep normal records. If someone were to get hold of them it could cause a lot of problems.

It didn't take long for Dr. Penmann to knock on the door and stick her head in.

"Hello," her raspy voice filled the silence that had fallen over the room. Her beaming smile faltered when she took in Violet's face. "Oh dear, what happened?"

Violet sighed. Her back slumped and she resisted the urge to facepalm herself. "I tried to stop my brother from attacking someone."

The doc eyed Patrick. "Did it work?"

He nodded. "It ended quickly after that."

Gesturing to herself, Violet added, "His elbow said hi to my face."

Dr. Penmann's lips pinched into a thin line and Violet tried not to look at the two scars running horizontally along the doctor's neck. Rumor had it that the female wolven's throat had been slit when she was younger. If it hadn't been for the healing power of her wolf, she would have died.

Supposedly, it had taken years for her to be able to speak again.

"With your birthdays drawing near, I'm afraid Jax is feeling the pressure of his alpha bloodline. He's been wound a little tight lately," she explained as she grabbed a few things from one of the cabinets and brought them over to the exam table where Violet sat.

"A little?" Violet mumbled then flinched when the doc pressed something cold and wet to her cheek. "That stings."

"I have to clean this out, but you don't need stitches." There was no apology and Violet was okay with that. It's not like the doc was purposefully trying to hurt her.

Patrick cleared his throat from his position leaning against the counter with his arms crossed. "Does she need to be worried about a concussion?"

The doc finished with the cut on Violet's cheekbone, then checked out her eye before answering Patrick's question. "Has she shown symptoms?"

"I felt like I was going to throw up—"

Dr. Penmann's hand froze against her cheek and worried lines deepened across her forehead.

"I'm fine now. I haven't felt that since before we got in the truck."

Seeming pleased with that answer, the doc continued working on her cheek.

"I just have a really bad headache and light and sound hurt," Violet offered, looking between Patrick and the doc when she finished. "Do those count?"

Dr. Penmann nodded. "Those are common symptoms. If you were anyone else, I'd say you'll be fine by morning. For you, it could take a couple of days before you feel like you have a clear head again. You need to rest. Avoid screens, light, sounds... anything that aggravates your head."

"So, what am I supposed to do then?" Violet growled, not liking the sound of this.

"Nothing." She smiled at Violet and patted her knee. "I know how much you love that, but get some rest. Rest is the best thing for you right now."

"But I need to train," Violet argued.

Patrick stepped forward, shaking his head. "A couple days off won't hurt. Besides, Doc knows best." He gently rested a hand on her shoulder. "I'll walk you home."

"Actually, there are a couple of other things I need to discuss with Violet." Dr. Penmann smiled apologetically at Patrick. "Ones that you are not privy to."

His jaw pulsed, but he nodded. "Understood. Do you want me to wait outside?"

The question was clearly directed at her, but it took Violet a moment to realize that. "Oh... uh... no, I'll be okay. I'm going to go home right after this."

With another nod, Patrick said goodbye and left.

"I was going to call you in for a follow-up, but seeing as you're already here and I don't have another patient at this moment, why don't we meet right now?" Doc clasped her hands together in her lap and smiled softly.

Violet shrugged nonchalantly even as her heart thundered in her chest. "Sure."

Dr. Penmann wet her lips, taking her sweet time to start talking. "We need to go over the results of your blood work."

The doc's grave tone shot spikes of fear through Violet's limbs. "What? Do I have cancer or something?"

Humor lit Dr. Penmann's eyes and she raised a brow. "Wolven don't get cancer."

"Well," Violet mumbled, shifting a bit uncomfortably on the exam table. "I'm not exactly a normal wolven, now am I?"

"No," she sighed, "You're not."

When the doc didn't continue, Violet raised her brows, waiting for an explanation.

With a huff of laughter, Doc said, "You do not have cancer."

"That's a relief."

"However," Doc's serious tone stamped out any relief Violet had been feeling. "There are some abnormal markers in your blood work."

Panic flooded her veins. "Like what?"

"I... don't know," Dr. Penmann admitted, pressing her fingertips to her forehead and rubbing the spot between her eyebrows for a second. "It's something I've never seen before."

"What... what does that mean?"

"I honestly don't know," the doc repeated.

"But you know everything about wolven blood."

Dr. Penmann's face took on a grave expression.

"Wait." Violet's brows pinched together. "Am I not entirely wolven?"

The older female didn't respond.

"That's not possible." Disbelief colored her voice as she continued, "Both my parents are wolven. My *twin* is wolven."

"I understand." The doc nodded, holding up her palms in a peaceful gesture. "And I agree. It shouldn't be possible."

Violet's eyebrows shot toward the ceiling. "Shouldn't?"

A large sigh deflated the doctor's chest. "You are aware that twins are unheard of in the wolven community, right?"

Violet nodded. "Jax and I are the only ones I know of."

"You are the only ones *at all*." Dr. Penmann clasped her hands in her lap again. "I've been researching everything I could get my hands on about wolven twins since I took this position. There isn't much because twins don't exist. Not as a complete set, anyway."

At least four blinks happened before Violet managed, "What?"

"It's only a theory, because there is no science to back it up, but the theory is that only one wolven spirit is given by the goddess to each pregnancy. That spirit then goes to whichever wolven child is stronger and the weaker of the two doesn't survive."

"For how long?" Violet's eyes widened. "Am I dying?"

"No, Violet... they don't survive." The doc paused, but seeing that Violet wasn't understanding, she tried again. "In all the accounts of wolven twins, not one reported both babies surviving. One of the twins always passes away. Most die before they are born, by miscarriage or stillbirth. A few live hours. The longest I have ever found is a day."

"A day?" Violet repeated. "So... what?" Her head shook as she tried to process this information. "I'm not supposed to exist? I'm some kind of fluke?"

The gray stool the doc sat on squeaked when she stood. "I honestly don't know. We are dealing with uncharted territory here. I think it's safe to say, you will never heal as fast as we do..." she pressed her lips together, as if realizing her mistake in words, "... as fast as the rest of us do."

Violet's gaze lowered to her lap. "You say that like I'm not wolven."

"I misspoke. You are wolven. You have the genetic markers. No one can question that." A gentle hand landed on her shoulder and Violet looked up into the doc's brown eyes. "Most wolven your age, actually *all* wolven your age have made contact with their wolf spirit by now. They have linked with their pack, or at least their families and alphas. The only person you are able to link with is your twin. You haven't connected with your wolf. Your eyes have not changed color. You show no signs of completing the transition."

"What is it you're not saying?"

"Violet," Dr. Penmann sighed, and for whatever reason, that made Violet's entire body tense. "It is very possible that you will never have a wolf."

There were no words to convey the void that filled Violet.

"You have heightened strength and speed. Heightened senses. You heal faster than the average human. But your wolf traits..." the doc trailed off, shaking her head.

Anger punched through Violet at an alarming rate. "So, I'm basically just a souped-up human."

"I believe so. You are stronger, faster, and have better senses than humans. As big as that advantage is, you have just as much of a disadvantage compared to wolven." The sad tone in the doc's voice cooled Violet's simmering rage. "We will continue to monitor you, run more tests if that helps, but... there is another thing you need to know and consider."

"And what would that be?"

Dr. Penmann closed her eyes briefly as if steeling herself before giving the news. "Without your wolf, it's possible that you may never find a mate."

Silence roared in Violet's ears. When she found her voice, a whisper came out, "What?"

"There is still a chance. Wolven have found mates in humans before, but those occasions are extremely rare and there is no record of them being able to reproduce. Now, none of this is..."

The doc's voice faded away and a ringing filled Violet's ears. All this time, and she'd been worried about the wrong thing.

For more than a year, she'd stressed over the possibility of finding her mate and having them reject her for being weak. No one wanted a weak mate. A lot of wolven wanted to better their bloodlines. Sure, she had alpha blood coursing through her veins, but if she didn't have a wolf and couldn't have children... there weren't very many who would even consider her. Which made her chances of finding a mate even less.

She could always go the route of finding someone who had been rejected or lost their mate, but those had a bad track record of being unstable and ending very badly.

Dr. Penmann patted her knee, making her jump. "There is too much that we don't know right now."

How long had she been zoned out?

She felt oddly hollow. Even the throbbing in her head was dulled.

"I understand," Violet heard herself say, but her voice was raw.

"Would you like me to have someone come get you? I could inform Alpha and Luna for you..."

"No," Violet shook her head, regretting it instantly as the room spun and her head pounded in protest. "I'm fine."

With a nod, the doc patted her knee again, gave it a soft squeeze, then led her to the door. "Your mom should be home. I don't want you to be alone right now."

"Okay."

"Rest for a couple days. Take time to process this. Then you can resume your usual schedule."

Violet heard herself agreeing with the doctor before she stepped outside into the dark cold January night.

The biting chill usually nipped at her nose and fingertips, but she felt numb as she made her way toward Alpha House. She thought someone called out to her at some point, but her focus was on the red home looming over her. With a sigh, she walked across the stepping stones to the porch and opened the front door with drooping shoulders.

"Mom, I'm home." She kicked off her shoes to the side of the door, just inside a small sitting room before walking through the entranceway.

The family room in the Alpha House opened up into the kitchen and dining area. Off to the side, through an archway was a small pentagon-shaped breakfast nook where Violet was often found on rainy days. She loved listening to it fall while she sat inside, dry and cozy, wrapped in a warm blanket. Everything was decorated modestly in a farmhouse style, but other than her mom, people rarely stayed here long. Alpha Draven's office was through a door to the right of the dining area so wolven were seen coming and going day and night from the back door. They used to have a kitchen table, but it was just in the way so they gave it to another family. Typically, they were too busy to eat together so they ate at the counter or on the go.

Evalyn Draven sat at a small desk she had placed between the kitchen and the family room. Her real office was upstairs, but she'd always preferred to be where all the hustle and bustle was.

Violet smiled when her mom's head snapped up, making her glasses slip down her nose a fraction. "There's my little miracle."

With the enhanced eyesight of the wolven, glasses weren't needed, but her mom spent eight or more hours staring at a screen every day, and she swore the blue light filter helped with any eye tiredness. She ran communications between other clans and handled a lot of the finances for their clan as well. Her ability to type was unmatched. Even now she sat at her desk with her laptop, tapping away at the keyboard furiously while looking at her daughter. Sometimes that freaked Violet out, other times she thought it was really cool.

"What are you working on?" Violet asked as she closed the door, wanting to talk about anything other than herself. She crossed the room and wrapped her arms around her mom's shoulders. Their dark chocolate hair fell together over her mom's shoulders and Violet stared at the similarity in color.

"Jax informed me about the altercation between him and Vikter Stravek. I'm trying to get ahead of the fallout and send an email to Stanislaus' Luna. Hopefully, we can talk it out over lunch or something."

"The duties of a Luna never end. You should let Dad handle it."

As the mate of the alpha, the luna was widely respected. As the female alpha, she supported and worked beside her mate, taking care of things he didn't have time for. Unfortunately, Violet had never seen it reciprocated.

Evalyn sighed and finished the last sentence before sending it. "You know your father would turn it into some sort of championship tournament. Alphas run too hot-blooded."

Violet snorted, then pinched her eyes closed against the pain it caused, "You married him."

After flicking her arm playfully, Evalyn worked on closing multiple windows on her computer.

Marriage wasn't necessary with wolven, and beyond a quick court appearance to receive a paper that the human government demanded, most didn't bother with any fanfare. The government allowed them to continue as they were because they followed certain rules. One of those was that each mated couple be documented. It was stupid, but it was a small price to pay to be left alone.

"Honestly," Violet thought aloud, "a tournament may not be the worst idea. Jax needs to work out some tension."

With a final tap to the keyboard, Evalyn's lithe fingers wrapped around Violet's arms and lovingly squeezed. "Then he can do that in the arena, here. I don't need him beating another future alpha into a pulp."

A quiet chuckle left Violet before she leaned over her mom's shoulder and kissed her cheek. "Do you have a minute to have some hot chocolate with me, Mom?"

She spun so fast in her seat that Violet had a hard time tracking it. Her large gray eyes searched her daughter's face, lingering on the cut along her cheekbone before she smiled softly. "I always have a minute for you."

That's all it took. An offering of hot chocolate and they knew the other needed to talk. Their own mother-daughter code.

Evalyn took Violet's hand and placed a gentle kiss on her knuckles before leading her to the kitchen.

Both mugs were nearly made—Violet's doubled the size of her mom's—before either of them broke the silence.

"Do you remember the frozen hot chocolate I brought you?"

A smile tugged at Violet's lips. Gently stirring her hot chocolate, she nodded. "It was incredibly hot outside and you thought a cold dessert drink would be better than a hot one."

Evalyn laughed, "It was a brilliant idea, you have to admit it, and it was delicious."

"It was!" Violet agreed and her own laughter mingled with her mom's. "But it wasn't the same."

"No, it wasn't." She reached over Violet's shoulder and sprayed a heaping amount of whipped topping in her mug. "Warm things are always more comforting."

After thanking her mom for the creamy deliciousness, she cradled her mug close to her chest. "You can't discount a pint of ice cream and a good movie."

"Of course not, but those are for when you need to cry it out." Evalyn winked.

They made their way to the couch, both sitting with a leg tucked under them so they could see each other. A couple minutes passed while they enjoyed their hot drinks.

With a sigh, her mom nudged Violet's foot with her own. "Are you going to talk, or did you really just want a cup of hot chocolate?"

Chuckling sadly, Violet shook her head. "No... I mean, yes, I always love hot chocolate, but I really do need to talk to you."

Over the course of the next few minutes, Violet explained what had happened at the tourney event, then her conversation with Dr. Penmann. Evalyn sat quietly, only snorting at her alpha-blooded boy and complimenting Patrick for knocking some sense into him. Her expression remained mostly impassive, ever playing the part of the Luna, until Violet mentioned the possibility of never having a wolf.

Tears lined Evalyn's eyes. "You'll have a wolf, my little miracle."

"You don't know that," Violet's voice was near a whisper.

Her mother didn't often express her emotions so visually—a trait learned and needed for leading an entire clan. She had to keep her face clear of emotion when dealing with clan issues.

"I do," she promised. "You are the daughter of two alpha bloodlines. It would be impossible for you not to have a wolf."

"I'm turning eighteen in two months, Mom. I haven't even felt her presence. I can't connect with anyone other than Jax, and I..."

"I know what Dr. Penmann said," Evalyn interrupted and placed a reassuring hand on Violet's knee, but to her, it felt like denial. "I'm telling you... She. Is. Wrong."

Violet shook her head. "How can you be so sure?"

She shrugged. "I'm your mother. I know everything."

A snort, that thankfully didn't feel like it was stabbing her brain, left Violet as she lifted her mug to her lips and took a long drink. "What about the mate thing?"

Evalyn's brows pulled together. "Wolven can go most of their lives without meeting their mate. They could be in the same clan or they could be halfway across the world. There is no guarantee you'll find them. It's not like a homing beacon goes off in your head the minute you turn eighteen."

Even with her tumbling emotions, a smirk lifted one corner of Violet's mouth. "Who would want a mate like me anyway?" She was half-teasing, but her mom's contemplative expression turned stern. "I'm the shortest wolven I've ever known. Not even counting all the other stuff, I am really short."

A slow smile spread across her mother's face, easing the serious expression, and her eyes sparkled. "I believe Patrick calls it '*fun-sized*'."

Violet's eyes bugged. Heat flooded her face and she felt it cascade down her neck.

"I think it's cute." Her mother raised a brow as she took a drink of her hot chocolate.

"I um... how do you know..."

The back door burst open, making Violet jump and slosh hot chocolate over the rim of her mug and onto her hand. Lightning quick, Evalyn grabbed a napkin off the little coffee table in front of them and handed it to her. A towering man with broad shoulders stepped into the kitchen and eyed them.

"Hot chocolate night..." he grumbled, scratching the scruff on his chin. "I'll make myself scarce."

"Nice to see you too, Dad."

Alpha Draven's eyes narrowed on his daughter. "Next time, don't step in the middle of a fight between alphas. It could get you killed."

"Noah," chided her mom. "Now is not the time to have that conversation. You should be saying you're glad it wasn't any worse."

Just like that, his gaze slid to his wife and mate, and the hard edges softened. He took five large strides and pressed a kiss against her lips that made Violet look in any other direction she could.

"Sorry, Evalyn," he whispered. "My beautiful Luna."

"I think I lost my appetite," Violet grumbled. Although it was nice to see her father actually had a soft side, considering he'd never directed that kindness toward her, it was also disturbing.

When her parents ignored her, her gaze settled on the black wolf sticking his nose through the doorway. He dipped his chin respectfully then moved out of sight. A few seconds later, he stepped into the kitchen barefoot with a shirt dangling from his teeth as he tightened the strings of the too-big sweats he was borrowing.

He pulled the shirt from his mouth and smirked when he noticed she was still watching him. "Hey, Violet. How's the face?"

She had no idea if he was mentioning the swollen eye and cut across her cheekbone or the fact that her face was practically in flames at this point, after being caught watching him... so she ignored his question altogether. "You're Justin, right?"

He chuckled and pulled the shirt over his head. "Yeah, the one that rattled your boyfriend's truck earlier. He's fun to mess with and that truck was just too tempting."

"I don't have a boyfriend," Violet answered automatically in a near robotic tone.

"Uh, huh." He winked as he walked around the counter and grabbed a cup from the cupboards. While he filled it to the brim with water, he studied her face. "That's why he's always around you, huh? Cause he's *not* your boyfriend?"

Violet cast an uncomfortable look at her parents. The mated couple were saying things so quietly in each other's ears that even with her slightly heightened hearing, she couldn't understand from three feet away. She probably didn't want to know.

With that disturbing thought, she pushed off the couch to join Justin in the kitchen.

"Actually, that's exactly why he's always around me. Jax ordered Patrick to guard me." Violet leaned her hip against the counter and shrugged, but Justin's brows creased. "He's been guarding me since he showed up three years ago, and I'm pretty sure he would kill anyone who tried to be my boyfriend—on Jax's command."

Justin dipped his nearly empty cup toward her face. "Doesn't look like he's doing a very good job."

Ducking her chin did nothing to hide the smirk that jumped across her face. "I may have threatened Patrick a couple of times to let me do my own thing." She lifted her gaze to find Justin grinning from ear to ear. "I don't like being controlled."

"You have the wrong brother for that." His warm laughter lifted the last of the chill that had settled over her since talking with the doc.

"Don't I know it," she chuckled.

Another man walked through the back door, just as broad as her father, but a few inches shorter. Graying hair along his temples and a hard weathered look in his brown eyes were the only indicators of his age. He greeted her mom with a nod of his head, and reverently said, "Good evening, Luna."

"Good evening to you too, Beta Paul." Evalyn smiled at him before he disappeared to his left, into the clan office.

Alpha Draven pressed a gentle kiss to Evalyn's forehead before moving for the office as well. "Justin, I believe you have reports to give?"

The young man nodded, quickly setting his cup in the sink, then said goodbye before stepping through the office door.

Alpha Draven grabbed the door handle, but before he disappeared, he cast his gaze on Violet who lifted her chin defiantly. The look in his nearly dark blue to white ombre eyes was as confusing as ever. Disgust. Disappointment. Anger. There were even times Violet would have sworn she saw hatred. Right now, the most prominent ones were disappointment and a look of defeat.

He opened his mouth, as if to say something, but seemed to think better of it and disappeared into the office.

"He does love you, Violet. I hope you know that." Her mom's soft voice pulled her attention away from the door.

She snorted. "*You* love me. He tolerates me."

A sad smile lifted her mother's lips. "Do you still want to talk?"

Sighing, Violet lowered her half-finished hot chocolate into the sink. "Nah, I'm tired. I think I'm just gonna head to bed."

"Okay." Evalyn placed her own empty mug beside Violet's then wrapped her in a hug. "I love you. Everything will be just fine. You'll see."

"Thanks, Mom." Violet buried her nose in her mother's hair, breathing in her scent of vanilla and cinnamon. "Love you." she kissed her mom's cheek then made her way up the stairs.

"I'm sorry." Jax's voice rang through her mind just as she made it to the second-floor landing and she crashed to her knees, clamping her hands over her head. *"Are you okay?"*

A quiet whimper left her as she leaned against the wall. *"I get it. You're sorry for being a jerk and hitting your twin sister. Please, don't talk to me like this."*

His anger stabbed through her mind, *"Excuse me?"*

"I have a concussion!" she snapped at him. *"You're hurting my brain, dufus."*

The scorching pain his anger had caused eased. *"Sorry. I'll talk to you later."*

Groaning, Violet pushed herself off the floor and managed to make it to her room. She wasn't quite sure if she closed the door or not before she collapsed onto her bed.

Chapter 3

Patrick

FURY SWEPT THROUGH PATRICK IN WAVES, *making his hands shake every so often as he stalked toward his apartment.* Going for a run hadn't cooled him off like he'd hoped it would and then he punched a hole through one of the bags at the gym. He was going to have to pay for that.

To top everything off, his newest fan-girl stepped in front of him just before he made it to the commons building.

A nasty snarl snapped out of him, "I'm not in the mood, Genie."

Disappointment sank the brunette's shoulders as he pushed around her and grabbed the door handle. "How many times do I have to tell you, Patrick? My name is Gianni."

Releasing the door, he clenched his fists as his wolf fought for control.

"Let me out." The deep voice that was eerily similar to his own held a promise of violence that Patrick desperately tried to control.

Patrick shook his head. "You shouldn't want to be with someone who can't be bothered to remember your name."

She tipped her head side to side, making her perfectly curled, brown hair sway. "You'll get it. It's not that big of a deal."

"I won't get it, because I don't care."

She flinched and guilt dug at Patrick's chest.

A snort of derision sounded in his mind. *"Don't feel bad. She isn't our mate."*

"If I have anything to say about it, we will never have a mate." Patrick fought back against the darkness inside his mind.

"You cannot keep me from my mate!"

"I will do everything in my power to keep you away from everyone till the day I die," Patrick promised, then refocused on the girl in front of him who was watching warily.

"What if we're mates?"

Patrick ran a hand down his face. "Do you really think we are?"

"I don't know." Gianni shrugged. "Neither of us are eighteen yet."

Annoyance rolled through him on a wave of anger, announced through the growl that escaped his control. Gianni quickly withdrew a step, fear swimming in her blue-eyed gaze. Another stab of guilt made Patrick close his eyes, draw in a deep breath, and imagine a steel wall blocking his wolf half.

When he opened his eyes again, that wary look was back in Gianni's eyes, but the fear wasn't completely gone. "You're afraid of me."

She parted her lips to deny it, but no sound came out.

"Why are you chasing after a guy that scares you?" Patrick shook his head at her. "I am not trying to frighten you; I've had a really bad day, and don't want to deal with this right now."

Even a blind mind would have been able to see the shift in Gianni's tactics. She pulled her shoulders back, sucked her lower lip between her teeth, and batted her lashes flirtatiously as she stepped toward him, but the movements were unnatural and made him tense. "I could take your mind off things. You could kiss me… take me to your room…" Her fingers walked up his chest as she spoke.

A disgusted groan left Patrick. He grabbed her hand and not so gently shoved it away. "When have I ever given you any indication that I wanted to be with you in any way?" His low growl darkened each word. "I haven't even accepted any of the free scones you've offered me when I come into the cafe."

Tears lined Gianni's eyes. "I should have listened to the other girls. You just toy with us before dismissing us. Why are you dating at all? Do you even want a mate?"

"No!" Patrick snapped and she took another quick step away from him. "I have no interest in ever finding a mate. I thought that not paying attention to all of you would have made that clear, but you keep showing up until you get frightened enough to leave. I don't want a relationship with any of you, but more and more girls keep clinging to me."

Confusion and then anger pinched Gianni's face. "Nobody stays away because you act as if you're searching for your mate. You haven't taken any girl on an actual date, you haven't kissed anyone, you haven't gotten too handsy—which some of us have been very disappointed about. The worst you do is get angry, scare us, and forget our names!" She stomped toward him and stared up into his tense face. "No one believes you're off the market. All you're doing right now is brewing curiosity."

"I'm not trying to brew anything," Patrick growled, and his voice slowly rose in volume as he continued, "I have no interest in completing the bond. Even if I did, neither of us are eighteen yet, so we wouldn't know if we were mates, anyway."

Resentment passed over Gianni's face. Her shoulder slammed into his bicep when she pushed past him. "In case you weren't about to end whatever this was, I am. Good night, Patrick."

Annoyed and flabbergasted, Patrick waited until her footsteps began to fade before he continued to his room. 'Whatever this was', indeed. It wasn't anything! Plus, she was wrong. He had taken a few girls on dates and even kissed a couple—all outside the Sentinel Clan and all he regretted.

Patrick burst through the commons door, startling a young woman who, by the look of her tactical gear, was on her way to patrol. He mumbled an apology as she darted around him, then continued his musing.

The first girl he took on a date was from Stanislaus Clan. He thought a casual relationship would be a good distraction—It wasn't. The second time was a girl from Whisky Clan and it filled him with indescribable agony.

The third, was by Alistair's doing and Patrick vowed to never allow his wolf half to have that much control again.

It didn't help that the beautiful, dark chocolate-haired girl that filled his mind was one he shouldn't have been focusing on.

Patrick unlocked his apartment door and slammed it behind him, making the picture in the commons hallway fall to the floor. He grumbled, opened his door again, and placed the picture back on the wall. Thankfully, this particular picture didn't have any glass.

He made sure the frame was centered, then returned to his room. This time, he closed his door much softer.

If he'd had any sort of decorations in his place, they probably would've crashed to the floor, too. As it was, his apartment looked more like a showroom than a lived-in space.

In the small sitting area to his right, rested a faux leather couch that faced off two armchairs. To his left, was a space for a tiny table, but it was left empty and the only chairs available were pushed under the island top. A small kitchenette was there, but he typically ate in the Clan House with Jax, so it didn't hold much of anything. The small hallway allowed for a tiny coat closet, then led into the only bedroom with an attached bathroom. It was a small place, and often felt confining, but he didn't need anything bigger.

Right now, the area felt suffocating.

"I wouldn't mind having a couple females in here." A low, rougher version of his own voice echoed in his head and Patrick growled. *"It would even out your stench, at least."*

"Don't pretend you would be comfortable having one of those females, Alistair. I've felt your discomfort right alongside mine," Patrick snapped at his wolf.

"Of course, I would prefer Violet, but..."

"Don't say that! Don't even think that. She is off-limits," Patrick snarled and the sound echoed in his living room.

Alistair's dark chuckle filled his mind. *"Maybe for you."*

"Where is Jax?" Patrick grumbled out loud and Alistair laughed at him again.

The future alpha had said he would meet Patrick at his apartment so they could talk, but when Jax'd returned to clan territory two hours ago he said it could be a while. That's why Patrick had gone for a run and then hit the gym... to keep from tracking his friend down and punching him in the face.

Patrick ran a hand through his curly, dark hair. Hopefully, that drive didn't take over when Jax actually did show up.

"He'd deserve it."

"Shut up," Patrick growled at the dark, tantalizing voice in the back of his mind. *"Stop reading my thoughts."*

"That is entirely impossible. We are one. Your thoughts are my thoughts."

"Yeah, right. I do not want the same things you do."

"Come on. You know he'd let one good hook slide," Alistair pressed. *"If you hit him just right, you could even knock him out and—"*

"I'm not having this conversation with you again, Alistair. I don't want Jax's rank," Patrick snarled. *"Back off!"*

Alistair's menacing laugh vibrated through Patrick, and he tried to shake off his darker half. His blasted wolf never seemed to understand Patrick's dislike for power. He didn't want to be alpha. Even *if* he could take it. And *if* that happened, then what? A lycan king would show up to try and approve of his reckless act to appease the clan.

They'd look into his past.

All Hell would break loose.

He'd lose everything.

Again.

The click of his door opening snapped his reflexes into action. He was at the door before it fully opened, grabbing a fistful of Jax's shirt without thinking.

"You'll be right here, huh?" Patrick growled and Jax carefully set his expression in neutral. "It's almost midnight."

"You know I had to debrief my dad. Come on, let go." Jax tapped Patrick's hand, but the light gesture lit fire to the gallons of gasoline pumping through his veins.

Slamming the door shut with a kick, Patrick shoved Jax toward the couch. Patrick took a step back as well, wanting to distance himself from his best friend in case his wolf decided to try and take that swing.

"What is going on with you tonight?" Jax asked, straightening his shirt before he slumped onto the arm of one of the chairs and rested his hands on his legs. "Actually, it's not just tonight. It's been the last few days."

A growl rippled through Patrick.

Jax raised a brow then rolled his palms over to face the ceiling. "Really?"

"Sorry," Patrick snarled, not sounding remotely as apologetic as he felt. "But you've had this coming."

"What?" Jax snorted. "Why?"

"Aside from ten other reasons I could give you—you hurt Violet today. Remember?"

He shrugged. "She's fine."

Ringing filled Patrick's ears. "You hit her hard enough to draw blood, Jax." His eerily calm tone threatened violence. "You gave her a concussion."

"And she will heal. Besides, it's not like I did it on pur—" Jax doubled over when Patrick's fist connected with his stomach. "Geez!"

Satisfaction and mortification twisted Patrick's insides as he stepped away, breathing heavily while he ran his hand over the back of his neck. "You hurt her, Jax! You asked me to protect her and I always have. I always will." Frustration beat down the mortification and he rounded on Jax again who glared at him. "I never thought I'd have to protect her from you, but I will if I have to."

Jax blinked. Shock rippled across his face, dropping his jaw a fraction.

With a shake of his head, Patrick shoved his hands into his pockets. Maybe that would keep him from punching his best friend again.

"You know I didn't mean to hurt her. I would never do that."

"But you did," Patrick grumbled, his shoulders sagging. "And you have been. You've hurt her more than you realize with how much you've isolated her. You think you're protecting her, but it's causing more harm than good."

Jax's gaze flared liquid gold. "I'm protecting my little sister, Patrick! I don't want her to have bad friends or fall in love with a guy that isn't her mate. There are so many guys around here that would take advantage of her simply because of her bloodline and the girls are even worse—thinking they will get special privileges for being her friend, or get closer to me."

"She can make those judgment calls on her own. Violet's smart."

"You think I don't know that?" Jax yelled, making Patrick pause. "You think I don't realize how smart my own sister is?"

Patrick's eyebrows pulled down. "No, actually I don't."

Jax glared and opened his mouth to retaliate, but Patrick wasn't finished.

"When was the last time *you* sat beside her while she worked on homework a normal fourth year in college should be doing? When was the last time you stood behind her while she helped another pack member figure out the mess of emotions they were going through or a messy relationship? When was the last time you watched her fight, Jax? You know she's witty and can dish out just as well as she can take it, but do you have any idea how great of a warrior she is?"

"In the training ring, maybe."

"Because you won't let her do anything else! You're not protecting her, Jax. You're trying to control her."

Jax blinked at him several times, purple slowly overtaking his gold irises, but wisely kept his mouth shut.

"I gave my word to you that I would protect her." Patrick's voice trembled with the effort it took to fight Alistair back as he raged that Jax didn't care. He did care. Patrick knew that. "But I will not be her jailer." Shoving his hands deeper into his pockets, he stalked toward Jax. "And if you ever harm her again—"

Turning his palms forward, Jax's answer was soft and cautious. "It was an accident."

Alistair pounded against the wall built in Patrick's mind, snarling to be let out. He could feel the shift in his eyes and molten gold swirled within Jax's gaze in response. He stared, slightly wide-eyed, back at Patrick.

"I. Don't. Care," Patrick growled through clenched teeth. "It happens again and *you* will be the one unconscious on the ground."

Shock registered for a second across Jax's face before he lowered his brows and growled back, "Did you just threaten me?"

Well, crap.

That was exactly what Patrick had just done. He had threatened his future alpha.

His knuckles ached from clenching his fists so tightly inside his pockets.

"I don't want your position, Jax. I never have. If I ever did knock you out, I wouldn't press my claim, but yes… I did."

Their staredown lasted longer than it should have. Patrick wouldn't back down, but Jax *couldn't* until he did. With Alistair snarling in his head, Patrick forced his gaze to lower with a grunt. A challenge like that would only lead to a fight for power, which was exactly what Patrick didn't want.

Clearly, they both needed a minute to cool off.

Patrick turned on his heel and strode to the fridge, nearly ripping the door off its hinges when he opened it. He winced, took a deep breath, and pulled out two water bottles. The tremors in his hands had subsided by the time he tossed the second bottle at Jax, who caught it in one hand.

With a huff and a shake of his head, Jax dropped his gaze, not something a future alpha should do, but it showed he still trusted Patrick and that meant more to him than he had words to say. "You know, sometimes I think there's more to this than just protecting her. Unless you take all your jobs this seriously. Maybe I should rescind my order and make you my bodyguard instead."

A snort escaped Patrick and he took a long swig of his water. "You don't need a bodyguard. You need a conscience to beat you over the head with a stick."

Word had spread through the nearest clans about what Jax did to those who were interested in his sister. Whether they were guy or girl, it never ended well for them. Some of guys consequences had even been dealt out by Patrick's own fists.

When Jax didn't pick up on the fact that Patrick had ignored the first part of his statement, he allowed his shoulders to relax a little. He was playing a dangerous game. His feelings went way beyond *interested,* and if Jax ever realized that…

"Then I guess I better get you a stick to beat me with."

Pulled from his thoughts, Patrick blinked at his friend. A smirk had lightened Jax's face. Slowly, Patrick released a tense breath and allowed a smile to slip over his own face.

"I'd rather use my fist."

A burst of laughter left Jax. "I'm sure you would." He sobered up a bit before continuing, "I am sorry about earlier. I already spoke to Violet about it and we're good. So, what about us?"

"You know I'm going to confirm that with her," Patrick warned, then shrugged. "But yeah. We're good."

Jax finished off the water bottle and eyed Patrick suspiciously before slipping off the arm of the couch to take a seat on the cushion. "Seriously, what's up with you lately?"

"I could ask you the same thing."

"Easy," Jax answered while Patrick made his way to the armchair across from him. "My dad is pushing more and more responsibilities onto me, I have a constant headache, and apparently I'm running a little hot-blooded since Dalim is getting stronger and can't fully connect with me until my birthday." He scrubbed a hand down his face. "He wanted to lay into you for punching me in the stomach, by the way."

"Alistair wanted me to knock you out," Patrick grumbled. "I figured your stomach was better than your face." Sighing, he slumped back into the armchair. "I get it. I feel like I'm constantly on the edge of biting someone's head off."

Jax crossed his arms and shrugged. "Try to give me some warning before you hit me next time."

A dry chuckle left Patrick. "I'm trying to make sure there isn't a next time."

"You've only got two weeks left. It will go fast." Jax slapped his hands on his knees. "Speaking of—we have a party to plan!"

Patrick groaned. That was the last thing he wanted to do.

Chapter 4

Violet

WHILE EACH OF THE HOMES IN SENTINEL CLAN *had a kitchen, most wolven preferred to gather for meals in the centrally located Clan House.* Unless the area was being used for other social events, round tables were set up across the large, gymnasium-sized room and staff members were always working to provide free, fresh-cooked food. Who would turn that down?

Not to mention the massive walk-in pantry was always stocked with the best goodies. The kitchen staff were extremely protective over it—they had to be with a pack of hungry wolven roaming around—but Violet had special privileges... or at least she used to.

Violet stretched as far as she could, rose up onto her tiptoes, then lifted one leg as if that would give her the extra five inches she needed. With a groan, she planted her heels back on the ground and put her fists on her hips. A low growl rolled within her.

Her head still ached from the concussion she received two days ago.

Her emotions were everywhere.

Cookies were needed.

Chef Mira had stepped down last month and the guy who replaced her seemed determined to deprive Violet of all her M&M cookie needs. He was seriously pushing his luck.

Opening her twin-link, Violet mentally screamed, *"Jax!"*

"Ow!" hollered a familiar voice within the Clan House.

Clamping her lips together, Violet peeked around the pantry door to find her brother seated a few tables away with his hands clamped over his head.

"Violet!" he yelled, quickly turning on her as his eyes flashed liquid gold.

A few people ducked their heads, even some on the second-floor mezzanine, submitting to the pressure thrown by his alpha aura.

Violet looked at her brother innocently and shrugged her shoulders. "Sorry."

Jax shoved away from the table, followed by his shadow, Patrick—who reluctantly pushed away from his meal.

"I thought you said link communication hurt your head?" Jax snapped. "And how many times do I have to tell you not to abuse it?"

"It's not like I can link to anyone else." Violet crossed her arms and kicked a hip to one side. "And yeah, when you used it, it made my head throb, but apparently I can use it just fine today without any problems."

Being twins, Violet and Jax had been able to communicate wordlessly since before she had memories. Their mom would swear by the light of the moon that they were communicating the moment they were born. Like a true future alpha, Jax had been able to connect with more and more people in the clan as the years went by.

Angry, bitter feelings mixed with an unhealthy dose of jealousy swirled within her chest. Two days was not enough time to process the doc's news, especially the part where Violet wasn't even supposed to exist.

"I just need someone tall to grab the M&M cookies. Chef Merik is being unfair," Violet grumbled.

Jax glared down at her. "You couldn't just ask?"

"I didn't know you were in here!" Violet snapped back, frustrated that he was mad at her and that she was jealous. She hated being jealous.

"Maybe next time you should look before attempting to explode my brain!"

His volume made her flinch as pain sliced through her head.

Patrick growled a warning, but she had no idea who it was directed at.

Rolling his shoulders back, Jax grumbled an apology, surprising her. "I'm glad you're doing better."

Violet squinted her eyes suspiciously. She was starting to wonder what was wrong with her twin when Patrick sighed and moved around them both. He squeezed his way into the pantry and the smell of chocolate peppermint filled the smaller space. Violet pressed her back against the shelves and tried to hold her breath. His scent was intoxicating, and it wasn't fair in the slightest.

The crackling of a package of cookies drew her attention, and made Violet's mouth water even before he lowered it to her.

Feeling more than a little embarrassed for throwing a tantrum over cookies, Violet ducked her head and whispered, "Thanks."

"Goddess forbid anyone deprive you of your cookies." A smirk lifted one side of Patrick's mouth when Violet craned her neck back to look up at him. "I kinda feel sorry for Merik."

She bit her lip to keep from saying something flirtatious, and held her frozen position while Patrick ducked out of the pantry and headed back to the table.

"Don't even think about it."

Violet's gaze snapped to Jax as he watched with a raised brow and crossed arms.

"What?" Violet shot back, then ripped open her package of cookies.

"Patrick's birthday is less than two weeks away. He's going to be bonded. You know he's off-limits, so don't..."

"Jax!" Violet shrieked out loud, making her head throb and her twin shrug.

"Remember the promise you made me, Violet." Jax leveled her with his best alpha glare, but it had no effect on her. It never had—well, except once.

"You never let me forget it." Violet glared back.

Jax's eyes narrowed even more before he left to return to the table where Patrick was waiting.

It's not like he had anything to worry about. By Jax's order, Patrick was her dutiful bodyguard. He'd never looked at her any other way... at least she didn't think he had. There were moments when her mind played tricks on her, thinking he smiled just for her or teased her as a way of flirting. That his hands lingered on her a second longer than they should when they trained together. Those were the moments her heart betrayed her... and her brother.

But ultimately, Patrick never gave her a second glance.

Holding two cookies between her teeth, Violet closed the package then tucked it under her arm. Chef Merik was done interfering with her cookie stash. Plus, she was probably going to eat them all anyway.

Two steps out of the Clan House and a friendly voice called her name. Her eyes widened as Tucker, decked out in workout gear, caught up to her while she still had a cookie dangling from her mouth.

"You know there are more nutritious meals inside, right?" He chuckled, reaching for the cookie.

A vicious growl rolled out of her as she jumped back.

Amusement lit his eyes and his brows raised.

Pulling the cookie from her mouth, Violet glared at him. "No one touches my cookies."

Tucker laughed. "Understood."

"Good." She bit another piece off and tilted her head to the side. "Was there something you needed?"

"Uh, yeah." He shuffled his feet a bit, making him look nervous and cute. "Listen, I know you have a head injury and all, but I've been thinking a lot about our conversation during tourney and I was wondering if you wanted to hang out sometime? Or go see a movie, or spar, or... something?" He chuckled at himself and shook his head.

A soft smile tugged at the corners of her lips. "Actually, I would really like that."

"Yeah?" Silver swirled within his eyes, showing off just how excited he was by her answer.

Violet nodded. "Yeah. I should be able to spar again in a couple days. I just have to get clearance from Doc, but I can let you know."

"I'd give you my number, but I know your family doesn't really do the whole cell phone thing."

"Oh!" Violet shuffled her cookies to one hand, wiped her fingers off on her jeans, then reached into her back pocket. "Mom gave me one this morning! Since there doesn't seem to be any progress in clan-linking with anyone other than Jax, she thought it was time I had another way to get in contact with people. The concussion freaked her out a little bit even though Jax and Patrick both filled her in. She said she should have given me one sooner, but I'm always around people who can communicate with each other, so it didn't seem necessary." She handed the phone to Tucker who flipped it over in his hand, eyeing it like it was some sort of trophy. "I haven't done much with it since I don't really know how. I've only messed with Lexie's phone a few times. Plus, I don't know anyone's number."

Tucker's thumbs flew across the screen and a couple seconds later he handed the phone back to her. He pulled out his own phone and pointed to her screen. "Hit that button. It'll call me so I have your number."

Excitement charged through her veins as she hit the phone symbol. Seconds later, his phone rang. He declined her call but continued tapping away. Her phone dinged and when she looked down there was a text message waiting for her from Hot Stuff Tucker.

- Hey gorgeous

Violet snorted, then chuckled. "My first text message! Aw, thanks."

She was definitely changing his name later.

He laughed and pocketed his phone. "Glad I could make it a good one. Now you can tell me what the doc says and we can set up a training session. Maybe after that sometime I can take you on an actual date?"

The thrill of being asked on a date was quickly stomped out as she thought about Jax. "I don't know if that's a good idea. Jax—"

"Is an overprotective brother that doesn't scare me."

She nibbled on her lip nervously for a second. "I'll think about it."

The grin that broke across Tucker's face was infectious and she soon found herself smiling as well. "That's all I can ask for. I gotta run, but I'll talk to you later."

He darted off in the direction of the training facility and Violet watched him go before turning toward Alpha House with a goofy grin on her face.

Sentinel Dome loomed in the near distance behind the house, providing protection and a beacon for the clan. The Yosemite landmark was where their clan name came from. Nestled under its towering form, they were mostly out of human contact and away from prying eyes.

Rumor said their clan was almost named Firefall, after the Natural Firefall event at Horsetail Fall. Others said they were almost named Horsetail, which always made her laugh. A bunch of wolven with the clan name of Horsetail. Ha! They'd never hear the end of it from other clans.

Violet chuckled to herself and shoved another bite of cookie in her mouth, happily chomping down on the sugary goodness she'd confiscated from the pantry. She gasped, nearly choking, when a large gray wolf darted around her, narrowly avoiding a collision on its way toward the Clan House. It scampered behind one of the stalls built along the side of the meeting hall. Some clans didn't have a problem with nudity, but Violet was very grateful her father had put a hard rule on not shifting out in the open. She really didn't need to be seeing a bunch of naked people. Not to mention the scarring on the children! No little kids needed to see people's junk hanging all out and about.

A few seconds later a girl popped her head out from the stall and waved to Violet. "Sorry!" She disappeared behind the stall again but kept talking, "I've been on border patrol for twelve hours, and I'm starving. That doesn't excuse nearly running you over, though." She grinned when she appeared again, wearing clan-issued sweats, and padded barefoot toward the doors. "I'll be more careful in the future. Good reflexes, though! Especially for someone who hasn't connected with her wolf yet." With a wink, she turned and darted into the building.

Violet's shoulders slumped. Connecting with your wolf spirit for the first time wasn't an announced thing unless you went around blabbing it. Most people didn't because it happened to coincide with puberty, and no one wants to talk about that. After a while, people started to notice Violet didn't ever mention her wolf spirit, then one day, everyone knew. She suspected her father had announced it. If she was being mature, she recognized the safety in the clan knowing she needed more protection than others. That didn't make it suck any less.

A few more wolves came and went while Violet stood in front of the Clan House. All of them followed the same routine as the young woman, disappearing behind the stalls and reappearing in their other form before moving off to their next destinations.

She wondered what it felt like to walk on four paws… and if she'd ever get the chance to find out.

"Hiya, Violet!"

A high-pitched shriek left Violet and she nearly tossed the cookie package into the air. Clutching her chest, with saved and nearly crushed cookies in hand, Violet turned on the girl behind her with round eyes.

"Lexie!"

The girl usually stood five inches taller than her, but right now, they were almost the same height since Lexie was doubled over with laughter.

"Oh… my goodness…" she spoke through bursts of mirth. "I haven't been able to scare you like that in forever."

"What the heck?" Violet tried to feel angry, but seeing her only human friend folded over laughing, made it impossible.

Lexie's nose scrunched when she laughed, and it was quite possibly one of the most adorable things Violet had ever seen. Coupled with her model height, which was average for female wolven, and her nearly white-blond hair… the girl really should have been on the runway.

"How long have you been here?" Violet chuckled, submitting to the humor of the moment.

"A few minutes." Lexie shrugged, then snatched the cookie package out from under Violet's arm. She was one of the only people who could get away with that. "I'm surprised you didn't hear me. I saw some cute guy run away from you and watched you nearly get run over by a ravenous wolf."

"I was a little distracted."

"Trying to see through the privacy stalls?" Lexie tsked at her, took a large bite of her cookie, then continued, "Here I thought you were only interested in one guy."

Violet snatched the package of cookies back. "Don't go there."

When Violet entered middle school, she was one of only three wolven children to still be going to public school. Lexie's elementary fed into the same middle school and for whatever reason she attached herself to Violet. A couple months into the school year, Jax connected with his wolf, Dalim, and his alpha gold eyes reacted to Lexie teasing him. That was that. It was all over. Lexie wanted to know everything, and no amount of avoiding her was going to stop the tenacious human.

Jax was removed from public school immediately, but Violet was allowed to stay for a few more years and continue her friendship with Lexie. She had to follow strict rules about what she could and couldn't tell her best friend... so naturally, she had broken all of them, and Lexie knew almost everything. Including her forbidden crush.

"Fine." Lexie polished off her cookie before shoving her hands into the pocket of her hoodie. "Are we all ready for tonight?"

Violet blinked.

"Girls night?" Lexie hinted, then groaned. "We made these plans a week ago, Violet! When we went out to lunch?"

Oh yeah... that sounded familiar.

Violet winced. "I totally forgot. I'm so sorry. I kinda got a concussion, and I'm still feeling the side effects and..."

"Woah, woah, woah. You did what?" Lexie shrieked, making Violet flinch. "Sorry. Loud noises, right? You got a concussion and didn't tell me?"

"I could say I forgot again, but is there really a point?" Violet nodded toward Alpha House, and Lexie hurried a few feet away to grab the bag she must have dropped before scaring her. "Anyway, I'm glad you're here. I could really use a girl's night."

"Mya's coming too."

"Oh good!" Violet nodded, not having remembered that at all. "Hey! Look what Mom gave me this morning."

Nothing could have stopped the squeal of delight that left Lexie and, even though it killed her head, Violet loved her friend's overzealous excitement. Lexie happily filled in all her details on Violet's phone and did pretty much the same thing Tucker had... but when she saw the message he'd sent her there was a whole other explanation that needed to happen. Violet assured her she would explain later and changed the subject to ask about how public school was going.

Lexie filled her in on the day-to-day life of public school while they walked. A few of the newer members to the clan shot glares in Lexie's direction, one in wolven form even snarled, but after ten years of friendship, the two girls were used to the odd looks they received. They were complete opposites. Violet was tiny in every sense of the word, and Lexie was considered a tall girl. Where Lexie was light, Violet was dark.

Lexie could have passed for an elf with her fair skin, light hair, high cheekbones, and blue eyes. Meanwhile, Violet basked in a healthy tan, dark-chocolate hair, and purple eyes.

However, in the wolven community, all they saw was that Lexie was human. One of the very few trusted to be within the community.

There was a time when Lexie had begged to be turned into a wolven, and she'd been broken-hearted when she found out that wasn't how things worked. Wolven were born, not bitten. There were accounts of a human being bitten and turning, but that hadn't happened for over a hundred years and every story ended the same—with the turned wolves losing their minds. People suspected this was due to the fact that usually when a human was bitten, it was because the wolven had gone insane, then transferred that unstable mind to the person they turned.

"Oh, Ian wanted me to say hi to you." Lexie winked as they reached Alpha House.

"Who's Ian?" Jax grumbled from behind them.

Lexie's casual smile turned into a full, wicked smirk as the two girls pivoted to face her brother, only he wasn't alone. Patrick stood to Jax's right, just a foot behind him.

"Violet's boyfriend. Didn't you know?" She *did* love messing with Jax.

Patrick's jaw pulsed once, but if Violet hadn't been staring at him, she wouldn't have noticed. Shaking her head, Violet nudged her friend. "Let's go."

"Violet doesn't have a boyfriend," Jax answered dryly.

"How would you know?" Lexie teased, crossing her arms over her chest. "You weren't around when she went to school with me. She could easily have a nice, hunky, human boyfriend."

"From what I remember, he wasn't nice." Violet admitted.

Jax's eyes flared liquid gold and a hard edge sharpened Patrick's face.

"Did he do something to you?" Jax growled.

Lexie laughed. "You're worried that a human did something to your wolven twin sister?" She shook her head. "You're always good for a laugh, Jaxy."

Annoyance flitted across Jax's face. "What are you doing here, *Lex*?"

Her eyes narrowed and she stomped down the steps until she was nearly toe to toe with him. "You know I hate that name. You also know that I am welcome here, whenever I want."

Jax snorted. "No, you're not. You're only welcome here, *girl*, when Alpha or Luna Draven say you are. Even Violet couldn't bring you here if they said no."

A sickly-sweet smile passed over Lexie's face. "I guess it's a good thing they both absolutely adore me then." She flicked Jax's nose, surprising both Violet and Patrick. He could have easily moved out of the way, but he'd allowed the contact. Lexie stomped back up the stairs. "Don't bother us tonight. It's girl's night. We'll be talking about hot guys and periods and things like that."

Shaking his head, Jax grumbled, "And cackling like a bunch of newborn witches."

"Better than smelling like a couple of dogs."

"You know what," Violet interrupted. "I bet Mya is waiting for us in my room. Why don't we say hi to Mom really fast, then join her?" Violet gently wrapped her fingers around her friend's elbow and tugged. "Come on, don't want to keep girl's night waiting."

Lexie snorted. "I think girls everywhere would approve of this."

"I think you meant witches," grumbled Jax.

Lexie opened her mouth, but Violet jerked her through the front door before they could keep going. "Mom! Look who's here!"

Looking up from her laptop screen, Evalyn grinned heartily at the two girls. "Hello, Lexie!" She set her blue light filtering glasses down and rounded her desk.

"Hello, Luna." Lexie bowed her head respectfully while the older woman made her way toward them.

She wrapped Lexie in a warm embrace and chuckled, "No need for formalities. I'm glad you could make it for girl's night."

"Me too." Lexie returned the hug then stepped back with her palms raised. "I promise I won't get into any more fights with Jax while I'm here."

Amusement lit up Evalyn's gray eyes. "Any *more*?"

"I'm not done with you, *human!*" Jax burst through the door with Patrick hot on his heels, looking regretful.

"Jax!" their mother snapped at him.

Jax's cheeks flamed pink and he dipped his chin. "Oh, hi, Mom. I thought you'd have your headphones in."

"So, you think it's okay to speak to her like that when I'm not listening?"

Lexie and Violet both snickered and Jax glared at them.

"It's not like she's innocent." Jax crossed his arms. "She called me a dog."

"Then perhaps you should stop acting like one," Lexie retorted, and Violet wished she'd let it go when Evalyn turned on her.

"Lexie," the older woman chided. "You two..." She shook her head. "I don't know what I'm going to do with you. Girls, Mya is waiting for you and I think she may have brought an entire candy store with her. Boys, leave the girls alone for the night."

Lexie gave a small air fist pump, then quickly hugged Evalyn for a second time before bounding up the stairs.

Sighing, even though she was smiling, Evalyn looked between her two children. "Behave, both of you. Patrick, keep him out of trouble."

"Easier said than done, Luna, but I'll do my best," Patrick smirked and bowed his head respectfully to her.

The older woman gave him a brief hug and reminded him he didn't need to call her that, before sending them all on their way. Violet dutifully ignored Jax's mental jabs as she made her way up the stairs with the two boys trailing behind her. When she reached her room, she sent a smug smile over her shoulder and closed the door in Jax's face.

"Girls night!" Mya called and Violet turned to see her two friends with sour gummy worms dangling from their mouths.

A bubbly laugh left her as she stared at her two best friends standing on either side of a giant box filled to the brim with an assortment of tasty treats. "Thanks for waiting for me," she teased and kicked off her shoes.

They'd turned on the twinkle lights that offered a gentle glow behind the sheer white curtains draped around her daybed—which was now covered in fluffy blankets and pillows.

Mya shoved a couple more worms in her mouth and shrugged. "We knew you'd be up here sooner or later."

"Besides," Lexie threw a gummy worm at her, but before it could peg her in the forehead, Violet grabbed it and bit it in half. "You can eat more than either of us. We needed to get a head start on the goods before you got your hands on them."

"We weren't talking about much. Mostly just boys." Mya shrugged again as she pulled the dark green, blackout curtains closed over the window.

"I like boy talk," Violet mumbled.

"Since when?" Both girls said at the same time.

"You avoid boy talk like wolfsbane," Mya said with slightly widened eyes as she took a seat on the bed, tucking her legs beneath her.

"You always shut down or change the subject." Lexie turned toward Mya. "Wolfsbane is that plant thing that you guys are allergic to, right?"

"Uh, yeah, kind of." Mya ran a hand through her coiled, lion mane hair. "It's poison."

"Right." Lexie nodded, then they both looked back at her.

Unease settled over Violet and she shifted her weight a bit before claiming the other side of the bed and leaning against the footboard. "I like boy talk," she defended lamely, "as long as we aren't talking about the boy I like."

Laughter burst from her friends, making her smile. Lexie settled into the desk chair so they created a triangle of friendship as they shared a boatload of sweets.

"I think Mya should tell us about Aiden," Violet offered and Lexie turned to stare wide-eyed at the blushing girl.

"Oooh, do tell!"

"There's nothing to tell," Mya defended, then shoved a handful of cheddar popcorn in her mouth.

Violet snorted. "Bah-loanie! You have been beside yourself every time we've been around him lately and I have my suspicions why." She brandished a gummy worm at Mya who held up her hands in surrender.

"Okay, quiet! I don't want the boys to hear us."

Lexie giggled and snuggled into the desk chair, ready for a juicy story.

Sighing, Mya confiscated a pillow and clutched it to her chest. "I never really noticed him until a couple months ago—a few weeks after my birthday—and now every time I see him, it's like this magnet pulling me to him. I can't stop thinking about him, and I often dream about him—"

"Have you kissed him yet?" Lexie interrupted, bouncing a little in her chair until Violet threw a pillow at her.

"Aiden isn't eighteen yet. If Mya is suspecting what I am, then she needs to keep her distance until his birthday."

"Which is right after the field trip to Moaning Caverns, so I shouldn't have to wait too much longer," Mya interjected hopefully.

The mega blond girl leaned back and watched her caramel friend for a long moment. "Do you think he's your mate?"

No one moved.

Lexie technically wasn't supposed to know anything about mates other than the fact that wolven had them.

Mya slowly nodded and a grin split her face when the two girls oooh'd. "It's not definite yet!" she defended. "But I'm really hopeful. He's so sweet and kind and strong and *so* cute..."

"Okay, okay, we get it. You're madly in love and will soon run away into the sunset with a fated match made by the moon or whatever." Lexie teased, but Mya eyed her warily.

Violet sent her a warning look and her human friend shrugged. Too late now. Lexie wasn't supposed to know all the intimate details of mates and how they were gifted or chosen, but she did, because Violet couldn't keep anything from her. Mya knew Lexie had more knowledge of wolven life than she was supposed to, but had no idea the extent.

"So, there's this boy," Lexie was the first to break the slightly tense moment which thankfully made Mya giggle and Violet groan. "He's super cute and as tall as any of the guys here, which means he's obviously perfect for me, right?"

Violet lifted a brow. "I don't know, looks aren't everything."

"Is he sweet?" Mya eyed the last of a Milano cookie before popping it into her mouth. "Cause then he would be perfect for you."

Lexie shrugged. "I haven't talked to him yet. He just moved into the area."

Shaking her head, Violet snagged another treat before leaning back against the footboard. "Maybe you should do that before you start planning your wedding."

"Hey, finding a human guy is nothing like you wolven." Lexie shook a nerd rope at her, then smiled apologetically as a few nerds flew off into the plush, soft pink rug that covered most of the wooden floor. Any bare floor it missed, Violet's clothes took care of. "Sorry."

"You're vacuuming before you leave. I don't want ants in my room."

Lexie rolled her eyes, took a bite of her candy, then said, "We don't get mates. We have no guarantee that the person we fall in love with will love us back or stay in love with us or be a good match for us. For us humans, it's trial and error."

"Maybe, but there isn't a guarantee we'll find our mates either." Mya played with one of her chestnut curls as she eyed the box of sweets. "I mean, I've been eighteen for three months now and I think I may have found mine, but there are wolven much older than us who haven't found their mates."

"Some never find them," Violet muttered quietly, staring down at the cookie in her hand.

Her friends were quiet for a while until one of them cleared their throats.

"That's bleak," Lexie admitted. "But don't you guys know like the second you see your mate?"

"You know we're not really supposed to talk about that." Mya tossed a warning look at the blond girl.

"But you're going to tell me anyway." Lexie stuck her tongue out and threw the pillow she'd been cuddling at Mya.

Violet laughed dryly. "You know too much for your own good."

"Okay, I'll answer you, but then we are talking about something else," Mya relented. "If both wolven are over eighteen, then yes, they'll know the moment they make eye contact. It's not immediate love, though, and definitely not immediate lust like those horrid werewolf books I've seen out there."

A disgusted groan escaped Violet.

"For those who are eighteen and find their mates before their other half is…" Mya shrugged. "I've heard a few different versions. Some say they know as immediately and intensely as if their mate was eighteen already. Others say it's more of a hunch or a feeling that the person will be their mate, but it isn't confirmed until their other half turns eighteen. For me, if Aiden is in fact my mate, it's more like this steadily growing admiration and confirmation. It's also considered incredibly rude to tell someone they're your mate before they feel it too. They may just end up thinking you're crazy." She shot Violet an apologetic look.

"Zander is the first and last of those examples. From the moment he turned eighteen, he has insisted he's my mate." Violet shuddered.

Both girls gave her sympathetic looks.

Zander had been one of her closest friends before his trials, but those memories felt like they were a lifetime ago now. Some wolven wondered how he made it out of the trial ring, if he even went at all. He'd gone alone, which was unheard of, but her mom hadn't approved of Violet going with him, and even then he refused to go with anyone else. He'd come back a completely different person… or maybe his shift had just amplified the feelings that were already there.

Mya reached over and patted her knee. "Zander kind of lost his mind when he shifted. I don't think he's your mate."

"What if he is?" Lexie asked quietly. She had only met the wolven male twice, but that had been plenty for her. Zander could be intense.

"Then I'll reject him," Violet answered just as quietly. "I'd rather be alone than be mated to him."

The three girls were quiet for a minute.

"Well, that was depressing," Mya grumbled, making Violet chuckle sadly.

"So, what happened to your face?" Lexie asked, settling back into the chair again. "Is that how you got the concussion?"

Violet's eyes widened and her fingers feathered over her cheekbone. It was a nasty yellow-brown today with a few darker spots here or there, especially around the corner of her eye. The cut had scabbed over last night so it would probably be healed tomorrow or the next day.

"Jax hit her in the face at tourney."

"What?" Lexie yelled, jumping up from her chair and starting for the door.

"No! No, wait." Violet leapt over her footboard and blocked the door from the raging girl.

Mya chuckled. "I should have popcorn, not candy."

"Lexie, it was an accident."

"He hit you in the face. How is that an accident?"

Violet tilted her head to the side. "I was standing behind him and his elbow got me when he pulled back to hit someone else."

Lexie blinked a few times before her shoulders lowered and the tension in her face disappeared. "Well, that was stupid."

"I was trying to stop him." Crossing her arms, she glared at her friend.

"Did it work?"

"Considering Patrick knocked Vikter out and pinned Jax to a tree after that..." Mya chuckled, "Yeah, I'd say it worked."

Astonishment dropped Lexie's jaw. She shot Mya a saucer-eyed look and squealed, "Shut up, he did not!" Her gaze snapped back to Violet. "I can't believe he did that for you!"

"Yes," Mya answered, at the same time Violet denied it, "It wasn't *for* me."

Lexie's head swung back and forth between the two girls. Her brows rose and she lifted her hands. "What the heck happened? Since when does he beat up your brother over you?"

"He didn't beat him up!" Violet insisted.

Mya snorted. "He would have if you hadn't stepped in."

"You are not helping!" Violet hissed at her.

Mya held up her hands in surrender.

"Nothing has happened. Patrick is the same defensive bodyguard Jax has always ordered him to be. It just so happened that Jax was the person he needed to defend against at that moment."

One corner of Lexie's mouth quirked up. "Pinning him to a tree sounds like a little more than just defending you."

Frustration coursed through her and Violet threw her arms out to the sides. "This is why I hate boy talk!"

Both of her friends laughed then Mya shook her head. "Okay, okay. We're sorry... right Lexie?"

The tall blond laughed, "Not remotely."

Violet glared.

"Who's Vikter?" Lexie asked Mya, ignoring her glare.

"The future alpha of the clan we were up against at tourney."

"Ah, got it. On another note, what's tourney?"

"Oh." Mya blinked, looked at Violet who blinked back, then shrugged. "It's short for the Clan Games tournament."

Lexie nodded. "What are the Clan Games?"

One of Mya's brows lowered. "Of all the things you know that you shouldn't, you don't know about the Clan Games? It's actually something you probably *are* allowed to know!"

Violet shrugged. "We've never talked about it. Probably because I'm not allowed to play, and Lexie doesn't care all that much for sports."

Shaking her head, Lexie eyed the door one more time, then returned to the desk chair. It thumped against the weathered white desk when she plopped down.

"You know the rules for Capture the Flag, right?" Violet asked. Feeling pretty confident her human friend wasn't about to chase Jax down with a stick, she reclaimed her seat on the bed. "Each team has a flag they hide. The other team tries to find it. Right?"

"Basically," Lexie agreed and opened a mini Reese's cup.

Mya's eyes bugged. "Oh wow, that's it?"

"For the most part." Violet waved a dismissive hand. "The Clan Games are a bit more complicated and a lot more brutal. Take Capture the Flag, add in an oval field the length of a football field that has a layout that changes with every game, a center zone with paintball snipers, a cage for the people those snipers hit, and regular points being scored with a ball and lacrosse stick."

Lexie rubbed her forehead. "So it's a mix between Capture the Flag, Lacrosse, and Paintball?"

"With a dodgeball aspect as well," Violet explained, "due to the cage once a person gets shot. Although, now that I think about it, Capture the Flag has a jail doesn't it?"

Lexie shrugged. "I think so?"

Letting that go, Violet turned to Mya. "Be thankful you were never subjected to dodgeball. Even being faster than the other kids, I hated playing that game."

"She was short so she got targeted."

Amusement lit Mya's eyes, "Was?"

"Oh, shut up." Violet hit her with a pillow, only to be smacked right back. "And I was just as tall as the other girls! They just picked on me because I came to school in the weird twelve-passenger white van that had a bunch of carpool kids in it."

That van was how the clan kids were able to explain where they came from. If anyone asked, they were in a carpool group.

"This game sounds incredibly complicated," Lexie admitted, ignoring the comment about the clan van.

"It is." Violet nodded. "It's easier to explain if you actually see it."

"Too bad that's never going to happen."

"Weeellll..." Both girls turned to Mya who had another glint in her eye, but this one read mischief. "We could sneak her into the next game."

Shock rippled through Violet. "What? She would be found out in a heartbeat."

"Not if we walked in as a group." Mya continued, "We could even get Robin in on it. With a trio of wolven females, no one will even pick up on the fact that she is human. You look more human than she does."

Narrowing her eyes, Violet growled, "Thanks."

Lexie laughed, "This sounds amazing. I'm in."

Looking between her two friends, Violet felt a smile tug at her lips. "This is insane, you know that, right?"

They both nodded.

"Alright," Violet caved after shaking her head. "I guess we're sneaking you into the next game. Do *not* wear any perfume and don't use scented soap. You know how sensitive we are to those."

"I thought my soap was fine?"

"For us, yes, but you're welcome here and we know you're human. It's a dead giveaway to anyone else." Violet waited until Lexie nodded before continuing, "And before that, I have to survive our field trip on Wednesday."

"What's so hard about that? It's just the Moaning Caverns, right?"

Mya dipped her head toward Lexie and sighed, "It's a tri-clan field trip.

Vikter will be there."

"What's the deal with Vikter, aside from the fact he is a future alpha?"

Violet crushed a velvety dark green pillow against her chest. "Like Jax, Vikter is running a bit hot-headed these days and seems like he has something to prove against Jax—"

"And the entire world," Mya interjected.

"True," Violet agreed. "It's almost as if he thinks Jax will take over the Stanislaus Clan."

"If it gets to his head too much, he could look for other ways to weaken Jax. Like hurting someone close to him." Mya's saddened gaze fell on Violet. "It's happened before."

"To you?" Lexie asked, sounding like she wanted to go after someone again.

"No." Violet clarified. "In history... in other clans... it happens when an alpha feels threatened."

Worry hardened the edges of Lexie's face. "Jax and Patrick will be there, right?"

"Patrick, yes. Jax, no. He has some future alpha duties to attend to," Violet explained. "Alpha Draven has been pulling him from more and more social events as our birthdays get closer."

"You have nothing to worry about." Mya patted Violet's shoulder. "It's not like Patrick will let anything happen to you."

Sighing, Violet fell backward onto the mattress and stared at the ceiling. "I can't wait to graduate. Then I won't have to deal with this."

"Graduation can*not* come soon enough," Lexie agreed, picking up on the new topic as if it were a lifeline and continuing on for a few minutes. "Being back from Christmas break sucks and Easter is still months away. I just want to graduate and move on with my life. Then we can go to college together and make our own rules..."

With the online courses Violet was taking, she would be graduating shortly after Patrick's birthday. This wasn't the first time Lexie had talked about going to college together, but with the recent news from Doc it was sounding pretty amazing. Beside Lexie, Violet could blend in with the human population. If she really didn't have a wolf or a mate, then maybe living outside the compound would be for the best.

Not as a rogue, of course. Rogues were lone wolves, not belonging to any clan, and they were known to fall into trouble. If they stayed alone long enough, most of them started to go a little crazy, too. Violet would keep her clan and check in every so often. Her mom wouldn't have it any other way—if she let Violet leave at all.

Chapter 5

Violet

***A COUPLE OF CHILDREN CUT VIOLET OFF** on her way to the training facility as they raced toward the parking lot.* One boy with orange-red hair turned to wave and apologize, but they were clearly in a hurry and didn't have time to talk. Pulling her phone from her pocket, Violet checked the time.

7:25

Yup, one of the clan's vans would be leaving any second to take the kids to their public schools. All high school aged wolven finished their schooling through online courses in the study hall within the compound, so the driver would only stop at the junior high school and elementary school before heading home again. Even with the very tinted windows, a large white van was easier to explain than a bus that came from nowhere. A carpool group was much easier to explain than a secret compound hidden in the forest that provided homes for what humans called werewolves.

Sending wolven children off to human schools helped them learn how to interact with the human world and also teach them how to protect each other and their clan's secrets. Occasionally, something would happen, but children believe all sorts of things, and "no sane adult" would believe there were packs of werewolves living amongst humans.

There was always the exception though, like Lexie.

Violet smiled to herself and shook her head as she thought about her friend.

Having Mya and Lexie over a couple of days ago had been the break she needed. They kept her thinking about anything other than her problems for most of the night. She wished she could be back there, laughing over Lexie's complaints about senior year, instead of heading to a training session she was now dreading.

At first, when Tucker had asked her to spar, it seemed like a fun idea. Now, all Violet could picture was the slightly disappointed look on her mom's face when Violet told her who she'd be training with... and the image of Patrick. Only a few weeks after he arrived in Sentinel Clan, Patrick started training her. He explained things in a way that made sense, and Violet was finally able to progress after being at a standstill for two years. Under his tutelage, Violet started winning against some of the weaker wolven teens, and her running surpassed some adults.

A shiver raced through her as she entered the training facility, but she was immediately met by warm air and the sounds of combat. Off to the right were larger areas with artificial grass where people typically sparred in their wolf forms when there were bad weather conditions. There were a few there now, swiping at each other, wrestling, and lunging. Directly ahead of her were loads of machines for muscle building. Plenty of people were using those and often rotated around each other for use of the same machine.

Violet's favorite area, though, was to her left. The floor was padded, some of the walls, too, for training in human form. Sparring was her favorite type of training, and since wolven didn't shift until the first full moon after their eighteenth birthday, she'd never been on the other side of the facility. She imagined that once she shifted, though, she would train over there a lot... *if* she shifted.

Her shoulders dropped at the reminder that she may never be able to take a wolf form.

"Violet!"

Tucker's voice punched through the darkening clouds in her mind, and she looked to see him smiling at her from the sparring area. He'd already worked up a good sweat with the dummy he was standing beside, and his bare chest glistened as it rose and fell with his slightly quickened breathing.

"I was beginning to wonder if you were going to stand me up." He tucked one of his basketball short strings back into his band, and tossed his head to the side to get the dark blond strands of hair that had fallen from his high man bun out of his face.

"Oh, was this a date?" she teased, making her way onto the mats.

He smirked as she dropped her bag next to his and walked over to grab a towel from his bag, patting over his neck and chest. "If this is your version of a date, you may just be the girl of my dreams."

A burst of laughter left her, making his smirk grow into a smile. "Sorry, you'll have to try a little harder than that."

With a shrug, he tossed his towel back into his bag.

"I would have been here sooner, but I needed to eat something, and Luna wanted to talk for a minute," Violet explained while she kicked off her shoes and began stretching.

Tucker watched until she looked at him with a raised brow. He cleared his throat and mumbled something about finding his water bottle before burying his face in his bag. "So, uh... is everything okay at home?"

Violet changed positions and took a moment to tighten her long, high-ponytail. "Yup. She was just being a mom."

Keeping his gaze averted, he nodded. "My dad's been on my butt about finishing school soon."

"How much more do you have?"

Tucker shrugged and briefly caught her eye. "I'm on track to graduate by late May, but he wants me to get done sooner."

Confusion bunched her face. "Why? That's when most seniors graduate."

He turned away and started moving the dummy to the side of the mats. "He wants me to take training more seriously and learn about his position. He is dead set that I take a post at lockup."

"That'll be fun." Violet snorted, thinking about the clan's personal prison set a little way off behind Alpha House and down a steep hill. She snagged her green padded training gloves from her bag. "Hardly anything ever happens there."

"More happens there than you realize," Tucker's defensive tone made her look up from her bag. He was in the process of tightening his own gloves. "More than anyone in the clan realizes, really. Why would they want to know about the wolven who are kept there?"

Adequately put in her place, Violet tipped her head to the side. "Fair enough." She shoved her hands into her gloves as she stood.

He looked over her from head to toe. "Ready?"

"Patrick never asks that, he just attacks."

He laughed, "I guess in a real fight, they wouldn't be asking if you're ready."

Violet did as she'd been taught.

She attacked.

Tucker's eyes bugged. The slight hesitation cost him a solid punch to his shoulder, but he managed to shift so she didn't hit his jaw. He collected himself, dropped into a defensive stance and blocked her next attacks. After training with Patrick, Tucker felt slow. Violet was able to connect a number of strikes. After a few minutes, she noticed Tucker telegraphed any left-handed attack. A couple more minutes, and she picked up on a pattern.

Jab. Cross. Jab. Jab. Cross. Hook. Kick.

Violet dropped to the mat, whipping her leg out to knock Tucker off his stationary leg. His back smacked hard against the mats.

"Ow," he grunted. "I thought you were supposed to be slower and weaker than the rest of us."

Frustration simmered in her chest while he made his way to his feet. "You shouldn't underestimate your opponent. I don't know who you've been talking to, but there's a reason I train with Patrick. He pushes me and doesn't let me use the fact that I don't have a wolf as an excuse." She threw a series of punches that he barely managed to block or dodge. "I may be a little slower and weaker, but I've trained to compensate for it. My size makes it easy to slip into the openings in people's defenses."

Another grunt left him when she demonstrated. Her fist slipped through one of his openings and landed against his ribs.

"It shows." He brushed some hair away from his face as his eyes flashed silver. "You're pretty good."

"*Pretty* good?" Violet growled, feeling competitive.

Tucker smirked and his eyes remained silver while they continued. Tapping into his wolven strength and speed was kind of cheating, but it pushed Violet to work harder, so she didn't mind... until she was the one on her back and he was kneeling over her.

Both their chests rose and fell heavily as they stared at one another. His eyes were still silver, making Violet wonder what he was feeling. They should have slipped back to his natural blue seconds after he knocked her down, but if his emotions were heightened, that would make them stay silver longer.

"Can I ask you a question?" He wiped at his forehead with the back of his hand.

This was kind of a weird position to be in for questions, but Violet shrugged a shoulder. Her tank top didn't do much to keep her from sticking to the mat and it made a weird noise as she shifted. "Sure."

"Are you and Patrick..." Tucker trailed off, looking a bit sheepish.

"What?"

"My buddies said you two are together. You're not... are you?"

Violet laughed, "Even if I were the last girl on the planet, Patrick wouldn't want me. He'd never go against Jax's orders."

If it were possible, Tucker's eyes flared a brighter silver. "Good."

She swallowed the knot constricting her throat when he lowered his head toward hers. Discomfort made her squirm, and she awkwardly interrupted his attempt to kiss her. "Um, can you let me up, please?"

Tucker barked a laugh, right in her face, then pecked her on the cheek and stood. "Never been kissed before?"

"What kind of question is that?" Violet grumbled as she rolled into a seated position.

"You were more afraid of me kissing you than getting hit in the face." He offered her a hand to help her stand.

Grabbing his hand, Violet frowned. "Maybe I was just caught off guard."

Tucker quickly pulled her up, but didn't back away. She gasped and braced her hands against his hot chest.

"Sorry," he muttered, but he didn't sound it. His hands slid to her elbows, softly holding her as she tipped her chin back to look at him.

"You did that on purpose."

His smirk returned, "Maybe."

"Hi, Violet!" called a female voice, pulling them both out of the moment. A perky redhead girl waved at her from the aisle.

"Hey, Robin" Violet pointed at her hair, "Decided to go red this time?"

No one knew what Robin's natural hair color was because she was constantly changing it. "Yeah, it's a color I've never tried. I'm not a huge fan of it, but it does make me feel like a mermaid sometimes."

Violet laughed and took a casual step away from Tucker. "That's understandable."

"Anyway, I just wanted to say hi. I've been so busy lately that we haven't seen each other in a while, but I need to hurry off to work." She wiggled her fingers as she started walking away. "By the way, you two make a super cute couple!"

Heat flooded Violet's face and she looked down at the blue mats beneath her feet.

Tucker cleared his throat.

When she managed to bring her gaze back to his, he was grinning like the Cheshire Cat, which made Violet laugh. "Don't go getting any ideas."

His grin widened. "I've already had these ideas for a while." He wrapped a hand around her arm and pulled her toward him. "Robin's right, we do make a good couple."

"Uh-huh," Violet muttered, tugging lightly against his hold. "Like a fish and a bird."

"What?" Tucker laughed, the sound a bit deeper than normal. "No, we are both wolven."

With a sigh, she shook her head. He didn't understand what she was saying. "This isn't a good idea," she told him softly when he slid a hand over her hip.

Tucker lowered his head toward hers. "Why?"

Violet's heart hammered against her ribs when his gaze locked onto her lips. He was right, she'd never been kissed before. That's how overly protective Jax was. She was nearly eighteen and had never been kissed...

and she wasn't sure she wanted Tucker to be her first kiss.

"Because, I don't..." Words failed her as his breath fell over her mouth.

"You don't want this?" Tucker asked, frozen in place with his lips skimming hers.

"No, that's not what I meant."

"So, you do want this?"

"Tucker, I'm trying to tell you th—"

He was gone.

Just like that Tucker was slipping down the padded wall ten feet away from her with Patrick looming over him.

"You were already warned once, Tucker," Patrick snarled.

"What?" Violet shrieked, hurrying toward them, but Patrick held out his arm to stop her from going to Tucker. When she still tried to get around him, he grabbed a fistful of the back of her shirt. "Let go of me!"

Tucker sucked in a wheezy breath then coughed, making her freeze. He'd hit the wall hard enough to get the wind knocked out of him? She punched Patrick in the side and he released her shirt long enough for her to dart forward.

"Are you okay?" she asked Tucker as she dropped to her knees beside him.

Anger blazed in his still silver eyes. He wasn't looking at her as he chuckled darkly, "Beating me up because you can't have her, Cowen?"

"I threw you off her because Jax doesn't want you anywhere near his little sister."

Violet spun on her knees and glared at Patrick, whose shoulders were rolled forward and muscles tight beneath his workout top. "Seriously? I was born five minutes after him!" she yelled, frustrated that she was being ignored and had a stupid twin. "Jax does not control my life."

Patrick's hardened gaze looked over her. She knew that look. He was assessing her, making sure she wasn't hurt. Golden flecked, hazel eyes met her glare and softened ever so slightly. "I follow his orders."

"This order is stupid," she snapped.

Tucker huffed a laugh and made his way to his feet.

"Are you okay?" she asked as she stood beside him.

He nodded. "I'm fine." His hand slipped over her lower back. "It's gonna take a lot more than that to keep me away from you."

"That doesn't surprise me." Patrick snorted, crossing his arms. "Do you want to tell her why you're so determined?"

"Isn't it obvious?" Tucker answered, but something was off with his tone. It almost sounded… mocking. "I like her."

Tucker's hand slid across her back to snag her side and pull her against him. It wasn't sweet like he'd been trying to be before. This was possessive and felt like he was taunting Patrick.

"Get your hand off her." Patrick's face contorted with rage. "Jax is your future alpha. You will obey him."

"Or what?" Tucker asked, keeping his hand where it was.

Violet squirmed uncomfortably beneath his hold and Patrick uncrossed his arms, resting his fists at his sides.

"He can't officially tell me to do anything because he is the *future* alpha. You can't beat me up for liking his sister." Tucker huffed a laugh. "And Violet likes me. She should be with me."

Nope. That was it.

Violet ducked away from Tucker's possessive arm and moved to Patrick's side, wanting the comfortable protection he would always give her. She didn't touch him, but she was close enough to feel the heat radiating from his body.

"Really?" Tucker growled, his brows slamming down.

"Flirting was one thing, Tucker, but…" Violet rubbed her arms, hating that Patrick was here for this conversation. "You don't know me well enough to know what, or who, I like and you don't get to speak for me, either. I have enough males trying to control my life; I don't need you doing it, too." She tucked some stray hair behind her ear. "Besides, I'm not really girlfriend material. And I'm definitely not mate material."

Patrick sucked in a breath and froze.

A snort left Tucker. "I think you'd make a perfect mate."

"Why?" Violet snapped, surprising herself and Tucker, based on his slightly widened eyes. "You hardly know anything about me."

"I know you're gorgeous," Tucker tried to defend.

She rolled her eyes. Robin was gorgeous. She was just averagely pretty with her slightly round face, button nose, dark chocolate hair, and purple eyes.

"You're fast, too," Tucker continued. "You're stronger than people think."

"You're not saying anything important!" Violet threw her arms out to the sides, narrowly avoiding Patrick. "What do you know about me, my personality, that you actually like?"

Tucker stumbled over his words for a moment. "Y-You-You're... fun. You aren't a pushover—"

She held up a hand. "Let me stop you." She shook her head. "Letting all this go, I'm not the one you want to be with."

He took a step toward her, making Patrick growl. "I *do* want to be with you."

Violet shook her head again. "No. You don't. You're looking for a mate and I will never have one."

Tucker blinked. "You would reject yours?"

"No," she sighed and cast a quick, nervous side glance at Patrick who was watching her. With a deep breath, she looked back at Tucker and exposed her new secret, "Doc told me I don't have a wolf, which means I will never shift, and I will never have a mate. I will never hold an official position or rank in the clan."

Tucker's eyes narrowed as he searched her face, looking for something that wasn't there. "You're not making that up, are you?"

Anguish sank Violet's shoulders. She looked at the floor, nibbled on her lower lip, and shook her head. Her voice was tiny when she spoke, "I really wish I was."

A moment of tense quiet passed between the three of them before Tucker stomped toward his bag. Violet watched as his threw his training gloves in with the rest of his gear and slammed his feet into his shoes. He snatched his gear off the floor and cast a last look over his shoulder.

Something like anger hardened his gaze, making Violet's brows pull together in confusion.

"I'll see you later," he grumbled, walking away without waiting for a response.

Violet didn't know if she wanted to cry or throw something at Tucker's retreating form. Her eyes stung with the threat of tears, but her blood boiled. "I don't understand," she whispered, through clenched teeth as she fought off her explosive emotions.

"Vi?" Patrick lightly touched her shoulder.

"Don't," she snapped, jumping away from him. She stormed toward her bag as a tear slid down her cheek. Angrily swiping it away, she shouldered her bag. "I'm so sick of you and Jax interrupting my life."

"What? Where did that come from? And where are you going?" Patrick came up beside her. "We have training to do."

"I'm not training with you today." Violet shouldered past him, but he grabbed the strap of her bag. "Let go."

From the corner of her eye she saw Patrick shake his head, making his longer, curly top hairs sway. "Violet, talk to me."

"I don't want to!" Violet shoved her bag at him and he held it against his chest. "I don't want to talk about Tucker or the results I got from Doc. I've been trying not to think about the fact that I'm even more of a freak than I thought I was!" Thankfully, her anger had stopped her tears, but as she stared into Patrick's gorgeous hazel eyes, her anger ebbed. Her voice took on a trembling tone, and she hoped he would understand what she was about to say. "I want to be with someone. I want to kiss someone without Jax interrupting or sending you to do it. I should be able to live my life and find joy in being with someone. Even if it can't be forever. I don't want to be alone."

His face pinched before he ran a hand through his hair to rub the back of his neck. Her bag dangled from his other hand, at his side. "You're not alone, Violet. I'll always be here. I just have to follow Jax's orders, as well."

Violet shook her head and backed up a step.

"We are trying to protect you. Tucker isn't the sweet guy you were trying to make him out to be."

"That is *my* decision to make!" Frustration poured through her and she would have fully screamed at him if they were outside. Instead, she stepped so close that their bodies nearly touched and craned her neck back. She glared up at him, making him swallow hard. "I don't want your protection. And if that's the only reason you're around me, then I don't want you anywhere near me!" Her palms smacked off his chest, but he didn't even budge an inch, making her more frustrated. "Tell Jax to obsess over someone else, because I'm done."

The tears were back, building quickly as she waited for him to respond.

"Vi," Patrick breathed the nickname he had given her shortly after joining the clan. He was the only one who called her that, and she loved it. It was his, and the way he said it made her want to melt.

Her bag hit the ground with a thud.

The feather-light touch of his hands sliding up her arms made goosebumps ripple across her body. His fingers settled around her upper arms, holding her as if she would crumble in his hands.

Violet drew in a shaky breath, leaned forward—

"Don't forget your promise." The memory of Jax and his stupid promise, snapped her out of it and she took a jerky step back.

She focused on the one thing that could push down her feelings for Patrick. Her anger. "I can take care of myself."

"Violet," Patrick's voice hardened a fraction as warning dripped into his tone. "You know I—"

"I can take care of myself, Patrick." She bit out each word, making them sharp with her fury.

A storm of emotions swirled in Patrick's eyes. His mouth slowly closed, pressing into a thin line. He didn't try to stop her again when she snatched her bag off the floor.

That was how Violet knew, even if he had some sort of feelings for her, he didn't feel the same way she did about him. She would do anything for him. Patrick would always choose loyalty and obedience to Jax over her.

Something broke between them when Violet walked away. Her chest felt like an anvil had landed on her, making it hard to breathe. The tears that hadn't fallen in front of Patrick cascaded down her face on the hurried walk back to Alpha House.

Evalyn Draven was in the kitchen with another wolven female when Violet opened the front door. She almost made it to the stairs before her mother caught up to her.

"I smell tears. What happened?" Evalyn practically dragged Violet into the kitchen, waving the female away.

"Luna." The female nodded respectfully, then hastily ducked out the back door.

Violet saw the female's tawny wolf race away from the house before a mug was shoved into her hands. "I wasn't crying, Mom."

"You're lying."

"It was just a few." Violet set the mug on the counter. "I feel like I've been on the verge of a torrential downpour for days. They were bound to come out at some point."

Sighing, Evalyn handed her the tub of hot chocolate mix. "You've been through a lot in the last week. It's bound to have a toll on your emotions."

With a nod, Violet popped open the lid and began scooping the brown powder into her mug. "Sure, but I've never been the girl who cries over her problems."

"No. You usually yell and hit things," her mom teased, leaning her hip against the counter.

Silence fell over them until the microwave beeped. Evalyn kept a twenty-five-ounce mug for these occasions, when hot water was needed as fast as possible. When it wasn't an emergency, they would use a teapot.

"I've..." Violet started, but her voice broke. After clearing her throat and allowing her mom to pour water into her mug, she tried again, "I've always thought I would have a mate one day. The idea terrified me. I mean, what if they saw me and rejected me? That would be horrible."

Evalyn nodded. "They say the pain of being rejected is second only to having your mate die."

She shuddered at her mother's words. What an awful fate.

"I guess I can find some relief in the fact that I don't have to worry about that now." Her words sounded cold and hollow. "But that also means I'll be alone. I... don't want to be alone."

Evalyn set her mug down and wrapped Violet in a tight hug. "Oh, my little miracle. You will never be alone." She kissed the top of Violet's head. "I believe you will have a wolf and a mate someday. It just might take a little longer than most."

"I think you mean longer than everyone," Violet's muffled voice against her mom's shoulder made the older woman laugh and release her. "How can you be so sure?"

"On which part?"

Violet scoffed. "All of it?"

"Jax would never allow you to be alone. He loves you, even if he has a funny way of showing it. And Patrick..."

"Don't..." Violet shook her head. "I don't want to talk about Patrick."

Evalyn was quiet for a moment and took a sip of her hot chocolate before speaking again. "You still have feelings for him, don't you?"

Violet swirled her mug in her hands and stared at the rich brown liquid within as if it could reveal all the answers she needed.

"It's written all over your face when he walks into the room, or another girl throws herself at him, or the way you worry over him."

"Mom, I can't..." Violet's voice broke. She'd never told her mom about the promise Jax had scared her into making.

Evalyn settled a hand onto Violet's arm, stilling her swirling mug. "Feelings are messy, my little miracle, but he would never leave you to be alone, either. I've seen the way that boy looks at you when he thinks no one else is watching."

A soft snort escaped her, making her mom raise a brow. "One, you're crazy if you think he is looking at me any other way besides wanting to keep an eye on me. You know Jax made him promise to protect me. Two... how did you know something happened with Patrick?"

"One," her mom teased, "no other guy affects you the way he does. Two, his scent is all over you."

Violet's eyes bugged. "Seriously?"

A chuckle shook Evalyn's shoulders. "Yes. There is another scent on you too, I'm guessing that's Tucker's, but I'm not too familiar with his scent and it's faint."

"That doesn't make any sense. I was sparring with Tucker. If I am smelling like anyone, it should be him."

Her mom shrugged. "I'm sure you've noticed some wolven have stronger scents than others, and every scent is slightly different. Some compliment each other more than others, as well. From what I'm smelling, Patrick's scent definitely compliments yours better than Tucker's."

Violet frowned.

Having finished off her drink, Evalyn set her mug in the sink. "Take the rest of the day to relax. Work on something you enjoy. Give Patrick a couple days and things will be back to normal. You'll see."

Violet's shoulders dropped. "I'm not really sure what my normal is anymore."

Evalyn kissed the top of her head again. "You'll figure it out. You always do." With that, she left Violet standing in the kitchen and returned to her desk.

Chapter 6

Violet

THE FIELD TRIP TO MOANING CAVERN *came too quickly, and Violet was slow to pull herself from bed and load up with the rest of the teens.* So slow, in fact, that she ended up stuck in the middle seat of the back of someone's car she'd never spoken to. For once, she was grateful for her small size because the guys on either side of her didn't leave much room to wiggle.

One of them let out a giant fart when they were almost to the cavern, and while they were all laughing it up, Violet felt as if she were going to barf. Someone seriously needed to go see the doc because the rotten egg smell could *not* be a good sign.

The moment the car stopped moving, Violet pushed against the guy to her right, shoving him into the door. He grumbled, but made his way out of the car. She hurried a good fifteen feet away before gasping for air. She'd been holding her breath as much as possible since the rotten egg was released. With her hands on her knees, she breathed the clean air until her head stopped spinning then looked up to see the other teen wolven gathering around a group of adults.

Hazel eyes caught her attention from the crowd. Patrick took one step toward her before she stood straight and shook her head.

He actually stopped. That was a first.

His shoulders sagged ever so slightly, but he turned away.

They hadn't spoken in two days. It may not have been fair, but she wasn't ready to talk about their fight—if that's what he wanted. She'd barely seen him since then. Jax had been more present though, which was not a welcome change. He was constantly telling her how stupid she'd been for even considering Tucker, but never explained why.

Not that it mattered anyway. She'd ended whatever had been starting, and he hadn't looked twice at her since.

Patrick looked at her again and anger pooled in her belly. He was keeping an eye on her, just like Jax had told him to. He was being a loyal guard dog... and she didn't want that.

With a final deep breath, big enough to raise her chest and shoulders, she joined the group of teenagers.

A deep voice from the Whisky Clan's male chaperone rose above their chaotic din, "Listen up! We need to go through the names we have to make sure everyone arrived safely. You never know with you crazy teenagers driving."

None of the clans had a bus and the possibility of exposure was too risky to rent one. The adults were busy with their other duties, and most of the teenagers were trustworthy and mature enough to handle carpooling. That being said, Violet was definitely finding a different car to ride back home in.

"I want you all to keep an eye out for the others around you," the short-haired female chaperone from Stanislaus Clan eyed everyone as she spoke. "Help us make this a good, memorable experience for everyone, and we'll be able to continue doing events like this in the future."

Violet groaned.

Thankfully, this would be her last field trip, as this one was going to be sad, lonely, and very long. Mya had already graduated, Jax was stuck at home due to future alpha duties, and Patrick... well there were more issues there than she wanted to think about right now. Plus, he would be eighteen soon and no longer welcome on these excursions. She would have even been okay having Robin around right now, but she'd been eighteen longer than Mya.

"Also, please remember that after the tour we are heading to Natural Bridges. The water will be cold, but you're a bunch of hot-blooded—" She looked around, seeming to remember there could be humans around and then said, "special teens. You'll be fine. Half the adults will lead the way and half will stay in the back, since we'll be traveling by foot. We'll make it a quick run." She winked, and a few whoops and hollers went off at the announcement.

No one had told Violet they were going to be getting wet. In her jeans and hoodie, she was not dressed for that, and quickly made the decision she would not be entering the water.

The group moved toward the gift shop and a young woman stepped forward. Her eyes were wide as she looked over the group. "I was told we would have a few larger individuals, but I see that number was exaggerated."

A few of the boys around Violet chuckled.

"Please be careful as you descend the first flight of stairs. It's a small opening and we wouldn't want any of you getting stuck."

More laughter answered her, and two guys in front of Violet elbowed each other.

"That being said, if there is anyone who is claustrophobic, I suggest you consider staying behind. One of your guides will remain on the platform at the top of the staircase, while the other will meet you at the bottom. With that, welcome to Moaning Cavern, and enjoy your climb."

The young woman stepped aside, and their two guides, who apparently had just come up from the stairs, introduced themselves. Six-foot-something boys made an excellent wall, which left her with the only option of imagining what the guides were talking about.

Wondering how long they'd be standing there, Violet sighed heavily.

A male voice explained a few more things, something about a steep spiral staircase and how if there was anyone who didn't think they could make the trip, now would be the time to step back—but they were all in excellent condition, so no one moved. He also said something about total darkness, but Violet wasn't paying attention. The back of Patrick's head was a lot more interesting.

Not talking to him didn't feel right, but she didn't want to feel like a chore anymore. She wanted him to talk to her because he wanted to, not because Jax told him to. They'd been really good friends when he first joined the clan, but over the last six months, or so, he'd pulled away and only interacted with her when he needed to.

The group moved toward the cavern entrance, shifting until they were single file. Their footsteps clattered against the metal staircase and Violet was grateful she didn't have a concussion anymore because this would have sucked.

"Whoa!"

Violet looked up from her feet to see one of the guys ahead of her crouched so he didn't smack his head. The stairs were almost like a bunch of ladders linked together. It was important to watch your step—and your head—many of the guys had to go down sideways and crouched.

For the second time in one day, Violet was extremely grateful for her lack of height.

"Looking tasty today, snack."

A shiver rolled up her spine as Vikter's hot breath trailed over her neck. He must have crouched real low in order to do that because she had already gone down a couple stairs.

"Why did *you* have to end up behind me?" Violet growled as she looked over her shoulder at him before taking another couple steps.

"Oh, I'm exactly where I wanted to be. No one was going to stop me."

"What do you want?" Violet asked through clenched teeth as she moved to one side to put her foot down on the next set of steps.

"I wanted a minute alone with you. With this single file business, you're stuck with me until we reach the bottom."

"Oh goody."

"I like that you're feisty." He chuckled and her head tipped back when he tugged on her ponytail. "I bet we could have a lot of fun. You should let me take you on a date sometime."

"I know at least two people who would probably kill you if I agreed to that," she warned as she moved to another set of stairs.

Vikter chuckled darkly and his voice sounded much closer when he said, "I'd like to see them try."

Violet groaned. She would have rather been lonely than have to deal with his chatter the whole time.

"Ack!"

Laughter filled the fissure behind her and many wolven in front of her turned around and began laughing as well. Confused, Violet secured her footing and turned to look back, expecting to find Vikter in her face.

Instead, a smile lifted one corner of her mouth at the sight of Vikter stuck a few steps behind her. He jerked about trying to get free, but his shoulders had wedged perfectly between the sides of the fissure. Panic began to settle over his face when he realized he really couldn't move forward.

"Stop laughing and get me out of here!"

That only made them laugh harder.

"I guess you should have been paying more attention to where you were going instead of messing with me, huh?" Violet lifted a brow and smirked at him.

Vikter's face started turning red and she briefly wondered how long it would take before it turned purple, but the fear in his eyes clawed at her soul.

Closing her eyes, she shook her head and drew in a deep breath. "I can't believe I'm about to do this." She climbed the steps between them to get a better look at how his shoulders were positioned. "You need to go backward, not forward."

"I tried that. It didn't work. What do you know, anyway?" Vikter snarled.

His eyes were fading in and out of gold which shortened their time to get this solved. If word got out that one of them was stuck, an employee would come help. The humans couldn't find out, or even suspect, what they were.

"Vikter," she tried his name and thankfully it pulled his attention to her instead of the laughing teens around them. "Try again, but this time move one shoulder like you're moving sideways instead of trying to get both out at the same time."

"Why should I listen to you?"

"I'd be happy to leave you here to get laughed at by everyone. My brother hates you and I can't stand you, but I care about the clans." She lightly punched his stomach. "Now do what I said. Turn your left shoulder behind you."

The order made his eyes flare gold, but he listened and tried to do what she said.

"You're still moving both shoulders." She ducked her head around his legs and glared up at the guy behind Vikter. "You! Stop laughing, or I'll make sure you're the next one to get stuck." The guy sobered up quickly, and his buddy behind him snickered. "Hold his right shoulder in place so we can move his left one."

"I can do this by myself," Vikter growled.

"Shut up." Violet snapped at him and moved to stand by his left side. "On the count of three: one, two, three!" She pushed as hard as she could against his left side while he moved and the other guy held and pushed against his right shoulder in place.

The rip of fabric filled the fissure that had gone quiet and a small yelp followed. Vikter was free, but he held his left shoulder tightly and glared at her.

"You're welcome." She rolled her eyes and continued down the steps telling others to keep moving as she went.

A second guide's voice called out to them as they appeared on the upper platform, "Ah, I thought we lost half our group for a minute there. Come on, file in here and make your way down the stairs to the second platform at the base of the cavern."

Violet tried to push away from Vikter, but he kept annoyingly close. She finally settled along the railing and stared at a sign that read, 'Moaning Cavern - Calaveras California.'

She tried to listen to the guide because he was a fountain of knowledge, but she kept missing bits and pieces.

"... this staircase we are standing on was one of the first arc-welding projects to ever have been completed... built in 1922... scrap metal from a World War One Battleship... It's one hundred feet tall and spirals seven and a half times..."

"Knock it off, Vikter," Violet growled when the irritating wolven male flicked her ear. She winced when her voice echoed in the cavern.

"Is everything alright up there?" called the guide from below and Violet looked down to see him staring up at the stairs from the base platform.

"All good!" Violet answered and gave a thumbs up, but with how far up she still was, she would have been surprised if he had seen it.

They all clambered onto the base platform, and the guide waited for them to settle down before asking, "Who knows how many steps we just took?"

No one answered.

"You just walked down one hundred and forty-four stairs. You are welcome to look around. Take a few minutes to enjoy the cavern before we make the trek back to the top, but first, I want to show you something."

Violet ducked between two wolven males and around a couple holding hands to distance herself from Vikter. Someone stepped into her path and she ran into his chest with a quiet, "Umph."

Sweet, chocolate peppermint wafted over her with a hint of cedar and she breathed deep, letting the smell calm her down.

"Violet?" Patrick whispered her name and she shoved away from him as fast as she could, but he held her arms to keep her from knocking into whoever was standing behind her. "Easy."

"I'm sorry, I didn't mean to bump into you and I'm sorry I smelled you, gah, that's so weird and—"

"Shhh," Patrick placed two fingers over her lips to stop her rambling before leaning over to whisper in her ear. "Wolven already have good hearing and now you're in a place that echoes."

Heat poured over her face and down her neck. Turning her head, she placed her lips near his ear and whispered, "Thanks for stopping me."

A shudder rolled through Patrick. He shook his head as a response, then slid his hand down her arm and wove his fingers through hers.

Her heart hammered in her chest and she was so grateful wolven didn't have *that* good of hearing, otherwise everyone would have been staring at her tomato red face and telling Jax she was holding hands with his future beta.

That thought alone should have made her pull away from Patrick, but the connection felt beyond incredible and Jax wasn't there. Holding his hand, breathing in his scent... it was the piece of her that had been missing since he backed off months ago.

He wasn't guarding her. He wasn't following any orders. He was simply being in the moment with her. Something she wasn't sure she had ever seen him do.

"So, if everyone is ready," called the guide, drawing her out of her thoughts, "I will turn off all the lights."

"What?" Violet asked, clearly having missed something.

Patrick chuckled and leaned over to explain, "It's to show what it was like for the miners who only had one lantern."

All the lights went out.

Complete darkness surrounded them.

Wolven eyesight required a hint of light to be able to see at night. Even starlight was enough. Granted, Violet's abilities weren't as strong as the others, but she couldn't see a thing.

A few growls went off and she thought someone was crying, but with the amount of echoes the cavern created it was hard to tell for certain. One thing was sure, though; she was not the only wolven uneasy without the ability to see.

Patrick's fingers squeezed her hand lightly, making her jump. She'd forgotten they were holding hands. Her free hand wrapped around his forearm and clutched it to her chest like he was her lifeline.

His body shook with a silent chuckle, and he slipped his arm free of her grasp to wrap it around her waist. There, in the pitch-black cavern, Patrick held her against his chest. His warmth and sweet, intoxicating smell relaxed her and she leaned into him. Something touched the top of her head and she was about to ask if he had kissed her when the guide spoke up again, ruining the moment.

"Settle down, please." Once everyone was quiet, he lit a single flame lantern.

Violet looked up at Patrick to find he was staring above her head. She turned around and his arm moved with her so his hand ended up on the front side of her hip. She leaned her back against him as she looked around with awe.

Even with some light to allow her wolven eyes to work, she could tell the drastic difference. She imagined what it must have been like for those human miners and how trusting of their ropes they had to have been. This was only a third of the cavern and the flame was so small… coupling that with all the noises they must have heard was disconcerting.

"I can't imagine what those miners had to go through," Violet whispered and Patrick tugged lightly on her hip.

His voice was gentle against her ear, "I will forever be awed by your compassion for others. These miners are long gone, and yet you feel for them."

"Of course I do," Violet turned in his hold again so she could look up at him. "Without them, none of this would be here. I'm grateful, but I also feel for the trials they had to endure."

A soft smile lifted one corner of his mouth. Here in the darkness it was like a whole new person was coming out of him. Or rather… the original one. The one she'd first met all those years ago and had immediately fallen for.

Patrick opened his mouth to speak, but the lights turned back on, driving out the dark. The light brought back his painfully familiar shield, blocking the emotion he'd been showing. Whatever he'd been about to say had been chased away with the darkness.

His hand fell away from her hip and he took a step away from her. "I'll stay by you on the way back up. That way Vikter will have to stay away."

Disbelief made her jaw drop. She couldn't believe he could just flip a switch like that. The anger she'd felt earlier bubbled up inside her. "No need," she snapped and stepped away from him. "I got it."

And she did.

When they were told to start the trek back to the surface she was one of the first ones up the spiral staircase. A couple of the chaperones were waiting for them in the trees when they exited the building and excitement charged through the group. One thing all wolven had in common, they all loved to run.

Including Violet.

Running was one of the only things she was good at. She didn't need super speed or strength to run. It just so happened that it was one of the only areas she excelled at. Chalk it up to training, or actually having some kind of wolven ability, but she was even able to keep up with some of the adults in Sentinel Clan.

The male who had spoken to them when they first arrived nodded after a minute. "Looks like we've got enough to start. Let's run!"

Adrenaline surged through her, and she took off after the chaperones as they darted through the trees.

Chapter 7

Violet

***ONLY A FEW MINUTES HAD PASSED** before they reached the trailhead, and only a few more until the Natural Bridges.* Violet beamed at one of the chaperones who gawked when she kept up with them the entire way. Many of the teens had fallen behind, left to follow their scent trail. The chaperones at the back would make sure everyone arrived safely.

Violet found a log to sit on and watched the river while she waited for others to show—she still had no desire to enter the water.

Teen wolven trickled in and many stripped down to swim wear they'd hidden beneath their clothing. Some jumped in fully clothed, making riotous laughter explode throughout the area. There were even a couple guys who had forgotten swim trunks, but went in their boxer shorts.

It didn't take long for Patrick to arrive, but instead of joining the others in the water, he found a spot in the trees not too far away from her.

She was starting to wish she had brought her phone, so she could at least text Lexie back and forth, when a fully clothed Aiden ran full speed into the water, hollering like Tarzan.

Genuine laughter shook her shoulders, and a grin split across her face. She had honestly forgotten that he would have been on this trip. Maybe she could get a ride home with him. That would be a lot more fun than being squished between two farty boys.

Aiden trudged from the water and shook out his light brown hair, grinning like a mad man. His gaze landed on her and an air of mischief surrounded him.

Violet's eyes bugged and her smile disappeared. "No! Aiden, I am not going in that water."

"Oh, yes, you are." He reached for her, but she held up a hand to stop him. He paused, shrugged, and grabbed her arm to pull her off the ground. "Come on!"

"Aiden!" she screamed when she flew into the air. He caught her in his arms with ease and turned toward the river. "No! Don't you dare!"

He laughed, tipping his head back and swung her around a few times. "You look like the most miserable person in the world. Well..." He turned so she could see Patrick who had sat down and was looking away from them. The tendon in his jaw somersaulted a few times when Aiden continued, "except for him, but I can't do anything about that."

"I'm not miserable," she lied, and a squeak left her when he turned back toward the water. "I just don't want to get wet! That water is freezing!"

Aiden scoffed, "Please, with your warm blood, you won't even notice."

Kicking her legs did nothing, Aiden tightened his hold and gave her a toothy grin. "Don't make me hit you."

"At least explore the caves with me?" Aiden asked, giving her the most ridiculous puppy eyes ever.

"Does that work on Mya?" Violet asked without thinking and wanted to smack herself. Mya was being exceptionally careful not to reveal anything to him before his birthday.

Aiden's brows lifted and he released her legs. "Mya, huh?" A light rosy color tinted his cheeks. "Nah, she's pretty good at keeping to her word. My begging has no effect on her."

Violet nodded and stepped out of his hold. "Would she go in that cavern with you?"

"If I say yes, will you go?"

"Aiden..."

"Come on!" He tugged on her sleeve. "Just come take a peek and then I promise I'll let you come back here and be your miserable self."

Violet chewed on her lip and eyed the water. She didn't have a change of clothes, which meant her jeans were going to be soaked... running in wet jeans was not fun and the drive back would be miserable, but the caves did look pretty cool.

"Please?" Aiden asked once more, giving her his best big ol' brown puppy eyes.

She sighed, "Let me take my hoodie off."

He whooped and bounced beside her while she took her socks and shoes off and pulled her hoodie over her head before tossing them at Patrick. He caught the bundle of clothing with a raised brow. "Hold on to those for me."

She only had time to see Patrick nod before her arm was nearly yanked off.

Aiden bolted toward the water with her. She was about to dig her heels in when he let go and jumped into the water.

At least he didn't pull her in.

She laughed and followed along on dry land while he raced upstream. The first bridge came into view and the shore ended. A small groan left her as she peered into the cave. She didn't want to get wet, but it looked amazing and she wanted to see more.

"Yeah! She's getting in!"

Violet laughed at him and stepped into the water. She sucked in a sharp breath and glared at Aiden who was grinning like the Cheshire cat.

"It's freezing!"

"You're not getting in that deep, what are you complaining about?"

Violet shook her head, but decided just to go for it. They continued up stream, pausing to gaze up at the wonders of the bridge. Most of the teens stayed near the chaperones downstream, away from the cave, so they were pretty much alone.

"This is amazing," Violet admired, staring up into the cave. She watched hundreds of water droplets fall from the natural ceiling into the river then looked at Aiden who was up to his neck in water and smiling from ear to ear. "I don't really know why you did this, but thank you. I needed it."

He nodded and looked around where he was treading water. "It gets really deep over here, so if you don't want to get any wetter, I'd stay where you are." He swam closer, found his footing, and stood up making her have to tip her head back a little. "So, I know we aren't the closest of friends, but Jax and I are good, and I think Patrick and I could be if he would relax a little—"

Violet huffed a laugh.

"They love you. Mya completely adores you. I think you're pretty cool, and that's good enough for me." He looked deeper into the cave for a bit before gazing back at her with pinched brows. "I know you and Patrick aren't really getting along right now, and you don't have anyone else here that you typically hang out with. I wanted to make sure you had fun."

A gentle smile spread across her face and she shook her head. "You're pretty awesome. Anyone would be lucky to have you as a friend."

His pinched expression turned into a beaming grin. "Thanks." He jumped into the water, splashing her in the process. His head popped back up and he was still grinning. "We should go on a double date sometime. I've been meaning to ask Mya out anyway. I think she'd be more willing if you were there."

Excitement rushed through her, and she bounced on her toes, "That would be awesome!" She tipped her head to the side, hoping what she was about to say wouldn't give too much away. "I don't think you need to worry about Mya saying no."

Aiden's own excitement showed through the silver that pulsed in his brown eyes. "I really hope not. Who would you bring?"

She opened her mouth to answer, but froze... Jax wouldn't tolerate her dating anyone. Well, that put a damper on her excitement.

"I'd be happy to join," Vikter's voice echoed through the cave, and she spun around, wide-eyed, to see him stomping through the water toward her.

The splashing behind her let her know that Aiden was swimming as fast as he could, and a moment later he showed up nearly in front of her.

He growled at the intruder, "What do you want?"

"I want to go on a date with my snack." Vikter shot a toothy grin at Violet. "Rumor is your twin won't let any guy near you. What better way to get revenge?"

"There's a problem with your plan. I don't like you," Violet spat back.

Vikter shrugged, making the torn fabric on his shoulder flutter. "That would have been the easy way. I have no problem with the harder course of action. In fact, I will probably enjoy it more."

"What is your deal with my brother anyway? He's never done anything to you."

"I've been wanting revenge on Jax since he broke my nose in the last duels and threatened to take over Stanislaus," the crazed young alpha announced and stepped closer. "He's not here, so I can't take it out on him. Your little bodyguard has been quite the pain lately, too, and his feelings for you are obvious. Going after you will be killing two birds with one stone."

Fear widened Violet's eyes when he spoke the worry that Mya had voiced a few nights ago. "Jax doesn't want Stanislaus! And you're crazy if you think Patrick has feelings for me."

Aiden snorted, and as much as she wanted to question him about that, there wasn't time with the hot-headed, bloodthirsty future alpha threatening her.

She shook her head, "Besides, you should know territory advancements don't work like that anymore. It hasn't for centuries. Just let this go and we can all move forward and build some solid groundwork for the future."

"You lie!" Vikter yelled, clenching his fists as his eyes flashed gold. "You're in on it, too. The only way to protect my clan is by taking Jax down. I'll start by going after the closest thing to his heart." He lifted his arm and pointed a finger at her. "You."

"You touch her and Jax will hunt you down," Aiden spoke up and Violet glared at him, wishing he hadn't.

Vikter chuckled darkly, "I'm counting on it. I would love to beat that overgrown mutt into oblivion."

"You'll start a clan war if you do this!" She moved in front of Aiden, who hissed at her to get back, and tried once again to reason with Vikter. She couldn't believe he was truly willing to push the rules so far. "You're really paranoid enough to risk bringing that kind of trouble down on us? On all of us?"

Gold swirled in Vikter's eyes, threatening to take over. He shook his head. "No. The kings and queens will understand. My clan has been threatened. I must defend it."

Aiden yelled for her as Vikter dove forward.

His attack was slowed down by the water lapping at his legs. Violet ducked around him and delivered a precise jab to his kidney.

Vikter roared, arching his back, and swung blindly behind him allowing her to dance around and position herself for another well-aimed shot.

She landed a few more hits before Vikter seemed to realize she wasn't as easy a target as he'd suspected. His movements tightened up, and his openings nearly disappeared.

Aiden wisely stayed back, but he watched them like a hawk from the sidelines; circling with her when she moved, ready to take over if she needed him to.

Playing on the defensive was not in Violet's favor. She wasn't strong enough to block properly and her arms began to ache and it stung whenever his attacks made contact. Thankfully she'd managed to avoid getting hit in the face—because that was a sure-fire way for her to be knocked out.

Her strength was beginning to wane, so she shifted tactics. Instead of blocking, she tried to dodge which thankfully worked most of the time. He was bigger and slower than she was. She just needed to hold out a little longer.

Vikter threw a low punch, which she pushed through the water to avoid, and with his lowered position took the perfect opportunity to jab his face. The connection of her fist to his eye was solid and Vikter staggered back a couple steps, howling.

"That's enough, Violet," Aiden called to her, rushing forward to push her out of the cave. "You need to get out of here. I'll stall him as long as I can."

He was crazy if he thought she was going to leave him.

She turned on him to tell him just that, but her eyes widened as Vikter's fist rose into the air, "Aiden!"

Violet tugged on his shirt, but she heard the impact of Vikter's knuckles against Aiden's skull.

He stumbled into her and she barely braced against his weight. He held the back of his head and turned to face Vikter who sneered at them both.

"Want a broken arm again, huh?" Vikter raised his fists. His knuckles were white from how hard he was clenching his hands.

Violet shifted back and forth anxiously. She was wearing out, but she couldn't leave Aiden to deal with him.

"You can run if you want, little snack, but I'll catch you." Vikter laughed, "I might enjoy a good chase."

Trying to ignore him, Violet pulled on Aiden's arm, "Let's go."

They'd taken two steps when the crazed teen lunged for them.

Aiden shoved her deeper into the cave, out of the way of Vikter's attack, and her feet couldn't find ground.

Her head went under and she cursed the weight of her soaked jeans as she struggled to break the water's surface again. She had to get back to him. In pushing her, Aiden had left himself unprotected.

She gasped for air when her head rose above water level, then searched for the two boys. She struggled against her jeans and turned in a circle to find Vikter pacing like a caged animal while Aiden stood still, waiting. Blood dribbled down his chin from a split in his lip, it would be healed soon, but Violet wondered how many hits Vikter had gotten in while she was underwater.

"Violet, go find Patrick!" Aiden's silver eyes found her when she started toward him.

Annoyance fell over her and she glared at him, "I'm not going anywhere." She finally found the ground and started wading toward him as she lowered her voice, hoping their attacker wouldn't hear the next part, "He's not stable, Aiden."

He snorted, "Ya think?"

"Not stable?" Vikter laughed and Violet cursed the echo in the caves. "I promise I'm thinking clearly." He motioned to Aiden. "You really wanna try and take on an alpha?" He smacked his chest and Violet was seriously starting to wonder what he was on. "Think you'll move up in rank? I was holding back before; I won't do that again."

"I know very well that I'm not strong enough to take you down," Aiden calmly admitted, and ice filled Violet's veins. It was true. She'd even beaten him when they'd sparred weeks ago. "But I'll hold you off long enough for her to get out of here."

The ice in her veins reached her heart. She threw her twin mind-link open and screamed, *"Jax, I need Patrick, now!"*

Vikter dipped his chin and snarled, "So be it."

"No!" Violet yelled when Vikter launched at Aiden.

She shot in front of her defender, connecting her fist with Vikter's stomach... but she wasn't his target anymore. He roared at her and threw her downstream. A rock impacted her stomach and she struggled for air.

Aiden used the distraction to get into position and delivered a well-timed combo of punches to the raging teen's exposed ribs.

Once she'd caught her breath, she stumbled out of the water and ran toward them, but time had run out.

Vikter landed an uppercut, knocking Aiden's head back.

It was like one of the nightmares where you're running, but never get any closer to your destination... she couldn't reach him in time.

Dazed, Aiden took a couple steps back, but Vikter gave him no quarter. He stepped into Aiden's space and hammered his abdomen with his fists. Water droplets flew from Aiden's hair when he doubled over and bloody spit fell from his lips. Vikter grabbed a fistful of her friend's hair and pulled his head up.

"Stop!" she cried. She tried to get to them, but the water dragged her legs down.

A sickening crunch twisted her stomach into knots.

Aiden slipped from the boulder Vikter had thrust him into and sank beneath the water.

Vikter turned toward her, chuckling like a maniac. "He'll be fine. I can't guarantee the same for you."

Lightning struck her feet. It was as if the water didn't exist anymore. She raced forward, jumped at the last second and slammed her fist into Vikter's shocked face as gravity reclaimed her. His head twisted to the side as she landed, splashing water everywhere.

"I believe my twin showed you that move last time!" Violet snarled at him and was surprised at how animalistic she sounded. "We learned it from Patrick."

As if on cue, the cave rattled with the force of Patrick's roar. He zipped past her and slammed into Vikter, taking him down into the water.

Relief sagged her shoulders before she turned to search for Aiden. She didn't need to worry about Patrick, she knew he would be just fine.

Aiden had traveled downstream a bit, but she caught up to him quickly, grabbed his shoulder, and rolled him over so he faced the sky. "Come on, Aiden." She tapped his cheek and began pulling him toward the river bank.

Once more than half his body was out of the water, Violet fell to her knees and searched for signs of breath.

"No, no, no..." she cursed and began chest compressions.

From the moment Sentinel Clan kids could understand what they were learning, and why, they were taught how to help someone if they were choking. The lessons grew more complex as they aged, and over time they also learned CPR and first aid techniques.

She never thought the lifetime of lessons would come in handy around a clan of supernatural wolven, but here she was, tilting his head back into the correct position so she could breathe into his mouth.

Aiden coughed and Violet rolled him onto his side, right before he spewed water. His eyes didn't open, but he was breathing.

She sank into a crossed-legged position and cradled his head in her lap, keeping him on his side. Blood oozed from a gash cutting across his temple and forehead. "Mya is going to kill me if you die. You need to wake up, Aiden."

It didn't take long for Patrick to beat Vikter into submission. The future alpha cowered on one knee beneath Patrick. His eyes were swollen, both his nose—which wasn't straight anymore—and his lip, were bleeding, and his breathing was labored while he held his side.

There was a conversation happening, but Violet's ears weren't able to pick up anything more than angry tones. Vikter's face twisted in rage and Patrick slammed his fist down.

It was over.

Vikter's body slumped, but Patrick caught him before he fell into the water.

He carried the unconscious teen to the riverbank near her and dumped him by a tree before heading in her direction.

"Are you okay?" His hazel eyes roamed over her before landing on Aiden. "Is he okay?"

Worry trembled her lower lip and she shook her head. "He's not waking up."

Patrick lowered to one knee and looked their friend up and down. "One of the Stanislaus chaperones is almost here. One of ours ran back to grab their car. They'll get him home to doc as fast as possible."

"The drive home is too long. He needs to see someone now."

"Violet, we can't take him to a human doctor, and it might take longer to get permission to enter another clan's territory than it would to drive home." He pulled something from her hair, then looked back at Aiden and grabbed his wrist. "I saw you give him CPR. He's breathing, it sounds like his lungs are clear, and his heart rate is normal."

She stared at him, wondering how he could hear that. Could others hear as well as he could?

"He's a fast healer. He'll be okay."

Seconds later, the female chaperone from Stanislaus Clan skidded into the clearing with her short hair sticking up in every direction. She patted her hair down and looked between the two unconscious teens then back to Patrick with a raised brow.

Patrick returned to his feet to greet her. "Everything is taken care of..." He gave a brief, but full report of what happened between himself and Vikter.

"And what happened with you two?" The woman asked, stepping toward Violet.

Patrick tensed, but remained still, allowing her to approach.

"Aiden and I were exploring upstream. He wanted to show me the bridge cave. Vikter found us, started saying some crazy things about Jax wanting to take over Stanislaus, and said he was going to stop him... and that he was going to start with me. We fought. Then Aiden tried to hold him off so I could get away."

The woman eyed Vikter warily when Violet was finished. "I'll make sure to report this to our Alpha and Luna. You make sure to do the same when you return home. Vikter's been warned too many times. I can't imagine this will end well for him." She looked down at Violet and Aiden again, "Any news on transport for your friend?"

Patrick nodded. "They are almost here."

"Alright. You seem responsible enough," she sighed and walked over to Vikter then kicked his shoe. "I'll take him back and leave you in charge here."

Instead of answering, Patrick watched Vikter very closely as he woke up, shook himself out, and stood up. Grunts and groans left him and he clutched his side, wheezing for air. His head stayed bowed, not meeting Patrick's gaze, and he nodded when the female scolded him. There was only an angry sideways glance at Violet as he trudged away.

Once they were out of sight, Patrick returned to her side and sat so close that his arm brushed hers.

Violet combed her fingers through Aiden's light brown hair, pushing it away from his head wound. Quietly, she broke the silence, admitting what was in her head and heart, "I really needed you, Patrick."

It took a second for him to respond. "I'm sorry," he shook his head. "I was trying to give you space, like you asked."

She huffed a laugh and turned her head to look at him. "You pick now to finally listen to me?" Violet elbowed him lightly. "Now? When I'm surrounded by other clans and a crazed teen who has it out for my brother and me?"

Patrick's jaw clenched. "I know, I didn't really think that part through. I thought you would be safe with Aiden. When I realized Vikter wasn't anywhere to be found, I got up to find you. Aiden contacted me shortly after that and I was more than halfway here when Jax practically exploded my brain." He nudged her with his shoulder. "You can't have it both ways, Vi. I can't be around you and not protect you."

She looked down at Aiden to avoid Patrick's stare. "Because of Jax?" Violet asked, hating how small her voice sounded.

"No." His answer was firm and left no room for question.

When she didn't answer or look up at him, his fingertips touched her chin, guiding her toward him. Patrick's gaze searched hers, searing her soul. No matter how many years passed, she knew she would never forget those hazel eyes and the golden flecks that drew her in.

His throat bobbed when he swallowed hard before practically whispering, "I will always protect you. Jax's order for me to do so just made it easier."

She didn't know how to answer that, and her heart was tripping over itself. After wetting her lips, she forced herself to look away and tucked an invisible hair behind her ear.

Patrick bumped her lightly with his shoulder again and she leaned against him, telling herself that resting her head against him for just a minute wouldn't hurt anything.

A short time later, the male chaperone from Sentinel Clan came crashing through the trees toward them. His silver eyes showed his wolf was lending him power. "Is he alright?"

"He's stable," Patrick answered while he stood. "I'll help you carry him back to the car. We'll head home as soon as we get to my truck."

The man nodded and moved into position to pick up Aiden's legs.

Patrick waited until Violet wiggled out from under Aiden's head then grabbed their unconscious friend under the arms. Aiden's head fell forward and Violet bit her lower lip, hoping his neck would be okay.

Together the two males easily made their way through the trees with Violet sticking close to Patrick's side. She waited patiently while they laid Aiden in the back seat of the car, and watched anxiously as they drove away at lightning speeds.

Patrick sighed once the car disappeared around a bend. "I should have asked before assuming; do you want to head home with me?"

"Yes," she answered firmly. "I want to check in on Aiden." She grimaced and added, "And I really don't want to ride back another two-plus hours with a bunch of stupid teenage guys who fart."

Amusement slowly lifted the corners of his mouth. "I promise no guys will fart in my truck."

"What about stupid guys? Will they be in your truck?"

His smile spread, melting her heart. "It's just you and me. Unless you consider me stupid?"

A cute, flirty comment opened her mouth, but common sense held her tongue back. She lowered her gaze and shook her head. "I don't think you're stupid, Patrick."

Chapter 8

Violet

SHE WAS RIGHT.

Running with wet jeans sucked.

She felt bad for soaking Patrick's truck, but he didn't seem to mind. Besides, he was pretty soaked as well.

Patrick maneuvered his truck through the second compound gate and she hugged her hoodie to her chest. He had the forethought to tell Eric—that was the name of the chaperone, apparently—to put her things in the truck bed so they were waiting for her when she and Patrick made it to the truck.

"You're probably gonna want to put your shoes on," Patrick reminded her as he turned his truck into the community parking lot.

"Right." Violet ducked down and did just that then hopped out of the car and threw her hoodie over her head. Even with its added protection, the cold air nipped at her wet clothing and skin. "I'm going to check in on Aiden," she told him as they headed toward Alpha House.

He shook his head and shoved his hands into his pockets. "You should talk to Luna first. Aiden can wait."

Violet stared at him, "You know my mom doesn't like it when you use her title."

A smirk lifted one corner of his mouth. "All I'm saying is, she needs your report. Aiden is already awake and with the doc."

She stared at him wide-eyed.

"You do remember he's wolven and they tend to heal quickly, right?"

"Why are you always reminding me about that?" she asked, pausing her feet so she could turn and look at him. "Of course, I know that. This is just one of those moments that I'm insanely jealous of your clan-link."

Patrick shrugged. "Having a bunch of people being able to enter your head isn't the greatest." He rubbed the back of his neck, "Why are you always so worried when someone gets hurt?"

Violet's cheeks flushed and she kicked at a small rock as she started walking again. "I don't heal as fast as the rest of the clan, and I always appreciate it when people check in to see if I'm okay. Mya and Lexie came over for a girl's night after Jax hit me..."

A growl rolled out of Patrick, surprising her. "Sorry," he muttered and looked away from her. "I'm still upset about that."

She snorted. "Me too." She shook her head and then let out a huff of laughter. "His apology sucked.... Anyway, I was just meaning that I want him to know I care about him and to see if he needs anything. There isn't anything wrong with that, is there?"

"You care about Aiden?" The surprise in his voice almost made her smile.

"Not like that, but he's a good guy. Mya likes him, and I like Mya, so..." she shrugged.

Patrick nodded.

They both stopped just before reaching the stepping stone walkway up to the house.

"Jax needs to work on his apologies," Patrick grumbled.

That *did* make her laugh, and one side of his mouth quirked up. "I don't think that is something he is going to improve on any time soon."

"I think you're right." His lopsided grin grew and he opened his mouth to say something else, but a loud siren went off, making them both cover their ears.

When it stopped, Violet looked at him with wide eyes. "A breach? That is what that siren means, right?" she asked, disbelieving what she'd heard.

Rogues didn't usually make it through the compound walls. They weren't organized or mentally stable enough to think that far ahead, so she'd never heard the sound accept during drills… where everyone knew it was a drill.

Patrick nodded, confirming her question, but his gaze was a little unfocused. He blinked and looked toward Alpha House. "Jax says they had some trouble on the border, but they're handling it."

"Trouble?" Violet spun around, looking down the road for her twin. "What kind of trouble? Is he okay?" Worry forced her to take a few steps before Patrick's hand landed on her shoulder and he pulled her back around to face him. "I should go help."

"No. You're worrying over nothing. We just talked about this. He is wolven. He'll be fine." He gazed down at her with a warmth she'd only seen on rare occasions, and her breath caught in her lungs. "I promise. They are just bringing in a couple of wolves who wandered too far into the territory."

"Patrick…"

"Vi." The way he said her nickname made her freeze. Warmth spread through her chest, the way it always did when he addressed her with that breathy tone. "I told him I'd keep you safe."

"If what they're doing isn't a big deal, then why do I need protecting?" Violet growled, then ducked under Patrick's arm.

"Violet, stop!"

His fingers snagged her shirt, but she kept going, grinning when she'd made it a good thirty feet up the road before Patrick's arm encircled her waist, pulling her against his hard chest. She gasped and tried to wiggle free, but he held her tight.

"Let me go!" She squirmed around to push against his chest.

"Not until I know you're not going to run away again," Patrick growled at her, his hazel eyes darkened making the golden flecks stand out more as he stared down at her.

"My brother could be in danger," Violet growled back, but held very still.

Patrick's head tilted sideways. "If he was in any real danger, do you think I would still be here?"

Blinking, Violet's lips parted as she thought about that. The answer was simple. Patrick would give his life to protect Jax. That had been put to the test last year when Patrick had shoved Jax out of the way of a crazed crossbow hunter and taken a bolt to the side because of it. He wouldn't tell anyone why, but his wolf had refused to help him heal. Thankfully, even without the wolf spirit, they still healed faster than humans; otherwise, he would have died. It was days before he woke up from what should have been a fatal wound. Patrick had come close during that time, twice... Only the doc and Violet knew how bad it had gotten.

She hadn't left his side until he'd woken up—when she'd played it off that she'd just been checking in.

"You're right," Violet relented and her hands slid down his chest to rest on either side of his waist. "I'm sorry. I won't run off again."

Patrick's hold on her waist loosened, but he didn't remove his arm. His gaze held hers and Violet hoped she wasn't imagining things when his eyes dropped to her lips for a fraction of a second.

"Come on." He dropped his arm, stepped away from her, and nodded toward the house. "Let's go talk to your mom."

They were less than ten feet from the walkway to Alpha House when a heavy weight dropped over her chest. Placing her hand over her heart, she took a deep breath, but the ominous feeling didn't dissipate.

Patrick turned to look back at her, and his eyes darted back and forth between her hand on her chest and her eyes, "Hey, you okay?"

She shook her head, then nodded. "I think so. I'm having a little bit of a hard time breathing."

"Maybe Vikter hit you harder than you thought?"

Shaking her head again, she continued toward the house. "No, he didn't ge..."

Her words trailed off as four warriors marched up the road toward them. They circled two males and a female, all in zip-tie handcuffs, while Alpha Draven walked behind them with Beta Paul & Jax on either side.

One of the three prisoners looked their way and terror chased down her spine as she watched red seep into his eyes.

"Blood Moon," she whispered as Patrick pushed her behind him.

"Violet, get inside now," Patrick growled over his shoulder.

One pair of red eyes turned into three and they snapped their zip tie cuffs. The warriors lunged at the red-eyed prisoners, desperate to keep them under control.

It didn't take long for the Blood Moon trio to gain the upper hand. A snap of bone rang into the air when one of the warrior's knees was kicked sideways. Alpha Draven's snarl rose above the scream of his clan member and he joined the fray, throwing a red-eyed male a good ten feet down the road.

Another warrior fell, and Jax darted into the fight to protect a male warrior from a life-threatening bite to his neck.

A set of red eyes turned on Jax, and Violet sucked in a sharp breath. She darted under Patrick's arm and sprinted toward her twin.

"Violet, don't!" Patrick called after her, but her feet only carried her faster. A sense of calm settled over her as she neared the closest prisoner, who'd grabbed one of the female warriors by the head, on her way toward Jax.

Years of training kicked in, and when the intruder turned toward her, Violet's fist met his jaw. By the time he turned back to snarl at her, she had dived between his legs.

Her back hit the ground and she kicked up as hard as she could. Yelping, the guy dropped like a sack of potatoes. She swung her legs in a helicopter rotation, knocking his head to the side, and rolled to her feet to continue toward Jax.

Locked in combat, her twin didn't notice her. He threw a punch only to have his opponent dodge, lock his arm in place, and thrust against the back of his elbow.

"Jax!" Violet's shout mingled with his cry of pain. She held her elbow, feeling as though it was on fire, and rushed toward him.

Her name was called, but the warning was too late. Hit from the side by a wolven-shaped semi-truck, she flew a few feet and landed hard on the ground. Her hip burned when she pushed away from the ground, but her attacker landed on her legs. She wriggled underneath his astounding weight, trying and failing to throw him off.

Panic seized her as he scaled her body like a rock wall and clamped his powerful hands around her head. He drove her head to the side, exposing her neck and lowered his mouth to her throat. She screamed, frantically trying to get out from under him, but he was so much bigger. His hot breath burned the sensitive skin of her neck...

Then the weight was gone.

Violet blinked, momentarily stunned, then launched to her feet, ready to attack. Two of the three Blood Moon wolven were pinned face down in the dirt with a Sentinel warrior or guard—reinforcements must have shown up while she was down—kneeling on their back while another replaced the broken zip-ties with multiple reinforcements.

She spun, looking for the one who had attacked her.

Off the road, in a shallow ditch, the guy was now pinned under Patrick's weight. He hammered her attacker's face and she winced at the sound of bone cracking before her feet were moving her toward Patrick.

"Violet, don't!" Alpha Draven ordered.

Years ago, when her mom noticed Violet could defy the alpha, she stepped in and taught Violet to pretend she felt the effects of the alpha aura. So, that's what she had done since. She felt the pull of his power, sure, but the pressure to submit had never been there. Chalk it up to not having a wolf or whatever, but she didn't have to obey—and in that moment, she chose not to.

"Violet! I order you to stop!" The alpha aura swarmed over her and she hesitated, knowing if she continued it would ruin the ruse she'd built over the years.

"Patrick, he's had enough!" she cried out to him, hoping her voice would calm him.

It didn't.

His elbow flew back again as the guy's body went limp and his head flopped back. Blood covered his mouth and nose, and ran down his throat. Red splattered the area with each hit.

"It's true," laughed the first guy Violet had kicked where it really counted. One of the warriors lifted him to his knees, since his hands were bound behind his back now. "You have a reaper in your midst."

A different kind of panic surged through Violet.

"Paul, grab her!" Alpha Draven ordered when she took another step.

Neither Alpha, nor Beta, could stop her as she ran forward and launched herself into the ditch.

Patrick pulled his arm back again.

The sound his knuckles made against the guy's bloodied face made her stomach twist.

Violet grabbed his arm when he readied for another hit. "He's out. Let him go!"

Oblivious to her pleas, Patrick shook her off and repositioned his arm. His breathing was uneven, labored and heavy, as he trembled.

Knots twisted in her gut when his fist landed another punch and blood dotted the ground. She shifted around his side, attempting to meet his gaze, but his dark, wavy hair hung obscuring his face.

Drawing in a quick breath, Violet dropped to her knees, and leaned over the Blood Moon guy—placing herself directly in line of Patrick's fist.

He froze, arm still raised to strike.

Slowly, Violet placed a hand on the unconscious guy's shoulder and threw all the authority she could muster into her voice, "Let him go."

A low growl rumbled out of him.

Well, that didn't work.

"Patrick." His name left her lips with a breathy note. If she couldn't get through to him... if he didn't stop... they'd throw him in Lockup. Who knew when her father would feel generous enough to let him out?

His breathing slowed, but his position didn't change. She tried to catch his eyes, but he'd pinched them shut. Torment was etched into every hard edge along his face.

Gently, Violet pressed her free palm against his cheek. A giant shudder ran through his body and his raised fist dropped a fraction. His skin was flushed, warm beneath her palm as she ran her thumb over his cheekbone.

"Please," she whispered. "Let him go."

The immediate thump of the guy's body made her cringe, but at least he'd let go.

Seconds later, the body was dragged from beneath her hand, between Patrick's legs. A guard appeared on either side of Patrick and a slight shift of her body let her see two more guards behind him.

Their gazes were locked on Patrick.

With one hand on Patrick's cheek and her other now free, she slid her free hand up his arm to grip his jacket sleeve. She made eye contact with each guard member and shook her head. They didn't move. One even took a step closer to Patrick.

Patrick's arm shifted and his hand gently clasped her arm, drawing her attention. Relief flooded through her, nearly driving her to tears, when her gaze was met by golden flecked, hazel eyes.

The guard to her left aimed a cattle prod looking thing with electricity sparking between two points at Patrick's side.

Violet threw herself into Patrick's chest. Her arms wrapped around his waist and he took an unsteady step backward before freezing. If it weren't for his pounding heart under her cheek, she would have thought he was a statue. The tension around them intensified.

A few thoughts ran through her mind; they wouldn't shock him if there was a chance she would be electrocuted as well, him being able to hug would show he was in control, and she just really wanted to hug him.

"Are you okay?" she asked, her voice muffled by his jacket. "Please, tell me you're okay."

The stiffness in Patrick's body eased. A small huff of laughter bounced her head before one of Patrick's hands cradled her head against him while the other circled around her shoulders. "You're the one who was pinned, and you're asking if I'm okay?"

Violet lifted her chin and found Patrick staring back at her with the warmth of the sun in his eyes. A small smile tugged at the corners of his mouth.

Why did he have to smile like that?

"Back off, Violet." Jax interrupted her thoughts, but his words felt weak in her mind.

"Jax!" Violet jerked away from Patrick, who quickly let her go, and bounded out of the ditch.

Her twin sat in the dirt with one of his arms bent at an unnatural angle. She slid to a stop in front of him and dropped to her knees.

"Your arm..." Violet reached out to him, but pulled back at the last second, unsure how to help. "What... what can I do?"

Molten gold eyes turned on her. "You can follow orders."

Violet jerked away as if he had slapped her.

A female warrior came to his side, looked over his arm, told him to brace himself and shoved his elbow back the way it should have been. Jax's face drained of color and his cry was short, but it tore at her soul. Once there was color back in his cheeks the female helped him stand before moving on to the next person.

Confused and hurt, Violet shook her head. "I was trying to help."

"Help?" Jax yelled and a few people around them ducked their heads. "You aren't even supposed to be here! Why are you home early from the field trip?"

"I didn't realize I needed permission to come home!" she yelled back, hating how he was treating her.

He ignored her and continued, "If you really wanted to help, you would have followed protocol and gone inside instead of freezing in the street like a child!"

She flinched at his words. They stung because she *had* frozen.

Jax wasn't done, though. "Our clan brothers and sisters were hurt because you didn't follow orders! One of them is dead!" He thrust his good arm out to the side and pointed at the only body lying in the road.

A long pale-blond braid spilled out from under the jacket someone had laid over her head. She was one of the gate guards. The one whose name Violet could never remember the name of.

"That's enough!" Evalyn Draven's voice sounded over her twin's antics.

Jax's chin lowered in respect and submission.

Many of the wolven lowered to one knee as the group greeted her in unison by saying her title, "Luna."

Evalyn walked toward their group, her wolven eyes nearly luminescent as she assessed situation, nodding to those who called out to her as she passed. From a distance, it was hard to place an exact color on the luna's eyes, but the power surrounding her was impossible to ignore.

Alpha Draven brushed a kiss over her cheek when she stopped to check on him.

When she turned to address everyone, multiple people stood up a little straighter. "Jax and the rest of those seriously injured, head to Dr.

Penmann's. The rest of you will follow Alpha Draven and take these Blood Moon scouts to Lockup." Her voice lowered in volume as she eyed her daughter. "Violet and Patrick will follow me."

"Paul will stay with you," Alpha Draven added.

"No. He won't," Evalyn countered, leveling her husband with a stern look. "He is needed with you at Lockup."

By the way the alpha's jaw shifted, Violet knew he wasn't happy, but he agreed anyway.

Before Violet could move, Jax stormed past her, slamming the shoulder of his good arm into her as he went.

Wanting to fix whatever she had broken, Violet turned to call after him, but the wake of destruction turned her stomach.

One bloodied, unconscious prisoner, two injured, three hurt warriors, Jax's arm was definitely broken, and then there was the body of the female guard.

Patrick lowered his head and followed Evalyn toward Alpha House.

"Violet."

Startled, she jumped at the sound of her name coming from Alpha Draven. "Yes?"

The dark blue to white ombre of his eyes had always been unsettling to her. Maybe it was the color that made him always look so intense, or maybe it was the fact that his icy eyes had never held warmth in them for her.

Slowly, Violet lowered her gaze, like she was supposed to, and stared at his chin.

"What you did was reckless."

"I know," Violet said quietly.

"You don't know what that boy is capable of. He could have hurt you."

Confusion jerked Violet's gaze back to his. "What?"

Alpha Draven rolled his shoulders back, exposing a rip in his shirt across his chest. "I'm talking about Patrick."

Violet shook her head while her brows pinched together. "Patrick would never hurt me."

"You don't know that." Hearing his name, Alpha Draven looked over his shoulder, nodded at whoever had called him, then turned back to her.

"An out-of-control wolf is a dangerous one." He turned his head to look at Patrick who was following Evalyn with two guards still flanking him. "Patrick lost control today."

Shaking her head again, Violet crossed her arms. "A wolf who has lost control, a true reaper, can't be pulled out of it. Patrick came back. He stopped himself."

Gold flared in Alpha Draven's eyes for a brief moment, but never fully consumed the blue there. "Did he?"

Without another word, he turned away from her and headed up the hill, following behind the group leading to the holding cells.

Anger surged through Violet and she stormed toward the guards who had stopped Patrick from entering Alpha House. "Get out of here!" One of them jumped at her harsh tone. "Why don't you do your job and go make sure the Blood Moon Pack members don't try to attack again."

"It's okay, Violet," Patrick sounded tired. He stared at his bloodied fist, relaxing and clenching his hand over and over. "They're here to protect Luna and make sure I don't do anything stupid again."

"That's what I'm here for," Violet snorted, and Patrick looked at her with a raised brow. "And anyone crazy enough to think that you would attack my mom needs to have their heads checked. I told you to leave!" she yelled at the two guards again and after some hesitation, they both followed after the other group.

Sighing, Violet grabbed Patrick's hand and pulled him into Alpha House.

The door hadn't even closed before Evalyn approached them with crossed arms. Her eyes had already reverted to their natural gray, but her aura was still pulsing through the room. "What happened?"

Patrick lowered his chin. "Where would you like us to start, Luna?"

"Why don't you explain what happened at the Bridges with Vikter first." She directed them both to the couches.

Violet startled when Patrick gently squeezed her hand and led her to the couch. He let go as soon as she was sitting, so he could lean against the arm of the couch, putting as much space between them as possible. The hurt that built inside her chest annoyed her, and she quickly shoved it down.

"How's your arm?" She asked Jax, hoping that thinking of him and the

promise she'd made him would help keep those feelings at bay. She really did hope he was okay, though.

His response sounded grumpy. *"Doc double checked to make sure it was set properly. That wasn't fun. I'm already healing. She's moved on, but she'll be back in a minute."*

Even if he was mad at her, she was happy he was being tended to. *"I'm glad you're healing."*

"Violet will have to explain what happened before I arrived, but I made sure to end things quickly when I got there," Patrick started, interrupting her telepathic conversation with Jax. "He is sounding more and more paranoid every time I see him."

"He's convinced that Jax wants Stanislaus and that he needs to defend his clan. He came after me because Jax wasn't there." She decided to leave out the part when Vikter had said it was also to get back at Patrick. "Um, he also got stuck in the entrance to the cavern, and I helped him. Apparently, that didn't do anything to earn trust because he came after me, anyway," Violet grumbled and fiddled with the strings on her hoodie. "Although he did try to convince me to go on a date with him—as a way of getting back at Jax."

It took a lot for her mother's wolven eyes to shine though—typically only coming out for moments like before, when a display of power was needed. Her eyes glowed brilliantly at the mention of her daughter being attacked. At this distance it was easy to see that Evalyn's eyes where not simply one color. Liquid gold swirled with silver and a little bronze—no other wolven had eyes like that.

"Vikter attacked you?" Evalyn's voice was hard and her luminescent eyes darted to Patrick who lowered his gaze. "You let this happen?"

"It wasn't his fault." Violet leaned forward, drawing her mom's attention once again. "I pushed him away. He was only trying to respect my wishes."

Her mother's brows pulled together. "Why would you do that?"

Violet could hear the hidden messages and questions her mom wasn't saying... Why would she tell the guy she liked to leave her alone? Why would she risk not having protection? It had been incredibly reckless.

Not for the first time, she wished she could clan-link with her mother.

"I did something stupid." Patrick answered for her and she started to shake her head, but he continued. "I reacted badly to her sparring session with Tucker."

"Reacted?" Evalyn tilted her head to the side, "Or were you told to intervene?"

"It doesn't matter," Violet interrupted as her heart pounded. She wouldn't let Patrick take the blame for this. "I shouldn't have said the things I did. Patrick *did* stop Vikter. Aiden held him off long enough for Patrick to get there. Have you heard anything about his condition?"

Her mom nodded to confirm she had, and turned her unique eyes back on Patrick, who was staring at the floor.

"After all of that," Violet continued, "I didn't want to stay there, so Patrick brought me home. We were almost inside when the siren went off, but I was so worried about Jax that I rushed off without thinking to make sure he was okay. Patrick stopped me, convinced me to come home, but the Blood Moon wolven saw us first. He stopped one of them from biting me." She looked at Patrick, but he was still looking at the ground, so she turned back. "Mom?"

Slowly, the older woman looked at her again.

"This isn't his fault."

From the corner of her eye, Patrick whipped his head toward her and stared, but she refused to break eye contact with her Luna... and that's who her mom was right now. She was the Luna of the pack.

To her surprise, the swirling colors faded from her mom's eyes and the harsh lines softened. "Honey, I'm not mad at Patrick. I don't blame him for any of this."

Patrick's head spun back toward Evalyn.

Violet's heart stuttered. "Do you... blame me?"

"No." Evalyn leaned back in the armchair she'd claimed earlier and rubbed her forehead. "It was a bad situation all around. Things happened that didn't need to, but they did and that's that. We need to move on. Your brother needs to learn some control over that blaming habit of his before he takes the official alpha position, though." She sighed and closed her eyes. Violet wasn't sure she had ever seen her mom look so drained before. "I'll speak with Stanislaus' Luna again. Based on what she told me last time, it sounds like Vikter probably passed the point of no return with this debacle."

Relief flooded through Violet so rapidly that a wave of dizziness washed over her.

"You're both all right?" Evalyn asked, straightening back up to gaze at both of them since they had been silent too long.

Patrick nodded, "We're fine, Luna."

With a snort, her mom waved a hand at him. "Stop with the title, you know you don't need to call me that."

A twitch of a smile tugged at the corner of his mouth. "I appreciate your concern, but I'm fine... really." He added that last part when she gave him a pointed look. "I can't really speak for Violet."

"I'm fine." Violet answered, her voice a little softer than usual.

Satisfied with their answers, Evalyn leaned toward them again. "Good. Aiden had a severe concussion and a broken rib, but Dr. Penmann says he is recovering well. He is resting right now, so I suggest you visit him later. Jax and the others are also recovering just fine." Sighing, she gave a small shake of her head and her hands relaxed in her lap. "The young woman we lost today... she will be mourned. I'll be notifying her family contacts as soon as we are done here."

"She was one of the gate guards, wasn't she?" Violet asked. She had to know who had given their life to protect the clan and her.

"Her name was Orla," Evalyn answered reverently. "And yes, she was one of our lead guards."

Violet's face scrunched up as guilt washed over her. "I'm so sorry."

"It's the worst part of being Luna. Her family has no doubt already felt her loss, just as I, and your father, have felt the loss to the clan, but having to deliver the official news that their daughter and sister will not be returning home..." She swept a hand over her weary face. "Feeling that kind of raw pain radiate from them... I wouldn't wish that job on anyone."

"Do you—" Violet bit her lower lip, not sure if she was even allowed to offer what she was about to, but the questioning lift of her mother's brow made her continue. "Do you want me to tell them?"

A soft, sad smile raised a corner of the older woman's mouth, but she shook her head. "It's part of my duties. They may see it as an insult if I'm not present."

Violet lowered her chin, wishing she could take this hardship from her mother's shoulders. "I understand."

"This isn't the best moment, but unfortunately there hasn't been one lately, and we are running out of time. Patrick—" She turned her attention to the young man who raised his brows in question. "Have you settled on anything for your birthday yet?"

He shifted uncomfortably in his seat. "Not yet."

"Maybe Violet can help you. She's been a huge help to me the last several solstice celebrations." Rising from her seat, Evalyn headed back to her desk with long, elegant strides that Violet would forever be envious of. "Now, if you'll both excuse me, I need to prepare to meet with Orla's family. Be-sides, you both need to clean up."

They knew they were dismissed, but Violet and Patrick looked at each other before standing and heading toward the front door.

Violet looked back at her mom before leaving, and worry poured over her. Evalyn tossed back whatever medication was sitting on her desk then rubbed her temples, completely oblivious to her daughter watching her.

Something was very wrong.

Drawing in a breath, Violet started back toward her mother, but Patrick yanked her out the front door.

"What are you doing?" he asked.

"My mom just took medication."

Patrick sighed. "With all the work she has to do, I'm surprised we don't see her take medication more often."

Violet blinked at him.

"She deals with everything that happens between the clans, plus every-thing that happens here, on top of handling Alpha Draven, and being a mom." He shook his head. "I think she's entitled to a headache every once in a while."

Well, when he put it that way, it made her sound like she was being paranoid.

"You should go clean up," Patrick nodded to the front door. "We can catch up later."

Ignoring him, she headed up the road toward the commons. "She also said we need to discuss your birthday and you lied."

"I did?" Patrick easily caught up to her and gave her a confused look.

"You're injured." Violet eyed the gash in the arm of his sweater.

He shook his head, "It's just a scratch. I'll heal."

"Not if the wound isn't clean."

"A shower will easily take care of that."

She glared at him. "Will you stop?"

A guarded expression passed over Patrick's face, but he stayed silent.

"I don't want to be alone in my room right now, okay? I've been on the losing end of two different fights today, my body hurts, and..." She looked away from him and let out a shaky breath. After deciding she didn't want to finish that sentence, another fled across her lips before she could stop it. "I'm worried about you."

There was no response to her confessions and the longer the silence remained, the more self-conscious she became.

Violet was about to turn back toward the house when Patrick said, "Come on."

He nodded toward the commons when she looked at him, then led the way toward his apartment.

Chapter 9

Violet

***THE COMMONS WERE FILLED WITH DIFFERENT** sized apartments ranging from one bedroom to three.* If you were single, you could pay extra rent for a bigger one, but generally, those were reserved for small families. Not every clan member lived inside the compound, but most did. There were over a hundred houses as well, making up their self-sustaining community. Many clan members never left, while others came and went as they pleased. Those who lived off the property checked in every once in a while, to let the clan know how they were doing, follow any directions from the alpha and luna, and keep their status as clan members.

Three years ago, when Patrick arrived at Sentinel Clan, he was only two months shy of fifteen, but was set up in the commons to live in his own apartment. Luna Draven looked out for him, and with the clan mentality and connections he was well cared for, but Violet often wondered if he felt lonely in his apartment all by himself.

He opened the door and gestured for her to enter before following her in. She'd only been there one other time a couple of years back when she was helping her mom with something.

It hadn't changed much.

A small sitting area to the right, an even smaller kitchen to the left with a bar as the only table, and one bathroom inside the single bedroom. No decorations or personal touches anywhere to be found. If she didn't know better—and if chocolate peppermint didn't fill the air—Violet would think that no one lived here.

Patrick led her through the bedroom into the bathroom, which was definitely not made for two people to be in. After washing his hands and taking extra care with the cuts across his knuckles, he pulled out a few dark-colored cloths, disinfectant, and a first aid kit from the cabinets, then turned toward her.

"You can clean up first, I'll step ou—"

"Absolutely not." Violet stepped in his path, blocking him from leaving.

He gave her a quizzical look and raised a brow.

"You're the one who's injured. We're taking care of that first." She pointed to the tub/shower and told him to sit.

Sighing, he shook his head then did as she said and sat on the edge of the tub.

She turned the sink water to warm. "You'll need to take your sweater off."

"Already did." Patrick dropped his sweater on the floor and she couldn't stop herself from turning to look.

She was both grateful and disappointed that he hadn't removed his shirt as well. Maybe a tad more disappointed.

"Thanks," Violet muttered, then returned to washing her hands before grabbing one of the cloths and running it through the warm water. The tremors in her hands hadn't stopped. She stared at them, shaking in the water. Her breath hitched.

"Hey." His voice snapped her out of it and she looked over at him. "You okay?"

Nodding, she stepped toward him. "I'm fine."

He leaned back. "You don't have to do this. I heal fast."

"Not if the wound isn't clean," Violet repeated her words from before as she stepped to his side and motioned for his arm.

With another sigh, Patrick turned his arm so she could reach the gash left by her attacker's claws.

"Why didn't you say something about this before?" Violet grumbled, as she grabbed the disinfectant and started cleaning the wound.

"I… didn't feel it…" he admitted, and wouldn't meet her gaze when she looked at him. "When you pointed out I had a cut in my sweater, I thought it was just a scratch."

She shook her head. "This is more than just a scratch… but it looks like it's already healing." She shifted her weight as she finished up his arm then stepped away to rinse the cloth out.

"Thanks."

"I'm not done." Not allowing herself to think about it too much, she stepped into his space, so she was standing between his spread legs.

He sucked in a sharp breath at her close proximity and snatched her wrist when she raised the cloth to wipe the blood from his face. "That's not mine."

Heart pounding, she held perfectly still and stared into his hazel eyes. When she spoke, her voice was nearly a whisper, "Just let me do this."

After a long moment, Patrick reluctantly released her and she gently ran the cloth across his forehead, clearing away the blood splatter. "Are you really okay?"

"Why do you keep asking that?" Violet wondered as she passed the cloth over a small cut just above his brow.

"Ow."

"Baby," Violet teased.

Patrick grumbled, but one corner of his mouth twitched as if he were trying not to smile. "You would tell someone if you weren't, right?"

Sighing, Violet rested both hands on his shoulders. "I promise, I'm fine."

"I can feel your hands shaking every time you touch me." Warmth seeped across her cheeks. Yeah, she was touching him. A lot. She was also standing way closer to him than Jax would have approved of. Her gaze involuntarily dropped to his mouth, and the filing cabinet in her heart labeled *Patrick* rattled violently.

"He was close, Vi, are you sure he didn't bite you?"

Violet jerked away from him as she pressed a hand over her throat. It *had* been close. That jerk nearly had his fangs in her. A shudder ran down her spine at the memory of his breath against her skin. If he'd been any closer—

"Hey," Patrick called to her softly. She jumped when his fingers curled around her other hand before guiding her toward him. "It's okay."

Her breathing was coming and going in short little gasps.

"Do you want me to check?" He whispered, watching her intently.

You wouldn't think that a bite from another wolven would have much of an effect, other than causing pain, but being bit by a Blood Moon pack member had dangerous side effects. Many of the symptoms reflected that of someone who'd contracted rabies. The extremely heightened irritability and aggression had been fatal many times in the past.

There were stories of bitten wolven attacking their loved ones or clan members, often killing them, which was a problem of another kind. If a wolven killed someone, their wolf eyes would glow red for the rest of their lives. They would succumb to the darker impulses of the wolf, and eventually lose all humanity. Somehow, that didn't happen when a war was going on or if someone killed a Blood Moon pack member.

Finally, she nodded and pulled her hoodie over her head.

Patrick went rigid as his gaze trailed over her. She had blood on her shirt and bruises marred her arms. She was about to look in the mirror to see just how bad she looked when he reached for her, making her freeze.

He hesitated when she stopped moving, and looked at her eyes for confirmation. Another nod was all he needed, and his fingers slipped under the collar of her shirt, pulling it down an inch or so. Her trembling kicked up about a hundred notches for a whole other reason. Feather-light touches brushed over the same area the jerk-faced Blood Moon guy had been going for, and a shaky breath left her.

"I don't see anything."

Violet nodded and stepped back. When did it get so hot in there? "See, I'm fine," she answered, trying to buy herself some time so she could compartmentalize her feelings. Hoping the brief smile she'd given was believable, she turned to rinse out the cloth until the water ran clear.

"My turn."

"Wha—eek!" Patrick lifted her, making her squeak like a little mouse, and placed her on the counter before grabbing a clean cloth and getting it wet.

When she opened her mouth to protest, the look he gave her was enough to make her close it. Stepping close, he gently ran the warm cloth over her face and neck. He rinsed it out a lot more than she had, keeping it borderline hot, which felt amazing.

She soon found herself closing her eyes and relaxing into his touch.

"Is the blood yours or..."

"It's Aiden's," she answered, sounding tired while she slowly looked at him. "Vikter didn't draw blood."

Patrick's jaw clenched and he lifted one of her arms. "Yes, he did."

Small cuts had already begun to heal up and down her arms. She rotated her arms to try and see them better. "I didn't realize... It started stinging when I was blocking, but I figured that was just because I was getting hit so much. He must have been wearing a ring or something. Or maybe there was a zipper on his jacket that got me."

Patrick gripped the counter's edge on either side of her hips and looked away, letting out a long, tense breath.

"I'm okay," she said and brushed her fingers through the longer part of his hair on top to grab a tiny twig that had lodged itself there.

His gaze met hers and she sucked in a small breath. Ever so slowly, he leaned forward and rested his forehead against hers. "I'm sorry I didn't get there faster."

Violet closed her eyes. "I'm sorry I pushed you away."

They stayed that way for a minute, comfortable with each other's presence, then Patrick went back to washing down her arms. He was extra gentle over the cuts, but made sure each of them was clean.

"Was that your first one?" Patrick's voice was so quiet Violet almost thought she'd imagined it.

"First what?" She asked, still sitting on the counter while he rinsed the cloth out for the last time. "Fight? Or nearly having my throat ripped out?"

He shook his head. "Body."

Violet shook her head. She'd been trying not to think about the female guard, Orla, who had been lost today. "Nope. I've seen them before," she answered, pushing off the counter and heading out the door.

"Violet." Patrick followed her into his bedroom.

She spun around on him, throwing her arms out to the sides—which hurt. "What? What do you want me to say?"

"I want you to talk to me. I know something's bothering you."

"Ha! A lot of things are bothering me, you'll have to be more specific."

He didn't answer.

She bunched her lips together, but the feeble barrier only lasted a few seconds before words began flowing from her mouth at lightning speed. "I don't know what you want me to tell you. That I'm probably going to have nightmares because my stupid decision cost a girl her life? That I thought I was about to die when that guy's teeth were nearly in my throat? That I was scared for you when they called you a reaper or when you weren't responding to me or when they were going to shock you with a freaking cattle prod?"

Patrick watched her calmly until she mentioned him, then his eyes widened. He closed the distance between them.

"It's okay," he assured her, grabbing her hands which had started trembling again. The knuckles of his right hand had almost healed, looking more like angry raw skin than split open wounds. "It's normal to feel all those things after what happened."

"Jax was right," Violet whispered. "If I had followed protocol, if I hadn't frozen, none of this would have happened."

"You don't know that."

"How can you say that?"

"Because you don't." He squeezed her hands a little. "They didn't attack because you froze. It was an attack of opportunity. They could have attacked even if we'd been inside. If that had happened, and we weren't there, the only thing that would have changed is maybe another body being on the ground."

Violet blinked at him. "What?"

Sighing, he shook his head. "Orla was dead before you got to them. I'm surprised you missed it. He snapped her neck. Without your distraction, he probably would have done the same to James as well."

James had been the other wolven leading the group. He'd taken a good beating, but he was still alive. Thanks to her dirty kick, he'd been the one to secure that guy.

"Jax had no right to yell at you like that." Patrick released one of her hands and gently tucked a hair behind her ear. After two fights and being thrown into the water, her ponytail was practically falling out and pieces hung around her face. She closed her eyes and forced herself not to lean into his touch. "Things could have been a lot worse without you there."

Peeking up at him, Violet asked, "Are you saying that because of the Blood Moon scouts, or your reaction to them?"

Patrick's eyes warmed. "Both."

Releasing a shaky breath, Violet looked over him again, "Were you bitten?"

"Not unless you count my fist colliding with his mouth, but I don't think that's the same thing."

Violet grimaced, and he apologized.

"Do you want some shorts and a shirt to wear?" Patrick asked, backing away from her as he rubbed the back of his neck. "I need to get out of these and I imagine you're just as uncomfortable as I am."

"Yeah. Wet, dirty clothes aren't that great," she agreed. "If you wouldn't mind, that would be nice. I'll return them to you tomorrow."

"I don't mind," he said as he rummaged through a drawer and pulled out a pair of long basketball shorts, then moved to the closet and grabbed a shirt off a hanger. He handed them to her, nodding toward the bathroom. "You can change in there."

She mumbled her thanks and hurried to do just that. A small moan left her when she had finally wiggled out of her wet clothes and put the dry ones on. Even though she was practically swimming in them, they were comfortable and a lot warmer. Plus, they smelled like Patrick, and that scent was intoxicating.

"Seriously, why did you have to make him smell like chocolate?" Violet grumbled under her breath to the goddess as she balled up her dirty, wet clothes. "That's completely unfair."

Once she made sure she had everything, she opened the door and nearly dropped it all. Her lips parted when her jaw fell as she found herself staring at a half-naked Patrick.

That thought made her snap her mouth shut. Seriously? She had seen guys without their shirts before, it wasn't a big deal... but it was. Patrick never took his shirt off while they sparred, so the last time she'd seen him shirtless was last summer; the one time they'd gone swimming together. The boy had filled out very nicely since then. Which was obvious even through his shirts, but wow.

"I think you're drooling." Patrick's laughing tone made fire erupt across her face.

Could this moment be any more embarrassing?

"I am not." She shook her head, feeling flustered, and grabbed the bathroom door handle. Pinching her eyes shut, she started pulling the door closed. "I'll just wait, you can tell me when you're ready. Sorry."

A low, rich chuckle filled the room, "It's fine. Look."

She peeked one eye open and caught the last glimpse of his lower stomach before he finished pulling the shirt down. Those low V lines were not something she should be looking at... and yet she couldn't stop herself from wanting to see them again.

"Thanks for the clothes," Violet muttered and had to stop herself from darting out of his room.

Forcing a facade of calm, she made her way to the sitting area and curled up in the corner of his couch, awkwardly holding her wet clothes. A minute later, he appeared with a bag and took them from her, setting it all by the door.

"Can I ask you something?"

Patrick shrugged as he headed into the kitchen. She heard the water run before he came back with two glasses and held one out for her. "Go ahead."

She took the glass from him and downed nearly half of it before holding it between her hands. "What happened to you? I've never seen you like that. You knocked Vikter unconscious and pinned Jax to a tree, but you let it go. And today with Vikter you were in complete control."

Sighing, Patrick dragged a hand through his hair, then sank onto the couch on the opposite end of where she sat—as far away from her as possible. "I wish you hadn't seen any of that. Today with Vikter was fine, but how I acted at the tourney and then with that Blood Moon guy..."

"Well, I did." She swirled her water around. "So, spill."

He finished his water, set the empty glass on the wood floor, then rested his elbows against his knees. "I have a hard time reigning in my emotions sometimes."

"I'm pretty sure the whole clan knows that, Patrick. That isn't a big secret." Violet drained the rest of her cup and copied him, placing her cup on the floor, before resting her head against her hand. "A lot of adolescent wolven do, especially as we near our eighteenth birthdays. It's like we hit puberty all over again, but this time with a wolf spirit."

"Right, well..." Patrick released a huff of laughter then blew out a heavy breath. "My parents taught me to be better. They'd be disappointed if they saw me act the way I have been, but when the scout pinned you, my blood felt like it was boiling. All I could think about was getting him off you. Before I could get to you, his mouth was on your neck, and..." Patrick shrugged. "I don't know. I don't remember what happened after that."

Violet's brows rose. It was extremely rare for him to speak about his family. She could count the number of times on one hand, and although she wanted to know more about them, she'd been down that road before. Asking him would only make him clam up.

"First of all," she pointed at him, "his mouth did not touch my neck. If it had, I'd be showering for the next year."

A half smirk softened the hard lines of Patrick's jaw.

"Second, how can you not remember?" Violet relaxed her hand back into her lap and leaned toward him.

"I think Alistair took over. I've been careful to keep him from doing so, but without remembering everything, I can't tell you if that's what happened for sure."

Violet studied him for a moment before asking her next question with a scared reverence, "Do you think you're a reaper?"

Patrick's golden-flecked, hazel eyes held her violet ones. "I don't know," he whispered. "I don't think so. Not me, anyway. I'm not sure I can say the same for Alistair. I heard you call my name and felt you try to stop me. It wasn't until you stepped into the line of my attack that I regained control. The thought of hurting you..." Patrick drew in a deep breath through his nose and let it out slowly. "I could never do that. Even Alistair shrunk away from that thought, which I guess is a good sign he isn't a reaper either."

True reapers lost control and couldn't regain it without extreme measures. In unfortunate cases, they're never able to. If Patrick was a true reaper, he wouldn't have been able to stop. He wouldn't have cared who was in his path. He would have killed them all, but he didn't kill anyone.

Violet snorted and settled back against the couch. "Jax would throw you in Lockup and bury the key, if you hurt me."

A dry laugh left Patrick. "That's an understatement. I don't think you realize just how protective your twin is over you."

Violet's eyes narrowed as she thought about all the times he'd interfered with her and Patrick… or any other guy for that matter. "I think I have an idea. The first guy who ever tried to kiss me nearly wet himself when Jax suddenly showed up and threw him against a wall."

Surprise shot across his face, "I didn't know he did that."

"I should also mention that's not the first time. Thanks to Jax, I have never been kissed. I have a sneaky suspicion Jax has threatened every guy here, just to keep them away from me."

Shaking his head, Patrick smirked. "He has. I've watched him do it."

Anger flashed through Violet, and she found herself leaning toward him again. "Are you kidding me? Is that why no one in the clan has even asked me out on a date?"

Patrick gave a single nod.

"Well, other than Tucker, but we know how that ended."

"Tucker isn't a good guy, Vi."

"You and Jax keep saying that, but neither of you will explain why."

Patrick sighed. "You like to look for the good in people, but with Tucker, you only saw what he wanted you to see. I can't tell you how many times I caught him making bets to see how far he would get with you or telling the other guys that he was hoping to up his rank by being with you. Every time, Jax or I would try to warn him off. All he cares about is rank and power. Why do you think he hasn't talked to you since you ended any chance of being mates?"

Grabbing the pillow beside her, Violet smashed it over her face and groaned. She should have known. "Why do I even bother?"

Patrick remained silent.

"Between guys like that and Jax scaring everyone away, I'll be lucky if my mate even sticks around." Realizing what she just said, Violet groaned again. "Not like I even have one according to Doc, but still I'd rather Jax not scare him off if he does exist."

Embarrassment passed over her. Why was she being so open with him?

It took a bit for Patrick to respond and when he did, it was not what she was expecting. "Do you really want one?"

Slowly, she peeked around the pillow to find him staring at his knuckles again, which were now a dry pink.

"Doesn't everyone?" Violet asked, her voice sounding small. When he didn't respond, she figured she might as well tell someone. "To be honest... I was always terrified of meeting my mate, but now, knowing that I probably won't ever have one..." She shrugged, searching for a way to explain. "At least before, I had a chance at the love and happiness they talk about mated couples having. Now I might as well walk around with a sign on my back saying 'Doomed to remain alone forever'."

Patrick stared at her for a long, quiet minute, then laid his arm across the back of the couch. "Not everyone wants a mate. I don't. I'm better off without one."

Violet shook her head. "Is that why you've had so many girlfriends over the last three months?"

Patrick's head tilted to the side. "Have you been keeping track?"

Mortification burned her cheeks. "What? I... no... I mean... it's hard not to notice when you flaunt them around everywhere!"

"I'm not flaunting anything."

"Tell that to the twenty girls whose hearts you've broken."

"You're exaggerating."

Violet snorted. "By what... three?"

Patrick's jaw pulsed and he turned his head away.

"You do know you could meet your mate at your party, right?" Violet's voice had softened as she started fitting puzzle pieces together. "That's why you haven't settled on anything, isn't it? You don't want that to happen."

Only Patrick's eyes moved, giving her a fantastic side glare. "It doesn't matter."

A dry laugh escaped her, "Yes, it does, and I'm sorry, but you're gonna have to get over it. My mom is pulling the mother card and making you have a party whether you want one or not. Plus, everyone has a mate—well, except me—and it makes them better. You know, the person being their second half and all..."

"And you're just repeating what we've been told our whole lives!" Patrick's voice rose and Violet snapped her mouth shut. He curled in on himself, leaning his elbows against his knees again, and dropped his head in his hands. "Sorry, but... not every mate bond ends with happily ever after. Not everyone wants to be bonded."

Agony tore at her heart. As much as she did not want to see him with someone else, she wanted him to feel that blissful happiness. "You won't feel that way when you meet her. She's going to be everything you could ever want and she'll light up your eyes and make you do that warm smile..."

"I doubt that."

"Patrick—"

"Mates can be rejected."

Violet's mouth hung open as she stared at Patrick who had just voiced the reason she'd been terrified of meeting her mate. "Do you know what they say about a rejected bond?"

Ever so slowly, Patrick turned his head toward her. His guarded expression and clenched fists made her heart hurt. Why would someone like him be so worried about his mate? He had everything going for him; personality, looks, brains, future status.

"They say the pain of being rejected is second only to having your mate die." Sorrow dripped from her words as she nearly whispered, "You would never make someone go through that."

"Trust me." Patrick lowered his head again, dropping his hands between his knees. "No one wants to be my mate."

"I can think of more than a dozen girls who would disagree with you." She didn't need to say she was one of them.

Patrick shrugged. "I can't help that. It's not like I asked for a mate."

"It's not like you're telling the world you don't want one either!" Violet snapped, resisting the urge to chuck her pillow at his face. "If you don't want to be bonded, then why are you dating every girl who looks your direction?"

Mischief flashed in Patrick's eyes as he turned his head to look at her. "Jealous?"

Violet snorted. "You wish."

Lies. She was extremely jealous. Not that she would ever admit that to him.

After participating in a minor staring contest, Patrick's lips tilted in a slight smirk before he shook his head and leaned back against the couch.

"So that's it? That's your big reason for worrying over your party?" Anger laced her words and Patrick's brows raised.

"Why are you upset?"

"I'm not upset, I ju..." Violet bit her lip and looked off to the side.

Everyone she knew was excited to find their mate. It was one of the things they looked forward to the most, including Jax.

"I don't know what time I was born," Patrick admitted, not waiting for her to finish her thought.

Sighing, Violet closed her eyes and shook her head.

Their wolf counterparts were particular about when they fully joined with their human halves. Sure, people could be in sporadic contact with their wolf for years, but it wasn't a permanent thing until they turned eighteen... to the minute. Some people waited to throw their party until they were officially eighteen, others threw countdown parties, and some partied all day, and night.

"Patrick, that isn't a big—"

"It is to me," Patrick growled. "I don't want that happening in front of everyone."

Shaking her head again, Violet shrugged. "I don't understand. Why not? It's a time to celebrate."

"Not for me. I struggle with Alistair as it is, I don't—"

Violet nearly leapt off the couch when the door to Patrick's room burst open. Patrick, on the other hand, did jump up to plant himself between her and the door.

"What is *she* doing here?"

A whole new kind of frustration hit Violet like a brick wall and her hands shook as she shouted, “That’s what you have to say?”

Jax threw the door shut and glared around Patrick, who slowly moved out of their way. He knew better than to get in the middle of a verbal argument between them. Years ago, he’d tried to settle them and they both turned on him instead.

Violet pushed off the couch and stomped toward her twin. His purple eyes swirled gold as he took in her appearance, then glared at Patrick.

He was about to say something when Violet stepped toe to toe with him and jabbed a finger against his chest. “I just got confirmation that you’ve been sabotaging every single relationship I could have possibly had since the moment I told you I thought someone was cute!”

To Jax’s credit, he didn’t even glance at Patrick when she mentioned that. Instead, he crossed his arms and waited.

“Not only that, but have you ever heard of knocking?”

“Patrick doesn’t make me knock.”

“Fine, how about a, hey sorry for yelling at you in front of a bunch of people, sis?”

“Nope, not sorry about that.” Jax’s lips pinched into a thin line.

“Or how about, sorry that happened to you, I’m glad you’re not turning into a raging Blood Moon monster!” Violet slammed her palms against Jax’s chest when he shot a look at Patrick. “Don’t look at him! I haven’t even started on the things you should be saying to your best friend!”

Warmth spread down her arms when Patrick’s hands rested over her shoulders. “Down, girl.”

“Get off me,” she grumbled and rolled her shoulders, but Patrick’s hands didn’t move. “This is a long time coming.”

“I’m not going to apologize for anything.” Jax was irritatingly calm, making Violet want to punch him even more. “My duty is to protect you. You stepped out of line tonight. I already knew you were fine, so I didn’t think I needed to bring it up.”

Violet stepped back, trying to bury the hurt that flashed through her, and crashed into Patrick who released her shoulders to quickly step away. “Dad would be proud. You sound just like him.”

The hard glint in Jax’s eyes wavered, but he didn’t respond to her jab. “I’m here to talk about Patrick’s party.”

"Funny," she snarked, harnessing her hurt and churning it into rage. "That's why I'm here."

Confusion contorted Jax's face and she felt a small zing of triumph.

"We were just talking about that," Patrick informed Jax. "Luna told her to help."

"Why in your apartment?" Jax growled and his voice grew louder and louder as he continued, "You could have stayed at Alpha House and talked about this and why the he—" He cut himself off and drew in a deep breath. "Why is my sister wearing your clothes?"

Violet smacked his arm and pointed to her bag of clothes by the door. "My clothes were soaked from our fight with Vikter in the river. They were really uncomfortable and even more gross after the encounter with the Blood Moon scouts."

While she spoke, Patrick plopped back onto the couch. To the unknowing eye, he looked like he didn't have a care in the world. She knew better though. His hands were in fists as he tucked them behind his head and his muscles were strung tight, anticipating the need to jump into a fight at any given moment.

"I had a couple of cuts that needed to be cleaned and figured we could do both at the same time," he shrugged.

It was difficult, but she managed to keep the shock off her face as he lied for her. That wasn't why they'd come here. Sure, talking about his party had been an excuse and they had cleaned up, but the fact that he would cover up her fear and worry warmed her from the inside out.

Jax didn't look fully convinced, but he made his way to the armchair across from Patrick and took a seat. Both boys acted like she was no longer there, leaving her standing by the door.

"She helps Luna with all the solstice parties, and she's pretty good at problem solving. She could help with our puzzle."

"I can't help if I don't have all the pieces." Violet crossed her arms and sat on the arm of the couch near Patrick's feet. "If I try, there will be holes in the finished picture."

Patrick's dry laugh shook the couch. "I see you're sticking to the puzzle analogy."

"You started it." Violet smirked and a pillow hit her in the face.

Jax, the pillow launcher, looked like his head was about to explode. He may have accepted this was happening, but he wasn't happy about it.

After chucking the pillow back at him, she continued with the birthday talk, "I don't know all the details, but I was thinking about moving his party to the day after his birthday. That way we don't run into any surprises."

"Except the possibility of running into my mate," Patrick grumbled then caught the pillow before it smacked him in the face.

"You've got to get over that," Jax grumbled. "We've been over this a hundred times. You can't live your life worried you're going to meet your mate. Most people are excited for that moment, you know? The bond is as much for your benefit as it is for your mate."

"You need to stop throwing pillows at people," Patrick growled. He tucked the pillow behind his head, which made Jax frown.

Violet watched their exchange, then stared at the ground as her heart thundered away in her chest. Watching Patrick find his mate and bond with them was going to be torture, but she wouldn't wish the pain of rejection on anyone and she couldn't imagine he would do that.

Feeling someone's gaze on her, Violet looked up to find Patrick watching her. She rolled her shoulders back and shot him an uneasy smile.

Patrick clenched his jaw and he returned his gaze to Jax. "It will be easier on everyone if we just leave the party the way it is."

That clearly wasn't a good option. "What if..." Both boys looked at her and Violet swallowed the knot in her throat. "What if we move it back to ten? We'll make it a ringing in your new stage of life kind of party. That gives you twenty-two hours for Alistair to merge with you and if it still hasn't happened... we'll be right by your side."

Jax's eyes narrowed when Violet's tone turned soft and gentle, but Patrick was holding her gaze, and that was all that mattered.

He nodded. "That's the best plan I've heard so far." He turned to Jax who was staring her down.

"Patrick will be with me the entire day. You just focus on getting everything planned and set up."

Violet ground her teeth and glared at Jax. *"If you think I'm missing one of my best friend's birthdays and not helping when he needs it, then you don't know me very well."*

Jax's fingers curled into the arms of the chair. *"You've been getting too close to him. I don't want to see either of you get hurt when you find your mates."*

"Well, the joke's on you because I probably won't ever have one!" she snapped at him out loud, and Patrick threw the pillow back at Jax.

He either picked up what she meant or he just really wanted to get him back with the pillow.

It hit Jax in the chest and dropped lifeless to the floor. "What?"

"I don't have a wolf, so Doc thinks I won't have a mate." She shook her head and sighed. "It doesn't matter. I'll let mom know the changes to the party time. Is there anything else you want me to handle?" She stood up and looked at Patrick whose worried expression made her chest hurt. She really wished he wouldn't look at her like that. It made it really hard to keep her feelings in check.

"There's um..." Jax's tone was almost flat. He'd sounded angry with her for so long that not having that there was unsettling. He was clearly still trying to process the bomb she'd just dropped on him. "The decorations. We haven't really talked about that."

"Got it." She walked to the door and picked up her bag. "Do you want a theme or not?"

Patrick shook his head.

"No theme. That makes this super easy." Opening the door, she called over her shoulder, "I'll give your clothes back tomorrow. Thanks, again."

Closing the door behind her, she stepped into the commons hallway and rested against the wall.

"I'm sorry." Jax's voice entered her head. *"Why didn't you tell me?"*

She leaned her head back. *"We haven't been that close lately."*

"Yeah... Even if you don't have a mate, Patrick will. I don't want to see you get hurt."

"I'm just trying to be a good friend, Jax."

"Seems like you're going for a lot more than friendship lately."

Violet's mind emptied as her twin closed their conversation and her shoulders fell. She stayed, sagging against the wall, until someone walked by. Without a wolf, she would never hold an official rank in the clan, but she still shouldn't show any more weakness than she already had. She straightened her stance, squared her shoulders, and nodded to her fellow clan-mate before heading back toward Alpha House.

Chapter 10

Patrick

THE SECOND VIOLET CLOSED THE DOOR, *Jax growled at him,* "It's a good thing I like you enough to let you explain why my sister was in your clothes."

Patrick rolled his head to the side and gave him a bored look, "Are you wound up so tightly right now that you think I would actually do anything to her?"

Jax shook his head, then shot up from the armchair and began pacing across the sitting area. He started going off about everything that had been bothering him lately, including Violet. He may not have been able to hear her heart beating frantically from the hallway, but Patrick could. It tore at him—knowing he couldn't help her.

He was meant to protect her.

Nothing more.

He had to remind himself of that every day. Lately, it seemed like he needed that reminder multiple times a day.

Patrick remained quiet while his best friend continued to rave about the Blood Moon scouts and the events that followed. Allowing Jax time to vent, he listened to Violet's heartbeat until it faded away before interrupting.

"She was worried about you."

Halting his pacing across the sitting area, Jax stared at him with his mouth hanging open.

Patrick had no idea what he'd been talking about, but apparently, he'd interrupted mid-word. "That's why she ran into the fight."

Jax turned toward him. "What?"

"She was worried you were going to get hurt."

Throwing his arms out to the sides, Jax glared at Patrick, "I did get hurt! My arm was broken!" He pointed a finger, "You could have stopped her."

Patrick lifted a brow, "I think you underestimate how fast she is."

"You're faster," Jax grumbled. "You and I both know you are."

Irritation prickled Patrick's skin. "I won't use Alistair's abilities unless I absolutely have to."

"It would be fun to chase her down."

"Shut up." Patrick snarled at his wolf counterpart.

"You didn't think you had too tonight?" Jax's voice rose. "You could have been inside where it was safe!"

"Nowhere is safe with Alistair!" Patrick yelled back, making Jax's jaw clench.

"Rude."

"Prove otherwise and I'll take it back." Patrick hated when Alistair commented on his conversations. It was like having a constant commentary running in the background.

"You don't understand," Patrick sighed, letting the tension drain from his shoulders. "You get along perfectly with your wolf, Dalim. You agree on everything—two halves of the same coin."

Jax's brows furrowed. "That's how it's supposed to be."

"It's never been that way for me." His hands curled into fists. "I know you want me to be your beta, and I've accepted those duties, but I need your word that you will release me if I feel it's necessary."

Jax sighed and made his way back to the armchair, "Once you pass the trial, you'll have more control over him. He'll be your other half instead of a random personality trying to take over."

Fear trickled down Patrick's spine, making the hairs on the back of his neck rise. "Alistair is not going to give in without a fight."

"Then you'll beat him," Jax leaned back against his seat as if that was the easiest thing in the world. "You're stronger and faster than anyone in the clan. You'll beat Alistair, too."

"You don't..." Patrick ran a hand through his hair and growled. "You've been in contact with your wolf since you were thirteen, right?"

Jax nodded and shrugged as if that information was common knowledge.

"Have you ever had a fight with him?" Patrick asked, leaning forward to place his elbows on his knees. "Does he contradict you in the middle of conversations? Have you ever worried he was going to take over and make you do something you didn't want to do?"

Confusion pulled Jax's brows together. "Of course not. You said it yourself, we agree on everything." He flinched and corrected himself, making Patrick wonder what Dalim had said to him. "Almost everything. He's my partner. We work together."

Shaking his head, Patrick let out a dry laugh. "I fight with Alistair every. single. day. I have to be aware of my thoughts at all times because if I lose focus, he has an easier time. I'm always on guard, waiting for him to try and take over. That's not an *if*, Jax, that's a *when*."

Alistair chuckled darkly, confirming what Patrick had just said, and goosebumps fled over his arms. Closing his eyes briefly, he drew in a deep breath while reinforcing his mental shields.

"Is that what happened with the Blood Moon scout?" Jax asked, leaning forward as well. "I would have come over, but my dad told me not to. I can't disobey the alpha."

"More like he didn't try."

"Violet did." Patrick spoke without thinking, a rare occurrence. It made him wonder if it was him or Alistair speaking, but the glare Jax was giving him didn't allow time to figure it out. "I don't know how, but she did."

"She's always had some weird ability to choose to listen or not. I'm not sure how that works." Jax grumbled.

"Did you fight against Alpha Draven?" Patrick asked and could practically see Alistair's victory dance in his head.

"There wasn't any point. No one can break an alpha command."

"Except a future alpha who's about to take over," Patrick reminded him. He was both proud and appalled at what he was saying to his friend.

A soft growl rippled from the future alpha. "Yeah well, my arm was broken, too."

A smirk tugged at the corner of Patrick's mouth. "Your arm, not your legs."

His friend's eyes narrowed.

"How is your arm?" He asked, eying the previously injured arm. It looked fine, but that could just be superficial.

"My elbow was destroyed. Everything is mostly fused back together now." Jax held his arm out to examine it while he explained. "The pain is minimal. Doc just had to check and make sure there weren't any floating parts or anything. Thankfully there weren't."

"You heal really fast," Patrick stared at Jax's arm. "Faster than most fully matured wolven."

Jax beamed, "Thanks, but stop trying to change the subject."

"I wasn't. I was following the conversation."

"Answer my question, Patrick." Jax ordered, his eyes flashing gold. "Is that what happened with the scout? Did Alistair take over?"

Sighing, Patrick shook his head and pretended that his friend's alpha eyes didn't feel like a threat to him. "You know that doesn't have much of an effect on me."

Jax growled. He couldn't help it. Any perceived threat to an alpha would make them react aggressively. At least, that's what Patrick had observed during his time as a Sentinel Clan member.

After another shake of his head, and forcing a fake calm to settle over his exterior, he shrugged. "I'm not really sure what happened. I'm assuming it was Alistair attempting to gain control, but I didn't feel him like I normally do. Usually there is a heavy presence in my mind when he is forcing his way to the surface."

"Maybe he didn't have to force so hard this time." Jax wondered. "You were defending Violet."

"Bingo. As much as I would love to take credit for that little display, it

wasn't all me." Alistair's delighted chortle made Patrick want to punch something.

He tilted his head to the side instead. "Much to your dismay, I assume."

One of his friends' brows lifted at the sharp tone he used, but Jax sighed, "Don't do that."

His brows rose, reflecting his friends, and even Alistair settled. "Do what?"

"Assume something and then get mad at me for it."

"Sorry," Patrick grumbled, gesturing to his head. "I've got commentary happening in the background."

"Tattling isn't nice, Boy Scout."

"Then leave." Patrick snapped, imagining a three-foot-thick wall of steel going up between them. He hated that nickname. It was one of the first things Alistair had called him when they'd made contact years ago.

Jax watched him for a moment, and when he spoke, his voice was a fraction softer. "I'm grateful you stopped him. I don't like the toll it took on you, and I think it could have been avoided… but I am grateful you saved her."

"I will always protect her." Those words were an automatic response at this point. He'd been saying them for years. It was also a helpful reminder. Her protector. Nothing more. "I gave you my word."

"I know." Jax nodded. "I'll always be grateful for that. Her mate may not be," He smirked, but a shadow fell over his face shortly after. "Well… I guess that won't be an issue after all."

Not sure how to answer that, Patrick remained quiet.

"Did you know?"

He pressed his lips into a hard line and clenched his jaw before nodding. "That's how she told off Tucker."

Jax leaned back in the chair and ran a hand over his face. "Why didn't you tell me?"

"It wasn't my place to do so."

"Yeah, I guess not." With a sigh, Jax stood and headed toward the kitchen. "We'll figure this out, with Alistair I mean." He patted Patrick on the shoulder as he passed. "I'll be there to help you through your trial. You'll pass, and then you'll take your place as my beta."

Having Jax out of sight, Patrick didn't have to force a smile. He wasn't sure it was going to be quite so easy and who knew what he'd be like after his trials.

"Hey, are you playing in the upcoming game?" Jax called while rummaging through the fridge. "Coach said he hadn't heard from you."

Happy to have a different subject, Patrick pushed off the couch to join his friend in the kitchen. "I don't know. Vikter seems to have it out for Violet. I was contemplating sitting this one out to watch over her."

"That's not a bad idea, but mom told me the Stanislaus Luna has reprimanded him adequately—whatever that means. I don't think he'll be a problem." He closed the fridge with a grumble. "Why don't you have any soda?"

"Because it's not good for you, and you do weird things when you've had that much sugar."

A goofy grin passed over Jax's face. "Sure do."

Patrick shook his head, "Do you think it would be smart for me to play?"

"It's your last game before your birthday. Are you really going to pass up your last chance to play?"

"I will, to watch over Violet, if that's what you want."

Jax lifted a brow. "I'll leave it up to you. We could use you though. You're the best scout we've got and we're going up against Whisky Clan this time. I've heard they have a fantastic offense this year and brutal snipers."

Nodding, Patrick drummed his fingers against the counter. "I'll think about it. It would be fun to play again before my trials."

What he didn't say was that it would be good to do something he loved one last time in case he didn't pass his trials.

Chapter 11

Violet

***SWEET, PEANUT BUTTER MAPLE SYRUP FILLED THE AIR,** making Violet's stomach growl.* One of the kitchen staff smiled at her as they set a full stack of pancakes in front of her, complete with strawberries and cream, plus loads of bacon on the side.

"Geeze!" Lexie's eyes bugged. "How many pancakes are you gonna eat?"

Violet laughed, "There are five here, and I'm going to eat all of them."

The staff member put Lexie's short stack in front of her, practically dropping the plate the last inch.

"Hey," Violet snapped, turning her attention to the staff member who had the good sense to look a bit sheepish. He apologized before scurrying away. "Sorry about that."

Lexie grabbed a piece of bacon off her plate and took a bite before shrugging. "He's probably new." Lexie cut through her two pancakes, slicing them into bite-sized pieces.

Their sleepover had been spur of the moment, but it had been great. Unfortunately, Mya couldn't make it, but they spent the night watching romantic comedies... and Violet tried avoiding talking about her time alone with Patrick in his apartment. Blocking and dodging Lexie's curiosity was a full-time job, but thankfully the movies helped tone her down a little.

"So, we were talking about you and Patrick."

Violet choked. She hit her chest while she coughed, attempting to dislodge the offending pancake bit. "We were not," she wheezed.

"But now that we are," Lexie's blue eyes glimmered with mischief as she rested her elbows on the table and leaned forward. "I have been dying to know more details about your time in his apartment."

"Shh!" Violet glared at her. "Keep your voice down."

Even though she obeyed and lowered her voice to a whisper, Lexie wasn't about to let the subject go. "You can't tell me nothing happened between you two. There has been something sparking there for years, and you are head over heels—"

"I told you before, Lexie, there's nothing to tell because nothing can happen between Patrick and me." She shoveled a giant bite of pancake into her mouth.

"Yeah, yeah, because of Jax's promise. Seriously, what is up with that?" After another bite of bacon, Lexie turned her fork toward Violet. "And that doesn't stop you from wanting something to happen."

Violet shook her head, pushing her food around her plate, "Nothing's up with it. Jax made me promise not to date Patrick, end of story. I can't and won't break that. Neither would Patrick, if he knew."

A minute of silence passed and she thought the topic had been dropped, but the contemplative look on Lexie's face told her that she'd been thinking things through. "Did he force you to make this promise? Is it binding? I can't imagine any promise you made when you were fifteen would be, but you wolven have ways I don't understand."

Violet chuckled as she listened to her friend ramble, "No, it is not binding, but it would have been for anyone else, so I have to act like it is. Yes, he kinda forced me."

Lexie raised a brow, waiting for Violet to explain.

With a sigh, she obliged her friend, brushing over the details quickly, "Shortly after Patrick moved here, I made a comment about how cute he was during combat lessons. It was the first time I'd seen Jax's wolf eyes and it terrified me. He slammed me into one of the ruin columns and growled in my face that I was never to date Patrick. He didn't let up until I promised, and he's never explained why. It's not binding for me because… well, I don't really know why, but I'm betting it's because I don't have a wolf."

Shock held Lexie's mouth in a small "o" while she listened, then she cleared her throat and stabbed her pancakes with her fork, "That sounds a bit extreme."

Shrugging, Violet took another bite, "He is my brother and my future alpha. He's super protective over me, but yeah, that was crossing the line a little."

"What about the whole… mate thing?" Lexie asked, hesitating when someone walked by.

She glared at Lexie, who gave her a little wave.

"You know I'm not supposed to talk about that," Violet reminded her while the girl was still within earshot. Once she walked away, Violet dropped her voice to a whisper and leaned toward Lexie, "Mating is a whole different story. *If* I turned out to be bonded to Patrick, and *if* he accepted that fact, and those are both really big ifs, then Jax couldn't do anything to stop it."

"Even though he is going to be your alpha?" Lexie mumbled around a full mouth.

Violet's eyes drifted to Patrick who sat with Jax on the opposite side of the room. Having a mate was off the table for her, but at least as Jax's beta he would always be in her life.

"Even an alpha can't stop the will of the goddess," she answered softly.

Seeing him be with someone else—someone he loved and cherished above all else—was going to hurt.

Thankfully, Lexie dropped the subject and twenty minutes later she was arching back in her seat, "I don't know how you eat so much. You're tiny!"

"Food is my first and only love, Lexie," Violet teased around a mouthful of strawberry and pancake. "Don't question it."

Laughing, Lexie shook her head then stood, "I have to get to school. Thank your parents for letting me stay over and for the free meal. It's always appreciated." She grabbed her backpack and headed for the door.

"Will do!" Violet called after her then hurried to finish her food. She had schooling to get to as well. Her graduation was on the horizon and Violet was more than ready to be done with high school. With a smile on her face, Violet returned her and Lexie's dishes, thanked the kitchen staff, and went to grab her stuff.

"Heading to the study hall?" Patrick's lower tone sent a pleasant shiver rolling down her spine.

She lifted her bag onto her shoulder and turned to face him with a practiced smile lifting her lips. "You know it. Gotta get everything finished, so I can graduate."

Nodding, Patrick followed her when she moved for the door. "Because of recent events, Jax asked me to shadow you."

"Is that why you've been lurking around more than normal?"

The animosity in her tone was impossible to miss. She hated when Patrick was around her because Jax told him to be.

Things had taken a turn for the crazy lately and her bottled up emotions were near shattering point. Training didn't help because she trained with Patrick—aka the number one reason she was bottling emotions. She really needed a good, long run. By herself.

But the weather had been particularly nasty the last few days, making her spend a lot of time indoors.

While the sun was currently shining brightly overhead, Alpha Draven pretty much had her on compound arrest.

"I haven't been lurking. I've been keeping an eye on you."

Violet shouldered her way out the door and started on the path up the hill toward the study hall. "I don't need a babysitter, Patrick. Especially within the base."

He caught up with her and gave her an incredulous look. "In case you've forgotten, there have been attacks within the base."

"I haven't forgotten." How could she? She had nightmares about it nearly every night.

"Good, because you're stuck with me today."

The idea of being stuck with Patrick all day sounded really nice, actually, but the stolen glances at him and the little smirks when one of them would say something the other found amusing... didn't last long.

A few minutes after settling into the study hall, Kristina—Patrick's newest arm candy—chose the armrest of Patrick's chair as her roost.

It was the weirdest thing to watch.

Patrick repeatedly told the girl she didn't need to be there, he only looked at her to intimidate her into stopping whatever flirtatious antic she was up to, and practically jumped out of his seat when she tried to slink into his lap.

After a while, Kristina had settled on pulling a chair up beside his and staring longingly at him. When the girl swung her model-long legs over his, he didn't hesitate to shove them off.

"Stop. Now."

With a pretty pout, Kristina leaned her elbows on his arm-rest and toyed with his jacket sleeve.

So many questions ran through her head, and none of them were about school. Did Patrick actually like this girl? If he did, why was he being so rude? And why did he insist on sitting right in front of Violet? He could just as easily have sat in the far corner of the room and still kept an eye on her. But no, he pulled up an arm chair and placed it on the opposite side of the long table where Violet sat.

Groaning for the hundredth time that morning, Violet dropped her head onto her folded arms.

This had to be some kind of torture.

"You okay?" Kristina's high-pitched voice put nails on a chalkboard to shame.

"Just having a hard time figuring something out," she mumbled into the table.

"I'm sure Patty could help. He's a genius."

Violet lifted her head a couple inches and glared. "You'd think so, but I'm not sure even he can answer this one."

Hazel eyes bored into hers as Patrick stared her down.

Kristina on the other hand, not picking up that anything was off, began swirling her fingers through his hair.

Ugly jealousy rolled through her. Violet ducked her chin, rereading the same problem she'd been stuck on for the last ten minutes, and not because it was hard.

Patrick grabbed Kristina's hand and Violet's head thudded onto her arms again.

Another groan and someone toward the end of the table shh'ed her, making her foul mood fouler.

Turning her glare on the study hall filled with clan kids didn't help anything. There was no way of knowing which one of them had shh'ed her and to be honest, she knew she was being disruptive. Not as disruptive as the short-haired brunette trying to slip her legs into Patrick's lap for the third time, but still.

It was days like today when Violet missed the mundane aspects of public school. Two years ago, Alpha Draven had told her it was time to start her home studies—with or without her wolf. Most clan-kids began online schooling between the ages of twelve to fourteen, when they connected with their wolf sides. It was easier to continue their schooling via online classes surrounded by a community of people who could help train and aid in controlling their wilder sides.

Without her wolf, Violet had been allowed to remain in public school. It was hard to transition to online. She missed Lexie so much that it hurt at first. At least at public school, no one expected her to be something more. No one was expecting her to live up to something she wasn't.

Violet jumped when her phone vibrated in her pocket. A smirk lifted one corner of Patrick's lips as she dug it out of her joggers. She still wasn't used to having one. She wasn't sure she ever would be.

Phones were kind of irrelevant amongst the clans. If someone needed one, they'd usually borrow one of the many in a community phone box at the Clan House. With the clan-link and being able to see in the dark... there wasn't much reason for it.

She couldn't do either of those though and had really been enjoying the convenience of communicating with her mom and Lexie. The light at night was nice as well. That didn't mean she was used to it though, and often forgot her phone in her room.

The screen lit up to show a message from Lexie.

- "I still miss you at school."

Violet's mouth tilted into a small smile as she typed her response. - "I was just thinking about how much I missed you when I first transferred."

- "Ugh. That was rough. Also, I don't know how you eat all of that food. I'm stuffed and feel like someone may need to roll me home later, and I didn't even finish mine!"

Violet snorted. -"Don't worry. I finished it for you."

- "Of course you did." A rolling laughing face accompanied Lexie's message.

Loud laughter burst from Violet, earning her some glares from the other kids studying around her.

Violet glared back at a couple of them before closing her laptop and holding it to her chest, "I'm going outside."

Patrick glanced at her while Kristina pouted for his attention. "Knock it off, Katrina," He growled at her. At least she had the decency to back off when he used the wrong name. "You're supposed to study in here, Violet."

"Yeah well, these conditions aren't ideal." She grabbed her bag and nodded toward the window behind her. "That blue sky though, is perfect."

Before Patrick could nicely convince Kristina to let him stand, Violet darted out the door. She took a deep breath as she left the room and tipped her head back, enjoying the warmth of the sun on her face. It had been too long. Her ponytail swung with each step toward her favorite spot until someone slid into her path.

Skidding to a stop to avoid smacking into the person, Violet growled at the intruder.

"Hey, Violet. Where are you going?"

With a roll of her eyes and a large sigh, Violet moved around the blue-eyed Zander, "Anywhere you are not."

Zander grabbed her arm, causing a growl to rumble in her chest, "I just want to talk… without your brother around."

Violet yanked her arm out of his grasp and ignored the sting that followed, "Right, because if he were here, you wouldn't be." She stepped away from him, back toward the study hall. She should have waited for Patrick. "When did you get back, anyway?"

That was a very good question that she quickly shot to Jax through their twin-link.

"Come on, Vi. We used to be friends," Zander trailed after her, ignoring her question.

Violet stopped abruptly, nearly causing him to crash into her, "It's Violet," she corrected, "and that was before you turned eighteen and started insisting I was your mate."

Anger rolled over his features, flashing his eyes silver, and he straightened to his full height. He'd grown over the last two months.

"You are."

"It's been seven months, Zander!" Violet pushed against his chest with her one free arm, but he barely moved a half step back. Apparently, he'd gotten stronger during his time away, too. "I've never had feelings like that toward you, and after what I've seen since your birthday, I don't think I ever could."

He reached toward her with a reassuring smile, "That will all change on your birthday, and then..."

Violet stepped out of his reach. "And then I will reject you, and we will be done forever."

Shock and hurt pulled his brows together. "You don't want to do that."

"I most certainly do," Violet promised.

"Just checked with Dad." Jax's voice filled her mind, putting a pause on what she'd been about to say. *"Zander was not supposed to return until the weekend. We were going to talk to you about it later today."*

"A little late for that!" Violet snapped.

"Violet, give me a chance," Zander stepped toward her again and she stepped away. "I've changed."

Shaking her head, Violet filled Jax in on what was happening before answering the guy in front of her. "The anger in your eyes tells me otherwise."

"I'm on my way. He was told not to approach you when he returned without our say so. Where's Patrick?"

Violet ignored that last part.

"I have." Zander promised, reaching for her once more. "This trip was exactly what I needed and I'm more positive than ever that we are meant to be together."

"I don't know what happened to you on your birthday, Zander, but you are not the same guy I was friends with, and the Goddess would never pair me with you." She stepped toward the study hall doors, hoping he would let her go.

He didn't.

Zander lurched forward, digging his fingers into her arms when she tried to walk away, "Violet—"

"Let go of me!"

"Zander!" Patrick's deep snarl reached them from the study hall doors, "Get your hands off her."

Releasing one of Violet's arms, Zander turned to face Patrick, who stormed toward them with Kristina on his tail.

"This has nothing to do with you, Patrick," Zander's voice wavered, but it was clear he was trying to stand his ground, "Go back inside."

Kristina's short hair blew in the light breeze and she grabbed onto Patrick's arm, trying to pull him away, "Come on, Patty… let's go. This is between them."

With hands curled into fists, Patrick pulled his arm from her grasp. "As Jax's future Beta, his sister is under my protection."

"Future. Beta," Zander reminded him and his grip tightened on Violet's arm, making her bite her lip.

If Violet hadn't been clutching her laptop to her chest, Zander would have been on the ground already. Even without contact with her wolf, Violet had been beating Zander in combat for almost three years—shortly after Patrick started training her. But this was the third laptop Alpha Draven had bought her in the last four months. He would kill her if she broke another one.

"I don't answer to you," Zander continued. "Besides, this concerns mates. That's not a beta's jurisdiction."

Patrick's knuckles had gone white. "Violet has no mate until her eighteenth birthday." He took a menacing step toward Zander. "And she has every right to reject you when and if that time comes."

"Which it won't, because according to doc I can't have a mate."

That got Zander's attention.

Violet swallowed the lump in her throat. "I don't have a wolf, so I can't have a mate."

Confusion pulled his brows together, and he shook his head. "Then she lied to you. I am your mate."

"No, you're not!" Violet pulled against his hold, but his fingers tightened to a bruising grip.

"Take your hands off her," Patrick growled. "I will not ask again."

Zander's blue eyes melted into silver.

Usually, Patrick had a decent fuse before he exploded, but lately that fuse seemed to be shorter and shorter. When his fists began to shake, Violet wondered just how short it was today.

"Patrick," Violet breathed his name, making Zander glare at her and tighten his grip even further. She flinched and a snarl ripped from Patrick's throat as he lunged forward. "Stop!" Violet's laptop clattered to the stones below when she dropped it to press her hand against Patrick's chest.

Zander took two fearful steps backward, pulling her along with him.

He may have been older than Patrick, but Patrick had always been stronger.

Pinned between a crazed boy who wouldn't let her go and a young man hell-bent on protecting her, Violet felt a tremor of fear travel down her spine.

With Patrick standing a full foot taller than her, she couldn't see much more than his chest, which vibrated under her hand when he growled, "Let her go."

"Patrick!" Jax's voice called from behind Zander, "I've got this."

Zander let go of her like she'd electrocuted him and frantically stepped away.

"Wh-what the... what's wrong with..." Zander stared at Patrick and Violet had never seen him look so afraid. His eyes returned to blue, submitting to whatever he'd seen in Patrick that had terrified him.

Violet craned her neck back to look at Patrick, but he'd ducked his chin and closed his eyes. She'd seen him do that before, when he knew things were okay and he needed to calm down. Sliding the hand that was resting on his chest, to his arm, Violet pushed on him a little. "Patrick?"

"Zander."

Violet looked over her shoulder to see Jax clamp his hand onto the unsettled wolven.

"We weren't expecting you for a few more days. You didn't debrief Alpha. Come, we can go together." Jax towed Zander along underneath his grasp. "Patrick, stay with Violet."

Patrick shot Jax a look, then nodded. A silent agreement before Jax and Zander walked away.

"Patty, are you okay?" Kristina's voice sent a spike through the tension.

A little twinge of regret for forgetting the girl was still there, made Violet wince, but Patrick held no such remorse. He glared at her when she came near enough to sneer at Violet's hand resting on her prospect of a boyfriend.

"Go away," Patrick spoke through clenched teeth. "I'm not interested."

"What?" Kristina stood dumbfounded, her pretty gray eyes blinking rapidly. "Why woul—"

"Get out of here!" Patrick raised his voice a fraction. The tone was the most threatening part because the growl of his wolf still touched each word he spoke.

Violet still held his arm and her thumb brushed back and forth along his bicep, hoping to help calm him, as Kristina hurried away, wailing.

Once his breathing slowed down, Violet lifted her gaze from his chest—which was still rising and falling dramatically... just slower... which may have made it more dramatic—to his eyes. She was surprised to see him watching her, and a knot formed in her gut. Why did he have to be so handsome?

The bulk of his curly, dark hair fell over his forehead, casting a shadow over his hazel eyes. He'd been keeping the sides short and the top a few inches long for five months now when she'd embarrassed herself by telling him how great the style looked on him. Warmth smoldered behind those usually closed off eyes and Violet bit her lip.

Stupid promise.

"That was rude, you know," she scolded him.

Patrick sighed, "Yeah... I know."

"Are you okay?"

A shocking huff of laughter left Patrick, "You're the one who was about to be kidnapped and you're asking if I'm okay?"

"Zander?" Violet snorted and let her hand fall from Patrick's arm so she could rub the spot Zander had bruised on her other arm, "He's a lot of talk and no bite. I can even beat him in combat."

Patrick's gaze fell to her arm and his hands curled into fists once again, but he continued the conversation, "It may not be a bad idea to remind him of that."

"I have no intention of getting close enough to him to touch him ever again," Violet teased, but Patrick didn't look amused.

"It isn't a joke. You need..." He let out a puff of air and looked around them before staring straight over her head as his jaw pulsed.

"You seem..." Violet started, but bit her lip, unsure which phrasing to use. It had successfully regained his attention, however, "Are you and your wolf, okay?"

Warmth filled Patrick's gaze again and he shook his head, "My wolf, Alistair, has his own idea of what I should be doing. He's..."

"Challenging?" Violet offered, lifting both her shoulders.

A dry laugh shook Patrick's shoulders and he nodded, "You could say that." He nodded toward her arm, "Did he hurt you?"

Violet glanced at her arm to see four purplish marks starting to form on her bicep where Zander's fingers had dug in. Thankfully, she healed faster than humans, but it would still take a day or two for the bruises to disappear.

"It's nothing," Violet tried to brush it off. "It's not like I haven't had bruises before."

Patrick's jaw clenched and he gazed off into the direction the other young men had gone.

Violet touched his arm again, "Hey, where'd you go?"

After staring at her for a few seconds, Patrick whispered, "Somewhere dark."

"Well, then let me drag you back into the light," She bent down, grabbed her sure to be broken laptop off the ground, and pressed it against his chest. "I broke this because of you, so you're coming with me to get a new one, and then we're going to get ice cream."

Patrick laughed before taking the laptop from her. "You do love your sweets, don't you?"

The warmth that spread from her chest to her cheeks when his fingers brushed hers was hard to ignore. She jerked her hand away to tuck an imaginary loose hair behind her ear.

Violet shot Patrick a grin and turned to lead the way, "Let's just say it's a good thing I have a wolven metabolism."

*****

While Sentinel Clan was pretty much self-sustaining with food, basic needs, and even some fun shops, it wasn't the best place to obtain new electronics. Leaving the compound was also a great way to avoid Alpha Draven since she couldn't clan-link with him. Getting ice cream on the way home was good for three reasons; spending more time with Patrick, avoiding Alpha Draven even longer, and duh—eating ice cream.

Sitting across the booth from Patrick sent a static charge through her strong enough to make her need to bounce her leg under the table. It was exhilarating being alone with him, without Jax telling him to be here. Him tagging along was probably mostly to protect her, but in that moment she allowed herself to pretend he enjoyed her presence as much as she enjoyed his.

Patrick leaned casually against his seat, but he'd chosen the booth in the corner so his back was to the wall and he could observe the whole diner. Violet often did the same thing. It was part of their training to be aware of their surroundings. His gaze would often wander off to things that were going on behind her, an act that would have made her nervous with anyone else, but she knew wholeheartedly that he wouldn't let anything happen to her.

"Here ya go!"

Violet jumped a little, having been pulled out of her deep musings, at the middle-aged waitress' cheerful announcement.

"Deluxe banana split for the lady and a chocolate malt shake for the handsome young man." She pressed her hands against her apron and looked between them. "Is there anything else I can get for you two?"

With her mouth already full of banana and ice cream, Violet shook her head as Patrick answered for them both, "I think this will be fine, thank you."

"Oh! So polite," The waitress beamed. "I love seeing a youngster who has been raised right." She rested her hand on Violet's arm and winked, "You got yourself a good one, sweetie."

Violet's eyes bugged and heat flooded her face as the waitress made her way back to the kitchen.

If she didn't know better, she would have thought Patrick's soft smile looked a little sad.

"How's the split?" He asked, lifting his drink to his lips.

The bell for the door chimed and his gaze snapped up, following whoever it was for a couple seconds before returning to her.

"It's good. Do you want some?" Violet asked, then shoveled another spoonful into her mouth.

Patrick shook his head and huffed a laugh. "No way. I've seen what you do to people when they take your treats."

"You wouldn't be taking it. I offered."

"That must be a miracle." He lifted a brow. "Or something is wrong with you."

Rolling her eyes, Violet jammed her spoon under a bit of banana. "Forget I asked."

He chuckled, but didn't say anything else.

Time passed in silence and Violet's ice cream began to melt.

"I've never seen you eat so slow before."

She looked up and found him eying the same spot she'd seen him look at multiple times. "I don't want to go home."

"Me neither. I have an uncomfortable apology to make when we get back."

Violet nodded.

He dragged his gaze back to her. "Why don't you want to go back?"

Leaning into her seat, she gave him a sheepish smile, "I don't want to confront Alpha Draven. He's going to kill me."

"He's not going to kill you," Patrick chuckled and leaned over the table. "He may chew you out though."

"Sometimes that feels like the same thing," Violet nibbled on her spoon, then set it down and folded her arms over the tabletop. "He isn't so great at lending an ear to his daughter."

Patrick lifted his glass, eyed the empty bottom, and set it back down, "Explain that Zander was involved. That should settle it."

Violet shook her head, "You must be thinking of a different Alpha Draven. That's something he would do for Jax. Not me."

"I've never understood why you two don't get along." His brows pulled together and he rested his elbows on the table.

She shrugged. "I don't know what to tell you. It's just how it's always been. He acts like I'm a curse on the family bloodline."

"You're not a curse."

Dropping her gaze to her soupy banana split leftovers, Violet mumbled. "It kinda feels like I *am* cursed sometimes."

Patrick reached across the table and tapped on her folded arms. The tension in her shoulders eased when she looked up to find warm, hazel eyes watching her. It surprised her when he didn't pull away as she unfolded her arms and fiddled with the arm of his leather jacket. The promise she'd made to Jax was fresh on her mind after her talk with Lexie that morning, and she couldn't bring herself to hold Patrick's hand. She'd been pushing that promise too far lately.

Besides, Jax was right.

Patrick would have a mate, and it wasn't going to be her.

"You're not cursed, Vi." He slipped his hand over hers, making her freeze. When she didn't respond, he sighed, "What are you thinking about?"

A sad huff of laughter left her, "That's not really something I can tell you."

Apparently, it was his turn not to respond. Violet lifted her gaze to his, but he was staring at that same spot as earlier with slightly narrowed eyes.

She turned to see what was happening, "What are you loo—"

"Don't look," his hushed words made her freeze halfway through her turn.

After playing it off like she was stretching, she gave him a look that said she was waiting for him to explain.

"Do you still have your phone on you?"

"Yeah, I'm getting better at remembering it."

Patrick pulled his phone from his pocket and his fingers tapped furiously across his screen.

A second later her phone vibrated, and a message came through from an unknown number.

- "There is another wolven here. Not Sentinel. He hasn't dropped his hood, but has been angled toward us since he arrived."

Violet forced her breathing to remain steady as she responded, - "He isn't causing any problems, right?"

- "No"

- "Do you think it's Blood Moon?"

- "I don't know"

- "Then let Jax know and try to breathe. We can't cause a scene here. This is technically Sentinel territory, but it's also human space. We can't stop him from being here. Let Alpha Draven work it out."

Patrick's jaw twitched. His thumbs moved quickly over his phone and Violet sighed. Maybe it would be better if they went home.

"Hi guys!" Robin pushed into the booth beside Patrick and his phone was suddenly gone. "I didn't expect to see you here."

"Oh, hey." Violet mumbled, wondering how he moved so fast.

As smoothly as he had made his phone disappear, a well performed half smile lightened his face. Violet couldn't help but notice that light didn't reach his eyes, but Robin didn't. She fluttered her lashes at him when he turned his body to face her. "I didn't know you were working today."

"Yeah, I was on dishwasher duties," she rolled her pretty green eyes then held up her hands. "Punishment for dropping a tray of dishes yesterday. Look at my nails."

Violet, who had never cared much about her nails, quirked a brow at the slightly chipped paint job. "I'm... sorry?"

Robin grabbed a perfectly curled lock of hair and pulled it over her shoulder to play with teasingly as she glanced at Patrick. "Nothing I can't fix."

The low rumble that filled Violet from within surprised her. She closed her eyes, pulled her hands under the table so she could roll them into fists and took a deep breath. When she looked up at her two friends again, it was clear Robin hadn't noticed. In fact, she was rambling on about one of the customers that had been here yesterday and led to her dropping the tray. Patrick glanced at her out of the corner of his eye, before returning his attention to Robin.

A wave of panic washed over her. Had he heard her? Would he piece it together?

"Oh, Violet!" Robin's eyes widened. "Another one bites the dust, huh?"

She blinked at the perky girl before realizing Robin was gesturing to the laptop package beside her. "Ah, yeah… I killed another laptop. You may start planning my funeral now."

Robin's head dipped to the side at the harsh tone Violet had used. "Someone's a bit touchy today." She pulled out a notepad from the front pocket of her apron. "What kind of flowers shall I arrange to be laid on top of your casket?"

Patrick huffed a laugh and a small smile spread across Violet's face.

It didn't last long. Robin reached across the table and snagged one of the three maraschino cherries Violet had been saving and pulled it off the stem with her teeth—all while eying Patrick.

Violet glared, "You know better than to mess with my food."

The fake redhead shrugged, "You don't usually leave food to mess with." Excitement burst through her and she waved her hands up and down. "We should catch a movie before heading back!"

Patrick's arm laid across the back of the bench seat as he answered, "Violet still has some school work to finish…"

"Then you and I can go." Robin leaned toward him and by the angle her hand disappeared under the table, Violet knew she'd laid her hand on Patrick's leg.

The mask he usually had around others slipped over his face. "I drove Violet. I should take her home."

Robin waved dismissively, "She knows how to drive. She can drive herself." She smiled flirtatiously, dipping her chin and looked up at him while she slowly blinked.

Violet hated the girl's perfectly dark, long, thick lashes.

"Unless you're one of those guys who won't let anyone drive their truck?" Robin teased, trailing her hand down his arm resting across the back of the seat. "I guess she could take my car if you're really that possessive."

Violet turned her head away and reminded herself to breathe… and not rip off Robin's hand.

No one except Patrick had ever driven that truck, as far as she knew. It was the truck he showed up in years ago, even though he was under driving age.

"I would let Violet drive it."

The answer surprised her and she whipped her head back around to stare wide eyed at him.

Robin had lost the ability to talk, momentarily, and gaped at Patrick.

"Well, then..."

"But I need to take her home. I promised..."

"It's okay!" Violet snapped, knowing the words he was about to say. She didn't want to hear him use the excuse of babysitting her. Embarrassment burned her from within and she felt the threat of tears in her eyes. Quickly gathering her things, she stood up from the booth seat, "I can take your truck back. I'll head straight home and it will be there when you get back."

"Are you sure?" Patrick's concerned tone hit her like a brick wall as he passed his keys slowly over the table toward her.

She swallowed the lump in her throat. Her lips were suddenly very dry. Wetting her lips, she tucked a hair behind her ear and nodded, "Yeah."

Curses... why did her voice have to break?

"Violet, are you sure you can't stay? We'd love to have you along." Robin reached across the table, but Violet pulled away.

She snagged the keys and took a step back from the booth.

It was a ruse; Robin played this game all too well. Pretending like she cared when all she wanted was Patrick to herself. The games she played were one of the reasons they weren't friends anymore.

Trying not to make a scene, Violet forced a smile to her face then stepped around the table to hug Robin and whisper-growl in her ear, "You owe me."

"Thanks, babe." Robin didn't bother whispering, but her hug tightened almost painfully around Violet's neck.

Without another word, or a glance back, Violet headed for the doors. Robin's loud laughter met her ears as she pushed against the door handle and headed toward Patrick's truck.

Chapter 12

Patrick

THE RAPID THRUMB OF VIOLET'S HEART *and the salty scent of tears clung to Patrick as he sat through the movie Robin had picked out.*

Why had she been crying?

Was she okay?

Did she make it back to the base safely?

That last question was answered with a quick message to Jax, but his friend wasn't happy Violet had arrived home alone.

"I can't believe you ditched my sister!"

Patrick rubbed his forehead. *"I didn't plan to. I was trying to get out of it. She insisted I stay behind."*

"Unless she tied you up, you have no excuse for not following her."

"I've been trying to respect her wishes more and give her space. You know she doesn't like having me guard her."

"Too bad!" Jax yelled, making Patrick's headache spike. *"She needs*

protection, and you're the best we have. Unless you keep letting her get away from you."

"I don't like hurting her." Patrick grumbled through their clan-link as he dragged his fingers across his forehead to his temple.

"She's going to get a lot more hurt one day if you keep this up." Jax's voice eased and Patrick could picture the sigh the future alpha was probably letting out. *"Get home as soon as you can."*

"Understood."

Other than his stalker wolf half pacing back and forth, his mind was quiet. He tipped his head from shoulder to shoulder trying to relieve the tension in his neck, but it increased a hundredfold when cold, clawed fingers wrapped around the back of his neck.

"Got a headache?" Robin whispered sweetly.

Barely stopping a shudder from racking his body, Patrick reached back and grabbed her hand, firmly returning it to her lap. "It'll go away. Jax was just chewing me out for not being home."

"Tell him you're on a date." Robin clicked her long, manicured nails together then leaned toward him. "I'm sure he would understand."

It took everything in him not to lean away from her… until she started walking her fingers up his arm. He pulled away from the arm rest and brought his hand up to run his fingers through his hair. Hopefully, it would look somewhat natural considering it was a habit he did fairly often.

The pout on Robin's lips told him she didn't buy it.

"There are two things that Jax doesn't have a tolerance for; ignoring duty, and anything that he deems isn't protecting his sister. I'm currently on both of those lists."

Robin snorted and threw herself back into her chair. She quickly got back into the movie, ignoring him once again, which he was grateful for.

When he turned back to the screen, he realized he had no idea what was playing, or happening, or why some girl was chewing out a guy who looked like his puppy had just died.

With furrowed brows, Patrick leaned toward Robin to whisper, "Isn't this supposed to be a romantic movie?"

The regret for leaning toward her was instantaneous. She immediately turned to him and pressed herself against his arm so she could whisper in his ear, which really wasn't necessary.

"Haven't you ever heard of..." she paused when he pulled away to look at her through narrowed eyes. Clearing her throat, she continued with a bit of a bashful look on her face. "... of enemies to lovers?"

"That's a thing?" One of his eyebrows quirked.

Robin nodded emphatically. "It's a huge romance trope right now."

"Trope?"

Throwing her head back, she groaned, "You're hopeless."

He shrugged and leaned against the arm rest on his other side. "Just have better things to do than watch movies or stay up-to-date on weird slang."

"You know..." She bit her lower lip and eyed him, making him instantly uncomfortable.

He slipped on the emotionless mask he'd practiced for years when she lifted the arm rest between them and shimmied onto the edge of his seat.

"I could show you how hopeless *I* am for *you*."

"I'm hungry," Patrick slid to the edge of his seat. "Do you want anything?"

Robin bunched her lips together and shook her head before settling back in her seat. "We can grab a bite after the movie," she patted the back of his chair invitingly.

"I can't. I'm expected back as soon as possible." He stood and asked once more if she wanted anything to eat before leaving.

A hint of annoyance had made her words a little biting, but she asked for an Icee, candy, and popcorn. He'd never seen her eat that much in the three years he'd been part of the Sentinel Clan, which made him think it was a bit of a punishment for not being the date she wanted. It didn't matter if he had to spend every last penny he owned on her, he was going to soak up every minute away while getting the food.

Relief swam through him the moment he was out of the room and on his way to the concession stand.

He lingered at a poster, sauntered slowly down the hall, offered others to go in front of him in the concessions line—anything to add time.

This was not what he'd wanted.

Using Violet's schoolwork was an excuse to try and get out of going to the movies. Not end up on an accidental date with a girl he couldn't really stand being around for more than a couple minutes. Not to mention being in a dark room with that girl and having to continuously avoid her touch.

Now, the idea of being alone in a dark room with Violet was... Patrick shook his head. He would not let his mind go there.

"Mmm, it would be exhilarating," Alistair practically purred in his mind.

"That's exactly why it's a bad idea." Patrick fought with the darker wolf spirit.

"Or the best idea."

Patrick growled and the couple in front of him gave him worried looks. Lifting his fist to his mouth, he faked a cough, "Sorry about that."

They turned back around, mumbling it was fine, but they moved closer to the group in front of them, anyway.

"Careful, Boy Scout. Your true colors are showing."

"If you think I will ever let you near Violet, you hav—"

"I'm around her every time you are." Alistair chuckled.

The sound was unsettling. Of course, anything Alistair did was. His voice was Patrick's voice only slightly lower, darker—rougher, more animal than man. Alistair was everything Patrick didn't want to be.

"She is intoxicating, and you know it. Her body, her scent, her laugh... I don't know how you ignore the tempta—"

"I respect her!" Patrick shouted at Alistair, gritting his teeth together so he didn't do so out loud as well. *"And I respect Jax. That's a whole lot more than I can say for you. All you care about is yourself."*

"If you respect her, then why do you keep telling her the only reason you stay around her is because you're ordered to? You're stupid, but you're not that *stupid."*

Patrick ran a hand through his hair and rubbed the back of his neck. Being chided by Alistair was new. He didn't like it. *"I know it hurts her. It also shows I'm more loyal to her brother than her."*

"Another lie."

"Shut up, Alistair."

Knowing that his stupid, black-hearted wolf side was right made Patrick incredibly uneasy. He shoved his fists into the pockets of his leather jacket, flexing and relaxing his hands to ease some tension.

The couple ahead of him was next and then he'd have to go back to Robin.

"Just ditch her. We can run home. Stick to the trees... I'll even help you

shift."

"Not possible." Patrick snapped, frustrated with Alistair's taunting.

"Dark corner. 10 o' clock."

Patrick's head snapped to the left.

There weren't many things Alistair was good for, but that was one of them. He had a habit of seeing or sensing things Patrick didn't.

In the shadows of the corner stood a wolven with his black hood pulled over his face, obscuring any defining details... but that scent... It wasn't Sentinel.

Every clan shared a scent—Sentinel's was Cedar—and then each individual person had their own as well. Violet always smelled sweet, like the cookies she was constantly eating, but somehow the two scents blended nicely. It almost reminded him of a Christmas cookie.

Alistair chuckled, and Patrick turned his thoughts back to the wolven in the shadows. Something about his scent was familiar, but he couldn't place it.

"It's the same scent from the diner." If Alistair could have rolled his eyes, he would have right then.

"I know," Patrick grumbled. *"But that's not what I mean. I know that scent from somewhere."*

"Next!" Called the concession stand worker. His fingers drummed along the glass counter-top as he waited for Patrick to step forward.

"Sorry," Patrick muttered, casting another look toward the hooded guy, but he'd left. Patrick whipped around, searching the room, but the stray wolven had vanished.

"Sir?" The worker tried to get his attention again. "Is there something wrong with you? Do you need me to call someone?"

Shaking his head, Patrick turned toward the counter. "No, I'm sorry. I thought I saw someone I knew." He gave an assured smile to the worker who rolled his eyes, but readily took Patrick's order anyway.

Carrying his and Robin's orders was a bit of a juggling act. The Icee had looked too good so he'd ordered himself one as well on top of the giant bowl of popcorn, her box of candy—which was tucked in his pocket—and his order of nachos. The fact that he didn't drop any of it was a miracle in itself.

Robin's eyes bugged when he approached, "I don't need that much popcorn."

"That's what you have to say?" He grumbled while maneuvering to set his Icee and nachos down… without any help from her.

She took the box of candies he offered then gestured to the rest of the items he was holding. "Is this why it took you forever?"

"You asked for half of this." He reminded her as he sat down before handing the popcorn to her as well.

"I do not need this much popcorn!" She hissed.

"Half of it's for me. Stop complaining."

"Ew… did you get extra butter?"

"Shh!"

Both of them turned to stare at the guy behind them.

"Would you two be quiet?"

"Excuse me?" Robin sneered at the man who sat alone looking like he'd just rolled out of bed and hadn't bothered to shower, or shave, in days. "We are on a date."

A loud groan left Patrick and he dropped her Icee into her cup holder.

"Date?" The guy looked between them, scratching the days of scruffy, unkempt growth under his chin. "Do you two even like each other?"

"No," Patrick groaned, at the same time Robin chirped, "Yes."

They glared at each other.

"You know, this is my tenth time seeing this movie?" The guy's eyes glazed over, becoming unfocused as he continued, "My girlfriend and I loved coming to the movies. She declared this was her new favorite, and we saw it three times together." He dipped his chin and the salty scent of tears made Patrick's nostrils flare. "She dumped me for some motorcycle riding orthopedic surgeon. How could I compete with that?"

"I'm sorry to hear about that." Robin didn't sound remotely sorry. "I say it's her loss if she couldn't see what a… wonderful… guy you are."

An exasperated sigh left Patrick as he glared at her.

"She was my world, ya know? That's how you two should be," the guy sniffed. "You should be with someone who makes every part of your life better."

Robin's large green eyes turned to Patrick and a sickly-sweet smile curled her mouth. "You may not be that for me, but you sure are pretty to look at."

Annoyance filled him, and he turned away from her, staring at the exit sign. How much longer did this movie have?

A hooded figure rounded the corner. Patrick's body tensed as the guy from earlier headed up the stairs.

"He's here."

"I can see that." Patrick snapped at Alistair while he followed the strange wolven's movement.

"Don't take it out on me just because you're on a date with wolven-barbie."

"I thought you said you did whatever I did?"

"I would choose to do anything else other than being here with her."

Patrick snorted. *"For once, we agree."*

The guy ended up two rows behind them, but three seats away from the stairs, which was good. Any closer and Patrick wouldn't have been able to sit still. As it was, having the guy behind him made it impossible to relax for the remainder of the movie.

Robin's annoyance with him grew every time he turned his head to watch the guy and when the credits started, it was nearly at a palpable level.

"You are the worst date in the world." Robin growled, when the lights came on and people began to leave. "You bought all this stuff and didn't help me eat any of it so I'm going to be working my butt off like crazy in the gym for the next couple weeks. You're more interested in that wall than me. I was even willing to have an epic make out session with you, and you acted like I was electrocuting you every time I touched you."

Patrick eyed the empty popcorn bowl in his lap—she'd maybe had two handfuls of it. Shaking his head at her ridiculousness, he looked over his shoulder once more to find the hooded guy making his way down the stairs. He looked relaxed as he followed the crowd and didn't look in their direction even once.

Maybe Patrick was being paranoid.

It was possible the guy was just passing through the area and ate at the same place he and Violet had been at. Seeing a movie after grabbing something to eat was also a very normal thing. It was weird he was here without a date to see a romantic movie, but maybe he'd just gone through a break up like the guy behind him and Robin. He'd heard from a few wolven that being in a relationship with someone just to have it end when their significant other found their mate really sucked.

"Are you even listening to me?" Robin nearly shrieked, smacking his arm.

Patrick turned toward her with raised brows. Had she been talking this whole time?

"Forget it!" She abruptly stood, leaving her garbage behind and shoved past his knees. "I don't understand what Violet sees in you! Ugh! I'll meet you at the car."

"Wait, what? Robin, hold on!" He scrambled to grab everything and follow after her. What did she mean? Was Violet interested in him?

She quickly left the room, but Patrick was relieved to find her standing in the hallway… Even if she had her arms crossed over her chest and her hip kicked out to one side as she tapped her toes on the ground.

Patrick sighed. He wasn't going to get any information from her about Violet in her current mood. Knowing he'd messed up, he threw away the garbage and headed toward Robin. She hadn't even touched the Mike and Ikes she'd asked for, so he held those out to her like a peace offering when he approached.

"I'm sorry."

After eying the candy, she snatched it from his grasp and shoved it into her purse. "Let's just go."

"Wait, let me explain." He let out a heavy breath and ran a hand through his hair. The shorter sides had been the result of telling the barber to do whatever he thought best, but after Violet had complimented him, Patrick had kept it that style. It looked nice and it was easy to care for. Thankfully his curls weren't crazy, but they were just enough to give some good lift to the longer pieces on top.

"Well?" Robin snapped. "I'm waiting."

"You caught me off guard." Patrick answered, trying to keep his thoughts from slipping back to Violet.

"I can think about her for the both of us." Alistair taunted, but Patrick

didn't have time for his disturbed wolf half.

"I had a job to do—"

"Lies."

"—and I don't do well when I can't complete my jobs. My duty to Jax as his beta is very important to me."

"Web of lies!"

"Shut up, Alistair!" Patrick snarled, hoping the commentary would end. It wasn't a complete lie anyway.

"Spontaneity doesn't work very well with my position."

As he spoke, the tension in Robin's shoulders eased and her angered expression turned to one of saddened understanding. "I guess that makes sense."

"I think I may be low on sleep, as well, because I very seriously thought someone was stalking us."

Robin's scoffed laughter managed to make him smile a little. "You thought someone was stalking us on our own territory? You really are sleep deprived. Jax needs to take it easy on you."

"I don't mind. I like feeling useful."

"I guess we should get you back, so you can feel useful then." Robin elbowed him lightly and started for the exit. "So, if we planned a date would you be better company?"

Another date with Robin? Patrick nearly groaned, but he had just apologized so he refrained. "I have a busy schedule."

"Right, following Violet around like a lovesick puppy. Seriously, why don't you just ask her out instead of going after every other girl in the clan?"

Her tone wasn't mean, in fact it was almost playful, which made Patrick eye her funny as she pushed out the door. Were her emotions really that unstable? "I protect her on Jax's order. You know she doesn't have the same abilities as—"

A human passed them and Patrick clamped his mouth shut.

"Yeah, I know the whole deal. She supposedly isn't as strong, or fast, or have as well-developed abilities, but have you seen her fight?"

He quirked a brow at her.

Robin chuckled, "Right. You're also her trainer." She pulled her keys from her purse. "See? You are always around her."

"That doesn't mean we belong together."

"Maybe not," she bumped her hip against him as they moved to separate sides of her car. "I think your bodyguard duties would make it hard to have a relationship with anyone else, though." She paused outside the driver's door, gazing at him with a flirtatious smile curving her mouth. "I'm happy to be a distraction for you, if you're interested. I know we aren't mates, so I won't let emotion get in the way."

"I'll keep that in mind," Patrick grumbled, then folded himself into her car. They couldn't get back to the base soon enough.

Chapter 13

Violet

"THIS IS INSANE!"

Violet glared at Robin, who apparently had enough of her red hair and was now a brunette with red undertones. "Would you keep your voice down?"

After she'd left to make way for Robin's impromptu date with Patrick, it hadn't been too hard to convince her to help… that didn't mean she was nice about it.

"Or better yet, just don't talk?" Lexie smirked at the fake brunette.

"Guys!" Mya chided all of them as the lights of the field gates illuminated the darkening forest. She bounced forward while the other three girls stayed a few paces behind. "Four tickets, please."

The guy inside the booth on their side of the gate winked at her and handed over the tickets as she slid the money across the counter.

Robin gaped as Mya sauntered toward them, flashing the newly acquired tickets. "How did you do that?"

Shrugging, Mya matched their strides and they continued along the tree lined dirt road toward the gates. "Ever heard you catch more flies with honey?"

Robin wrinkled her nose, "Why would I want to catch flies?"

Lexie's grin was sickly sweet. "She means you'll get more in life by being sweet than by being a..."

"By being snarky," Violet blurted, sending Lexie an exas-perated look.

Her very human friend chuckled, seeming oblivious to the danger around them. Lexie had not been happy when she'd heard about the date, which didn't make the situation between her and Robin any easier.

"Whatever." Robin shoved her hands into her jacket pockets.

Worried she would leave if they kept fighting with her, Violet offered a warm smile. "Thank you again for helping us with this."

Robin lifted her chin a little, but did give her a small smile in return.

"Tickets," ordered a grumpy looking teen male as he held out one hand. The front legs of his chair were about five inches off the ground while he propped the backrest against the fence.

His attention remained focused on a gaming device in his other hand, even when Mya handed the tickets to him. He bit one corner of the four tickets, tore them, then handed them back.

Mya grimaced and was careful not to touch the part of the tickets the guy had bitten while Violet let out a relieved sigh. One more barrier passed.

"Thanks," Mya muttered before the four girls shuffled past the distracted male.

"I can't believe we made it in," Robin's eyes widened after they walked through the gates and a roar from the fans reached their ears.

The smaller dirt road expanded beyond the gate to a path big enough for two cars to carefully pass each other. Thick forest remained on either side as they walked the remaining length into the concessions area of the tourney pitch.

Due to the noise and the space needed for the field, the Sentinel pitch was located a little more than a mile from the base. Still within Sentinel territory, but outside the compound fence line.

Lexie's excited giggle made Violet smile. "I can't wait to see this."

"I hate being late," Robin murmured.

Arriving late had been Violet's idea to minimize the number of people Lexie would be exposed to. Surrounded by a group of female wolven, her human scent would be masked while standing or sitting, but she'd still leave a trail to follow while walking.

For the most part, the meager crowd in front of them split to the right or left, home team and visitors. Some were gathered in the neutral zone in front of the concession stands chatting or eating whatever food they could afford.

"Looks like we have a good view tonight!" Mya exclaimed excitedly and hurried them toward the home side.

After climbing the stairs and moving high into the stands, Violet turned to see the pitch.

Sentinel Clan had done an excellent job of making sure both sides could see the field. The stadium lights at each end of the field were brilliantly lit due to the waning crescent moon dangling high in the sky. Hay bales were scattered through the pitch, creating little mountains here or there while four large ones were stationed in a zig-zag pattern through the Blood Zone.

Lexie sucked in a sharp breath when a Sentinel team mem-ber was slammed into the ground by the opposing team. "Is he okay?"

The three wolven females all nodded and Violet shrugged. "The Clan Games are a lot more violent than the sports humans play."

"They aren't wearing any pads."

"We heal quickly." Mya patted the human girl's arm. "Even a broken bone will be healed in a matter of hours to a day."

"Sure, but..." Lexie flinched as paint splattered across the front of a player in the Blood Zone. "That's got to hurt."

Robin smirked. "The velocity on the paint guns are set to the highest they go. It *does* hurt."

Surprised the high maintenance girl knew about paintball velocity, Violet's mouth fell open a bit.

"What?" Robin glared. "Don't look so surprised. I wanted to be a sniper; it's the one position that can't be hit."

"So, there are rules to this madness?" Lexie asked, sounding desperate as a few snarls lit up the field.

Two Whisky Clan members trudged toward the cage on Sentinel's side. One had a hand clamped over his arm and even from where they stood, they could see blood covering his arm.

"This can't be safe," Lexie whispered as she clutched Violet's jacket.

Violet chuckled, then shook her head. "Just watch. Yeah, he got hurt, but that's just a scratch. By the time he gets to the cage, the medic will be there, but they won't do anything. He'll probably be healed by that point."

Just as she'd described, a medic was waiting for the two team members when they arrived at the cage. He wiped down the teens arm then signaled something with his hands and the game resumed.

"What was that?"

Mya answered that question, "He was signaling that no penalty was necessary and game play could resume."

Lexie pulled her coat tighter around herself. "Geeze, what warrants a penalty?"

"Needing stitches, a broken bone, or muscle or bone exposed," Violet offered, watching a familiar mass streak through the Blood Zone.

Patrick was nearly a blur with how fast he was moving. He leapt from hay mound to hay mound, ducking behind them as a paintball whistled past him. A curse flew from one of the snipers. If Patrick made it out of the Blood Zone, he would be off limits.

"What's Patrick doing?" Lexie asked, leaning down to whisper to her best friend.

After telling her more than a hundred times that whispering wouldn't help around wolven, Violet simply shook her head. "I'm surprised you saw him. He's fast."

"I only noticed him when he landed for a second on the hay bales."

"Patrick is the scout—and the best one I know," Violet explained, "His job is to make it into the Whisky Clan territory so he can look for their clan crest. It'll be on a thirty-by-forty-inch flag and will be hidden somewhere. There are specific rules on where the crest can be. Like, some portion of the flag must be visible so it can't be completely buried."

"That sounds like normal rules," Lexie shrugged.

"Right, but this version has three knights who are tasked to fight off the scout and any other teammates he brings with him. Which he is allowed to do once he finds out where the crest is."

"What happens if he loses that fight?"

"He goes in the cage," Robin answered with her eyes glued to the game. "I forgot how much I missed this."

Mya rolled her eyes at the weird, reddish-brown haired girl beside her. "The cage is just a penalty box inside the goal. You saw where those team mates went, right?" At Lexie's nod, Mya continued. "If anyone is inside the goal, no points can be made until you free your team members."

"Like dodgeball?"

Violet shuddered. She hated that game. "No. You can still progress in dodgeball as long as you have people in the game. You see the ones out there with the lacrosse sticks?"

Another nod was Lexie's answer as she followed the game-play on the field.

"Those are strikers. They score as many points as they can until the flag is captured and brought to their side. If they have teammates in the cage, they can't score points.

"So how do they get their teammates out?" Lexie asked, rising onto her toes to try and get a better view.

"Watch," Mya pointed toward the cage with the two Whisky Clan members stalking back and forth.

A few minutes later, a knight with a matching jersey darted across Sentinel's territory.

"What?" Lexie screeched. "He was just over there!" She pointed to where the knight had previously been on his own territory. "I thought the knights were supposed to protect the crest?"

"Yes, but their other job is rescuing their team members while the strikers fight off the other team."

The Whisky knight grabbed a Sentinel defender and slammed his knee up into the guy's face. All four girls flinched as the Sentinel crumpled, hitting the grass with a hard thud.

Punches, kicks, full bodied tackles... they were all happening as the three Whisky strikers went toe to toe with Sentinel's strikers and two defenders... well... now one.

"This is insane," Lexie watched with wide eyes as a Whisky teammate dropped to one knee. "They are actually fighting."

Mya snuggled against Lexie's side, "Think of it like a boxing ring. This is part of the game, but it's also a fantastic way to put all our training and self-defense into action without the danger of losing your life in a real clan war."

Tossing her head from side to side, Lexie agreed that was better and watching the fallen wolven rise from the ground helped ease her worries.

"There is also a rule to the fighting as well," Robin chimed in again. "Three hits and you go down. Even if it's a tap. If they get three hits on you, you take a knee and let them pass. You are not allowed to go after that team member until they cross back over the Blood Zone.

The jail keeper lashed out at the approaching knight, fending him off as he reached for his teammates.

"All he has to do is touch them and they can walk back onto the field." Robin snorted as the guide sacrificed a punch to the ribs for brushing his fingertips across his teammates out-stretched hand. "They are essentially ghosts until they make it back to their territory. They can't fight or be fought, no defending, and they can't score any points."

The freed teammate jogged toward the Blood Zone, ignoring all the brawling around them.

"I'm guessing only those hit by the snipers go in the cage?" Lexie asked as the knight took a knee before heading back toward his territory.

"Yup," Violet nodded, impressed that her friend was picking the game up. "That knight will have to either switch with one of the other knights or try again."

Mya cleared her throat and lifted her chin dramatically. When she started speaking, it was with this strange announcer's voice that made Violet and Lexie snicker. "Each goal is five points. Each prisoner is negative three points. The clan crest is worth fifty points, but often doesn't guarantee the team a winning score. The only thing that is guaranteed is once the crest makes it to the opposing team's territory, the game is over."

Shaking her head, Lexie chuckled. "Negative points. That's harsh."

"It really sucks sometimes," Violet agreed.

"Knowing the rules helps. Thanks," Lexie nudged her shoulder against

Violet. "I'm not cringing every time someone drops now."

Laughing, Mya wrapped her arm around Lexie's shoulders. "It's intense, huh?"

"Very," the human girl agreed, tipping her head to press it against Mya's. "Is Aiden playing tonight?"

Mya bit her lip and nodded, making her lion mane of curls bounce. "Did you know it's his birthday? He insisted on playing tonight since he doesn't officially turn eighteen until 11:21 and said this was the party he wanted." She pointed out to the field and tried to show Lexie where he was. "He's one of our strikers."

Meanwhile, Violet's gaze roamed the pitch for Patrick as she fiddled with the end of her long braid.

Even with all the rules and the fast healing of the wolven, any time Patrick was involved in a fight, Violet worried. It was ridiculous. He was one of the best on the team, if not *the* best, but seeing him hurt was never fun.

A head of curly, dark hair peaked up from behind a small mound of hay bales and a paintball splattered, narrowly missing Patrick's cheek. Smirking, he dove for the next miniature mountain of hay.

The sniper's abrasive female voice carried across the pitch when she cursed. She was quick, firing again as soon as the trigger released, but Patrick was fast, too. He moved in unpredictable patterns making it nearly impossible to hit him or guess where he would be next. When he finally slid behind some more hay bales, the cursing began again, making many Sentinel fans chuckle.

"I'm surprised she didn't open fire."

"She can't," Robin lifted her arm and pointed at the sniper. "Each gun is rigged so the trigger locks up for a third of a second after firing. Otherwise, the entire Blood Zone would be lit up with paint due to our fast reflexes. She is one of the fastest snipers I've ever seen. There was nearly no pause between the trigger release and her firing."

Violet turned her head toward her semi-friend and smirked. "I am surprised, Robin. I had no idea you were so into the Clan Games."

Tossing her long red-brown hair over her shoulder, Robin shrugged. "Because I never played. I wanted to. I did tons of research on it, but the idea of me playing really freaked my mom out."

Robin had shown up in Sentinel territory a year before Patrick, with her dad. Her mom had been killed in a border patrol that had gone horribly wrong, and the only reason Violet knew that was because she'd overheard her mom talking about it. Robin hardly ever mentioned her mom. She never mentioned what happened to her.

Knowing better than to press any further, Violet nodded and returned her attention to the pitch.

A couple more minutes and Patrick had successfully made it into Whisky territory, to the dismay of the sniper who let out a string of curses so impressive that one of the adults scolded her from the stands. A few more minutes and Violet was sure he had to be getting close to Whisky's Clan crest. He was quick and thorough, moving from one position to the other with stealth and ease.

Mya gasped, startling Violet into looking away from Patrick.

Aiden was on one knee, holding a hand up in surrender. He must have taken a pretty good hit to make Mya react like that. The four girls watched, waiting for him to stand and return to game play. It took a couple minutes, but he did rise and the crowd went wild.

A happy smile spread across Violet's lips as Mya took a bunch of deep breaths, trying to settle herself down.

Red flickered in the corner of her gaze, drawing Violet's attention away from her friend. Her breathing sped up and her heart raced as two bloody eyes beamed from across the stands. Shaken, Violet blinked. She stumbled back into the person next to her who snarled at her to stay in her own seat. When she looked back, the red eyed person was smiling and cheering on the game, like everyone else.

"Hey." Lexie grabbed her hand.

How long had she been shaking?

"You okay?"

Swallowing the knot in her throat, Violet nodded. It felt like someone had dropped a twenty-pound weight on her chest. "Just thought I saw something. It's been a rough couple weeks."

"Do you need to go home?" Mya asked, leaning around Lexie. "We can walk you back."

"Speak for yourselves," Robin mumbled, focused on the female sniper again.

After shooting her a glare over their shoulders, Lexie and Mya turned back to Violet, waiting for her to answer.

She shook her head, "No. I think I'm just gonna grab something to drink."

"We'll come with you." Mya chimed in, glancing back at the pitch. "Besides, it looks like Aiden is being switched out and I want to say hi."

Violet laughed. "Sounds like a plan."

Without Robin and her snarky remarks trailing behind them, the three girls made their way to the neutral zone with plenty of laughs.

Another pair of red eyes stopped Violet in her tracks, but once again, she blinked and the crimson filter was gone.

"What the heck?" Violet's brows pulled together as she ran a hand over her other arm.

"Violet, are you okay?" It was Mya who asked this time and the look of concern on her face made Violet wonder how bad she looked.

Her stomach was in knots, she had a headache, her heart was racing, and she was seeing things. "No," she answered honestly. "I don't feel so good."

Lexie's eye bugged. "Like you're sick? You never get sick."

"That's because we don't get sick. At least, not like humans do." Mya explained in hushed tones as she stepped close to Violet. "What are you feeling?"

Violet tried to explain, but ultimately shook her head and simply said, "I think it's residual trauma from the Blood Moon scouts in the compound."

"The what?" Lexie shrieked and both the female wolven shushed her. "You didn't tell me that happened!"

"I've been trying to forget about it." Violet shifted uncomfortably and rubbed her neck where the Blood Moon scout had nearly pierced her flesh with his fangs. Another set of crimson eyes glowed from a wolven walking away from a concession stand, but again the color disappeared.

"Yeah... I think I need to go home," she agreed, forgetting about the drink she wanted and just wanting to be in her bed.

Mya wrapped an arm around her shoulders. "Do you want me to tell Luna?"

"No. I actually remembered my phone tonight so I can call her if I need to. I'll talk to her when we get there." She gave her best friends a grateful and apologetic smile. "Thanks, guys. I'm sorry we aren't staying."

Lexie shrugged, then weaved her arm through Violet's. "I've seen enough. It's exciting, and definitely different, but a little intense for my tastes."

Laughter tipped Mya's head back. "Glad you got to experience it."

"What about Aiden?" Violet asked, feeling guilty for taking her away.

Mya shrugged, "I'll see him later. We're going to meet up and watch a movie at my apartment to finish up his birthday."

"Oooooh!" Lexie teased, but Violet didn't join in the merriment.

Ringing filled Violet's ears and she could hear her blood pumping. Three sets of blood eyes zeroed in on their little group, freezing Violet in her tracks.

"Lexie?" questioned a familiar voice and she blinked.

The three wolven who did *not* have red eyes passed by them, looking at her like she was losing it.

"Oh no," Lexie groaned.

"Violet, why is *she* here?" Jax growled and came to a stop nearly toe to toe with his twin.

"Something isn't right," she whispered to herself, ignoring the fact that Jax was fuming in front of her.

His bruising grip on her arm snapped her back to reality. "Are you stupid? Bringing a…" he glanced around anxiously. "Bringing *her* here?"

Violet wrenched her arm from his grasp and ignored the sting that followed. "Don't worry, we were just leaving, but something—"

"You had some pretty decent plays out there, Draven."

Both twins turned to stare wide eyed at Vikter. Had he actually given Jax a compliment? Violet's gaze traveled over Stanislaus' future alpha… something was terribly wrong with him. His shoulders were slumped, his blond hair disheveled, his shirt was creased and didn't appear to be clean, even his jeans looked like they hadn't seen a washer in a while.

"What happened to you?" Violet asked before she could stop herself.

Vikter snorted, "You did."

"No, Vikter," a deep authoritative voice sounded over the grumpy, wrinkled teen and a neatly put together young man stepped into the conversation. "This was a long time coming, and you brought it on yourself."

Vikter's nose scrunched in a snarl as his eyes flared gold.

Mya was the only one who audibly responded. Her gasp filled the area enough to draw Vikter's gaze. Future alphas, and alphas alike, had eyes that resembled liquid gold. Vikter's eyes no longer held that magical quality—they were muted, dull, and matte.

The newcomers' light brown eyes swirled molten gold in response and Violet knew if she looked at Jax, his eyes would be the same.

"Stand down, Vikter." This new future alpha's tone was calm, but the authority rang through and Vikter's chin dropped a fraction. "You can go home, or you can go enjoy the tourney."

Resentment twitched across Vikter's face as he looked around their group. His gaze settled on Lexie, making Violet's heart race. He couldn't pick up her human scent, could he? Not with this many wolven around, right? She knew if she made a move to defend her friend, Vikter would react. She was about to send Jax a link when her twin stepped in front of Lexie, his shoulders tensing and his gaze threatening violence.

"Leave, Vikter," ordered the new guy. His dark, thick eye-brows added a scary effect to the stern look written across his toasted almond face. "Now."

Unable to resist his alpha's order, Vikter snarled and stomped away.

The atmosphere around their group sighed with relief at his departure. Jax's shoulders relaxed before he turned his attention on the new guy who was dusting off an invisible speck of dust on his nice black coat.

"Let me apologize for my clan member's attitude and introduce myself." He held out his hand toward Jax. "I'm Talon Break, future alpha to the Stanislaus Clan now that Vikter has been removed from his previous position."

The wind played in Talon's dark hair, pulling it out from behind his ears so it laid about an inch longer, while the two future alpha's shook hands.

"Always a pleasure to meet the alpha's I'll be working with in the future." Jax nodded respectfully. "Thank you for addressing that situation."

Sighing, Talon tucked his hair behind his ears then shoved his hands into his coat pockets. "Vikter has been a bit of a handful since losing his position. To be honest, I feel like I'm babysitting most of the time. His paranoia has made things... difficult."

Violet snorted. "I think you're being nice."

A pleasant grin slipped over Talon's face and he ducked his chin as a chuckle rolled out of him. "I may not be able to stand the guy, but he is still part of my clan."

"Doesn't mean you have to be *that* nice."

Humor lit his eyes as they drifted over her, making Jax tense. "You must be Jax's twin."

Violet raised one shoulder and smiled, "The one and only." Unease twisted her stomach as another set of red eyes flashed at her. She shifted her weight and glanced back at her friends. "We were just heading out, but I'm glad to see Stanislaus has a stable future leader."

With a respectful nod, Talon looked over their group. "Thank you. I look forward to working with you, Jax."

"Likewise," Jax returned Talon's nod with one of his own before the new guy walked away in the direction Vikter had disappeared.

"Okay, you're starting to worry me," Mya admitted, grabbing Violet's hand. "That guy was hot and you want to walk away."

"Mya," both Violet and Jax said at the same time.

"I just don't feel good, okay?" Violet repeated her previous answer then looked at Jax. "I think that encounter we had a couple days ago is still affecting me."

Jax's gaze settled on her face as if searching for the answers to what she was really feeling. *"Anything I need to know about?"*

"Not unless seeing red tinted eyes everywhere I turn is something you need to know." Violet sighed internally.

His face tensed. *"Are you actually seeing them?"*

She shook her head and shrugged. When she wouldn't reveal anything else, he grumbled to Mya, "Get her out of here."

"I'll keep a lookout, but I haven't seen anything." He assured her through their mind-link. He passed a look over Lexie, who had her arms crossed and a brow raised, then headed back toward the game.

Mya sighed, "We're going to the doc's and getting you chec..."

"I don't need to see the doc. I just need to go home."

"Violet..."

"Really. I'm just tired and stressed. It's nothing to worry abo—"

A blood curdling scream ripped through the air.

Goosebumps flooded across Violet's skin. Mya spun around, on the defensive. Lexie backed away, but Violet snagged her arm before she could get too far.

"What w-was that?" Lexie's eyes were wide with fear as she cowered between her two wolven friends.

Moments later the thunderous sound of footsteps grew louder and louder. Screams, growls, and snarls filled the air. Fear permeated the atmosphere with its stench and Violet scrunched her nose as the first wave of wolven rushed for the gates.

"Move!" Mya yelled, shoving them both to the side so they wouldn't be trampled.

People rushed past, knocking into them in their frantic attempts to leave.

"What is going on?" Lexie asked with a shaky voice. "Should we be leaving too?"

"If we try to leave right now, you'll be taken out. We could survive this frenzy, you'd get trampled to death." Violet shoved Lexie's head down when her friend tried to see what was happening. "Keep your head down!" A snarl ripped out of her on the last word when something jabbed her kidney.

"I have to go find Aiden," Mya looked around frantically as the last of the wolven passed by. With the crowd gone, Violet expected there to be silence, but there were still sounds of snarling and growling coming from the tourney pitch. "I have to make sure he's okay."

Lexie nodded, "We'll come with you."

Although her bravery was admirable, Violet also felt it was stupid. She grabbed her arm when she tried to follow after Mya, "You need to be as far away from whatever is happening back there."

"Mya needs us."

"You need to stay alive!" Violet growled and Lexie's eyes bugged. Typically, she was careful not to react so... wolven... when around Lexie, but this was serious and her human friend needed to know that.

"She's right, Lexie. You need to get out of here." Mya walked backward away from them, back toward the pitch. "I'll send you a message when I know more about what's happening."

With that, she spun around and sprinted back the way they had come.

Patrick was back there. Jax, too.

They could take care of themselves, Lexie couldn't.

Heart pounding, Violet pushed her human friend back toward the compound.

"Let's go, Lexie. Now," Violet ordered.

She relented and they hurried for the gates.

"What do you think is happening?" Lexie asked quietly. "Do you need to tell your mom?"

Violet pulled out her phone and handed it to Lexie. "She has probably heard from Jax already, but you can send her a message. Tell her there is trouble at the pitch."

She had expected more wolven to come running for the gates, but there had only been one wave, which made her even more uneasy.

"So, what do you think is happening?" Lexie asked again after sending the message.

"I have two guesses, and neither one of them are good."

A twig snapped to her left and Violet twisted toward the sound, but there wasn't anything there.

"What is it?" Lexie hissed.

"Shh!"

Twigs didn't snap for no reason.

"Violet?" Lexie asked after a minute of agonizing quiet. "What are the two things?"

When no more movement was found, Violet sighed and hauled Lexie down the path. "A clan issued attack—which would be bad on multiple levels and unlikely. If it's unsanctioned, that would bring a world of hurt down on every clan involved. If it *is* sanctioned, that means the kings and queens are mad about something we did, and we're to be taught a lesson."

"So, either you're being taught one or you're about to be?"

"Those were kind of two issues tied into one," Violet's ear twitched at another sound to the side. "I can't decide if the other one is worse or not."

"What?" Lexie grabbed the back of Violet's coat.

The last rays of sunlight were dwindling and while Violet could still see all right, she imagined Lexie with her very human eyes was having a harder time.

Shaking her head, Violet tried to push the images of blood-red eyes out of her head. "I don't want to scare you."

"I can barely see in a forest that I'm not supposed to be in, surrounded by supernatural beings that are better than me in every way, and would probably take me out without hesitation if they found me here. I've been scared since we got here."

Violet shot a look over her shoulder at her best friend. "Why didn't you say something?"

"Because I was excited, too. Now, I'm just scared."

"I'm not going to let anything happen to you, Lexie," Violet turned and grabbed her friend's arms. "I promise. I'll take care of you."

After Lexie nodded, they continued making their way toward the compound. They'd only managed to make it about ten steps before Lexie's curiosity got the better of her.

"Okay, I need to know what the second possibility is because I'm going crazy thinking about all sorts of weird stuff now. Like chupacabra or witches or zombies."

A smirk tugged at Violet's lips, "I'm not really sure how those three things relate, but I can assure you that at least two of the three don't exist."

"Well crap… it's zombies, isn't it?"

Violet chuckled and shook her head. "Witches are very real. Zombies are not. I've never seen a chupacabra, but I'm pretty sure they don't exist, either."

"What about vampires?"

Movement in the trees made Violet freeze and Lexie crashed into her back.

"Seriously, are there vampires?" Her friend nearly squeaked, clutching her shirt.

"Shh."

The trees were still. They had been before, too. The little hairs on the back of her neck stood on end.

Something vibrated behind her.

"V-Violet?"

She turned around to find Lexie's pale face illuminated by her phone. She turned the device so Violet could see the message sent by her mom.

-Blood Moon. Get home. Be safe.

"Lexie," she gently took the phone from her friend, tucked it into her pocket, and held Lexie's hands which were shaking violently. "I need you to listen to me very closely."

Another snap of a twig and trembling of leaves and Violet spun around, keeping one hand on Lexie. She couldn't see anything, but she knew they were out there. A dark feeling had settled over her chest, making it difficult to breathe.

"Vio—"

Her hand clamped down over Lexie's mouth, against her groans of protest and trying to remove her fingers. "We are being hunted," she hissed, making Lexie freeze.

"What?" she mumbled against Violet's hand.

"I'm so sorry." Violet released her face. "We just have to focus on making it back to the compound. It's not far."

"You try not being able to see, it makes this a lot harder," Lexie hissed.

Frustration zipped through Violet and she hissed back, "If we don't get out of here soon, I won't be able to see either! My eyesight is not as good as other wolven, but the light from our phones will draw attention and without the moon..." She tugged on her friend's hand. "I just need you to move quickly. I'll be your eyes, but we have to go or we are going to be dog chow."

"Now that's not very nice," a deep voice from the trees shot goosebumps flooding up Violet's arms.

Chapter 14

Violet

"WHAT'S WRONG WITH THEIR EYES?" *Lexie whispered, clutching Violet's arm as two blood-eyed males stalked toward them through the trees.*

Violet positioned her small body in front of her friend and leveled the two men with her best glare, hoping she would give the air of dominance.

A long scar ran down the length of the closer one's face and neck, disappearing under the collar of his shirt. The sadistic smirk that lifted a corner of his mouth made Violet's body tense—apparently, her acting had no effect on him. "You must be really desperate to die, little human, if you're trudging around these parts."

"Little?" Lexie snorted, her fear evaporating in an instant. "I'm just as tall as any of the females here. Well," she nudged Violet in the back. "Except for this one."

Violet would have rolled her eyes if there weren't two killers in front of them.

A cold laugh drew her attention to the second one, whose long, blond hair had started to slip from the ponytail at the base of his neck. "She's got fire in her soul. I'm gonna take pleasure in breaking it."

Another snort left Lexie. "You can't break fire, idiot. You can douse it. Blow it out. Smother it. Ste—"

"Shut up, Lexie," Violet hissed after seeing Ponytail Guy's eyes glow brighter.

The first one, Scar Face, looked up and down Violet's body then took another step toward her, which Violet mirrored, pushing Lexie back a step as well. "Aren't you that twin?"

"The miracle?" asked the other. Curiosity tilted his head to the side as he looked at her.

Violet's heart skipped a beat.

"Yeah. You fit the description," Scar Face nodded then rubbed a hand over the five-o-clock shadow dusting his jaw. "Boss is curious how that happened."

Confusion pinched her brows together. Boss? Not Alpha? And why would some random Blood Moon guy care who she was?

She shook her head, "How should I know?"

"Well, you're her, aren't you?"

It would've been stupid to lie at this point. If they really had heard of her, it would probably be pretty obvious who she was. After all, she was really short for a wolven which was kind of hard to miss.

"That doesn't mean I know how I'm still alive when all the others have died."

"What should we do?" Ponytail Guy rubbed his hands together like he was suddenly nervous, "Boss will have our heads if we kill her."

Another smirk twisted Scar Face's mouth again, exposing one of his fangs.

Hold up, since when did they have fangs? She'd never heard of wolven having fangs before. Her brows pinched together in confusion as she stared at him. If they made it out of this, she had so many questions to ask her mom.

"I wasn't thinking about killing either of them," Scar Face replied, looking to his partner.

Without anything more than a brief nod of agreement from Ponytail Guy to give her warning, Violet narrowly dodged the attack from Scar Face. She threw her arm back, shoving Lexie backward and the 'umph' that resulted told her she would need to apologize later.

"Quick reflexes for a girl without a wolf," sneered Scar Face, frustrated he had missed.

"And you're pretty slow for a murderer," Violet snarled, trying to back away as he stalked closer, but Lexie was still on the ground blocking her path.

He laughed and began circling them, breaking away from Ponytail guy. "So, the rumors are true then? Violet Draven doesn't have a wolf of her own?"

The split attention was not good.

Feeling Lexie move, she tried once again to back up so she could keep both of them in her line of sight… unfortunately, Lexie was not trained in combat and only took one step back when Violet bumped into her.

"What do you care?" She asked. Two faster, stronger, Blood Moon wolven against one tiny wolfless girl were not good odds. If she could keep them talking, she might be able to hold them off until someone came along.

Scar Face shrugged, feigning a relaxed gate. "Just curious."

"Careful," Violet quirked a brow. "I've heard it's a killer."

His eyes narrowed a fraction, but she thought she caught a hint of humor before he growled, "I'm not so easy to kill."

"Me either!" Snarled a familiar female voice from behind her.

"Robin?" Lexie's surprise jerked Violet's attention toward the bloodied female rushing toward Ponytail Guy.

Pain lit up Violet's jaw and the ground kissed the other side of her face. Lexie screamed her name, but it sounded farther away than it should. A large hand grabbed her hair, scraping her scalp with his nails, and lifted her to her knees. She clawed at Scar Face's hand while he laughed at her, forcing her head back until her neck hurt.

A memory of one of her and Patrick's first training sessions came to mind. She had been so angry that hot tears had flooded down her cheeks when he restrained her for the hundredth time. He'd pinned her arms behind her back and leaned close to whisper in her ear. "I'm not trying to show you how weak you are, Vi. I'm trying to teach you how to use what you have. With your tiny, unsuspecting body, no one will expect you to fight dirty. If you're backed into a corner with nowhere to go, I want you to fight as rough and dirty as you can to get out of there alive."

Anger hot enough to feel like she was burning from the inside flooded her. She stopped clawing uselessly at his hand which made him stop laughing and gaze down at her curiously. Her hand balled into a tight fist and she socked him as hard as she could where it really counted.

The ache across her scalp eased when he dropped her to double over. He fell to his knees, clutching himself, and groaned.

"Lexie, get out of here!" Violet ordered, but the tall blond girl appeared frozen with horror. She pushed her friend, spurring her into action, "Go! Run!"

Lexie turned and ran, driving her long legs into the ground as fast as she could.

Scar Face brought one foot forward into a single leg kneel, attempting to get back in fighting shape. Using the opportunity of his lower position and slowed movements, Violet stepped closer, spun around, and delivered a solid roundhouse to the side of his head. His head whipped to the side, followed by the rest of his body crumpling to the ground.

Patrick had always told her that her tornado roundhouse was one of her strongest attacks, but it wasn't always the best option. Paired with her slower speed, most wolven would be able to counter the move, but staring down at the unconscious male unleashed a smug satisfaction that fell over her.

"Violet!" Robin's desperate cry pulled her out of her self-congratulatory moment.

Ponytail Guy was raining hit after hit down on Robin. She cried out as she blocked a bone-rattling hit.

Sprinting toward her, Violet drove her fingers into the tender flesh of his back just below his ribs. He arched back, snarling and swung blindly for her. Robin fell back against a tree trunk clutching her arm to her chest while Ponytail Guy turned his attention on Violet.

"This doesn't have to be difficult," he told her, throwing a hook that she ducked under and drove her fist into his side. With his teeth bared, she caught sight of his canines, which were longer than your average wolven, but not quite fang like.

The speed he used to throw his elbow back, blindsided her. Her already tender scalp burst with pain when his elbow made contact, and she stumbled a couple steps blinking, away her blurred vision. Pressing her fingers to her head, she felt something slick and pulled it back to see blood coating her fingertips.

"Robin, catch up to Lexie, please. Get her home safe."

"I can help," Robin offered, but her voice sounded weak.

Violet curled her hands into fists and squared off with Ponytail Guy once again. "He's not getting past me."

His laughter twisted her stomach into knots.

The sound of foliage crunching told her that Robin took the available exit and left. Running from a fight wasn't shameful. From the look of her, Robin had done her fair share of fighting just to get to Violet, and she wasn't a fighter. She had never been interested in becoming a warrior for the clan, but she trained a little to stay in shape—which may have saved her life.

Violet prayed to the Goddess that Robin would find Lexie as Ponytail Guy battered her with a series of punches. Pulling her elbows tight in front of her to protect her stomach, she crunched inward. Her arms shook with his hit and she clenched her teeth to keep from crying out.

A brief pause in his attacks allowed her to uncoil and jab his stomach. She sacrificed a hit to her side so she could grab his shirt and thrust her knee upward.

Some sort of groin attack had worked twice now on Blood Moon pack members, but he shifted to block.

"Nice try." He smirked, but he'd left his right side open.

With her close proximity, she flattened her hands and jabbed him with wicked fast repetition. A rib snapped under her fingers. He roared in pain. The resulting backhand across her face was too quick to do anything about.

The strength behind the attack was enough to spin her around and send her sprawling into the dirt while her vision spun.

"We were told you would be easy," he grumbled, stepping over her. He knelt down, driving his knee into her back and grabbed one of her arms.

"What?" Violet sputtered, tasting blood in her mouth. She struggled against his hold. "Am I the target?"

She tried to throw her free elbow back, hoping to hit his inner thigh, but he caught her arm easily and pinned it with the other. "Nah, but our buddies from the other night told us about you. Boss said if we came across you again, you were a bonus."

Panic raced through her. She didn't want to know what the 'Boss' wanted her for, but the more she struggled, the more she realized his strength and weight had her chest firmly locked against the ground.

"Jax! I'm pinned!"

Ponytail Guy called out to his companion, "Dev! Wake up!"

"Scorpion or horse." Jax answered and she knew it must have been a relayed message from Patrick. *"Where are you?"*

Taking a couple deep breaths, Violet settled her pulse before throwing her leg upward. It wasn't a strong attack, or really that great of one at all, but it was enough to be a distraction. Her heel hit him... somewhere... and he flinched, looking over his shoulder. His lack of attention cost him some grip strength and Violet rolled away from him, knocking him off balance.

He landed with a grunt against her stomach. She threw her arm up then drove her elbow down into his face. Blood spewed from his nose, his eyes watered, and his hands grasped his face.

"Violet!" Jax's worried voice called for her while she rolled away from Ponytail Guy and got back to her feet.

"Head home. You'll find me."

She semi-dodged a handful of attacks from Ponytail Guy's bloody fists, but he was pumped on rage and she was wearing out. Before long, his fist sank into her stomach, making her double over. She tried to catch her breath, but no air filled her lungs.

He walked around her, toying with her, while she struggled for air. Clutching at her stomach and chest, she willed them to work again.

The pressure on her lungs released and she gasped.

"I'll give it to you. You're a pretty decent fighter for not having a wolf to boost you."

"I had..." She sucked in a strangled breath, "a good teacher."

"Good," he came closer to her again, "That will come in handy after the Boss turns you."

Fear hit her like an ice bath. She threw a punch, but he swatted her arm aside like it was an annoying bug and shoved her away. He leaned back on his further leg and Violet saw the kick before he executed it. She stepped into it, wrapped her arm around his leg absorbing the impact against her side with a grunt, and drove her free elbow into the softest tissue she could find.

A scream shattered the air.

Ponytail Guy pulled away from her, beating his leg with his fist to release what she guessed was a pretty nasty dead leg as she looked in the direction of the scream.

Please, don't be Lexie.

"While you've been focused on me, Dev slipped away to play."

Breathing heavily, Violet turned to find the spot where she'd left Scar Face empty.

"Face it, you've lost. You're wearing out, and I could keep going for hours. As for your friend..." He clicked his tongue. "What was it you said earlier? She's dog chow." His wicked laugh was cut short by a sickening crunch.

Her knees nearly gave out on her when she turned to find Patrick standing over the Blood Moon member, whose head was no longer in the right direction.

"Are you okay?" He asked, eying her up and down as he stepped over Ponytail Guy's body.

Violet placed a hand to her stomach which still ached, "I'm fine, but Lexie..."

She was interrupted when Jax and Aiden came down the dirt road, supporting Mya who had blood running down the side of her face and chest.

"Mya," Violet started toward her, but her wolven friend was in good hands and would heal quickly.

Lexie was a human in a supernatural world. "We need to find Lexie."

Jax's wide, golden eyes turned to her.

"I told her to run, but one of them got away—"

She'd never seen Jax outrun Patrick before, but he bolted past her, leaving Mya in Aiden's arms. Patrick was hot on his heels and Violet tried to keep up, but her body ached all over.

"I've got her scent," Jax announced from up ahead and darted off the path into the trees.

Patrick cursed a minute later and swerved in front of Violet, stopping her in her tracks. "You might want to stay back."

"Yeah, right! My best friend is in trouble."

"Violet!" He grabbed her shoulders and lowered his head so he was in her line of sight. "There is a lot of blood up ahead. Just wait here until we check it out, please."

She opened her mouth to protest, but no words came out.

Slowly, he backed away from her, then turned to follow Jax. The wind shifted and the overwhelming sweet, metallic scent of blood nearly made her lose her dinner.

Tears welled in her eyes and she cast her face toward the moonless sky. Another couple minutes and she wouldn't be able to see anything. Starlight wasn't enough for her weaker eyes to go by.

"Please, Goddess," she prayed out loud, "let her be alive. I'll never endanger her like this again. Just please, let her be alive."

"I found her. She's alive." Jax's voice filled her head and her feet were moving, before he could warn her about what lay ahead.

She dug her fingers into a tree to slow down as the blood smell reached its peak. Sliding to a stop, Violet's mouth dropped open at the massacre that laid before her.

Bodies lay scattered across the ground from both Blood Moon pack and Sentinel Clan. None of the intruders moved or breathed. Thankfully, she saw some of her clan mates still making their way to their feet while others searched the bodies.

"What happened?" Violet quietly asked.

"We intercepted what we can only guess was the main group coming to attack the tourney," announced one of the guards, a female who often worked with Alpha Draven.

"Bunch of cowards," growled a male who was leaning back against a tree trunk, applying pressure to his abdomen. "Going after a group of teenagers like that..."

"It would have crippled both Sentinel and Whisky to lose their next generations," Violet mumbled and they both looked at her like they hadn't thought of that. She looked at the guy and motioned toward his wound, "Do you need help?"

"Nah," He shook his head and groaned. "It wasn't fatal. I'll be able to walk soon."

She nodded, then addressed the female again, "Did you see which way Jax ran?"

The female pointed her thumb behind her, "He asked if there was a human here. I told him we had seen her earlier and told her to keep running."

"Thank you," Violet moved through the sea of bodies and trees in the direction she'd been given.

By the time she'd made it up a small slope, the last of the sunlight disappeared, leaving her blind. She struggled to find good footing and when the ground quickly dropped out from underneath her, she fell. A loud hiss left her when she landed on her hands and knees. Rocks of all different shapes and sizes littered the ground beneath her, digging into her palms, knees, and shins.

"Jax thought you would have a hard time without the moon," Patrick's voice filled the… whatever she was in.

"He was right. I can barely see my hand in front of my face."

His hand curled under her arm to help her stand. Once she was on her feet, she turned to where she thought he was, wincing only a little when she put weight on her left side. "Where are we?"

Even with her jacket blocking his touch, the movement of his fingers sliding down her arm was enough to make goosebumps ripple across her skin. She bit her lip and decided it was a good thing she wasn't wearing a shortsleeved shirt. He intertwined his fingers with hers and gently tugged her forward.

"We're in a small ravine that's been dried up for a while. Lexie fell in here while she was running."

"Is she…"

"She's fine. A little scraped up, scared, and I'm worried she broke her ankle, but otherwise she's okay. The guy you said went after her never caught her. She ran into our warriors first."

Although the ankle sucked, it was better than being caught by one of the Blood Moon Clan. A relieved sigh left her, "Thank goodness."

Patrick pulled her along, acting as her eyes in the dark. "They are a little further down the ravine."

"What about Robin?"

Patrick hesitated and she really wished she could see his face. "I don't know. We haven't seen her."

The combination of worry and relief was an odd feeling, but when Lexie's face came into view, lit by the light from her phone screen—Violet rushed forward, momentarily forgetting about Robin.

"I'm so glad you're okay!" Violet nearly cried as she sank to her knees beside her friend. The pain from the rocks digging into her already bruised flesh didn't even chip the bubbly happiness welling up inside her. "How's your ankle?"

Lexie groaned, "It hurts." The bright light from the phone showed the dirt covering her face and the tear tracks running down her cheeks. "The warriors told me to keep running. They said the area behind them was safe, but I didn't realize I was running straight for a cliff."

"I'm glad it was a small one," Violet offered a small smile as warmth spread through her body. She wished she could take away her friend's pain, but she was alive and smiling. "I'll make sure you're never in a position like this again."

A loud laugh burst from Lexie, "The only way you can ensure that is if we stop being friends, which isn't an option. You're stuck with me. I like you and these crazy wolf-boys too much."

"Wolf-boy?" Jax asked, drawing Violet's attention.

Her eyes bugged when she saw him sitting near Lexie's feet with one of her legs in his lap. His hands worked gently into the muscles of Lexie's lower leg, making her mouth fall open a little. Who was he and what had happened to her brother because the Jax she knew would never have been caught massaging Lexie?

"It's better than calling you a dog," Lexie countered.

"Barely."

Trying not to let their almost friendly banter—and Jax's hands on her friend—disturb her, Violet tucked a hair behind her ear and looked back at Lexie. "What were you thinking egging them on like that? That guy really had it out for you."

"He was rude and annoying. I wasn't going to let him sit by and talk to us the way he was." She winced and Jax muttered an apology. Violet shot him a weirded-out look... Now he was apologizing?

Violet rested a hand on her friend's leg. "These wolven aren't the same as the ones you're used to."

"Do you really think Lexie cares who or what the person is?" Jax chuckled, "She just likes to vex people."

Lexie threw a twig at him.

"They're the ones you told me about, aren't they? You said the Blood Moon pack was really dangerous, I just didn't realize how dangerous they actually were. You wouldn't go into any details."

The glow from Jax's golden eyes drew Violet's attention, but it faded away quickly.

"There's a reason I didn't tell you more about them." Violet explained, gently squeezing Lexie's leg. "You're not supposed to know everything you do as it is, but I didn't want to scare you with something I thought you would never experience."

"Well, I have now and Jax filled me in on a few details."

"Not everything." Jax clarified, filling Violet's mind with his voice. *"I only told her they are more vicious and bloodthirsty. Not that they are all murderers and hold a very real threat to the rest of us."*

Violet nodded her understanding. "I'm really sorry, Lexie. You shouldn't have ever had to go through this."

"She wouldn't have if you hadn't gotten this stupid idea in your head to bring her to a tourney." Jax grumbled out loud.

Lexie leaned forward and smacked his arm, "Be nice. It wasn't her idea. I talked her into it."

"Then *you* shouldn't have such stupid ideas," he growled back at her and she folded her arms over her chest defiantly. "You have no idea the amount of danger you were in."

"Right, `cause my tiny human brain can't comprehend the fact that my life was in danger?"

Despite the situation, Violet found a smile lifting one corner of her mouth. If Lexie was able to muster up that kind of attitude and bicker with Jax after the night she'd had, she would be just fine.

"That's not what I..." Jax grumbled and looked away from her.

He muttered something under his breath that Violet couldn't pick up, but the huff of laughter that came from Patrick told her that he had.

"How's your ankle?" She asked, noticing Jax hadn't stopped his massage.

Lexie blinked, then looked at her foot like she'd forgotten about it. "It actually feels a lot better." A thoughtful look crossed over her face, "And really warm. In any case, it's better than my nerves. When Jax got here, I was a trembling, sobbing mess and couldn't put any weight on my foot. Whatever he's been doing is helping."

"You've never had a massage before?" Jax gave her a sideways glance like she was being ridiculous.

"I've had them before." Lexie snapped, then a wicked grin lit up her face. "Just didn't think you were capable of being so sweet."

Instead of snapping back, the tiniest of half smirks quirked up one side of her twin's lips, and he turned back to her ankle to roll her pantleg down. "I think that's all I can do. We should get you to the doc. She'll be able to determine if it's broken or not."

Without asking, Jax slipped one arm under Lexie's knees and another around her back and lifted her like she weighed nothing.

"I don't need to be carried!" Lexie protested, smacking his back.

"Can you walk?" Jax asked grumpily.

"Probably not," she replied, sounding just as unhappy.

"Then I'm carrying you. It's faster this way, anyway."

"If you think I'm going to—"

Jax jolted her in his arms, making her squeal and throw her arms around his neck. A dark, satisfied laugh rolled out of him. "I suggest you be nice or I'll throw you over my shoulder."

"What the heck is happening?" Violet muttered to herself as the two of them started toward the doctor's office.

Patrick came up beside her and with the fading light of Lexie's phone, she barely caught him rubbing the back of his neck. "He doesn't actually hate her, you know. I think he enjoys fighting with her."

She nodded, "I think so, too, but that was the nicest I've ever seen him with her."

With a shrug, Patrick started forward, "Let's catch up so we don't lose the light."

"Oh!" Violet pulled her phone from her pocket and pushed the button to turn the screen on. "Oh no. Mom's not going to be happy."

Spiderweb cracks lit up the screen, making the scrunched-up face Lexie had put as her background all warped.

"I think she'll be happy you're alive. A phone can be replaced."

He had a point, and it's not like she'd broken another laptop.

Chapter 15

Violet

***THANKFULLY, THE LIGHT FROM HER PHONE STILL WORKED** as a decent flashlight.* Lexie and Jax snapped at each other back and forth the entire walk to the doc's, but at least the commentary was entertaining.

The medical office was completely overrun after the attack from Blood Moon. None of them were bleeding excessively, or had fatal injuries, so they were told to sit and wait, which gave plenty of wolven an eyeful of Jax holding Lexie in his lap and her fighting to get away from him.

"Jax, do you really have to hold her like that?" Violet hissed at him nearly half an hour later.

"The other chairs are needed for our wounded clan mates," Jax grumbled when Lexie tried once again to get off of him. "Stop it. You're going to hurt yourself more… or me."

"Then let me go," Lexie glared at him.

He gave her a toothy grin and shook his head. "You're stuck with me until we get into one of those medical rooms. Next time, don't get hurt inside clan boundaries. You're under my care and protection until you leave. This is just part of those duties, so deal with it."

"Ugh!" Lexie threw her arms in the air. "Can I please have my leg looked at, so I can go home?" She yelled, drawing a lot of attention, but no one came to her rescue.

Sometime later, Violet was seriously starting to worry about the two of them.

Lexie had stopped struggling and was leaning back against Jax's chest, looking like she was about to fall asleep. Jax on the other hand, feigned relaxation by resting his head back against the wall with his eyes shut. The grip he held on Lexie's jeans and shirt told another story. His knuckles were as white as they had been when they'd arrived... other than the blood splattered across his hands.

Not wanting to start another argument, Violet kept her thoughts to herself.

Patrick pushed through the doors and sank to the floor in front of her chair. He leaned heavily against her chair before resting his head against her knee.

Surprised, Violet jumped and looked at Jax, but his eyes were closed, and he didn't seem to notice. She slowly leaned forward and whispered, "You okay?"

Patrick had disappeared for a while, not explaining where he was going, and Jax would only say he would be back.

"Yeah, just tired," Patrick whispered back. "We've been here a while."

"*We* have. You left." Violet poked his shoulder. When he didn't respond, she poked him again. "Where did you go?"

"Outside."

"Thanks." Violet snorted. "Do you know what time it is?"

Patrick pulled out his old phone, which he very rarely used, and her mouth dropped open. She was sure he had fought more than her, but his phone was magically unscathed? That was unfair.

"It's almost midnight." He yawned as he put his phone back in his pocket.

"Have you heard anything from Aiden and Mya? It's his birthday..." she blew out a quick breath, "what an awful way to bring in your eighteenth birthday."

"Yeah, this would suck," Lexie chimed in, sounding half asleep.

"They got here before we did," Patrick replied. "Mya was bleeding pretty heavily so they set her up in one of the recovery tents out back. As far as I know, Aiden hasn't left her side. He seemed fine, more or less, when we came to find you."

Violet looked around. The room had quieted down a lot. All the vitally wounded had been cared for. Now it was just a waiting game to see who'd come in first. Since they were one of the last ones to arrive, it was going to be a few more minutes.

"I'm going to go check on her." She lightly tapped Patrick's shoulder and he lifted his head off her knee. "I feel bad for running off on them like that."

"She'll understand," he assured her as she stood and stretched her arms above her head. "She's friends with Lexie, too."

Jax cleared his throat, "It could have been a lot worse. The warriors knew about the attack before I mentioned anything to them. They had already taken out quite a few. I was told they hit the west wall pretty hard. I'm betting that's why they were able to make it through the south side and into the tourney."

"Or they came in with the Whisky Clan," Patrick offered, lifting himself into Violet's now vacant seat. "No one would have thought to check for that."

"Do you think they'll cancel tourney?" Jax asked, grunting on the last syllable when Lexie elbowed him in the stomach.

"If you want me to stay here peacefully, stop talking."

Violet grinned and shook her head. "I'll be right back."

She'd taken two steps out the door when Patrick called her name.

"You shouldn't wander off alone tonight. There could be some of them still in the gates." He buried his hands in his jean pockets and tossed his head toward the side of the medical building. "The tents are set up in the back. I'll show you where Aiden and Mya are."

He walked past her and she spun around, took a few hurried steps to catch up, and looked at him quizzically. "How do you know what tent they're in?"

"I left earlier to help assemble more tents. They had run out." He explained as they rounded the corner. "There were a few minutes when I was waiting for more to arrive, so I dropped in on them to see how things were going. Mya was healing really well, and they were watching a movie on Aiden's phone."

Violet nodded, "she said they were going to finish the night with a movie. I'm glad they still did that even with everything happening."

They came around the back of the house and Violet gasped. Rows upon rows of tents filled the field behind the medical building. Lanterns had been placed periodically so people wouldn't be left in the moonless dark, but the dim light couldn't hide the blood splattering the ground, leading to many of the first tents.

"How many were hurt?" Violet whispered.

"Too many."

"Do we know what they were after?"

Patrick clenched his jaw as he shook his head. "We don't have a definite answer."

Silence lingered between them as they made their way through the makeshift medical area.

Patrick pointed to one of the last tents in the third row. "That's Mya's." He snagged her arm when she hurried forward. "I don't think you want to go in there. I promise she is fine. I can tell Aiden you wanted to check in."

"What? No." Violet pulled her arm out of his hold. "She's one of my best friends. I'm going in there."

He didn't stop her again, but he also didn't follow.

Snorting, Violet ducked into the tent.

The movie's loud music filled the small space, but the phone playing it had been forgotten about in the grass.

Violet gasped and threw her hands over her eyes, "I'm so sorry!"

Mya seemed just fine as she had practically been sucking Aiden's face off. It would take some time to burn the image of his hands trailing up her friend's side.

A trill of giggles rose over the movie noise.

Mortified that she'd walked in on her friend making out, Violet turned her cherry red face back toward the tent opening and hurried to leave. "Congratulations!"

"Hey, wait!" Aiden called through his laughter.

Ever so slowly, Violet turned and peaked through her slitted fingers. Thankfully everyone still had clothes on and hands were being kept to themselves.

Aiden bent down to retrieve his phone and a second later the movie stopped. He pointed at Violet, "Did you know?"

Lowering her hand, she looked sheepishly at her friends, "Sorry, I should have asked before barging in here."

"Know what?" Violet squeaked.

Mya laughed, "Violet, he knows! We're together! Do you think I would have let his tongue practically down my throat if we weren't?"

Violet's face scrunched in disgust.

"Geeze, was it really that bad?" Aiden asked, pinching Mya's leg.

The happy girl squealed and smacked his hand. "We'll talk about that later."

"I'm really glad this all worked out," Violet smiled. "But I think I'm gonna go."

"No, wait." Aiden stopped her again. "Did you know when we were at the bridges?"

Nodding, Violet shifted her weight a little uneasily, "Mya told me a while ago that she suspected you were mates."

"That's why you kept bringing her up," he nodded, piecing the puzzle together. "Why didn't you tell me?"

Mya slapped his arm lightly, making him laugh before he practically pounced on her to kiss her lightly on the forehead. She playfully shoved him off before returning her attention to Violet. Her green eyes were nearly luminous, catching Violet off guard.

There it was.

The pure love and joy that could only be found in a moon-blessed mate. Aiden's eyes matched his new mate's and Violet wondered how long that little glow would last. She'd never been close enough to someone who'd recently found their mate to notice.

"How's Lexie?" Mya asked as she weaved her fingers through Aiden's.

Violet shrugged. "She's alive and pretty much unscathed. Blood Moon never caught up with her, but she took a pretty nasty fall and may have broken her ankle."

"I'm glad they didn't catch her. She must have been running pretty fast."

Biting her lip, Violet shrugged again. "I got a cheap shot in and was able to knock one of the two guys out. She had a pretty decent head start. I'm betting he ran into our warriors."

"Good," Aiden grumbled.

The light in Mya's eyes faded a little. "I'm sorry I wasn't there to help."

"Don't apologize! You had someone else in mind," Violet gestured to Aiden.

"She saved me," Aiden explained, offering Violet a small smile. "She jumped on one of the guys' backs who had me pinned."

Mya winced, "That didn't end too well for me, but it worked out."

Nodding, Violet agreed with her friend. "I haven't heard anything about Robin, have you?"

"She's already back home—probably asleep," Mya explained as Aiden began trailing kisses down the side of her face that hadn't been hurt and lower to her neck.

Violet looked away uncomfortably.

A happy giggle filled the tent and Mya told him to knock it off. "I'm trying to talk."

"Talking is overrated," Aiden grinned at her, but she pushed his face away. With a disappointed groan he turned back to Violet and finished explaining, "From what I saw, she took out a couple of them on her way out. For someone who doesn't want to be a warrior, and would rather save her own skin, she's a pretty decent fighter." He looked back at Mya. "Happy now?"

Her brunette coils bounced when she nodded at him, grinning from ear to ear.

"Cool, I'm gonna go now." Violet fumbled behind her for the tent flap. "Congrats again. Mya, I'll talk to you whenever you surface for air."

Her friend's laughter followed her out of the tent, along with a delighted squeal that she did not want to know the cause of.

Patrick's smirk was equal parts adorable and infuriating. He lifted a brow as his mouth opened, but Violet lifted onto her toes and clamped her hand over his lips.

"Don't even think about it."

Amusement set his hazel eyes afire and his shoulders shook with silent laughter. His smirk spread into a smile beneath her hand, sending goosebumps rippling down her arm. A shuddery breath filled her lungs and she quickly stepped away, heading back the way they'd come without another word.

"How did you know?" Violet asked when he caught up to her a couple seconds later. "Could you hear them?"

A slightly pink tint covered Patrick's cheeks, "You couldn't?"

She groaned. "Just another thing I can't do. I can't even hear through tent walls."

"Did you try?" Patrick asked, tugging on her jacket sleeve to make her stop.

Disappointment laced the embarrassment that washed over her and she stared at the grass. "No." Her shoulders slumped. "I didn't think to do that. I was more focused on checking on her than keeping my senses at full capacity. It's hard for me to do that without actively thinking about it. I think..." an exhale deflated her chest. "I think that's why Lexie and I were able to be ambushed so easily. Even knowing we were being hunted, I still didn't try to amplify my senses. I didn't even think about it."

The longer it took for him to answer, the higher her unease grew. She was nearly crawling out of her skin when he sighed and shook his head.

"It's not your fault, Vi," he whispered.

"But it is. I failed her." She looked up at him as tears began to gather in her eyes. "I snuck her into the game."

He shook his head, "That wasn't your idea."

"I went along with it." She tipped her head back and stared at the moonless sky. "Jax was right—"

"Violet—"

"What if she had died?" She whispered.

The silence that followed was suffocating.

One stupid decision. That was all it would take for her very mortal, human friend to die. It was enough to make anyone second guess themselves—to wonder if they were actually worthy of friendship.

Her tears pushed past the threshold, spilling out the corners of her eyes, and dribbling down into her hairline.

Patrick's warm, long fingers touched her jaw on both sides of her head, then spread into her hair. He pivoted her head forward, ever so gently, and brushed away her tears with his thumbs before pulling her against his chest.

"She's alive," he spoke into her hair. "She's alive because you were able to hold two of them off. I know the doc says you're not as strong as the other wolven here, and some people believe her, but I have seen a strength in you that rivals so many here. It's hidden, but that strength comes out when it's needed most."

The warm, soft fabric of his shirt grew moist with her tears.

When she didn't respond, Patrick tightened his hold. "You've been through a lot lately, and somehow you're not totally wrecked."

Violet huffed a laugh and Patrick gently eased her away from his chest in order to look at her. "Oh, I am. I'm just trying to let it out in pieces. I don't have the luxury of falling apart."

He shook his head, making the curly, longer hair pieces on top of his head sway a little. "You're allowed to fall apart sometimes, Vi. Everyone does, that doesn't make you weaker than anyone else."

A shallow sigh left her, "I'm only as strong as I am because I have a really awesome teacher."

Patrick's face brightened with a half smirk that made her heart ache. "Interesting. My student is pretty great, too."

Flames licked her cheeks... and face... and ears. She ducked her chin and fiddled with the end of her long braid.

"By the way, Lexie saw the doc while you were with Mya." Patrick told her, breaking the moment. "She doesn't think it's broken—I don't know how because it sure looked broken. Jax and Lexie are heading to Alpha House where Alpha Draven is waiting to talk to all of us."

"Why didn't you tell me sooner?"

"I thought it would be better for you to let your emotions out here than in front of your dad. Jax agreed."

He led the way to Alpha House without another word, but Violet eyed him strangely every few steps. Everyone addressed her father as Alpha. It was near impossible to do otherwise. His position demanded respect and a certain amount of submission. This wasn't the first time she'd seen Patrick be able to disobey a command from his superiors, but each time it happened she grew more and more curious how he was able to.

Without a wolf, she wasn't surprised the alpha aura didn't have an effect on her… but Patrick definitely had a wolf.

"Can I ask you a question?" she asked quietly.

He gave her a side-glance, but didn't offer an answer either way.

"Are you okay?"

"What do you mean?"

"Well… you killed that Blood Moon pack member and—"

Patrick stopped mid-stride. His jaw was tense as he turned toward her, "It didn't bother me if that's what you're asking."

"It didn't bother you at all?" Violet blinked at him, not believing he wasn't affected. "You snapped his neck with your own two hands. Like it wasn't anything more than a branch."

An uneasy sigh left him. He looked at the ground, shoved his hands in his pockets, and shook his head. "I've killed before, Violet."

She couldn't have heard him right. "What?"

"You heard me." He lifted his gaze to look at her through his lashes. "If you're asking me whether or not it bothered me, if I feel bad about it, the answer is no. I was protecting you, just like I was protecting someone the last time. I would do it again if it meant protecting those I love."

Her lungs seized. He loved her? He didn't feel bad about killing someone?

The lack of response to his confession made his shoulders tense. He looked toward Alpha House, but surprised her by continuing, "What you need to understand is that there is a difference between being bothered by something and being affected by it. Just because it doesn't bother me that I took a life tonight because I was protecting you and the rest of the clan doesn't mean that I won't remember feeling his bones break beneath my hands for years to come…" He closed his eyes and let out a tense breath. "Or the sound that will haunt my dreams. Just like his lifeless body. Or wondering if this was a life he chose or if it happened to him."

Violet's brows pinched together, "Happened to him?"

After another sigh, Patrick shook his head. "It doesn't matter. What's done is done. I did what I needed, and was expected, to do. Just like the warriors. That doesn't mean we aren't affected by it."

Nodding, Violet stepped toward him and wrapped her arm through his. It took a minute, but his shoulders gradually relaxed before he looked at her again.

"Thank you for protecting me," she whispered.

His hardened expression softened and the tiniest hint of a smile lifted the corner of his mouth. "Always."

*****

The house was eerily quiet when they entered.

Part of Violet wanted to turn around and make a break for it. Especially when her mom didn't rush both her and Patrick the moment they walked in.

"Where's Mom?" She asked, standing in the doorway while Patrick held the door open.

"Sit." The pressure in the room grew, announcing Alpha Draven's aura.

Violet swallowed the lump that had swelled in her throat and repeated herself with a bit more force, "Where's Mom?"

Lexie squirmed against the arm of the sofa as Alpha Draven's heavily slouched form slowly straightened in his seat. His molten gold eyes swept over Jax, who lowered his gaze, before narrowing at Violet.

"**Sit.**"

The pressure to comply clamped down on her chest, making it hard to breathe. Hard... not impossible.

Following her mother's instructions, Violet obeyed Alpha Draven like any other wolven would. Like Patrick was doing right now.

They sat.

No one said anything for a long minute.

Looking around, Violet paused on the sight of Lexie's foot propped up on a pillow resting in Jax's lap. Her best friend offered her a small smile that Violet was positive was meant to be reassuring, but her heart thundered in her chest.

Risking it a third time, Violet gently asked, "Where's mom?"

The amount of annoyance that poisoned Alpha Draven's sigh was practically tangible. "Luna is resting after an instantaneous headache hit her a couple hours ago." He repositioned himself so he was leaning heavily against the arm of the chair, slightly toward them. "She waited as long as she could, made sure to hear how you all were fairing, before going to bed. I promised to tell you all how pleased she is none of you were gravely injured or killed."

Worry gnawed at Violet's insides. More headaches? "Is she okay?"

Alpha Draven's face pinched with anger, "*You* don't need to worry about her right now." He stood up, drawing all their attention—including Lexie—and clasped his hands behind his back.

Jax and Patrick both dipped their chins ever-so-slightly as their alpha's voice boomed and his aura pressed down on them.

"Violet Draven, you have been given the privilege of keeping a human friend with the knowledge that certain parts of our world were to remain secret. That rule has been broken countless times, but none have been as severe as tonight."

Violet closed her eyes and drew in a long steadying breath.

"What is our most important rule?"

She opened her eyes to find Alpha Draven—her father—glaring down at her. "Clan above all else."

"Second?"

"Remain hidden from the human world."

"Third?"

Violet's amethyst gaze found her best friend's worried blue eyes and held them as she softly repeated the last 'golden rule' she'd been taught from birth. "Protect humans, at all costs."

Blue eyes rounded to the size of saucers. Lexie had heard the rules before, but always played them off as non-consequential. Violet had never expressed just how important those wolven laws were.

Protecting humans was not their job, but if they ran across a situation where they could help—they were required to. This also meant never putting a human's life in danger.

"Violet Draven, you have broken one of the clan's most important laws. You endangered the life of a human."

Violet closed her eyes, worried what her punishment would be.

"By doing so, you risked your best friend's life and exposing the clan—"

"It wasn't her fault—"

Violet's eyes snapped open at the sound of Lexie's voice, strong and angered toward Alpha Draven.

"Silence!" The alpha's booming voice filled the room, making it seem small, and his eyes zeroed in on Lexie who shrunk against the arm of the sofa.

She opened her mouth to defend her friend, but another voice filled the silence.

"Do not speak to her like that," Jax growled, drawing Alpha Draven's attention. "I know you're angry, you have a right to be, but Lexie is not a member of this clan. She doesn't understand your aura the way we do, and you are frightening her."

Violet stared at her twin, jaw going slack as he spoke those last words through clenched teeth. Jax had never stood up for her that way, and the alpha's mistreatment was a near daily occurrence.

The tension in the air eased when Alpha Draven let out a large sigh. He shook his head and turned away to begin pacing, "You're right, Jax."

Violet's jaw nearly hit the ground. If she had been the one to speak up, he may have actually hit her with how emotional the alpha was being. It would be a first, but he'd threatened as much in the past.

"Let it go, Violet." Jax's remarkably calm voice came into her mind when she opened her mouth to give their father a piece of her mind against her better judgment.

"But I..."

"It's done. Don't start him up again." He interrupted her. *"Let it go."*

Anger simmered just beneath her skin, but she nodded curtly to him. This wasn't the time to get in an epic throw-down with her jerk of a father.

"In the light of today's events, Luna and I have come to an agreement," the alpha spoke from the other side of the room with his shoulder's turned ever so slightly toward them—always keeping those around him in his sight. "It's in Lexie's best interest to stay away from the compound."

"What?" Violet jumped off the couch only to have Patrick pull her back down onto the cushions before Alpha Draven turned his full attention on her. His glare told her enough—he'd seen her. She didn't know if she wanted to thank Patrick or punch him. "I've barely seen her over the last few weeks as it is!"

"That's irrelevant."

"Mom agreed to Lexie helping me set up for Patrick's party."

Patrick groaned.

"It's in two days!" Violet continued, "She was invited by Mom!"

Alpha Draven's shoulders tensed. "Plans change."

"What?" Violet shrieked, rose to her feet against Patrick's pull on her shirt, and ignored Jax's voice of warning in her mind when the alpha stalked toward her. "You're going to dismiss your mate's plans and go against her word?"

She never saw the attack coming.

Her head snapped to the side from the impact of Alpha Draven's backhand across her cheek. Her knee hit the floor with a loud thud.

"Dad!" Jax's protest rose above the ringing in her ears.

A low growl rumbled through the room, but no one addressed it.

Closing her eyes, Violet shifted her jaw around, and let her tears recede. She clenched her hands at her sides so she wouldn't touch her stinging face as she made her way to her feet and lifted her chin to glare at the man who'd only ever been her father by blood.

He pointed a large finger in her face. "*Never* speak to me about mate matters ever again. You have no idea what I'd do for her. Your human is not part of that deal." The hatred in his eyes as he drew closer called out her own ill feelings as if she had been challenged. "Do I make myself clear?"

She met his gaze with a steady glare of her own, ignoring the swell of power pressing down on her. He was trying to hurt her. To intimidate her. He'd done worse. Getting hit stung and she was sure to cry about it later... but she'd been on the receiving end of his verbal abuse all her life. Her face would heal long before some of those wounds would.

"Do I make myself clear?" He growled at her, his golden eyes swirling with rage.

"Transparently," Violet snarked.

Drawing to his full height, Alpha Draven flashed his teeth and snarled a warning, "Stand down."

Her blood boiled. "You challenged me."

"You nearly killed your best friend tonight. You have no ground to stand on."

Ice water flushed the heat from her body. A sadistic smirk tugged the corner of the alpha's mouth. He knew he'd buckled her defenses.

"Violet, it's okay," Lexie's small voice rose above the deafening pressure in Violet's head. "After tonight... I could use some time away."

She tore her wounded gaze away from the man in front of her and looked at her friend with worried brows. "Okay," she whispered her agreement.

Violet would do anything for those she loved—even let them go when they needed it.

"Besides," Lexie smiled softly. "You have a phone now, so we can keep in touch."

Violet groaned and pulled her phone from her pocket, showing the shattered screen to the room. "It took a hit during the fight."

"I'll get you a new one from storage tomorrow morning," Jax answered before Alpha Draven could object.

"Fine," the alpha grumbled. "Jax, take Lexie home. Violet—"

"Blood Moon could still be in our territory," Jax interrupted without apologizing. "It would be safer to take her in the morning."

An annoyed sigh left the alpha, but he nodded. "First thing in the morning. Do I make myself clear?"

A voice more animal than man interrupted Jax's answer, "Alpha!"

They all turned and both Patrick and Jax were instantly on their feet.

Beta Paul, with his mousy brown hair tousled about, and Justin—the guy who had pranced around in Patrick's truck bed—both stumbled through the door tying off the sweatpants they'd hastily put on.

"We have trouble." Paul crossed his arms over his bare chest. "I thought you'd want to hear this in person."

"What kind of trouble?" Alpha Draven asked, standing to his full height as he stared down his beta and the friendly wolven.

"Go ahead, Justin," Beta Paul nodded to the younger male.

Justin stepped forward and drew in a deep breath, "One of the Blood Moon members we captured is lycan."

Her father was always tense, but for a second, Violet thought he may have turned to stone. "Where?"

"He's at Lockup under heavy sedation," Justin answered, then looked at Beta Paul who gave him an approving nod.

Lycan were royalty to the wolven. To have one be part of Blood Moon...

"Upstairs. All of you. Now." Alpha Draven ordered without turning back to look at them.

Jax quickly lifted Lexie into his arms and carried her up the stairs, leaving Violet and Patrick to follow behind them.

"Don't get used to this," Jax grumbled, but the animosity his words usually held was lacking. "The next time I see you, I will not be carrying you."

"Thank goodness." Lexie lifted the hand behind his back and flicked his ear, making him growl softly at her. "You're worse than a trotting horse."

"You're barely moving."

"Because I'm clinging to you like a scared koala!" Lexie hissed at him. "I don't want you tossing me around or dropping me."

"I'd never drop you, Lexie," he replied softly before shifting her a little to one side in order to open Violet's door. He nudged it wider with the toe of his shoe then turned to crab-walk sideways into the room.

A warm hand wrapped gently around Violet's arm and she turned to find Patrick heavy gaze fixed on her. Two stairs up and she was looking straight into his gorgeous, golden-flecked hazel eyes.

"Patrick," she breathed his name, surprised at his close proximity.

Slowly, his free hand rose toward her face.

She glanced at his hand, then back to his eyes—exhaling to relax the tension in her shoulders. Her eyes snapped shut at his touch.

Just a feather-light caress, but it was enough to make her flinch.

He whispered an apology as the pad of his thumb brushed over her tender cheekbone. "I wish...

Violet's eyes found his again, brows drawing together in concern.

"I'm sorry I didn't stop him."

She wet her lips then bit down on her lower one. If she wasn't careful, those tears she needed to shed later weren't going to wait.

There were no words. So, she tenderly circled her arms around Patrick's neck. He readily enveloped her, cradling her against him. He released a heavy breath and nuzzled his face into her neck.

"Is everything alright out there?" Jax called to them after a while and they released one another.

Patrick's hand slipped down her arm and grasped her fingers.

"I hate to ruin this, but I need to ask something." Violet offered him an apologetic look.

"Anything."

Drawing in a deep breath, Violet asked, "Did you know lycans could be turned into members of Blood Moon?"

His gaze searched hers before he nodded ever so slightly.

A shaky breath made her chest fall, "Do they look different than wolven?"

He leaned close and whispered in an attempt to keep their conversation private, "How would I know that?"

"Do you?"

Patrick stared at her, their noses only inches apart. "Why?"

"Because the guy I knocked out had fangs and the tips of his ears were kind of pointed." She wet her lips before adding, "I've only ever seen a lycan once in my life, when I was really little, but I don't remember if that was a trait they had."

Surprise pulled Patrick back, "You… you've seen a lycan?"

Violet nodded. "A handsome man came here one time. There was a ton more security and everything was super formal. Alpha Draven was really upset when the man noticed me, but I don't know why."

Patrick's face twisted in thought. "The lycans I've come in contact with have all had fangs and the tips of their ears were more pointed. I think it's a good bet the guy you knocked out was lycan. If that's the case, you put a lot more power behind your attack than I thought."

Her head dipped to the side. "Why?"

"Lycan are…" Patrick hesitated, then shrugged. "Better… than wolven in practically every way. Faster, stronger, better senses, they transform instantaneously instead of the bone breaking process wolven go through, and they don't have a wolf spirit inside of them because they *are* the wolf.

Some even have unique abilities. I ran across one once who could produce fire from the palm of his hand, I learned later that he could also breath fire..."

"Like a freaking *dragon*?" Violet whisper-hissed at him. "How do you know all that?"

"My clan taught me a thing or two." He rubbed the back of his neck looking uncomfortable. "I learned the fire breathing the hard way. It's best not to tick off lycan."

Violet blinked at him. It was incredibly rare for him to mention his old clan or his past.

"Vi, to be able to render a lycan unconscious proves what I was saying earlier."

Snapped out of her musing, Violet shook her head. "No." She didn't want to give into that hope. "We don't know for certain he was the lycan. It could have been someone else."

"Violet—"

"No, Patrick." She shook her head again. "I can't believe there is more in me. I can't. I can't face that kind of disappointment again."

Hazel eyes clashed with purple. Understanding passed over his face and his already open expression turned soft.

"Hello?" Jax's voice rang out again, sounding slightly annoyed.

With one last shared look, they made their way into the room and Violet almost walked right back out.

Jax had set Lexie on the bed in the corner, which was her favorite spot, and was fluffing a second pillow to place under her foot. "What was going on out there?"

Violet glared at him. "Nothing."

"She had some questions about tonight and didn't want to bother you with them," Patrick answered smoothly and leaned his shoulder against the door frame.

"I have a question, too," Lexie held up her hand, making Violet grin. "What's a lycan? I thought you guys were lycans, but just went by a different name."

The situation could have been handled with an easy answer. It may have left Lexie a little disappointed, but she would have understood—

especially after tonight.

Apparently, Jax didn't see it that way.

He planted his fists on the bed beside Lexie's hip and leaned forward, invading her space... but Lexie just blinked at him. "There are a lot of things you should *not* know and there are some things you will *never* know for your own good. This is one of those things."

Intrigue sparked across Lexie's face.

Violet rolled her eyes. "Oh brother. Way to make it sound forbidden."

"It *is* forbidden." Jax snapped, turning his head toward her.

"Sure, but now she'll never let it go."

Lexie nodded. "It's true."

"Just tell her we are their descendants and leave it at that."

Jax straightened to his full height, "Violet!"

"It's better than leaving her curious," Patrick added, defending Violet's case. "Because wolven are descendants, their abilities are not nearly as refined as a lycan."

"Patrick!" Jax glared at his best friend who simply shrugged. "Well, now that you know all of that—" he turned back toward Lexie. "You need to stay away from anything lycan or Blood Moon related. Do you understand?"

Liquid gold from Jax's wolven eyes reflected off Lexie's pale blue eyes and she gave him a spastic little nod.

"And if you ever put yourself in danger again like you did tonight, I will make your life here unbearable."

The threat turned Lexie's slightly widened eyes into narrow slits. She shoved against Jax's shoulders, but he didn't budge. "Life is already unbearable enough with you around, but I'm still here because I love Violet. Now get out of my face, you stink like dog."

Violet moved closer and pulled against Jax's shoulder. "Back off, she's been through enough."

Reluctantly, her brother returned to his full height and stepped away from the human girl. "In case you weren't told already, there aren't any broken bones. Without an X-ray it's not a one-hundred-percent guarantee, but the doc is pretty certain."

"Why?" Violet asked, following him toward the door. She glanced at Patrick. "Weren't you positive it was broken? How did it just miraculously get better?"

Patrick raised his shoulders and shook his head.

Jax stopped in the doorway. "I don't know. Patrick and I were positive it was broken, but the doc was able to move it without pain and put pressure on it. The only time it hurts is when Lexie moves it herself, which led the doc to believe it was muscle, not bone."

Confusion pulled Violet's brows together as she turned to look at her friend. "Did it hurt when Jax was massaging you?"

Lexie shook her head. "He was up high enough that if there was any discomfort it was only a little."

"Something doesn't add up."

Patrick sighed, "Let it go, Vi. It's late. We're all tired. Our friends are still alive and Lexie isn't broken." He reached around Jax and squeezed Violet's shoulder. "Take the win."

Annoyance pinched Jax's face and he smacked his friend's hand off her shoulder. "Let's go."

"Goodnight boys!" Lexie called sweetly as they left the room, leaving the two girls alone.

Violet made sure the door was shut before joining her friend on the bed. "I can't apologize enough about toni—"

"Don't!" Lexie slapped Violet's leg. "I had fun. It was terrifying and I hope it never happens again, but before that, and even after, I had fun. Besides, I have so much material that I can use to torment Jax for years to come!"

Violet snorted. "You're horrible."

"No, he's horrible."

She nodded her head side to side. "True, but you don't help."

Lexie grew still and quiet as her gaze traveled over Violet's face. "Is your face okay?"

For the first time, Violet tenderly touched the cheek her father had struck and winced a little. "It's sore. Why? Does it look bad?"

Pinching her lips together, Lexie wrapped an arm around Violet's shoulders and squeezed. "You've looked worse."

A hearty laugh escaped Violet, completely unexpected and very needed.

"So, you're really not going to tell me anything else about these lycans?"

Lexie asked while shifting her position a little.

Violet shook her head. "For once, I agree with Jax. The kings and queens aren't to be trifled with and the less you know, the better."

"Oh, so that's what you meant earlier by kings and queens. You were talking about the lycan." Lexie tapped her chin thoughtfully. "That makes more sense now."

A small chuckle shook Violet's shoulders. "Alright that's enough. We have a lot to discuss since you won't be here to help me with the party."

Excitement burst through Lexie, making her bounce happily on the bed. "Let's do this."

She may not have been able to attend, but that didn't stop Lexie from having all sorts of opinions. Violet didn't mind. She wasn't sure when the next time she would get to see her friend, so she soaked up every minute until Lexie couldn't keep her eyes open any longer… then she stared at the ceiling, willing the horrors of blood-colored eyes and the sound of bones snapping to leave her mind so she could sleep.

Chapter 16

Violet

***PUTTING PATRICK'S PARTY TOGETHER** without Lexie's help made the days go by a lot slower.* Thankfully, Jax had kept his word and found her a new phone right away. It was nice to be able to communicate in some way, at least. The human girl had an eye for decorating, and although Violet had been helping her mom with clan parties for years, Lexie's ideas were fantastic.

Together, the two girls had decided to do a light faux-ceiling, exchange the wintery curtains for ones that matched the golden flecks in Patrick's hazel eyes, and have multiple tables with food, but only tall tables to stand at instead of proper seating. Without the excuse to sit and brood, they were hoping Patrick might get into the music and let loose a little.

That was going to be extremely difficult, seeing as the party had been going for a while now, and the guest of honor was nowhere to be seen. It appeared Jax had helped Patrick ditch his own party.

"Not cool, guys." Violet mumbled to herself as she leaned back against the wall and watched the throng of teens and newly adult wolves dance the night away. The pulse of the beat vibrated through the floor and walls, amping everyone up.

Too bad she didn't have anyone to party with.

Zander had caught her eye briefly earlier, but she was happy to see he had made himself scarce. Whatever Jax and Alpha Draven had said to him, must have left a lasting impression if he wouldn't even approach her when her brother was obviously not here.

She grumbled. Where were they?

She tucked her hair behind her ear, then pulled her phone from her pocket. Why had she even bothered to leave her hair down tonight? It was just in the way. Maybe she'd cut it. She always wore it up anyway.

Lexie would kill her if she chopped her hair off.

With that in mind, Violet quickly typed a message to her human friend, knowing it would get a rise out of her. - "I'm thinking about cutting my hair. Also, should I use the green candles or the traditional off-white?"

Lexie's response was immediate. - "NOT THE YELLOWY PUKE GREEN!"

Laughter bubbled out of Violet at her friend's over-reaction.

Lexie - "Hasn't the party already started? Why are you still decorating?"

Violet smirked and quickly typed her response. - "I'm not." She added the emoji with the winky face and the tongue sticking out. - "Nothing about my hair?"

According to Lexie, using emoji's was vital when texting, so people understood the emotion you were using, but you shouldn't use too many. Violet hadn't realized there were so many rules to texting.

Lexie - "Punk." She had also added a face with the tongue sticking out. - "And I know you wouldn't actually cut your hair."

Violet's amusement was short-lived. She looked up at the crowd, envious of their free movement, happiness, and especially of those who were obviously couples.

Feeling lonely, she sent another message - "I wish you were here."

Lexie - "Oh yes, because I would really be cutting the rug with my crutches."

A snort of laughter left Violet. The human doctors had taken X-rays and determined her ankle wasn't broken, but a sprain wasn't much better, and she was going to be on crutches for a while.

Her phone pinged again.

Lexie - "Now get off your phone and go party!"

After an hour of waiting, and having more guys approach her than she was comfortable with, all Violet wanted to do was make sure Patrick was okay and go to bed.

Mya waved at her from the crowd then tugged on Aiden's hand, who readily followed right behind her with a goofy grin on his face. Her friend's mane of coiled chocolate bounced as they made their way to her little table. "Hey babe, why aren't you dancing?"

The new couple's obvious happiness was infectious and Violet soon found herself smiling at them. "I'm waiting for Jax and Patrick. Besides, my dance partner is stuck at home with a bum ankle."

"I thought the doc said it wasn't broken?"

Violet blinked at her, "Oh, that's right. You've barely come up for air since that night."

Pink flooded across Mya's cheeks and Aiden had the good sense to look a little bashful as well. "Sorry about that. I guess I haven't been the greatest friend over the last few days, huh?"

Shrugging, Violet waved her hand nonchalantly, "Don't worry about it. Finding your mate right off the bat is pretty incredible. You guys are the lucky ones!"

Mya's smile fractured a little.

Realizing her mistake, Violet cleared her throat. Her friend was going to think Violet was down on herself about the whole mate thing, and that's not what she wanted. It was true! But not because of them.

"I'm really happy for you guys," Violet assured Mya, reaching forward to squeeze her hand. "Lexie is fine. She sprained her ankle, so she'll be on crutches for a while. But no cast, so that's good news."

"What about you?" Aiden asked. The concern in his eyes made Violet wonder how much of what he was feeling was his own emotions or an echo of Mya's.

Violet shrugged one of her shoulders, "I'm good, really."

The knowing glances the two of them exchanged made her uncomfortable.

"You should go dance!" Violet shoved off the wall and pushed them back toward the crowd. "I'm fine. I'll wait a couple more minutes then wander around the edges."

Aiden was more than happy to move back to the dance floor, but Mya was a little less convinced. "Violet..."

"Really!" She insisted, plastering a smile to her face. "Go enjoy dancing with your mate."

Pure joy chased away the worry in Mya's gaze, and she turned back to the guy she was obviously head over heels for. She sank into his embrace, tugging his shirt until he pressed his lips against hers. After the not so chaste kiss, they both waved at Violet and made their way into the crowd.

The song changed and many howls rose into the air as the volume increased. The thump of the base nearly rattled her bones!

Apparently, texting etiquette wasn't the only thing she needed to catch up on because she had never heard this song before.

As the beat pounded through the room, Violet nibbled on her lip. Patrick was more sensitive to sound than other wolven. If he ever decided to show up, the volume would be an issue. She'd told the DJ to take it easy, but apparently, he'd gotten carried away.

Her feet moved with a renewed action plan, driving her toward the guy in charge of the music. The mosh of people swarmed toward her, and she ducked under a balcony to avoid being carried off by the dancing wolven. She declined a couple people who beckoned her to come dance, keeping to the edges like she'd said she would do, and stepped right under a waterfall full of ice.

Gasping, Violet shook off her arm. Thankfully, her buttoned, plaid shirt was sleeveless so her clothing was minimally soaked, but there were a few pieces of ice she needed to shake out of her hair.

"Wow, they really got you, didn't they?" Asked a guy to her side. He was on the short side for a wolven—Violet guessed he was about 5'8". Dark blond hair had been pushed back over his head, and a slippery smile lifted the corners of his mouth, "Care to dance?"

Violet looked at him like he had two heads, "I just had ice water poured on me, and you're asking if I want to dance instead of offering me a towel?"

"Does it look like I have a towel, darling?" The guy laughed.

"What are you even doing here?" Violet asked, crossing her arms in front of her as the scent of fir trees washed over her. "This is supposed to be Sentinel Clan only."

"So, an attack happens during our tourney game and Whisky Clan isn't allowed to come to the party?"

"No one is allowed inside the gates except Sentinel right now. How did you get in?"

He shrugged, "My buddies and I have our ways."

Making a mental note that she needed to tell the guards about this annoying trespasser, Violet tried to push past him, but he grabbed her hips and pulled her against his body.

"Come on, just one dance."

"I can't," Violet grunted as she thrust her elbow against his ribcage, making him briefly struggle for air.

"Why not?" He asked through his teeth.

"If you really want to know, I'm waiting for someone."

"Like a boyfriend?" He eyed her again, "No mate would be stupid enough to leave you unclaimed."

Violet's brows rose as the song changed and the hard beat rattled the windows and shook the floor. She wasn't sure which part of his sentence she should be mad at, so instead she pushed him away when he tried to approach her again, "I don't have time for this."

"Why not?" He asked again, snatching her hand when she tried to pull away.

Shaking her head, Violet backed away from him, "I have a..." A familiar jolt of electricity cascaded down her other arm as someone grabbed her and spun her around, "Patrick!" Her hands automatically braced against his chest so she wouldn't smack her face into him.

A tingling trail was left in the wake of his hand as it slid down her arm then moved to settle around her waist. He scowled over her head at the guy who was now behind her before lowering his chin so he could look into her eyes, "Are you alright?"

Violet rested her forehead against him, "I am now." She tilted her head back and glared, "Where have you been?"

"With Jax," Patrick answered quickly then tightened his arm around her waist, holding her close. His lips curled back and he growled at the guy who'd been bothering her, "Leave. Now."

"Are you her boyfriend or something?"

Patrick's chest expanded beneath Violet's fingers as he gasped. He doubled over and groaned, "Vi..."

"Patrick?" Violet tried to move back so she could get a better look at him, but he'd gripped the back of her shirt, holding her in place. "Don't be afraid, okay? It's just your wolf. Welcome him." She pressed her palm to the side of Patrick's face and ran the tips of her fingers through his soft hair.

Patrick's other hand snagged her arm, holding on like she was his lifeline on a sinking ship. "I can't... go away."

Goosebumps flooded down Violet's arms at his menacing tone, but his hold tightened, making it impossible to do what he said. When she tried to look at him, Patrick buried his face in the crook of her neck and shoulder. The intimate hold made Violet suck in a breath, but after a momentary freeze, she wrapped her arm around his shoulders and rubbed his back, "It's okay. Listen to my voice and breathe."

Tremors wracked Patrick's body as Violet continued whispering to him. His body sagged a bit, and fear shot through her. She'd never seen this happen to anyone before. Every person she'd seen connect to their wolves acted as though it was this great power surging through them. Not some creature trying to take over.

The party raged around them, everyone missing the fact that the guest of honor was suffering, which was probably better for Patrick, anyway.

"Hey man!" complained the guy from earlier. "If she belongs to you, then you should keep a better handle on—"

"Back off!" Violet thrust an open palm into the guy's chest when he moved to grab Patrick. "This doesn't concern you."

Getting the message, finally, the guy stayed back... but his eyes flared silver exposing how upset he was.

Patrick was leaning heavily against her now and boy was he heavy. Worried he'd collapse on top of her, Violet shifted until she could cup both sides of his face with her hands. "Patrick, look at me."

He shook his head.

"Patrick, look at me," Violet repeated with more force. "You're stronger than whatever your wolf is saying to you. I know you. Open your eyes."

Two shaky breaths later, Patrick opened his eyes and froze as he stared into her purple gaze.

"Hey, there you are," Violet smiled at him, but he didn't smile back. She looked at the clock on the wall, then smiled again. "Looks like you were born at 10:59pm."

His wonderful hazel eyes scanned her whole face as he drew in a deep breath… then his face contorted in pain. He shook his head and slowly backed away, "I have to go."

"But you just got here," Violet reached for him, but he hurried away, leaving her alone with an aching heart.

"Looks like you're not *his* mate," the guy from earlier returned and anger pulsed through her, "wanna be mine?"

Any hurt she had just felt from Patrick's departure vanished as disgust washed over her, she grabbed the front of the guy's shirt and growled, "I'm not even eighteen, you pig."

The guy's eyes widened, supplying Violet with some brief gratification before she shoved him back and hurried after Patrick.

Jax!" She screamed through the link, angry that he had blocked her out all day in the first place, but then had abandoned his best friend after saying he wouldn't leave Patrick's side. *"You better not be shutting me out this time! Where are you? You little…"*

"What?" Jax snapped back.

Cold January air bit at her flushed cheeks and arms when Violet stepped outside. She'd been so set on following Patrick that she'd forgotten to grab her jacket and with the waxing crescent moon, she couldn't see much without the light of her phone.

"Do you know where Patrick is?" she asked.

"With me."

Violet froze a few steps from the doors of the Clan House and folded her arms to brace against the cold. Had Patrick known where Jax was the whole time? If so, why had he sought her out? *"Is he okay?"*

"He's a little shaken up," he paused and she could almost hear the sigh in his voice. *"He won't tell me what happened."*

"I was with him." Violet heard the venom in her own thoughts. *"He connected with his wolf. How could you leave him after saying you wouldn't? I've never seen anything like that before, he seemed terrified or... like he was fighting—"*

"You don't need to worry about it. I've got it handled." Just like that, Jax severed their link, blocking her out of his head again.

"What the...?"

Violet tried to speak with him once more, but the link remained closed like an iron gate.

The music in the Clan House died, turning Violet back toward the doors as Jax's voice rose above the complaining crowd. "Thank you for coming out to celebrate Patrick's birthday with us!"

A deafening cheer answered him while Violet silently fumed.

"Due to unforeseen circumstances, we will be ending the party early." The crowd complained, but Jax continued and they eventually quieted, "Your host was honored to have so many clan members show up, some even came from neighboring clans! It goes to show we truly are all part of a larger whole. Now if you will please find an exit and return home safely. Thank you and good night!"

Even through her anger, Violet was impressed. She would've just snapped at everyone to leave... which was why Jax was the one destined for Alpha. That and he actually had an alpha wolf within him. She would forever be the wolfless-mateless-wolven.

Chapter 17

Violet

THINGS SETTLED AFTER PATRICK'S BIRTHDAY. *He seemed more relaxed, even if he was ever-present, and pretty much ever-silent, since he'd barely spoken three words to her.*

The good news was, it had been over a week since anyone had seen or heard anything about the Blood Moon pack.

Violet shifted through a rack of overly elegant dresses in the third store of the day. Everything was prom level, but she just needed a nice dress for her graduation ceremony.

"I'm so jealous that you get to graduate now instead of having to wait until June," Lexie bumped her hip against Violet's side as she joined her. "Also, I think this store is too fancy."

"Agreed," Mya appeared on Violet's other side and crossed her arms over her chest. "And there's a guy at the cash register that won't stop eying me like I'm a piece of meat."

Having her two best friends with her at the mall was quite possibly the best thing to happen to her in a long time. Lexie's ankle was healed enough to walk on with a brace now, as long as they didn't move too fast, and Mya managed to slip away from Aiden for a few hours.

"How'd you pull off leaving your one true love at home?" Lexie asked over Violet's head as she continued looking through the last of the dresses on the rack.

"Aiden is working, and I'm off today." Mya grinned. "It was perfect timing."

"Are you able to keep breathing when you're together?"

"Lexie!" Violet hissed, sending her human friend a warning look.

The pale blond girl shrugged, "You're the one who says they can't keep their hands off each other." Her face twisted in confusion. "I thought you said it wasn't insta-lust?"

Mya scoffed. "It isn't. I thought Aiden was attractive before realizing he was my mate. Now it's just amplified." She pointed a finger at Lexie who was waggling her eyebrows. "And we can keep our hands off each other, thank you very much. We actually cuddle more than anything else."

"Awe. Aiden's a cuddler. How sweet." Lexie stuck out her bottom lip and Mya glared at her.

Violet shoved the dress hangers back in place and growled. "How many more stores do we have to go to before I give up?"

"You're not giving up," Mya insisted, wrapping her arm around Violet's as she steered her toward the door. "We'll find something."

"Hey guys," Lexie called to Jax and Patrick, who were leaning against the railing of the second floor as they started down the walkway toward the next shop. "We're moving on."

Violet tried to ignore the fact that Robin was hanging out with the boys and was too close to Patrick for her comfort. The now ebony-haired girl was practically velcroed to Patrick's side as the three of them moved toward their group. Robin had said she wanted to go shopping as well, but she hadn't entered a single shop.

Throwing his head back, Jax groaned, "Another dead end? How long are we going to be here?"

"As long as it takes!" Mya snapped and pulled Violet through another set of doors. "Come on. This place has a great vibe."

Jax had been banned from going into the last store with them by Violet because he had shot Lexie a flirtatious comment. It was the weirdest thing ever, and she didn't want to see that again.

The girls walked around, looking for anything that might work as a graduation dress. Violet had planned on just wearing a nice outfit until she texted Lexie who decided a shopping trip was in order. Her graduation was tomorrow, so if they didn't find anything at least she had a backup idea.

"Patrick, what is with you?" Robin complained loudly as they made their way into the store. "It's like you're not even here."

Violet looked over to see him staring out the shop windows.

"Just keeping an eye on things." He looked at Robin briefly. "I'm not here to hangout. I have a job to do."

"If I had known that in the first place, I would have just stayed home." Robin pulled her phone from her small purse that was crossed over her body. "It doesn't matter. I need to go anyway. My shift at the diner is starting soon."

Violet ducked her head when Patrick looked her way at the same time Robin rose onto her toes to kiss his cheek.

"Bye, girls!" Robin called.

Mya and Lexie gave half-hearted waves while Violet's gaze remained fixed on the rack of clothes in front of her.

"Good riddance," Lexie groaned.

"Lexie!" Mya chided.

"What? She's so fake, and she's moving in on something that isn't hers. She didn't even bother trying to act like she was here to be with us."

Violet shook her head. Patrick wasn't hers, but Lexie knew how she felt about him. "You still need to be nice."

"Yeah, Lex," Jax teased as he made his way toward them. He walked two fingers along Lexie's shoulders as he passed by her and she smacked at his hands. "Relax a little. This is supposed to be fun."

"It would be a lot more fun without you here."

"Awe, come on." Jax's lips tilted into a half-smile. "We have fun together."

It was official. Jax had been brainwashed.

Violet dropped a t-shirt that said 'Hangin' with my peeps' with a few peep easter bunnies beneath and grabbed her twin's arm. "This isn't the right store."

"Wait, but there are dresses over there!" Mya called after her, but Violet was already out the door with Jax in tow.

"Knock it off." She hissed at her brother and smacked his arm. "You're freaking me out."

He rubbed his arm mockingly, "What?"

"You're flirting with Lexie."

Disgust twisted his face, "Yeah... no. I would never do that."

"You just did! And you did it earlier, too! That's why I told you not to come into the stores with us anymore."

"Hey, are you two coming?" Mya called when she and Lexie headed off to yet another shop.

"Coming!" Violet called, then poked Jax in the chest. "Seriously, no more."

She looked over at Patrick who was looking behind them and didn't offer any kind of help or advice.

"So, what happened at Patrick's party?" Lexie asked when Violet caught up to her and Mya.

The crazy curly brunette shrugged. "Nothing much. Aiden and I danced the entire time while Violet pretty much just stood against a wall."

"I had ice water dumped on me, too," Violet grumbled. "Jax didn't even show up until the end when he announced the party was over, and Patrick was there less than five minutes."

"Oh, and some Whisky Clan members snuck in," Mya added as they passed by a soft pretzel place that smelled divine.

"Wait, wait, wait... You're telling me it was total lockdown and some Whisky guys still managed to get in?" Lexie asked.

Jax walked up and slung his arm around Violet's shoulders, "Apparently one of the guards is friends with them. He let them through the gate. Violet was convinced there was a hole somewhere in the fence line, but nothing was found and the guard admitted his actions. He was reprimanded with a weeks' worth of work at Lockup."

"Get off me," Violet ducked under his arm and shoved him away.

Lexie softly punched his arm after Violet moved out of the way. "You guys seriously ditched her? That's so rude."

Holding his hands up in surrender, Jax backed away a step, "It's not like we did it on purpose. At least, we didn't mean to wait that long. I got called into a meeting last minute."

"How last minute?" Lexie rounded on him, drawing the attention of a couple passing by.

"As in we were literally on our way to the party when my dad summoned me."

"So, what were you doing before that?"

Jax looked anxiously at Patrick who had made it his job to trail a few feet behind them for the last half hour.

With a small smack against his chest, Lexie pulled Jax's attention back to her. "Don't look at him!"

"Well, I—" Jax shrugged and looked at Patrick, anyway.

Sighing, Patrick put himself into play and entered the conversation. "It was my fault, Lexie. I should have told Violet I was waiting on something before coming to the party. Don't blame Jax. He tried to get me to go many times."

"See?" Jax gave Lexie a pointed look, "I wasn't being a—"

Violet and Mya both turned their full attention to him when he stopped talking, and Patrick stepped toward his best friend.

"Jax? What's going on?" Violet asked after a full minute of silence.

Her twin's face tensed, "Have any of you heard from Vikter?"

Mya was the first to answer, "As in… Stanislaus' ex-future alpha?"

Violet shook her head, and Jax eyed her, "I haven't seen or heard anything about him since the tourney attack."

"Yeah," Jax let out a large breath of air. "Apparently, that's the last time anyone heard from him."

"His body wasn't found on Sentinel territory," Patrick added as he looked behind them once again.

"I didn't like the guy, but his parents must be worried sick," Mya twisted a chocolate coil of hair around her finger.

"His alpha is as well," Jax shook his head. "They can't reach him by link or cell. So, either he's dead… or he ran away."

"I wouldn't put it past him to run," Patrick said quietly, his attention on something else. "After being removed from position like he was, it might be better for him to be in a different clan."

Violet nibbled on her lip in thought for a moment. "Is there anything we can do to help?"

Shaking his head again, Jax answered, "Not unless they call for a combined clan search, which they haven't."

Lexie cleared her throat drawing all of their attention. "Well, on that note, I think I know what store to go to next, and I'm pretty sure it will be the last one."

"Good," Jax grumbled as they all moved to follow the human girl. "I'm mall-ed out."

Violet rolled her eyes. "You haven't even done any shopping."

"Speaking of which," Jax fell behind to walk in step with Patrick. "Do we need anything for your trials while we're here? Anything I, as your anchor, might need?"

"Don't sound so smug about it," Patrick chuckled, "there isn't much for you to do."

"Still, it's cool that I get to do that for you. It isn't very often that I get to help you."

Violet grinned as they made their way into what was hopefully the last store. As annoying as her twin brother could be, he had a good heart, and he was a good friend to Patrick. As Jax's beta, it was pretty much Patrick's job to help Jax in everything. Being happy to do the same in return was yet another endearing quality that would help him in his future role.

"Oh my gosh, Violet! I think I found it!" Mya jumped up and down with an off-white sundress covered in sunflowers hanging from her hands. "Try it on, please!"

Laughing, Violet ran her fingers over the soft fabric. "It's cute, but I'm not sure it's the one I'm looking for. Maybe this place has something else, though."

"Like this?" Lexie asked, whipping a dress around in a circle as she approached.

When the seafoam green chiffon material settled, Violet smiled. The skirt was divided into four layers which were separated by small, outward seams. A cinched band a couple inches wide drew the waist in, and the bodice was covered by a flowy, off-the-shoulder top that ended just above the waistband.

It was a beautiful spring dress that looked like it belonged on a beach instead of the beginning of February, but it was perfect.

"Yeah. I think I'll try that on." Violet took the dress from her friend who squealed with excitement and headed into the changing room.

Lexie and Mya chatted excitedly as Violet changed and from the sound of it, Lexie had also found a dress. The changing room beside hers opened and closed as Violet was finishing adjusting the dress.

"I'm coming out!" Violet called.

"Congrats," Jax's droll voice called out to her, but Mya's squeal kept her excitement up. "Hurry up already."

"Wait!!!" Lexie cried and a thud against the changing room wall made Violet flinch. "Ow."

Violet fiddled with the end of her long, dark chocolate ponytail. "You okay, Lexie?"

"I'm fine, I just want to show them at the same time."

A laugh left Violet and she shook her head. "So, you can upstage me with your model height and figure?"

"Oh, please," Lexie scoffed. "You may be shorter than me, but your figure is so much better. You've got curves in all the right places. I'm flat and tiny in all the wrong places."

Violet snickered, "You're ridiculous and gorgeous."

"Ready?"

"Yes."

Violet opened her dressing room door and stepped out, looking to her right. A gorgeous red sheath dress fit perfectly to Lexie's lithe frame, making Violet's jaw drop.

"Dang girl!" Mya exclaimed loudly, making the girls laugh.

"Violet, that dress is gorgeous on you!" Lexie tapped Violet's shoulder and she spun slowly in a circle for dramatic effect. "Very nice. I think that's the one."

Excitement bubbled up inside her, and Violet swished the skirt of the dress around. "Thanks! I think so, too. What do you think, Jax?"

She looked up to find her twin brother's slightly widened gaze glued to Lexie, whose face was nearly as red as her dress.

"Jax!"

He startled and grew fidgety as he looked over Violet before crossing his arms and grumpily turning away, "Yeah. It looks good."

Patrick appeared from around a clothing rack, walking quickly toward them. "Guys, I think we may have a problem."

His feet slowed as his gaze landed on Violet. The tense expression on his face gave way to a slack jaw and wandering eyes before his jaw clenched. The way his face twisted was as if he were in physical pain. He turned away, making Violet's chest ache.

"What's wrong?" Jax asked, moving to Patrick's side.

"I wanted to be sure, so I haven't said anything until now, but there is a guy following us. Unfortunately, this isn't the first time I've seen him."

Jax turned toward the girls, his eyes determined, and an air of authority passed through him, making him stand a little taller. "Violet and Lexie, get dressed. If you're buying those, do so quickly. Mya, stay with them. Patrick and I will stand at the store entrance until you're ready, and then we will make it back to our cars as fast as possible."

"How fast?" Lexie asked quietly. Her face had lost some color and Violet couldn't blame her. She'd now witnessed firsthand how dangerous being friends with a bunch of wolven could be.

After looking down at Lexie's braced ankle, Jax sent her a quick smirk, "Fast enough that I may have to carry you again."

Lexie's brows slammed down and she crossed her arms over her chest. "No. Freaking. Way."

"Enough," Patrick growled. "We don't have time for this."

He stormed away, grabbing Jax's sleeve to pull him along.

The girls did as they were told, quickly changing and buying their dresses before joining up with the boys once more.

"Let's go," Patrick ordered, nodding down the walk toward the cars.

Their positioning shifted as they moved, forming an unspoken ring of protection around Lexie—who either didn't notice or didn't mind. Patrick led the way, Violet was on his right, Jax brought up the rear, with Mya on the left. They moved as one with either Violet or Mya grabbing Lexie's arm when they shifted directions quickly.

Patrick's head jerked to the side. His eyes narrowed as he looked down another walkway. "I'll be right back."

"Patrick!" Jax called after him, but the headstrong young man was already a good distance away. "You guys get to the car. I'll go after him."

Violet snagged her brother's arm as he stormed by. "Splitting up is not a good idea. If he really did see something, that is what someone would want us to do. We're coming with you."

Cursing under his breath, Jax reluctantly agreed and led the way after their wayward friend.

Patrick slammed his giant hand down onto a black hooded guy and pushed him into a small opening in the wall.

"Patrick," Jax growled low, quickening his pace.

"Guys, I can't—"

In one fluid motion that Violet didn't know he was capable of, Jax turned, scooped Lexie into his arms, and continued on.

"No! I didn't mean for you to pick me up!" Lexie screeched and pounded her fist against his shoulder. "Put me down!"

"Shh!" Jax glared at her. "You're drawing attention."

"*You're* drawing attention!" Lexie whisper-hissed at him.

Violet jogged ahead, ignoring them, and turned into the opening Patrick had disappeared into, only to come to a sudden halt. The only things in the little area were a couple janitorial supplies and a door with an "employee exit" sign over it.

With the only options being that he left the building with their stalker, or he somehow managed to make it past them undetected… Violet pushed through the employee exit and came to another sudden halt.

"You're not the owner of this! Where is he?" Patrick's voice was teetering between a yell and a growl as he held a blonde-haired guy against a wall with one fist twisted in the black hood.

"That's what I'm telling you! It *is* mine!"

Violet stalked toward them; her eyes fixed on the sweat beads gathering along the guy's forehead. "You're not telling us something."

His panicked gaze darted between the two of them and he pulled at Patrick's arm, but it didn't move. If the stench of cologne wasn't an obvious indicator, his lack of strength was. He was average height for a human, which put him several inches shorter than Patrick. There was a good amount of muscle on him—which meant he was probably involved in some kind of sport… but no matter how strong he was, it was no match for a wolven.

"What, now there's two of you? What did this guy do?"

Tipping her head slightly to the side, Violet grinned wickedly. "That's on a need-to-know basis. Now," she took another step toward them, holding the guy's attention. Even Patrick had looked her direction for a moment. "Tell us how you got this hoodie."

He released Patrick's arm and held his arms up in surrender. "I don't have much to tell you guys. He offered me ten bucks if I would wear it. I just wanted a free lunch!"

"Did you see which way he went?" Patrick asked with a calmer tone than before.

"Nah, he was gone when I looked back up after putting this on."

The fist Patrick had twisted up in the guy's hood slammed into the wall behind him. The guy flinched, curling in on himself, but Patrick had already backed away several steps. His breathing was heavy as his jaw pulsed.

Slowly, the guy stood back up. "Dude, what did this guy do to you?"

Violet stepped between the two young men, gaining the guy's attention once again. "I suggest you leave. Now."

It didn't take long for the guy to book it back to the door which opened to reveal the rest of their group just as he reached it.

"It was him, Violet. I know it." Patrick ran a hand through his hair as he paced.

Shaking her head, Violet moved toward Patrick. "Him who?"

"I do—" He growled and frustration cascaded off him in waves. "I don't know who he is. I just know that I know his scent. I know him from somewhere."

Violet snagged his coat, stopping his pacing. "I don't know what you're talking about."

His golden-flecked hazel gaze darted all over her face, as if he were rapidly trying to memorize every feature. "Remember the guy from the diner?"

She nodded.

"He was at the movies with Robin and me, too."

Confusion laced with worry pulled her brows together as he continued.

"I saw him, or rather caught his scent, the other day while running an errand for your dad. I haven't seen his face yet; he always has his hood up."

"Was it the same guy tonight?" Violet whispered as their friends closed in on them.

"Yes."

"You have a lot of explaining to do, Patrick," Jax growled.

Violet was pleased to see he was no longer carrying Lexie, but the worry that Patrick had a wolven stalker wasn't something she could let go of.

"I'll explain on the ride home," Patrick answered gruffly. "We need to go."

It didn't take long to find Lexie's car. The human girl threw her arms around Violet and squeezed as tight as she could, which made Violet laugh.

"I wish I could be there to celebrate your graduation," Lexie mumbled.

"Don't worry about it. I'll be there to obnoxiously cheer you across the stage in a few months," Violet teased, but closed her eyes and breathed deep. Lexie was her anchor when things went sideways. Her voice of reality and blunt, heartfelt honesty. Not having her around was hard. "Maybe I can come stay with you sometime."

Lexie jerked back and starlight filled her eyes. "That is the best idea ever! Now you have to!"

Violet laughed and shook her head. "Sometime. I have a few things to do before that can happen."

"Yeah, like graduating! Let's go, Violet!" Jax called grumpily as he leaned against the trunk of Lexie's car.

"You can wait!" Lexie snapped and rolled her eyes, but there was a hint of a smile tilting the corner of her lips skyward.

Shaking her head, Violet stepped back. "You guys are freaking me out. Drive safe, okay? Text me when you get home."

"Yes, Mom." Lexie stuck her tongue out as she sank into the driver's seat of her car. "Love ya."

"Love you, too," Violet answered, then patted the top of Lexie's car and stepped away so her friend could leave. She stood beside Jax, watching the taillights fade down the parking lot. "That red dress did look pretty great on her, huh?"

Jax's head snapped in her direction and he stared at her with one brow raised. When she smirked at him, he grumbled, "Shut up." He turned to climb into the driver's side of his car where Patrick sat in the front passenger seat and Mya waited in the back. "Let's get you graduated, so dad stops bugging me about it all the time."

"Oh, yes. Because I'm sure he cares about my graduation oh so very much." Violet slid into the back with Mya who gave her a sad smile.

"He does," Jax answered cheerfully. "He cares that you're wasting clan resources by taking your sweet time."

The news of that wasn't surprising, but it still hurt.

Patrick swiftly bent his elbow, lifting his fist into the air, then drove his knuckles into Jax's thigh.

"OW!" Jax viciously rubbed his leg while seething in his seat. "Dead leg!"

Mya snickered behind her hands, which of course did nothing to hide her laugh, but it was cute nonetheless.

"Need me to drive?" Patrick asked in an even tone, not apologizing or even acknowledging he did anything.

"No!" Jax snapped, still massaging and shaking his leg out.

Patrick nodded. "Good. Be nice."

Aside from Jax's mumbled complaints, and Patrick explaining about the guy who had been stalking him, the ride was uneventful... which Violet was grateful for. It gave her time to think through her plans for after graduation.

Chapter 18

Violet

VIOLET HAD ASKED THAT HER GRADUATION WOULDN'T *be turned into a huge affair.* Clan graduations happened twice a year, and she was happy to wait to walk with the rest of the graduates in May. However, being the Alpha and Luna's daughter meant that her mom had insisted on a separate celebration. It was kind of a nice thought… until her mom's condition had started worsening.

Since the tourney attack, Evalyn had mentioned more headaches than Violet could ever remember, and there was a certain weariness about her. She was concerned the planning would be too much for her mom. However, the large Clan House had been lightly decorated, anyway, with a congratulations sign, streamers, elegant white curtains, and chairs lined to cover the entire floor.

Violet looked out over the crowd, honored that so many would attend a simple graduation. Nearly every chair had been filled! As her gaze scanned over the crowd, her eyes lingered on the empty seat beside Jax.

Her shoulders sagged.

Since Alpha Draven was still in position, Patrick's future role as beta required very little. He shadowed Beta Paul from time to time, but his current job was as a clan warrior. Patrick said he would be there, but the chair beside Jax remained empty. He'd been given a last-minute shift patrolling the base borders.

"Over the last six months," Evalyn announced from atop one of the balconies, with Violet standing beside her. She'd been speaking for nearly ten minutes now telling everyone stories from Violet's childhood and the accomplishments she'd done throughout her life. "Violet Draven has worked extra hard on her studies, exceeding requirements day in and day out, to graduate ahead of her class."

A stream of light spread across the Clan House floor as the door beneath them to the left opened. It closed quietly as Evalyn continued and Violet's heart nearly leapt out of her chest when the scent of chocolate peppermint filled the air.

Patrick quietly made his way to Jax's side, claimed the seat beside him, ran a hand through his freshly showered hair, then looked up at her and smiled.

Her answering smile spread against her will, even with Jax's small glare burning holes in her face.

Patrick had come.

His shirt was only half-buttoned, his hair was a mess, and the light stubble along his jaw were all indicators that he had been in a hurry, and it set her soul on fire.

Her mom lightly pinched Violet's side, drawing her attention, as she continued, "...I am honored to announce our newest high school graduate! She'll be taking on new responsibilities inside the clan, and is excited to start college as soon as possible. I'm sure we are all anxious to see what her bright future holds. I couldn't be more proud! Congratulations, Violet Draven!"

Evalyn threw her arms around Violet and squeezed as the crowd below them clapped.

"Thanks." Violet squeezed back.

Evalyn turned her head so her mouth was close to Violet's ear as she whispered, "Sorry for pinching you. It was that or publicly wipe the drool from your face."

Flames ignited Violet's face. "I was not drooling," she insisted, pulling away from her mom to shake her head.

The older woman laughed as she handed over Violet's diploma. There may have been permanent light bags under her eyes, but her sense of humor was still intact.

"Yes!" Called the deep, resounding voice of Alpha Draven, making Violet's spine straighten. "We are all so proud of our little Violet."

With a tight-lipped smile, Violet turned to face her father who was now standing behind her with Beta Paul on his right side. The alpha held out his arms, a show of affection for all to see. She awkwardly wrapped one arm around him for a quick hug before stepping back and bowing respectfully.

"You may take your seat, Violet." Alpha Draven told her quietly, but the order was clear. She was dismissed.

After a curt nod, she left the balcony. There were a few whoops and hollers as she descended the stairs, making her smile. Mya, Aiden, Jax, and Patrick were on their feet clapping for her when everyone else had gone silent.

"Alright, now, settle down. While a graduation is an important occasion, I've gathered you all here for another reason..."

Disappointment shattered Violet's smile. As soon as her ankle boots hit the floor she turned to stare up at her father.

He was doing it again.

Using her achievement for his gain.

"Easy, Vi. This is important." Jax's voice filled her head.

She ground her teeth, resisting the urge to turn around. No one needed to see her outburst of emotion. *"It always is. He could've called a separate meeting."*

"Everyone is already gathered, and if you would just listen..."

Violet slammed through the Clan House doors, her graduation robes billowing behind her. She focused on blocking Jax out of her mind, which would effectively end their link... if she'd ever been any good at it. His voice was quieter, easier to ignore, but she could still hear him.

Halfway between the Clan House and Alpha House she stopped and looked over the field she and Mya would crawl around in as kids. The first place Patrick had ever taught her anything about combat. The place she'd seen Jax tackle a guy for trying to kiss her.

She couldn't recall a single happy memory involving Alpha Draven. Not in that field. Not in their home. Not anywhere or in any part of her life. Almost like she was an extra he never wanted and couldn't be bothered with trying to care.

Reckless rage poured over her as she lifted the diploma in her hands. The thought of ripping it in pieces flitted through her thoughts, but it was gone as soon as it came. She'd worked hard for that stupid piece of paper; she wasn't about to destroy it.

"Violet!" Patrick's voice made her spin around and she stared in shock as he made his way toward her. "Jax couldn't leave, so he sent me to check on you."

The shock was gone. "Oh."

More disappointment.

Ever since Patrick's birthday almost two weeks ago, he'd barely spoken a word to her. The shopping trip had been the most interaction they'd had, and even that was mostly relaying information about his new found stalker.

"Go back to the Clan House, Patrick," Violet grumbled and headed home. "It's not like you want to be around me anyway."

"What makes you say that?" He asked, quickly catching up to her before matching her stride.

With a snort, Violet shot him a nasty glare, "You really don't know?" He lifted a shoulder and the urge to smack him was nearly suffocating, "You've been avoiding me for weeks! You left me standing in the middle of your party with some creep breathing down my neck! You've barely spoken to me since then, shopping last night seemed like it was torturous for you, and you just said that you're out here because Jax couldn't be. Not because you wanted to see how I was."

Patrick lifted his hands in surrender. He didn't say anything, which made her even more angry.

"Seriously, do you even care?"

Patrick's hands fell to his sides and he sighed, "Of course I care, Violet."

"Then what happened?"

"How did this go back to my birthday?" Patrick ran a hand through his drying hair then rested it on the back of his neck, "I thought you were mad at Alpha Draven?"

Violet threw her arms out to the sides and stopped walking to glare at him, "Yeah, well, there isn't really anything I can do about my dad, is there?"

"Do you have any idea what he's talking about to everyone?" Patrick asked, his voice adopting a harsher tone as his hazel eyes locked onto her. "Do you know why he couldn't wait to bring it up to spare your feelings?"

Guilt weighed heavily on Violet's shoulders and she took a step back.

"There have been raids and attacks and kidnappings."

"Those things always happen," Violet shook her head. "That's nothing new. The Paladins always take care of those things."

"Except the Paladins haven't been able to stop it this time. They keep going missing."

"Missing?" Violet wondered out loud.

The Paladins were a nomad clan of wolven fighters. The best of the best. They traveled ensuring the safety of the clans and the laws of the kings and queens. Violet often wondered if Patrick would have joined their ranks if he wasn't in position to be beta for Sentinel Clan.

"Yes." Patrick's shoulders tensed. "And it's all happening in a direct path headed for our clan."

Realization dawned on Violet and she froze. She didn't even breathe, "Blood Moon?"

Drawing in a deep breath, Patrick broke his eye contact with her, "If you thought that attack at the tourney was bad... it's nothing compared to what's coming for us."

"No..." Violet didn't want to believe it. "The Paladins will stop them. Blood Moon wouldn't be stupid enough to expose themselves like this. They know what will happen if they do."

They would all be killed, that's what. The kings and queens would issue a combined clan attack to wipe the scourge from existence.

"If they believe they have the strength in numbers, I'm not sure anything would stop them. Especially if your father is correct."

"What do you mean?"

"He is pretty sure they're after someone." Patrick explained, his hands curling and uncurling at his sides before he shoved them into his suit pant pockets. "They're increasing their numbers. Rumor is the kidnappings are of wolven they believe would make good pack mates."

"Wolven that have a thirst for blood, you mean. Ones who are prone to violence. Maybe that's where the Paladins have been disappearing too as well." Understanding chilled the fire raging in Violet's veins. "I guess I can't be mad at him for that. He still could have picked a better time to do it, though."

"Could he?" Patrick's head dipped to the side. "More people came to this meeting because of your graduation. He received information about the attacks this morning. Is there a better way to spread the word than having a good portion of the pack in attendance? He can't clan-link with everyone at the same time."

Violet's mouth opened and closed, then did it again. No... she couldn't think of a more effective way. That was what her father excelled at. Finding the most efficient route, even if it hurt others.

"Did you know he's inviting all the neighboring clans to Jax's and my birthday party?" Violet released a dry laugh.

Confusion pulled his brows together. "That's a little off topic, but no, I didn't know that. Why does it matter?"

"It's not, actually." Violet continued when Patrick lifted one brow, "Off topic, I mean. If you were in my head the connection would've made sense."

"Okay, but I'm not... so explain."

She did and it only made Patrick shake his head.

"Being efficient is an excellent trait for an alpha. You can't fault him for that."

"It also makes him a really frustrating father," Violet grumbled. Growing tired of the conversation, she started toward Alpha House again.

Patrick followed her and sighed, "Why is he inviting so many people to your birthday?"

Violet lifted a shoulder, "He believes it gives us the best chance to find our mates. To create a bond right out the gate."

"Does he know you..." his words trailed off and he cleared his throat. "Does he know what Doc thinks?"

"Not unless my mom told him." Violet snorted. "So yeah, he probably does know and doesn't care."

"Did it ever occur to you that he might just be hoping you do have a mate and your bond will be with someone close to home?"

Shock pulled Violet's lips apart and she looked at Patrick as her previous guilt magnified. "You clearly see a different man than I do."

"Of course I do." Patrick answered matter-of-factly. "He took me in when no one else would."

Yes. Her father had done that, and she loved him for it. Rumor was no other clan wanted Patrick. Sentinel was his last resort, or he would have gone rogue. Something about that never sat well with Violet. She couldn't understand why someone would turn him away.

Shaking her head, Violet said, "Let's talk about something else. How are the preparations going for your trial?"

With a groan, Patrick ran a hand down his face, "Anything but that."

Violet grimaced, "That bad, huh?"

The wolven trials happened during the first full moon after you turned eighteen. It was the first time a wolven would be able to shift, making the connection between wolf and man complete... whatever that meant.

Patrick's trial was in two days.

"I've run into a bit of a snag," Patrick admitted. "I was told this morning that Jax can't be my anchor."

"What?" Violet jerked back, grinding to a halt about twenty feet from the stone walkway to Alpha House's front door. "Why not? That's been the plan all along."

Patrick rubbed the back of his neck. "It was our plan all along, but we didn't realize we had to confirm that plan with Beta Paul. When he asked this morning if I'd decided on an anchor, I told him it was Jax. He stared at me blank faced until he realized I wasn't joking."

"So, why can't he?"

"Because Jax is my future alpha."

"That's stupid," Violet scoffed and stomped toward Patrick. "Shouldn't he have even more right to be there? Especially since you're going to be his beta?"

"You would think that had some kind of sway on the decision, but apparently, it's an old rule that can't, or won't, be changed. It gives him and I an advantage."

Understanding dawned on her, making Violet nod. "As your alpha, he could coerce you with his aura, forcing you to pass the trial instead of letting you work through it."

"Right." Patrick sighed and ran a hand through his dark, curly hair. The curls had loosened a bit with how much he had been doing that. "It also means that he can't be an anchor for anyone in the clan. Ever."

Violet chewed on her lip as she thought things through, and tried not to focus on how good a little bit of scruff looked on the young man in front of her. "What does an anchor need to do?"

Growing up in the clan, and the alpha's daughter no less, she knew the basics... but it wasn't something people talked about until it was your own time. As the first full moon after your eighteenth birthday neared, the beta would take you aside, teach you what you needed to know and do, and how to go about it.

Patrick waved a dismissive hand. "You know some of it; keep an eye over the wolven going through the trial, be a look out for potential danger, relay how things are going to family, etc. What you may not know is sometimes the anchor acts like a tether back to this world."

"Why?"

Shrugging, Patrick swallowed hard. "Some wolf spirits are harder to control than others. Some would rather remain a wolf, not part human. Some people aren't strong enough to come back... or they don't want to."

"Which is why the anchor needs to be someone you care about." Violet nodded. "If that situation arose, having someone you care about would be a reminder of what you would be losing." A small laugh left her, "Thus the reason it's called an anchor."

Patrick was quiet, making Violet's nerves spike.

"Do you have a second choice?" Violet stared at the ground, trying not to get her hopes up.

"I haven't ever given a second choice any thought. It was always going to be Jax."

Violet looked up and found him staring at the nearly full moon.

She brandished the last ribbon of bravery she had and said, "I know I could never replace Jax and the brotherhood you both share, but..." She shrugged a shoulder as his gaze slid from the moon to her. "I could be your anchor."

It took a second before Patrick's eyebrows rose and a wry smile slid into place. "You, really?"

Violet jerked away from him like he'd slapped her. "Forget it."

"No, wait. Violet, I didn't..."

Too many emotions for one day. That's what Violet determined as she ran away from him. Her cap fell off just before she made it to the door, but it didn't matter. She'd embarrassed herself yet again, and all she wanted was to get to her room, bury herself in warm blankets and block out the entire world.

She knew it was childish. She knew there were more important things.

But she wanted to be noticed. She wanted to be wanted.

Chapter 19

Violet

"YOU'RE THE ALPHA'S DAUGHTER," *explained Andrew, a seventeen-year-old wolven with dirt-dusted blond hair and brown eyes spread wide with fear.* "If I hurt you..."

Violet growled, pacing around him. "You won't. Stop holding back!"

Andrew snorted and crossed his arms, "Violet, you're nearly a foot shorter than me. You haven't made contact with your wolf. I'm turning eighteen next week." He pointed a finger at her. "I'm stronger than you."

Using his opening, Violet grabbed his wrist and twisted—spinning under his arm to pin it against his back.

"Gah!" Andrew cried out as his knees buckled under the direction from her foot.

"Speed and intelligence will always win against brute strength," Violet growled in his ear.

Andrew's other arm reached around, and Violet had to credit him on his shoulder flexibility. After gripping her loose tank top, he dragged her in front of him, breaking her grip on his arm as he stood and flipped her around.

Typically, Violet avoided the flying triangle choke—it was a potentially hazardous attack—but with her legs already leaving the ground... she didn't feel like she had that much to lose.

Besides, Andrew was terrified of hurting her. He wasn't about to slam her head into the dirt.

Flinging one leg up behind Andrew's head while her other grappled under his arm, she twisted her ankles together and squeezed.

Another shriek left Andrew as her added bodyweight, little as it may be, threw off his center of gravity. Tipping forward, he let go of her and braced for the ground.

Violet's back hit the dirt before Andrew rolled over her, landing face up with his head and arm stuck between her thighs.

"Go easy on him."

The familiar voice lit a fire in Violet's belly and she pulled against Andrew's arm, making him protest.

"He was trying to be nice," Patrick's head came into view above Violet and she glared at him.

Andrew tapped her thigh frantically, "Can't... breathe..."

"Sorry," Violet immediately detached herself from Andrew and rolled away. She was standing before Andrew had made it to his knees.

"I'll take it from here, Andrew." Patrick helped the poor guy stand, who rubbed his neck and stared at Violet with saucer-sized eyes.

Without another word, Andrew waved goodbye then grabbed his gym bag and headed for the indoor training arena.

Violet crossed her arms as Patrick turned back to her with a raised brow, "What?"

"Using your tiny, unimposing body to beat up nice guys just because you're upset, is not very nice." Patrick chided and leaned against one of the ruins.

The combat ruins consisted of a broken-down mansion with what appeared to be stone pillars extending out in a large circle. Dirt filled the space between the crumbling pillar making it a fantastic place to train and spar in a more realistic setting than the padded artificial grass indoors.

"If they didn't underestimate me, then it wouldn't happen," Violet bit back, then rubbed a bunch of dirt off her arm that had stuck to the moisture on her skin. "That sort of thinking could get them killed in a real fight."

"Thank goodness they have you to correct them."

Anger pulsed through her, and she stared at him through narrowed eyes.

Patrick's gaze wandered down the length of her body then back up, "How long have you been out here? You're covered in dirt."

Violet shook her head, then went to retrieve her water bottle from the other side of the pillared arena. "I don't have time for your games right now, Patrick." She popped the top off her water bottle and took a quick swig, swished it around, then spit to the side to wash the dirt from her mouth. "My dad loaded me with all sorts of errands and things for the clan. I graduated two days ago, and I'm already wondering how I'm going to attend college and figure out my role in the clan with all the—"

"Will you be my anchor tonight?"

Violet froze with her water bottle near her mouth, then snorted, "Thanks. You don't need to be a jerk about a sincere offer."

"I'm not trying to be a jerk," Patrick explained while she downed a mouthful of water.

She hit the top back down before tossing it onto her gym bag. "Maybe you should have thought about that before laughing in my face."

"Vi..."

His hand touched her shoulder, triggering Violet's hypersensitive fight reflex. Her hand wrapped around his as she backed into him, preparing to throw him over her shoulder... but Patrick was a much better fighter than Andrew. He stepped to the side, avoiding her butt and throwing her off balance.

Violet regained her footing, only to find Patrick waiting patiently for her. Fury propelled her forward. She released a series of attacks, actually landed a couple, then threw her knee up.

"Woah!" Patrick protected himself, then tossed her knee out to the side. "That was low."

Smirking, Violet went back on the offensive.

After catching a roundhouse against his side, Patrick held her leg, stepped into her space and kicked her other leg out from under her.

Violet grunted as she hit the ground and again when Patrick pinned her there.

"Get off!" she growled.

Patrick snatched her hand away when she tried to attack him again, then pinned it against the dirt near her head.

"Not until you listen to me." His voice was irritatingly calm.

She tried to bend her legs to get her feet under her and throw her hips up, but he'd flattened them to the ground with his own.

"I only have thirty minutes to train. I'm not going to spend it listening to you back pedaling," Violet groaned as she wriggled beneath his weight, trying to find an opening, "... for something you're not even sorry you said."

"I *am* sorry!"

Violet froze and stared into Patrick's hazel eyes.

"The thought of you escorting me wasn't amusing. I was surprised by the offer, and handled it the wrong way." His grip on her wrists loosened, but he didn't move. "I've been trying to find some way to explain that to you. I thought returning your cap and giving you your graduation gift might have helped, but you acted like it didn't even happen."

Surprised, Violet sucked in a small breath. Once she had calmed down after having her feelings hurt, she'd found her cap on the entryway table. It sat atop an adorable graduation-bear's head with her favorite cookies... there hadn't been a note.

"What you did for me on my birthday..." words failed him and Patrick looked off to the side for a moment. His voice was much softer when he continued, "If anyone can help me get through this, it's you."

"I didn't do anything," she whispered.

One corner of his mouth curled into a smirk, "Yes, you did. You decorated the Clan House. You waited all night for me and weren't angry when I showed up last minute. You didn't let me give in to Alistair. You held on and called me back while fighting off some random guy who wouldn't leave you alone."

Violet's heart pounded, kicking her breathing into high gear like she'd just finished running five miles. Every time she drew in a breath, her stomach brushed his. Had he moved closer or had he been this close the whole time?

On top of that... He was complimenting her like crazy. Had he actually given her a graduation gift? One that took thought and not just a congratulations card?

The longer she took to answer, the more Patrick's eyes warmed until she saw fear begin to seep through.

"Are you scared I'm going to say no?" Violet whispered.

Patrick's gaze dropped to her mouth when she spoke, then he met her gaze again with creased brows, "Terrified."

"Do you really think I would?"

"With how mad you were, anything was possible."

A dry laugh left her and a relieved smirk softened the hard, worried edges of his face. "I'll answer you if you let me up."

Patrick launched himself off her, landing in a crouch a few feet away.

"Should have said that earlier," Violet mumbled as she rolled to her feet. Without exerting herself or having Patrick's body to warm her, the late-winter wind bit against her exposed skin. She shivered as she moved to grab her athletic jacket.

"Let me help." Patrick was suddenly behind her, dusting off the dirt from her skin and clothes.

Violet offered her thanks when he was done, then quickly pulled her jacket on.

"So, are you going to answer me or continue letting me have a mental breakdown?"

A smile spread across her face. "You're asking for my help. How could I say no?"

Relief sank Patrick's shoulders as a large sigh escaped him, "Thank goodness." He shook himself off and grabbed her bag off the ground. "You need to be ready to leave in an hour."

"An hour?" Violet called after him as he walked away with her bag. She stood frozen in place for a second, wondering what she'd really gotten herself into before hurrying to catch up with him. "Why an hour?"

Patrick shouldered her bag as they walked, "We are headed to the main trial arena. They've had to set up a second, temporary one for Aiden since we have two of us entering the trials. It takes about an hour to drive there.

The road is steep and has a lot of hairpin turns according to Beta Paul. I've been informed it will take about an hour on foot to find the trial area."

"Why can't we just run there. We won't have that much stuff, will we? And wouldn't it just be faster and easier to go through the trial in the woods behind Alpha House?" Violet asked, taking a few jogging steps to keep up with him. He was moving fast!

"I asked the same questions. After the shift, I'll be too weak to run back. It also needs to be a place where we won't be accidentally interrupted or found, so while it's still within Sentinel territory, it's deep in the forest near the base of the mountains. We will follow the road, then head down a hiking trail before veering off into the trees at some point that I will recognize when we get there.

The surrounding area has also been spelled. Nothing and no one will be able to hear, see, or smell us." Patrick glanced sideways at her. "It's just a precaution, but the trial area itself also has a spell on it. Only mentally stable wolves will be able to exit the area once inside. No one has gotten stuck in a trial ring in years, but it does happen."

"Right... I guess I would have learned about all that soon with my birthday coming up."

He set her bag on the front porch of Alpha House and turned to face her. "I'll be back in fifty minutes."

Violet nodded and he jogged down the road. Fifty minutes was not a lot of time to prepare. She grabbed her bag and hurried inside.

"Mom!" She shrieked when the older woman snatched her bag from her. "What are you doing? I have to get ready."

Her mom nodded. "I know. Patrick came to me to ask if he could have you as an anchor. I was the one who told him where you were."

Surprised, Violet shook her head and stood dumbfounded while her mom set her bag aside. "You... He... what?"

"Never mind," her mom waved a dismissive hand. "Go shower. I set out some clothes for you on your bed, but you're welcome to pick something else. I have a small bag of essentials already packed for you."

Violet nodded and hurried toward the stairs. She'd taken two steps when she turned around.

Evalyn was leaning heavily against the back of one of the couches, rubbing her temples.

"Mom?"

Her mom's dark hair swished with her sudden movement as she stood and folded her hands in front of her. "Hmm?"

"Are you okay?"

A soft smile brightened her mom's face. "I'm fine, my little miracle."

Worry seeped through Violet, but she knew her mom wouldn't tell her anything else. "You know you can talk to me. Hot chocolate is always waiting."

The soft smile on her mom's face widened. "I know, but right now you need to hurry."

"Why is it so important that we leave in such a rush?"

"Your father and brother are out of clan territory right now. If they find out before they return, they will try to stop you. That being said, I have the authority to approve this. So I am."

Evalyn's explanation made Violet's jaw drop.

"Besides," her mom continued as her gaze softened, "Patrick needs you."

Violet swallowed the knot in her throat. When was the last time her mother, Luna of the clan, had gone against her father… the alpha?

"I'll hurry."

And she did. Her hair was wet, but she was ready to go when Patrick knocked on the front door.

*****

Not a single minute was spent in silence while Patrick drove. Violet had a million questions, and he had a lot of information for her.

"I'm sorry for the flood of information," Patrick apologized when he finally put the truck in park at the head of a trail Violet had never seen. "This is all stuff you need to know."

Violet stepped out of the truck when Patrick did, then shrugged. "It's fine, just don't expect me to remember all of it."

"You need to try." Patrick looked at her from the truck bed. "You could need that information at any given time tonight."

Dragging her lower lip between her teeth, Violet moved toward the bed as Patrick reached over the side. He hadn't mentioned Alpha Draven or Jax the entire ride so she decided to prod, "I'm surprised Jax was okay with me being your escort."

Patrick's hand froze on her bag. "He's not." He handed over her bag, then grabbed his own before locking the truck.

"What do you mean he's not?" Violet asked, not bothering to hide the grin that rose to her face. Of course, her mom had already spilled the beans, but she wanted to hear his side of the story.

"Can you try not to sound so pleased?" Patrick walked toward the trail head, leaving her to catch up.

"No. I don't think I can," Violet laughed. "How am I here if he didn't approve?"

Patrick stopped, nearly causing her to run into him. "I went to Luna first. She was very enthusiastic about the idea, but encouraged me not to mention it to Jax until we were already on the road. So, I didn't. He's been chewing me out for the last forty minutes."

Pinching her lips together, Violet peered around Patrick's shoulder to find a slight smirk raising one side of his mouth. "Patrick Cowen... you surprise me."

A huff of laughter escaped him and he shook his head before continuing down the path. "Don't get too excited. I'm sure you're going to get an earful when we get back tomorrow."

"How did you keep up a conversation with me and him at the same time?" Violet hopped over a log that was a measly step for Patrick.

"I barely said anything. It was mostly him yelling." Patrick held a tree branch up for her to walk under then continued by her side. "He isn't that hard to tune out and it only gets you in trouble when he starts asking questions."

Giggling, Violet shook her head. "I had no idea you tuned him out."

"Pfft, all the time."

Violet stared at him wide eyed.

"You've heard how much he can talk. The guy's my best friend, and hopefully always will be, but sometimes..."

A half grin gave away Violet's feelings, "...you just gotta tune him out and let him rant."

"Exactly." Patrick smiled down at her, then jerked his attention away as though he had done something wrong.

Violet bumped into him to avoid a larger tree. "Can I ask you something kinda personal?"

"If you think a personal question isn't allowed then you really haven't been paying attention to what's going to happen tonight."

Blushing, Violet cleared her throat and looked away from him. "It's about your relationships."

"Oh."

"Oh?"

"Yes, oh. That conversation never ends well." Patrick pulled ahead and Violet thought he was angry with her until he hopped atop a fallen tree and reached down for her hand.

After thanking him, and making it over the tree safely, Violet continued, "I'm not trying to start a fight. I just want to know how your date with Robin went and how all that is going?"

"Are you spying on me for her?" Patrick teased, making Violet laugh.

"No. I actually haven't really talked to her since the tourney attack." Violet maneuvered around a few foresty obstacles, and Patrick followed, patiently waiting for her to continue. "She and I used to hang out a lot, but now she's in college and working full time at that restaurant and I'm about to start college… hopefully…"

"I don't know how the two of you are friends," Patrick interrupted, shocking her to silence. "You're nothing alike."

Violet tilted her head to the side. "Two people have to be alike to be friends?"

"No, that's not what I…" Patrick sighed. "She's loud and bossy and really into fashion—"

"Oh thanks," Violet muttered.

"That wasn't a dis on you," Patrick grumbled, then grabbed her arm and turned her to face him. "All I'm saying is I'd be surprised if the two of you have anything in common and to be friends… don't you need some kind of common ground?"

Violet smirked, "We have the same taste in guys."

Patrick's brows rose, then pulled together as his head tilted to the side and a smirk slowly grew across his lips.

Mortification burned Violet's cheeks and she walked backward away from Patrick. "I didn't mean… I… she… I know she was flirting with you, but I…

"Looked jealous."

"I did not!" Violet insisted and probably would have stomped her foot had she not been worried about tripping over something.

Patrick followed after her with that ever-growing smirk and mischief lit up his eyes. "You most certainly did."

"Stop looking at me like that."

"Like what?" Patrick shrugged.

"That. I was not jealous. Besides, we are talking about Robin, and how you don't understand friendship even though she and I aren't…" Violet shrieked when her heel caught on a root.

With the weight of her bag, she fell quickly toward the earth.

Patrick laughed as he pulled her back to safe footing and into the warmth of his chest. "You're clearly falling for me."

Violet glared at him, "That was cheesy and lame." She pushed out of Patrick's arms and returned to walking forward. "Besides, I'd never jeopardize anything for Robin. We were close friends for a long time and, even though we aren't anymore, it's hard to let that go." Curiosity pulled Violet's gaze back to Patrick, "I haven't seen you be so openly friendly with any other girl you've dated. You must be really comfortable with her."

"If I was that comfortable with her then she would be here instead of you."

"What?"

Sighing, Patrick looked up at the darkening canopy above them. "I haven't talked to Robin much since going to the movies. Having her with us at the mall was awkward. Everything with her is awkward. I know she's interested. She and everyone else it seems, but…" Patrick's words faded away.

"Right." Violet nodded. "I almost forgot your decree to be a lone wolf."

With another sigh, Patrick shook his head. "I don't think she would be able to accept every part of me. I'm not sure anyone could."

Violet swallowed the lump in her throat as Patrick stared into her eyes. After nervously biting her lip, Violet gathered the courage to ask, "Does that include me?"

Patrick's chest inflated with a long inhale. "We're about to find out."

They continued down the path until Patrick jerked to a stop and gazed left, into the trees. Violet was about to ask him what was wrong when he stepped off the well-worn path, into the brush.

"It's this way."

With the diminishing light, Violet had been having a hard time seeing where she needed to step on the normal path. How was she supposed to walk through that? If she had her phone with her, she'd use it as a flashlight... but she'd forgotten it on her desk in her bedroom.

Her night vision needed an upgrade.

"How do you know?" Violet breathed, feeling uneasy.

Patrick looked back at her and held out his hand, "It's just a feeling I have."

As Violet stared at Patrick's hand, she could practically hear Jax yelling in her head, but Jax wasn't there. In fact, she hadn't heard him all day. She was alone, in the woods, with the guy she was seriously crushing on, who was offering his hand like a perfect gentleman to lead her deeper into the forest to have a ridiculously personal night together.

Thinking about it that way sent a furious blush from her chest, to her cheeks, to her ears. Pushing those thoughts aside, Violet placed her hand in Patrick's and allowed him to lead her.

Violet tried to focus on anything other than the feel of her hand in his while they walked through the trees, but on a cold, winter night... there weren't many sounds in the woods—and she couldn't see much. Patrick had stopped talking and she was really starting to wish she had remembered her phone when Patrick came to a halt.

"We're here," he breathed.

As far as she could tell, the area before them just looked like a normal patch of forest. Violet was about to question him when he pulled her forward. Her movement slowed as thick, oily, invisible liquid enveloped her, making her gasp. The pungent smell of sulfur filled her lungs and she scrunched her nose. A relieved sigh left her as she was pushed out the other side and the compressing, liquid feeling left her.

That was a ring of magic if she ever felt one. A powerful one. They were now standing in a ring of trees spelled by a powerful, trusted witch. From inside the wall, Violet could see the pinkish smoke rising from the ground, and extended toward the sky beyond her eyesight. The only sounds within the circle were being made by Patrick and Violet.

Their breathing.

Their steps.

Their... hearts?

Violet tucked her hair behind her ear and concentrated on the thumping she heard. She recognized the rhythm of her own heart beat almost immediately since she was also able to feel it... but the second pulse... Violet's gaze lifted to Patrick who was busying himself around a dugout fire pit.

His pulse almost mirrored her own.

Violet's heart quickened, and Patrick froze, then turned to face her as his heart caught up to hers.

"You okay?" He asked, rising from his crouched position.

After spastically nodding her response, Patrick chuckled.

"Okay. We need firewood if we're going to stay warm tonight. I've always hated having a winter birthday, but this is just cruel."

Violet grinned. The idea of sitting around a cozy campfire with him sounded way too good. "I can find some."

"Isn't your eyesight a little..." Patrick's face contorted.

"I can see well enough to gather wood," Violet grumbled, then headed toward the magical wall.

"Violet," Patrick called and when she turned around, he was less than a foot away from her, making her jump. "We should go together."

"That's silly," Violet snorted. "You stay here and set up the site."

"If you run into any trouble, I won't be able to hear you." Patrick's hands curled and uncurled at his sides.

Hesitantly, Violet reached for one of his hands. He jerked back at first, but she couldn't ignore how he visibly relaxed when she didn't let go. "If you're really that worried, then let's go."

Patrick nodded and walked toward the wall.

Violet's shoulder was pulled back as she exited the trial sanctum. When she looked back, her hand had disappeared… and so had Patrick.

"Patrick?" Feeling panicked, Violet squeezed her hand and after a terrifying moment, Patrick squeezed back.

A relieved sigh left her and she stepped back through the wall. "What happened? Why'd you stop?"

Patrick's gaze was focused on the ground. His voice was barely a whisper, "I can't leave."

"Why not?" Violet asked.

"The spell put around this ring is a protection spell."

Violet shrugged, "Yeah, I know. We've been over that."

He released her hand and stepped away from her. "If you remember, part of that spell is to keep unstable wolves inside."

Violet's lips parted as she thought about that statement. Her head slowly started shaking, "Patrick, you are not unstable. It can probably tell you're the one here for the trial so it won't let you out. It's not a big deal."

"Maybe." He agreed, but it sounded half-hearted. "I wasn't sure how to tell you, but you need to know what you're getting into. You can still back out."

Violet snorted, "Don't be ridiculous, I'm not going anywhere."

Patrick backed up a few more steps. "Vi, I'm probably the most unstable wolf you've ever come across."

"You can't start thinking like that," coached Violet, stepping toward him. "You need to go into the trial thinking positively."

Patrick countered her steps, keeping her at arm's length. "I almost killed that Blood Moon scout, I barely stopped myself at only knocking Vikter out…"

"Stop it," Violet shook her head again, not wanting to hear him talk like this. He was always so confident. Why was he so afraid now?

"I had the thought to chase after Zander and…"

"Patrick!" Violet leapt forward and grabbed his arms to keep him from moving away from her. "Stop." She bit her lips as tears built in her eyes. "This isn't like you. You can't go into the trial like this. You're losing before you even begin."

Patrick's shoulders slumped. "That's just it, Vi…" His voice tipped toward more beast than man as he continued. "I've just been holding off the inevitable. The truth is—I lost a long time ago."

She was about to tell him she didn't understand when his hazel eyes swirled into an all-consuming deep blood red.

Chapter 20

Violet

FEAR PULLED VIOLET AWAY FROM PATRICK *with lightning speed.* Her back smacked against the trunk of one of the trees barely sticking into the protective ring. Unable to lock her brain around what she was seeing, Violet froze and waited for the immobilizing fear to pass.

Patrick hadn't moved.

Other than the pulse in his jaw, he could have been a statue.

Violet's pulse thundered in her ears, drowning out the sound of her rapid breathing as her heart raced a hundred miles an hour. Then the second heartbeat she'd heard earlier returned, faster and even harder than her own.

Fear rolled off Patrick in waves as he stood with his hands clenched at his sides.

Ever so slowly, Violet walked toward him. Only his eye color had changed, right? If his personality had changed, he would be attacking her… wouldn't he?

This was still Patrick… and he was waiting for her.

Patrick's nearly luminescent red eyes followed her, but he did not move. Not even when she laid a hand on his arm and gradually slid up to his shoulder.

It wasn't until her fingers brushed his neck that he swallowed hard, pinched his eyes shut, and spoke through clenched teeth, "What are you doing?"

"When did this happen?"

"Before I came to Sentinel Clan."

"Everything makes sense now."

Patrick opened his eyes and looked at her again with that reddened gaze, but confusion pulled his brows together, "What?"

Dropping her hand to her side, Violet shrugged. "How careful you've been with losing your temper, not wanting to have your wolf connect with you during your party, the look Zander gave you…"

Patrick groaned, "That was a mistake."

The longer she looked at him, the less scary his red eyes were. They weren't cold or hungry like the Blood Moon scouts she'd seen. They weren't filled with a never-ending hatred or lack of humanity.

Sure, his eyes were red. Which meant he had killed someone… but Violet had never seen so much fear and warmth at the same time.

"Are you trying to scare me away?" Violet finally asked, when it was clear Patrick was waiting for something.

His answer was almost a whisper, "No."

"Then what are you doing?"

"Showing you who I really am." Patrick's eyes narrowed in wonder, "Why haven't you asked?"

It took a moment for Violet to answer and when she did, her shoulders raised, "Because I already know who you are. If you want me to know what happened, you'll tell me."

"But… you're not scared."

"I was at first. That was very shocking and probably not the best way you could have told me," Violet admitted. "But like I said, I know you. I've lived with you and watched you for years. You're fiercely loyal, protective to a fault, sweet when you're not holding back, unbelievably thoughtful when you're not actively trying to be a jerk, and you're the best friend my brother has ever had..." Realization dawned on her, cutting off her train of thought, "Huh, that's why he did that."

Jax didn't know Patrick all that well when he'd forced Violet to make that awful promise... and even now he—if he knew, which he had to with being future alpha, son of the alpha, and Patrick's best friend—Jax would know that if news of Patrick's eyes got out, life would be very difficult for him and his mate. Jax had been protecting her this whole time.

"Who did what?" Patrick asked.

Violet shook her head. "Never mind. The point is, you are still you. It doesn't matter what your eye color is." She stepped into his space, making him draw in a sharp breath, and placed her hands on either side of his face. "You're still Patrick, and I trust you with my life."

Lowering his head, he closed his eyes and rested his forehead against hers. A weary sigh left him as his hands found her waist and Violet listened to his heart calm. "You have no idea how hard it's been keeping this from you."

"Considering you're around me a lot of the time, I can imagine."

A small chuckle rumbled in Patrick's chest.

"Now," Violet pulled her head back and when he opened his eyes, they were back to their beautiful hazel color. She gave him a serious look. "I don't know everything you're thinking, or feeling, or going through right now, but I do know that you have to get your head in the right space if you're going to make it through tonight."

Patrick gave a small nod.

"I know not being able to walk through that wall freaked you out, but after tonight, nothing is ever going to hold you back again. And in the morning, I am going to take your hand and we are going to walk out of here together."

"Okay," Patrick's voice was so quiet, she almost missed his response.

Violet planted her hands on his shoulders, "Now, I'm going to get some firewood while you set up the camp. I'm no good at that, anyway."

A small smile tilted a corner of Patrick's lips, but as she stepped away from him, his hand caught hers. "You're coming back, right?"

Warmth pooled around her heart. Violet threw her arms around

Patrick's neck. "I promise I won't ever leave you."

Patrick's arms encircled her waist, nearly lifting her feet off the ground. His embrace was entirely too comfortable and it took everything in her to push away from him.

She gave a reassuring smile over her shoulder just before stepping through the oily wall of magic. The moment she was through her knees buckled.

She stayed on the ground, thinking through everything until she was certain her brain had wrapped around... most of it. With a final deep breath, she pushed herself off the ground, dusted the dirt from her jeans and said, "Okay. Let's do this."

It didn't take long for her to find enough firewood to last the night. Every time she found a suitable log or stick, she would chuck it through the magical barrier and watch it disappear.

Violet stepped through the magical barrier with the last log and smiled, "Is that enough?"

Patrick looked at her with wide eyes, "I thought you were aiming for me a few times."

Gasping, Violet dropped the log she was holding and planted a hand over her mouth. "I'm so sorry, I didn't even think about that!"

"Clearly!" Patrick chuckled. "It was entertaining to watch."

"Oh," Violet's hand lowered as embarrassment flooded through her. "I didn't think about that either."

Patrick nodded as he bent over the sleeping bag, he'd been unrolling onto a camping mat. "You had me worried when you collapsed right after leaving. I really am sorry if I scared you, and I know that is a lot, too..."

Shaking her head, Violet stepped around the now full fire pit. "No, it wasn't too much. I mean, it was a lot, but I just needed a minute to process everything." She lifted her arms out to the sides. "I'm fine now."

Patrick looked over her as a small smile softened the hard lines of his jaw, "You really are, aren't you?"

With a nod, Violet turned toward the fire pit. "How do we get this going because it is getting really cold!"

"Here." Patrick removed his jacket and laid it over her shoulders.

The lingering warmth and the overwhelming scent of chocolate peppermint made her sigh. Even with her puffy winter coat that her mom insisted she take, Violet still felt the bitter nip of a forest winter throughout her limbs.

"I'll work on the fire next."

"Don't you need this?" Violet wondered as he moved around the pit.

"Not right now. I'm pretty warm."

Concern pulled Violet toward Patrick. He raised a brow when she placed the back of her hand against his forehead.

"You have a fever," Violet whispered and removed her hand before looking up at the stars. The moon had begun to peak over the canopy of trees. "It's nearing the apex."

Patrick let out a heavy sigh, "No wonder I'm feeling off."

A wolven's first shift was always the hardest and didn't happen until the first full moon after their eighteenth birthday when the moon was at its highest. Or in this case, the center of the ring of trees.

Violet's gaze drifted to Patrick, "Are you ready?"

"Whether I am or not, this is happening." Patrick tossed a lighter in the air and caught it without looking, "I better get this done."

Kneeling down, Patrick moved to light the fire. The lighter clicked, but no fire came out. A groan left Patrick. His knuckles pressed against the earth.

"It's not a big deal, just try it again."

"That's not..." The lighter fell from Patrick's as he doubled over. Dark claws spread from his nails, digging into the earth.

Violet dropped to her knees beside him and rested her hand on his back as it spasmed.

"Start it," Patrick growled, sounding more beast-like. "You need to stay warm."

"Your body is literally starting to tear itself apart to adopt a new form." She brushed the longer pieces of his hair out of his face, and her fingers lingered at the tips of his ears which had elongated. "I'm not focused on building a fire at the moment."

"Violet!" Patrick rounded on her with blood red eyes and she jerked back, that would take some getting used to. Two long fangs touched his bottom lip as he spoke, "The temperature is dropping. You will go into hyperthermic shock and then you won't be any help to anyone. Start the fire!"

Nodding frantically, Violet grabbed the lighter he'd dropped and clicked it over and over.

A painful howl made Violet jump, nearly losing the lighter in the process, and she looked back as Patrick pulled his shirt off, exposing the contorting muscles along his back.

"First stage," Violet whispered to herself.

A wolven trial happened over four stages. The first was often referred to as The Void. Most wolven never remembered this part, which was a blessing considering their bodies tore themselves apart to figure out how to shift. They all talked about how easy it was to shift back and forth after the trial with little to no pain.

Watching Patrick writhe in agony, Violet wasn't sure how that could ever be possible, and there was a part of her that was grateful she would never experience it.

He fell to his hands and knees, his shirt clutched in one hand as a nasty, ripple rolled down his spine. The bones swelled, enlarging his ribcage, then snapped back into place with a gut-wrenching thwack. Patrick fell to the ground in a trembling heap then lifted himself up onto his elbows.

Violet had only taken a step toward him when he growled, "Fire. Now."

"You need help," Violet countered.

"Then hurry up with the fire."

Frustration escaped her on the tail of a large sigh. "You're infuriating, you know that?"

A shaky, breathy laugh met her ears as the lighter clicked and fire came to life. It took longer than she hoped for the starter leaves and twigs to catch. Another sharp howl made her jump, and she nearly dropped the lighter into the fire.

"It's lit!" She set the lighter on one of the sleeping bags then hurried to Patrick's side as he convulsed again. Something snapped inside him and a very human cry tore at Violet's heart. "What can I do?"

Unable to form words, Patrick shook his head.

There wasn't anything she could do.

Nearly two hours passed in this violent agony. The worst was when

Patrick was stuck in a holding pattern for more than ten minutes, halfway between wolf and man. Salty tears had dried on Violet's cheeks now that Patrick's body had stopped ripping itself apart.

Black fur covered most of Patrick's wolf form as he lay, breathing deeply beside her outstretched legs while she leaned back against the trunk of a tree. There were some areas of brownish red, even a couple places of white like the strip on his chest or one of his back feet. Violet's hand was nearly swallowed by his thick, wavy coat as she ran her hand between his black ears and down his neck. It had taken a few minutes being in this form before Patrick's body had stopped trembling, then he'd collapsed and passed out.

He'd made it to the second stage—The Treaty. Even while passed out, Patrick would be finding a balance between him and his wolf as they figured out how to be two sides of the same coin. Some found this as easy as a handshake, while others mentally battled themselves to decide who was alpha—wolf or man. The third stage—The Pact—began when an agreement was made, then both sides worked together to return to human form.

Patrick's ear twitched when Violet ran her fingers along its velvety tip and a soft laugh escaped her. His body tensed, then he opened his eyes.

"Hey, you're awake," Violet smiled at him when he turned his large head in her direction. "Sorry if that was my fault."

He stared down his black muzzle, lined with brownish-red on either side, then blinked lazily at her.

Violet's smile faded. She couldn't talk with him in this form.

With shaky limbs, Patrick lifted himself off the ground so he was standing on all fours.

Violet made her way to her feet, as well, and practically stared straight into his eyes. "Darn, even in wolf form, you're still taller than me. Although your ears may be considered cheating."

A very human-like snort left Patrick, making Violet grin.

"At least I know you can understand me."

Patrick's eyes softened as he watched her, then he slowly pushed back onto his haunches.

"You look amazing," Violet told him and his eyes narrowed a little before his head tilted to the side, "That was almost too human for a wolf."

A huff of laughter puffed Patrick's chest.

"Don't let it go to your head, okay?" Violet teased. She stepped forward and extended her hand toward his muzzle. "I've never seen a wolf with your coloring before. I've seen all black or a combination of a bunch of colors, but yours is very unique. And your eyes..."

Patrick pulled his muzzle away and gave her a narrowed look.

"They aren't red," Violet told him, taking another step. "Your eyes are that gorgeous hazel they always are, but the flecks of gold are larger. Did you know that you had gold in your eyes?"

His gaze darted all over her as she closed the distance between them to less than a foot. Hesitantly, Patrick rested his muzzle against her hand. His eyes closed when she brushed her hand down the length of his muzzle and onto his neck.

"I'm sorry I can't hear you," Violet whispered while her heart ached.

Patrick's eyes opened.

"I wish I could." Violet shrugged a shoulder, "I'm sure being able to talk to someone during this would be easier."

Violet stepped back when he stood, but he stepped toward her and dropped his head over her shoulder. Her shoulders deflated with a sigh before she wrapped her arms around his furry neck.

Pulling away from him, Violet asked, "Are you ready?"

Patrick's body shook from nose to tail.

"I'm sorry you have to go through this again, but I'm here and I'm not going anywhere." Violet promised and ran a hand down his neck again. "Living here would be kind of weird though, so don't take too long, kay? I need you to shift back so we can go home together."

Trial wolven had until sunrise to complete stage three. More than a few wolves never turned back, which is why the anchor was so important. They helped remind the human side what they stood to lose if they gave in to the fear of pain or couldn't find an agreement. Even with that, some remained as wolves, which was where the myths of fantastical sized dire wolves came from.

Patrick used his nose to push her toward the fire, pulling her from her thoughts.

Laughing, Violet turned toward him and grabbed his mostly black face. "Are you still on about that? I'm fine." She released him and fluffed the fur on top of his head, "You're giving off an impressive amount of body heat. Plus, I'm starting to think the magic barrier helps insulate this area."

A tremor ran up Patrick's spine, making his hackles rise. His eyes closed and his lips curled back in a snarl exposing his sharp wolf teeth.

"I guess you're ready then?"

Patrick nodded through the trembling.

"I'm right here," Violet reminded him.

When Patrick opened his eyes again, they were blazing red.

Violet held his face and promised once again, "I'm not going anywhere.

He stayed in her hands as long as he could while his body shivered, convulsed, and broke itself to try and reverse the process. Eventually he had to move away, or his spasms could have caused her harm. His claws stretched and dug into the growl. Pained howls shattered the quiet of the darkened forest.

Two hours passed and Patrick was still in his wolf form, trembling on his side.

Hesitantly, Violet made her way toward him and sat near his head, "Patrick, can you hear me?"

The giant black wolf groaned in response.

As gently as possible, Violet scooted her legs closer and tried to lift his head onto her lap. "Why is your head so heavy?"

A huff of laughter expanded his chest before he maneuvered his body to be able to lay his head on her lap.

"You've been laying here for ten minutes," Violet ran her hand down his furry neck and shoulder. "I know you're tired. I know it's easier to give in, but you can't. I won't let you."

Violet thought Patrick had a good side eye as a human, but it was nothing compared to the look he was giving her now.

"Don't look at me like that. You're stronger than this. You have a life to live, promises to keep, a future as a beta... Jax needs you. You make him a better person and somehow manage to keep his head screwed on semi straight."

Patrick snorted.

"It's time." Violet hardened her voice in an attempt to sound commanding. "You're going to get up, you're going to put everything you have into this, and next thing you know you'll be standing a foot taller than me again. Now let's go."

He didn't move.

Violet rolled her legs out from under his head then knelt beside him and, before she could think about it too much, planted a kiss on his muzzle. "You can do this," Violet whispered as Patrick stared at her with wide eyes. "You need to do this! Get. Up!"

The rise and fall of Patrick's chest increased until he rolled back onto his paws. His body shook. His claws carved canyons into the dirt as his body contorted and began to reshape.

"Come on, Patrick!" Violet cheered him on. "You can do this!"

Patrick howled, and his body reverted back then started all over again. Blood red filled his eyes. He turned toward her, holding her gaze, and Violet repeated her encouraging words.

After a few more tries and slips, Patrick's light-colored skin returned. His claws retracted, shifting back to human nails. He shook his head as his ears slipped back to the sides of his head, but they still had pointed tips even after he dropped to his hands and knees, breathing heavily.

"You did it!" Violet screamed, then ran forward with a blanket and a change of clothes. "I'll hug you once you're dressed again."

Patrick's hoarse laugh made Violet dart away to find his water bottle. By the time it was in her hands, he'd pulled on some pants, but it took everything in her not to stare at his torso. His abs and chest were extra pumped like he'd been lifting weights for hours, and his veins were ever so slightly raised along his arms and near his waistband.

Taking care of his body had always been important to Patrick, and it showed in his physique, training, and combat. He outmatched more than half of the mature wolven before his birthday. Now that he'd reached maturity, Violet wasn't sure if there was any wolven that could beat him. She wondered briefly how much of that was due to the red eyes...

"Here," Violet held out the water for him, but jumped back when he aggressively snatched it from her hands.

After nearly downing the entire thing, he smashed the lid closed and tossed it on the ground.

Worry pulled Violet's brows down as she took a step toward him,

"Patrick?"

A deep chuckle shook her to the bones and Patrick's head turned toward her. The wicked half grin on his lips, that exposed a sharp fang, sent a shiver down her spine even before she noticed his eyes—which were still glowing red... and did not look friendly.

"Patrick can't come out to play right now."

It was Patrick's voice... sort of... but deeper and full of malice.

Violet swallowed the lump in her throat and took a step back, "Alistair."

When his half grin returned, a fang slipped over his bottom lip. "Hello, gorgeous."

"Well, you're creepy," grimaced Violet.

"Nice to see you, too." Alistair ran a hand through his hair. The familiar habit was disturbing, and the remaining pointed ears made it even more so. "It's so good to be free!"

"I thought the third trial was about finding balance between your two halves and working together," Violet grumbled, kicking her hip to the side as she crossed her arms. "I think you're breaking the rules."

"Actually, it was Boy Scout who broke the rules. You, my dear, are mixing up the second and third trials. He never let me out while he was using my wolf form, so there was no compromise to be made. Not that I'm complaining; it worked in my favor. Besides," Alistair winked, "I've never been a fan of rules. They make life boring. I've been stuck living that life for years."

"Patrick's life is not boring."

"Really?" Alistair chuckled and began circling her.

Although Violet remained where she was, she turned with him, keeping him in her sight at all times.

"When was the last time Patrick let loose? When was the last time you saw him with a side ache from laughing so hard? Have you ever seen his emotions run him instead of logically thinking things through? Or did something just because it was fun?"

Other than when he lost control defending her... no. She didn't think that was what Alistair was talking about, anyway. Patrick hadn't done any of those things. Violet looked off to the side.

Faster than she could process, he surged forward, and Violet sucked in a sharp breath. His bare chest brushed against her folded arms, making her fight against taking a step back.

"How do you move so fast?" Violet blurted.

"Pure, raw, wolf power. Something you haven't experienced yet, sadly." Alistair leaned toward her, "You know, without all of Patrick's rules, you and I could rule the world."

"World domination?" Violet briefly narrowed her eyes to show her sarcasm as she said, "How original."

"Ooh, I like you."

"The feeling is not mutual," Violet grumbled.

Alistair's deep, throaty laugh sent goosebumps up her arms.

"So, what's your plan?" Violet stepped away from him, but kept him in her peripheral vision as she moved to grab her water bottle.

"Easy," Alistair shrugged. He lifted a hand and started counting on his fingers as he moved toward her, "Get you to like me instead of Boy Scout, destroy Boy Scout at sunrise, leave this awful ring that reeks of witch, join up with Blood Moon—they seem more my speed—and live the life of my dreams with you and your own set of ruby eyes beside me."

It took everything Violet had not to react as he listed off his plan, but her fingers clutched her water bottle while she drank. She took her time, slowly drinking her water while she thought things over, then—just as slowly—closed it and tossed it back on the sleeping bag.

Sunrise wasn't for another two and a half hours, but from the easy way Alistair talked, and how quickly he moved, it was clear he wasn't struggling to remain in control.

"I'm sure you know this, but..." Violet shrugged, "...Patrick couldn't leave this ring before. What makes you think you can?"

Alistair rolled his eyes, "Boy Scout has been at war with himself ever since I showed up all those years ago." He shook his head and paced the width of the ring. "He hasn't been able to forgive himself for those three teenagers he killed..."

Violet's heart seized... three?

"... Oops. You didn't know that, did you?" Alistair chuckled. "In doing so, I was released. I won't lie to you, I enjoyed feeling another's life blood on my hands, but my goal is not to harm anyone. I only want to be free to do what I want. Instead of working with me, Boy Scout and I have fought ever since, but that will all end at sunrise." Alistair looked up at the stars. "He's too weak to fight me off now."

Panic made Violet's heart race. She hadn't thought about how weak Patrick would be after shifting, and then adding in the fact that he fought Alistair off the entire time he was in wolf form… did he even stand a chance?

Alistair's gaze slid back to her, and she knew he could hear her heart by the way his eyes narrowed.

"You didn't answer my question," Violet grumbled, hoping to distract him.

With a shake of his head, Alistair continued, "It's simple. Boy Scout has been fighting with himself for years, on the verge of mental collapse, really. Once he's gone it will just be me, and I can assure you, I have no issue with who I am."

Violet really hoped that wasn't how the ring worked. "Clearly you aren't going to hurt me."

"Glad to hear you trust me, gorgeous."

"Don't call me that," Violet growled then released a calming breath through her nose. "Sunrise isn't for a couple hours. What are we supposed to do until then?"

Alistair swaggered up beside her, "I can think of a few really fun ways to pass time. Bonus, it would drive old Boy Scout here berserk."

Violet snorted and her nose scrunched, "In your dreams."

Alistair's nasty grin exposed both fangs this time, "You have no idea."

Disgust drew Violet's chin back as her face scrunched even farther.

"Come on, you have to admit, I'm way more fun," Alistair trailed his clawed finger down her jaw and neck only to have her smack his hand away. He laughed, tipping his head back.

"I'm not some game to be played for your enjoyment," Violet snapped.

All amusement drained from Alistair's face. His hands slammed into her, knocking her back into a tree. Violet struggled for air, clutching her hand against her stomach. When she gasped, Alistair pressed one hand against the base of her throat to hold her there.

"Patrick will be gone when that sun rises," Alistair growled in her face, but the lack of pressure on her neck remained the same. He was threatening her, but allowing her to breathe. "I know you yearn for him. I see you, even when he doesn't, watching him… longing for him."

"Shut up," Violet's voice wavered. She did *not* want Patrick to know any of that.

Alistair pushed off her and headed toward one of the sleeping bags, "I'll give you some time to think it through." He flopped onto the sleeping bag and rested his hands behind his head. "I'm the closest thing you will ever have to him."

Chapter 21

Violet

***"PATRICK'S TIME IS RUNNING OUT,"** Alistair reminded her and pointed toward the open canopy.*

The sky was starting to lighten with the promise of a new day… and that promise weighed around her neck like a noose.

She'd tried being snarky.

She'd tried being sweet.

She even tried reasoning, which admittedly was not her strong suit.

Everything Violet did only made Alistair angrier.

"Alistair?" Violet softened her voice which immediately pulled Alistair's attention. She only had one trick left up her sleeve and she'd been hoping she wouldn't have to use it. "What was that promise you made me?"

Alistair raised a brow. His still shirtless torso curled, making his abs flex as he rolled onto one elbow. "Which one?"

"The one about you being similar to Patrick," Violet reminded him while playing with the bottom of her jacket.

With the same speed he'd had hours before, Alistair was suddenly standing in front of her, lowering his head toward hers. "No," he teased, trailing his clawed finger down her jaw like he had before. "I told you I could be a near perfect replacement."

Violet's skin crawled, but she bit her lower lip and leaned heavily against the tree behind her, hoping to mask her disgust. "How?"

Alistair blinked, "What?"

"Show me how." Violet gently commanded. "If I'm going to consider this, I need to know what I'm getting into."

Alistair's fangs slipped over his bottom lip when he grinned.

"How's this?" His voice smoothed out, replicating Patrick's. He stepped away, shoving his hands into his jean pockets. If his eyes had been hazel with the same warmth Patrick had been showing her lately, it would have been a convincing copy.

Shaking her head, Violet clutched the tree behind her. "Not good enough."

"Why not?" Alistair asked with Patrick's voice. "Isn't this what you wanted?"

"No..." Violet made her voice crack and she looked at the ground, "Because Patrick never wanted me. He never needed me. And I..."

Alistair walked into her space and Violet stopped talking. If this didn't work, he might be angry enough to kill her.

When his hand raised, Violet couldn't stop her flinch, but then his palm rested gently against her, his fingers spreading into her hair. Leaning into his touch, Violet closed her eyes.

The scary thing was... with how gentle Alistair was being—and with her eyes closed—Violet could almost imagine it was Patrick in front of her.

But when Alistair's body pressed against hers, they clashed in all the wrong places. Her body tensed. It didn't make sense, whenever Patrick held her, she fit perfectly. This was the same body... but it wasn't *him.*

"It's okay." His whisper sounded exactly like Patrick and it broke her heart. "I'm here. I've always needed you, Vi."

Electricity shot through Violet at the sound of her nickname. Whenever Patrick used her nickname, he spoke it with a breathy, almost reverent tone. Alistair's version was clipped, abrupt, and lacked warmth. Her head tipped back when he moved his hand to the nape of her neck and his hot breath touched her lips.

Violet's eyes shot open just as his closed. He lowered his head toward hers.

"There's something wrong," she breathed.

"What?" Alistair grazed her bottom lip with his fang and Violet dug her nails into the tree trunk. "Tell me and I can fix it."

"You're not him." Violet growled.

Alistair's gaze locked onto hers, but for the briefest second, his eyes were hazel.

"Patrick, I know you're in there." Violet tried to reach him for what felt like the hundredth time. "I know you're tired..."

Alistair's lips curled back in a snarl, "Stop."

"... but I can't leave here without you." Violet shook her head and stepped toward Alistair as he backed away. "I *won't* leave here without you."

Alistair growled. Stepping back into her space, he extended his claws and grabbed her shoulders painfully, "Don't you see the sun rising? Patrick is gone!"

Violet shook her head, "You think his silence over these last few hours has been his sign of giving up?"

Alistair's eyes narrowed. "It is!"

"Wrong!" Violet yelled back. "He has been biding his time. Regaining his strength, so he could take you down for good."

It was brief, but Violet caught the fear that flashed over Alistair's eyes. "He can't get rid of me. I will always be a part of him."

"Give him back, Alistair."

A sneer lifted Alistair's mouth, "I love the way you say my name."

"Give him back!" Violet threw an upper cut between his arms. Her fist collided with Alistair's jaw.

Surprised, Alistair released her shoulders and took two steps backward. Instead of being angry, he grinned, "That's more like it. I have always loved a good sparring match with you."

Anger pulsed through Violet's blood, "I'm not giving up on you, Patrick."

Violet spun around, ready to kick the crap out of Alistair, but he caught her foot and the next thing she knew, her back was pressed into the ground. Alistair straddled her hips and she struggled against his weight.

"Get off me!" She screamed at him, throwing a lazy punch while she shifted her position under him, drawing her feet closer to her butt.

Alistair laughed, "I can feel him slipping." His claws gripped her chin. "Do you see the light, Violet? You've lost."

"Never," Violet thrust her hips toward the sky, knocking Alistair over her. She rolled with him, using his own momentum against him, and landed in the same position he had been previously.

His hoarse laugh sent goosebumps up her arms, but he didn't struggle, which was exactly what she'd hoped for.

Violet's heart pounded as she pressed her hands against Patrick's bare chest and stared straight into Alistair's red eyes. She had to stop focusing on Alistair. This was Patrick, and she was getting him back.

"Patrick, I know you can hear me." Violet imagined Patrick's beautiful hazel eyes and the way they lit up whenever she embarrassed herself. She knew it was impossible to mind-link with him, but she projected her thoughts as loudly as she could anyway.

"What are you doing?" Alistair snared her upper arms, instantly bruising her.

She flinched, but kept talking, "Fight him, Patrick! I know you can win this! This isn't you."

Dry leaves crackled under his head as Alistair tipped his chin back and laughed, "Really? You're smarter than this. How do you think I have so much control? This is him."

Shaking her head, Violet tried again, "I know you."

Alistair sat up and she shifted her hands to Patrick's shoulders. Ignoring Alistair's nasty grin as his hands moved from her arms to her back. His claws dug into her jacket, shredding the material as his hands moved toward her hips.

"You're wasting your time, Violet. But I'm still willing to give you a chance."

Violet clenched her jaw, determined not to give him any attention. "You are good," she whispered, but her voice grew stronger as she continued, '... and kind and selfless and so incredibly frustrating at times."

Alistair's grin faltered.

"You are stronger than you realize. You're the strongest person I know." Violet's thumb grazed over Patrick's cheek as she stared into his ruby red eyes. "You're Jax's rock and best friend. You are meant to be his beta. You made a promise to him, Patrick. You cannot break that promise. Jax needs you."

Alistair snorted, but Violet caught the flicker of uncertainty in his eyes.

Laying it all on the line, Violet pressed her forehead against Patrick's as her voice faded to a whisper, "I need you."

Anger pulsed off Alistair. "I'm done playing games, Vi," he growled as his claws cut through her clothing and dug into the tender flesh of her back.

Pinching her eyes shut, Violet bit her lip against the pain. "Come back to me, Patrick."

Alistair cursed.

A fierce growl echoed off the spelled wall around them, shaking Violet to the core. Alistair grabbed her hips and a moment of fear shot through Violet. If he threw her off, that would be it. The sky was light now. If the sun hadn't risen already, it would very soon. All it had to do was crest over the mountains, and Patrick's fate would be sealed.

When he spoke again, his voice sounded like he'd been without water for days—gravelly and deep, "It's not nice..."

Violet's forehead slipped off his and crashed against his shoulder. A sob tugged at her chest.

They'd lost.

He cleared his throat and tried again, "It's not nice... to use your tiny, unimposing body against others."

Gasping, Violet jerked upright as tears streamed down her cheeks.

Hazel eyes stared back at her with the warmth of the sun that brightened the sky to a light blue, "But I think I'll make an exception this time."

Violet threw her arms around Patrick's neck, making him groan when she squeezed.

"That's a little tight and I'm really sore."

"Deal with it," Violet smiled against the crook of his neck and a huff of laughter shook his chest.

Patrick wrapped his arms around her back and agony shot through her.

Gasping as the lightning bolt of pain made her vision temporarily go black, Violet slammed her hands against his shoulders, pushing him away.

"What's wrong?" Patrick asked, his voice tipping toward frantic.

He held her forearms, then froze, staring at his hands. Blood tipped each finger and painted each nail. A string of curses left his mouth.

"What did he do?" Patrick lifted her off his lap with ease then made his way behind her. A sharp breath pulled through his teeth did nothing to calm her nerves. "He did this?" Patrick growled.

Violet dug her fingers into her thighs while Patrick examined her back. "If it's any consolation, I'm not sure he meant to. At least not to my skin. He was definitely destroying my jacket though," she grumbled.

"He destroyed more than that. I need you to remove your coat and shirt."

Even with Patrick's serious tone, the thought of undressing in front of him made Violet's heart skip.

"I have to clean this," Patrick continued, oblivious to her unease. "... and make sure no fibers got caught in the tears before I bandage it."

"Stop," Violet held her hands up when she turned toward him, the twisting motion pulled at her back and she winced. "I'm okay."

"You are not okay," Patrick argued, "Your back is drenched in blood and you are still bleeding."

"I know." Whatever adrenaline she'd had must have been wearing off because a sharp sting had settled over her back. "We were told to be out of the ring right after sunrise, weren't we?"

"Violet..."

"I don't want to chance anything!" Violet gripped his forearms. "I just got you back," she added softly, "I won't lose you again."

Patrick's gaze softened. "I'm not going anywhere." He sighed, lifting his hand toward his hair, but caught sight of the blood still staining his fingers and lowered his hand back to his side. "They only say that so people don't linger. Nothing bad is going to happen if we fix up your back before we go."

Realizing there was nothing stopping them now, Violet nervously shifted her weight, then flinched when it pulled against the cuts in her back.

Tension pulsed in Patrick's jaw. He held out a hand toward the fire pit, "Let's get you cleaned up."

"I don't want to do this," Violet voiced her fears in a whisper.

Careful not to touch her with his bloody hands, Patrick wrapped an arm around her shoulders. Her surprise nearly buckled her knees when he pressed a gentle kiss to her forehead. "Do you trust me?"

A smile tugged at Violet's lips and a small laugh escaped her, "More than you know."

"I think I have an idea." With his arm still around her, Patrick led her to a log next to the firepit. "I'm surprised you were able to keep the fire going all night."

"I'm not sure if I should feel pride in that statement or be offended." Violet grimaced as she sat down and started trying to wiggle out of her destroyed jacket.

"Pride." Patrick answered from behind her. "You had a lot to deal with."

Violet snorted, "I knew..." She froze as pain shot through her back. "I think I need help."

With Patrick's aid, they managed to pull the jacket off her before he threw it in the fire. There was no point keeping it and bad things had happened in the past when scientists got a hold of wolven blood.

"I knew," Violet started again, "if I let the fire die and you saw that, I'd never hear the end of it."

A strained laugh brushed the back of her neck, "So you kept it going out of fear?"

"Self-preservation." Violet countered while she undid the last button of her shirt. Exhaling a long, shaky breath, she slowly unbuttoned the cuffs.

Patrick took the moment to wash his hands, dig out a first aid kit from his pack, and grab a blanket for her before kneeling behind her.

Violet's hands trembled when she pulled the shirt off her shoulders.

"Do you want help?"

Violet bit her lip, then nodded. His fingers brushed her nearly bare shoulders, making goosebumps rise along her arms while he gently pulled one sleeve at a time.

"Are you alright?" He asked softly when Violet clutched the blanket against her chest.

"It's kinda cold."

"Sorry. I'll try to be as gentle and fast as I can."

Violet buried her face in the blanket when Patrick's fingers grazed her back. She was thankful she didn't need to remove her bra, but Patrick did raise the band a couple times while he worked. The sting she'd felt before turned into a blazing burn when Patrick started cleaning out the gashes across her back.

The blanket came in handy when the pain became too much, blocking out her whimpers and protecting her palms from her nails as her hands curled into fists.

"I'm almost done," Patrick assured her with a hoarse voice. "I'm sorry. If I had gained control sooner..."

"Don't," Violet grunted into the blanket, then lifted her head. "This was not your fault."

After a sigh, Patrick fell silent again. The next thing he said was a few torturous minutes later, "Done. Now just the bandages."

Relieved, Violet sank into the blanket.

"This is just gauze." Patrick's fingers feathered over her back and sides. "Apparently we need to replace the medical tape and a bunch of other stuff. The only thing we have to secure the gauze is a wrap."

Violet groaned, "I wish I healed as fast as you do."

He pulled the new wrap from the first aid kit and tore off the packaging. "You'll get there, but for now, we'll use what we can." He unwound the first two feet and looked over her shoulder for permission.

Sighing, Violet pushed the blanket down to her lap. "Alright. Make me look like a mummy."

With a smirk, Patrick slipped an arm around her.

Violet gasped when his fingers brushed her stomach.

Patrick stumbled over an apology as he continued wrapping her torso. "That should keep everything in place." He smoothed a hand down her back, careful to avoid any direct contact with her wounds. "Any chance you brought an extra shirt?"

Heat burned from Violet's chest, to her cheeks, and ears. "I wasn't expecting to need an extra one." She buried her face in the blanket. "You were the one shifting—not me."

Patrick's chuckle filled her with a different kind of warmth. "Here."

Peaking over the blanket, Violet sighed with relief. "Thank you," she took the dark green shirt he was offering and quickly slid it over her head. "I was worried I would be returning wrapped up in a blanket."

The long sleeved, V neck, men's shirt was far too big on her. The hemline touched the top of her thighs, the sleeves slid past her hands, and the neck line either slipped off one shoulder or exposed way more skin in the front than she was comfortable with… but it was soft and smelled faintly of chocolate peppermint.

"I would never let you go home in a blanket. I'm glad I had the sense to take my shirt off before I shifted, though." Patrick ran his hand through his hair then rubbed the back of his neck while Violet tucked the front of his shirt into her jeans. "Jax is already going to need to be held back with me going against his wishes and seeing you in my shirt. Once he finds out about your back…"

"Don't tell him." Violet suggested, opting for the exposed shoulder instead of indecent cleavage. "I'll be healed in a few days."

"Vi, I have to tell him."

Upon hearing his breathy tone speak her nickname, Violet closed her eyes momentarily. "Say that again."

"I have to tell him?" Patrick lifted a brow.

"No." Violet shook her head. "My nickname. I hated the way Alistair said it."

A ghost of a smile appeared on Patrick's face. "Vi."

She grinned.

"You know I'm going to tell him."

Her grin disappeared. "Then he really will kill you."

Patrick shook his head, attempting to hide his smile as he packed everything up. When Violet tried to help, he made her sit down on the log again, insisting she rest so the gauze would stay in place.

She would never admit it out loud, but when Patrick finally did put on a shirt, Violet was more than a little disappointed.

"I think that's everything," Patrick patted himself down and took note of his keys, wallet, and phone. "Let's get you home to Doc."

Violet nodded in agreement as Patrick rested his jacket over her shoulders and led her toward the magical wall. "Are you ready?"

Patrick looked around them for a moment. "When we came in here last night, I was terrified I wouldn't make it back out." He sighed contently and smiled down at her. "I'm not afraid anymore."

Seizing the moment, Violet wrapped her hand around his and tried to ignore the flip her stomach did when his fingers readily interlocked with hers.

"Good," was all she said before they left the trial ring together.

Chapter 22

Violet

***THE WALK BACK TO THE TRUCK** took a lot longer than Violet hoped.* Every time she had to stop, Patrick's jaw pulsed. It didn't matter how many times she told him it wasn't his fault, she could tell he was beating himself up for it.

"Can I ask you something?" Violet asked when they neared the end of the trail.

"Anything." Patrick shifted the weight of both packs, making her feel bad for not carrying one… even if she was hurt.

"Do you remember anything from last night? Or this morning?"

Patrick tilted his head to the side. "Bits and pieces. Why?"

"I'm just curious," she mumbled as they broke through the trees and the old red truck came into view.

"About what exactly?" He tossed the bags in the bed, then moved swiftly to her side and opened her door.

Violet grabbed the "oh crap" bar then looked at him over her shoulder. "Never mind. It doesn't matter."

When she climbed into the seat, Patrick spotted her by placing his hand at the base of her spine, just below the bandages. He handed a blanket to her once she was settled then lowered his chin. The sun cast golden streaks through his dark, curly hair while he watched her through unguarded hazel eyes.

"I remember more than I thought I would."

Nerves and excitement jumbled together inside of her and set her fingers fidgeting inside the over sized sleeves of Patrick's shirt.

"'Kay," was all she managed to whisper which brought a quick smile to Patrick's face before he closed the door and made his way to the driver's side.

Within minutes of being on the road, Violet's head started dropping forward. She tried to reposition, but every time she moved, her back would pull.

"Come here, Vi." Patrick softly ordered and patted the seat beside him. "You've been awake all night. The least I can do is lend my shoulder as a pillow."

Violet snorted, but after a few more minutes of her trying to stay away, Patrick undid her buckle, "Hey!"

He grabbed the waistband of her jeans and pulled her against his side, "Buckle up."

"I'll just move back," Violet complained, feeling competitive.

"I'll just pull you back."

Violet crossed her arms, "You won't win this."

Red flashed briefly over his mischievous gaze when he glanced at her. "Believe me when I say, I will."

Sighing, Violet buckled up, but didn't rest her head against his shoulder. She suddenly felt very awake. "How are you feeling?"

"Stronger. Faster. Like all my senses are heightened..."

"Weren't they already heightened?" Violet asked as she pulled the blanket over her lap.

Patrick nodded, "Yes, but now... it's weird. They are about the same as before unless I focus on one of them. For example, if I focus, I can tell you there is a deer up the road."

"What? Really?" Violet squinted her eyes in attempt to see better, but she didn't see any sign of a deer.

"Just wait," Patrick patted her knee then returned his hand to the gearshift. "You'll see it soon."

Violet settled back against the seat and tried not to flinch as her pain flared. "Any other differences you've noticed?"

Exhaustion pulled her eyelids down before Patrick answered and her eyes flew open when he spoke.

"I feel like I'm in control for the first time in my life."

Violet smiled at him and he glanced at her as a grin lifted one side of his mouth. "I bet that feels amazing."

Sighing, Patrick rested his head against the headrest. "You have no idea." He pointed out the windshield, "Here comes the deer."

Sure enough, three seconds later, they passed by a young buck and Violet gaped at him. "I can't believe you can see that far!"

"It's pretty incredible," Patrick admitted with a soft chuckle as he rubbed at the scruff darkening his jaw.

"It looks good on you."

He shot her a confused look.

"The facial hair." She explained. "I'm guessing you didn't have time to shave before my graduation because you were a little scruffy then, too. It looks good on you."

Patrick rubbed his jaw again. "Thanks."

After the excitement with the deer wore off, Violet's eyes began to drift closed again and Patrick's hand lightly pressed against her head, tipping it onto his shoulder.

"Get some rest. I'll wake you up when we get close."

Too soon, Patrick's voice was telling her to wake up again. "Hey. Violet."

"Hmm?" Violet mumbled, not wanting to open her eyes.

"We're nearing the clan gates."

Panic iced Violet's veins and she shot off Patrick's shoulder then winced as agony lit up her back, reminding her of her wounds. Her nails dug into the blanket while she attempted to breathe through the pain.

"Are you okay?" Patrick worried and rested a hand on her knee.

Violet shook her head. "That definitely could have felt better."

"Sorry."

"You really need to stop apologizing. This isn't your fault." Violet unbuckled and grabbed the 'oh crap' bar to pull herself back to the outer seat. She buckled then lowered the visor to look in the mirror.

"What are you doing?" Patrick wondered as they turned down the clan's private drive.

Violet looked in the mirror, fixing her hair and wiping away any mascara that had settled under her eyes over the night. "Trying to make it look like I wasn't sleeping on you." Violet's eyes bugged and Patrick's laugh did not lessen her mortification. "You know what I mean!"

Through his chuckling, Patrick said, "Just to warn you, Jax has been trying to talk to me for the past thirty minutes. The only thing I have told him is updates on our progress home."

"Guessing he is angry?" Violet grumbled.

"Beyond furious, but he did say he was happy to hear from me. So there's that."

Violet shook her head, "At least he was polite enough for that."

"Uh oh."

"Uh oh, what?" Violet looked ahead. "Uh oh is never a good thing."

"And this isn't either," Patrick grimaced as they pulled up to the first gate. "I think Jax is waiting for us in the parking lot."

Groaning, Violet tipped her head back against the seat. "He can't wait for us to shower at least?"

Patrick shrugged, "Maybe giving him updates wasn't the best idea."

They were waved through the gate with a welcome home from the guard, and Patrick directed the truck onto the wood and steel bridge. The image of Jax standing in the parking lot with his arms crossed tightly over his chest was easily visible while the truck rolled to the other end of the bridge and they waited for the second gate to open.

"Your heart is pounding." Patrick whispered.

Violet tore her gaze off her twin and looked at Patrick. It was the first time since leaving the trial ring that she realized she couldn't hear his heartbeat.

Sorrow pulled her shoulders down. "Is yours?" she asked, wishing she could hear it.

He nodded once. "Almost as fast as yours."

"At least I'm not the only terrified one then," Violet teased, making Patrick smile as they were waved through the second gate.

Jax followed the truck through the parking lot. Once they were parked, his hands flew in the air as he yelled, "What. The—"

Violet startled when Patrick turned up the radio so Jax's words were drowned out, but it was obvious he was swearing up a storm. A smile slowly spread across her face as her twin raged.

"Figured we didn't need to hear that," Patrick told her and she laughed.

Jax stomped forward and hit his palm against the window. "Get out here, Patrick!" His glare shifted to Violet. *"You, too!"*

Violet sighed. *"Yeah, I definitely did not miss you yelling in my head all the time."*

"I was trying to be nice and let you keep your head in the right space to help Patrick." Even Jax's thoughts sounded angry. *"Clearly, that worked."*

"Don't you dare take credit for the hard night we've been through!" Violet yelled at Jax when Patrick opened the driver's door and Patrick looked at her with wide eyes. "You don't get to do that."

"I could have come after you," Jax growled.

"No, you couldn't," Violet snorted, calling his bluff. "All that would have done was set Patrick up for failure, and you know it. Which is why you chose to chew him out instead of me and stopped the second he told you we'd made it to the trailhead."

Jax's gaze snapped to Patrick. "You told her?"

Patrick's warm eyes held hers while he answered, "She knows a lot of things now."

The warmth in his eyes spread through Violet's chest. Patrick stepped out of the truck and Jax lowered his voice so Violet couldn't hear while he followed Patrick around to her side.

"What are you doing?" Jax asked when Patrick opened her door and stepped toward her.

"Helping." Patrick reached through the truck after Violet unbuckled and helped turn her hips toward the door.

Violet grabbed the 'oh crap' bar and pulled at the same time Patrick moved her toward him. She winced, despite trying not to, and bit her lip. Black spots filled her vision until the pain settled. She could tell Jax was talking, but his words weren't clear until the spots faded away.

"... me what happened, now! Why is my sister in pain?"

"I was attacked by a demon." Violet rolled her eyes then moved away from the truck so Patrick could close the door. "I'm fine."

"Is that why I woke up this morning with my back on fire?" Jax growled at her.

Shoot. Violet had forgotten about the funky twin connection.

All throughout their lives, if one of them were seriously hurt, the other one knew. No one could explain it. When Violet fell out of a tree and broke her arm as a kid, Jax had dropped his chocolate chip cookie while standing in the kitchen and told their mom Violet was hurt while he clutched his arm.

"Possibly." Violet relented while Patrick grabbed the bags from the bed of the truck.

Jax's eyes narrowed as he looked over her. "Why..." his voice was now a growl and gold was beginning to seep through his purple eyes. "... are you wearing... Patrick's clothes?"

Violet pulled Patrick's jacket closed as she swallowed the lump in her throat.

Patrick stepped between the two of them, blocking Jax's glare and surprising Violet. "I will answer all your questions later."

She'd never heard Patrick speak to Jax that way... like there was absolutely no other option. No one spoke to an alpha that way. It didn't matter if they were current or future. She peered around Patrick to see Jax now glaring at Patrick with near hatred.

"She needs to get to Dr. Penmann."

"No. I'm fine," Violet insisted, making Patrick turn around to protest, but she kept talking. "Mom has proper bandages at home—"

"Bandages?" Jax's shoulders dropped.

"You've already cleaned it out—"

Anger gave way to concern as Jax looked over her, "Cleaned what out?"

Violet shot him a look, frustrated that he kept interrupting her, before continuing, "I just need clean bandages and sleep."

Patrick shook his head. "I'm not a doctor. I could have missed something and there is no way I cleaned it as well as Penmann could."

With a sigh, Violet lightly rested her hand on Patrick's arm. He slid his arm back and Violet was worried he was pulling away from her until his fingers caught hers. Out of the corner of her eye, Jax shifted uncomfortably.

"I'm fine." Violet gave Patrick's hand a light squeeze. "I promise, if it starts hurting more or it isn't healing like it should or anything like that, I'll go straight to Dr. Penmann's."

Patrick's gaze shifted back and forth between her eyes like he was trying to solve some complex puzzle. Finally he sighed, "Okay, but I'm gonna make sure those bandages actually get on you."

Violet smirked. "You don't think I can manage?"

"Enough!" Jax yelled. "Where are you hurt? Why are you hurt? And who hurt you, so I can beat their face in?"

Rolling her eyes, Violet ignored him and started the trek home with Patrick following close behind.

"Hey!" Jax shouted. "What makes you think you can just walk away? I'm not done asking questions!"

"Then I guess you better follow us," Patrick answered.

Violet looked over her shoulder and laughed. Patrick's gaze immediately slid to hers, and he smirked while a scowling Jax hurried to catch up to them.

"What did you do?" Jax growled through their link.

"What are you talking about?" Violet shook her head, but kept walking.

"Patrick has never dismissed me like that before," Jax explained. *"He is paying more attention to you than he ever has. What did you do?"*

Violet spun around, winced when the sudden movement made her back ache, and stepped into Jax's space making him take a startled step backward. Her jaw clenched and her brows lowered in quite possibly the darkest glare she'd ever given her brother. *"I helped him through what may have been the hardest night of his life. If you think something like that doesn't change any kind of relationship, then maybe you need to re-evaluate how you treat others and the relationships you have."*

Jax's brows lifted in surprise, but for once he didn't have a response.

"Don't worry." Violet snorted and shook her head. *"I kept my promise*

to you."

"Yet you're wearing his shirt."

"It's not like I kissed him!"

"You could have done a lot of other things without kissing!"

Anger flooded through her. Faster than she thought she was capable of, Violet's fist collided with Jax's cheek. Jax stumbled back a step, holding his cheek while he stared at her with wide eyes.

Violet's knuckles stung and she shook out her hand, "Thanks for having so much faith in us."

Jax's throat bobbed when he swallowed, but he stayed quiet.

Patrick watched their exchange with a tense expression. His face tightened further as he stared at Jax, then shook his head before following after Violet when she continued toward the Alpha House.

It took a little longer for Jax to follow.

*****

"Hey, Mom. We're home," Violet called as she stepped into Alpha House with the two boys close behind.

"Violet!" Her mom pulled the headphones from her ears and shot up from her desk in the corner of the room. She hurried across the room and threw her arms around her daughter in a crushing hug. "How did everything go?"

Violet's face scrunched as her mom's super-hug pulled at her back. She sucked in a sharp breath and fought the tears that built up in her eyes.

"Luna," Patrick's voice was soft and respectful as he rested a hand on Evalyn's arm.

Under Patrick's gentle direction, Evalyn released Violet who was pinching her lips together. Violet raised a trembling hand to rest on her lower back, trying to make it seem like everything was fine.

"I can't thank you enough for allowing Violet to come with me." Patrick addressed her mom with resounding admiration. "I don't think I'd be standing before you if she hadn't been there."

Evalyn wrapped him up in a motherly hug which he quickly returned. "I'm so happy your trials were a success." She pulled back and looked between the two of them. "I'm sure you're both exhausted, but after you've had some rest, I would love to hear how everything went."

"Of course, Luna."

"Patrick, you don't have to call me that."

"I know," he answered, but the smile on his face said that he wasn't about to stop. It showed the deep respect he had for Violet's mother.

Violet had always been in awe with how much love her mother had for Patrick. It'd been that way since the day he arrived. It wasn't until now that Violet understood why Patrick loved her parents so much. He had to ask their permission to join the clan after having to tell them about his past and what he was going to do about it. An incredible amount of planning had to have gone into him moving here... and without her parents, none of it would have happened.

"Thank you, Mom." Violet grabbed her mom's hand and squeezed. "For everything."

Her mom's eyes welled with tears before she shook her head. "I'm proud of you, my little miracle." With a dismissive wave of her hand, Evalyn moved back to her desk. "Now stop making me cry, so I can get back to work. You both should get some rest."

"We will." Violet promised her, then headed toward the stairs.

She opened the door to her room, then quickly slammed it shut again when she realized the boys were still tailing her. "You know what," her voice squeaked. "I can grab a change of clothes later."

Jax snorted and crossed his arms. "You're such a slob."

"And you're a clean freak," Violet shot back.

The difference in how the twins kept their spaces had led them to have separate rooms when they were still very young. Violet had never minded having an organized mess... until the boy she seriously liked was about to enter it.

"It's fine." Patrick grumbled and rested her bag against the wall. He'd left his bag out on the porch so now his hands were free. "I'm assuming we are going into the bathroom?"

Violet nodded, then moved down the hall.

Thankfully the bathroom was spacious because cramming three people, two of them being well-muscled wolven, into a small space would not have been fun.

Violet pulled the first aid supplies out of the cupboard to the right then held up the larger bandages for Patrick to see. "Which ones?"

Patrick's hand rested at the base of her back while he looked over her shoulder at their supplies. "These ones should work," he reached around her to hold the longer, thinner one up.

A shiver ran down Violet's spine as she looked at their reflections in the mirror. Patrick's head was so close to hers that if he had turned his head, his lips would have grazed her ear when he spoke. Then there was Jax who was watching their exchange from his position against the wall with unleashed rage. His eyes shifted back and forth between gold and purple and Violet briefly wondered how much more of this he was going to take.

"'Kay." Violet's voice was small as she pulled a few of those bandages out. "How many?"

Sighing, Patrick straightened to his full height and rubbed the back of his neck. "Let's start with three."

"Three?" Jax launched off the wall, "Was she attacked by a bear?"

Violet shot him a look through the mirror, "Knock it off."

Patrick's worried tone captured her attention, "Violet, I really think you should let Dr. Pen..."

"Would you just help me?" Violet grumbled and lifted up the back of her shirt.

"What are you doing?" Jax snapped when Patrick grabbed the hem of her shirt. "You are not undressing my sister!"

"Get out, Jax!" Violet snapped back and she was grateful their mom typically worked with headphones in because she would have been up there in an instant. Jax blinked at her a few times. "You can either deal with what's happening, or you can get out."

Patrick lifted the shirt up and helped hoist it over her head so the sleeves were still on her arms and she clutched the rest of the material to her chest.

Jax's face lost all color as he stared at her back while Patrick unwound the bandage.

"Some of the gauze slipped," Patrick informed her, then cursed. "You're still bleeding."

"What?" Violet stared at him through the mirror. "How is that possible? I heal faster than that."

Shaking his head, Patrick grabbed some gauze from the counter and pressed it against her back making her arch away from his hand. "Sorry," Patrick mumbled, but maintained the pressure.

"Violet, either you get over to Dr. Penmann's or I will carry you there myself." Jax's voice was harsh with concern. "You are not going to make Patrick do this when there is a perfectly good doctor here."

"Jax..."

"No!" Jax glared at her through the mirror. "I'm surprised you're walking with injuries like that. You're going to see Dr. Penmann."

Jax and Patrick both followed Violet to Dr. Penmann's office... and into the patient room.

"She'll be with you in a couple minutes," informed Nurse Jake, then he looked at the two boys before casting a worried glance back at Violet. "Are you sure you're alright?"

Violet rolled her eyes at the ridiculousness of the situation. "I'm fine. Annoyed!" She glared at both young men, but mostly at Jax. "But fine."

Nurse Jake smiled, then stepped out of the room.

Jax started up again as soon as the door clicked shut, "You better fill me in right now, Patrick, or I—"

"Give it a rest, Jax!" Violet raised her voice as she stood by the exam table. "Patrick helped me. That's all you need to know."

"Vi..." Patrick closed his eyes and sighed.

Jax's eyes narrowed. "You're lying to me, aren't you?"

"I thought you could tell when I was lying to you." Violet shot back and crossed her arms. When Jax's jaw clenched, Violet relented, "I'm not lying to you."

"She's not telling you the whole truth either," Patrick informed Jax. He leaned back against the cabinets and rested his hands on the counter. "I hurt her."

"*You* did not!" Violet growled before Jax could launch across the room.

"Violet, we've been over this!" Patrick raised his voice, above hers. "If I was in control, then none of this would have happened!"

"But that's the point! You weren't in control, Patrick! You didn't do this to me!"

Jax's eyes drifted back and forth between Patrick and Violet while they yelled at each other.

"Alistair freaked out right before Patrick gained control again," Violet hurried to explain so Patrick didn't try to make himself sound like a martyr. "His claws got me, but Patrick pulled through, obviously, and patched me up immediately afterward."

Surprise held Jax's mouth agape. He looked like he was just about to form a word when a knock sounded at the door.

"Hello," Dr. Penmann's raspy voice filled the room before she peeked her head in and shot them all a beaming smile.

They returned her greeting as she stepped into the room and closed the door.

"What's going on here?" The doctor wondered out loud as she set her laptop on the small standing height desk in the corner.

"Ridiculous over protection," Violet grumbled.

Dr. Penmann smiled sympathetically at Violet then settled onto the stool nearby before briefly holding her hands out to her sides, "Since it's obvious no one is dying, let me first congratulate you, Patrick, on completing your trials."

Patrick rubbed the back of his neck and mumbled his gratitude.

"Now, care to tell me why you're in my office once again, Miss Draven?"

It was embarrassing how often Violet sat in one of these rooms, but between not having a wolf and lacking the ability to heal rapidly she was often injured and/or going through tests.

Sighing, Violet pulled the sleeves of Patrick's shirt over her hands. "During the trial there was a..." she bit her lip and looked to Patrick for help.

"My wolf tried to take over. We did not come to an agreement, so I was fighting against him the entire night." Patrick explained and crossed his arms. "In the process of trying to regain control, I..." Patrick's jaw pulsed and he took a steadying breath before continuing, "*He* clawed her back."

With a raised brow, Dr. Penmann nodded and reached up to close her laptop, "I guess she knows then?"

"I'm not sure how she could have been my anchor and not know."

"You have a point," the older woman agreed. "Due to the sensitive topic, I'll be giving a handwritten report to Alpha later today. I'll hand it over as late as possible, so you have time to meet with him before he gets it."

"I will," Patrick assured her.

Jax cleared his throat, "Thank you for your discretion with Patrick's condition, Doc."

The doc moved toward Violet as she shook her head. "As I've told you before, thank you for keeping me in the loop. It makes it easier to treat my patients when I know the full story." Her gentle gaze landed on Violet. "Well, hun, let's take a look. Are you more comfortable sitting or laying on your stomach?"

"I think I'll sit." Violet glanced at Patrick, blinked, and he was by her side.

"Let me help," he whispered and held her elbow to support her while she climbed onto the exam table.

Dr. Penmann backed away and pulled on a pair of blue gloves. Once Violet was sitting the doc moved toward her again, "I'm going to need you to lift your shirt."

Once again, Patrick helped raise the shirt into the same position she'd had it in the bathroom.

"Who patched you up?" Dr. Penmann asked as she unwound the wrap Patrick had bound her in.

"I did," Patrick answered. He stood so close to Violet that the toe of her shoes pressed against his legs. "The kit I took with us wasn't restocked, so I improvised. I cleaned it as best as I could, but we only had water and tweezers."

"Tweezers?" The doc asked from behind Violet as she peeled one of the gauze strips off Violet's back.

"There were cloth fibers in some of the gashes."

"Not bad." Dr. Penmann complimented then apologized when Violet flinched. "Have you considered going into medicine?"

Patrick gave a small nod, "I've thought about it."

The surprise on Jax's face matched how Violet felt. Patrick had never mentioned he was interested in medicine before, but he always did seem to know a lot about the subject.

"Think about it more." Dr. Penmann suggested. "We could use another doctor here."

Patrick nodded, but didn't respond. If he was going to be beta that would make working as a doctor especially tricky.

"Well, Violet."

Violet clutched her sleeves. Whenever Dr. Penmann used her name, it was never good news.

"As well as Patrick did, I still need to clean these out. Water unfortunately does not get rid of bacteria. Also, there still seems to be something in one of these lacerations."

Dismay filled Violet and she closed her eyes. That was one of the reasons she didn't want to see the doc. It had hurt bad enough with water... A hand rested on her knee and she opened her eyes to see Patrick gazing down at her.

"You also need stitches for the center right one."

"Stitches!" Violet looked over her shoulder at the doctor. "Really?"

Dr. Penmann nodded. "Which means you need to rest for at least a week."

"But I..."

"Violet," Jax spoke up from his corner of the room, drawing everyone's attention. His voice was soft as he continued, "Listen to her. This is serious."

"You're going to tell Dad, aren't you?" Violet asked through their link.

Jax sighed, *"You know I have to. He needs to know. The doc and Patrick will be telling him anyway."*

"Patrick didn't—"

"Patrick is safe." Jax assured her. *"Dad still needs to know. If for no other reason, just because he's our dad. I'll let Patrick deliver the news, though. It will be better coming from him."*

While they were conversing, Dr. Penmann had gathered the supplies she needed and wheeled them over on a small tray. "I suggest you lay down for this."

Fear shot through Violet, but she obeyed and laid down on her stomach. Patrick shifted with her and knelt down in front of her.

"Mr. Draven and Mr. Cowen, you may both go," Dr. Penmann told them.

"Violet is in good hands."

Patrick looked over Violet's head, "I'm not leaving."

"I..." Jax's voice sounded a bit weak, but Violet didn't hear him move.

"It's okay, Jax." Violet told him softly. "You've got better things to do than sit and watch a needle go through my back."

Violet was one of the few people who knew Jax was terrified of needles.

"I'll come back." Jax promised as the door opened.

When the door closed again, Dr. Penmann apologized for what Violet was about to go through. "I could numb the area. I'm going to have to for the stitches, anyway."

"No." Violet shook her head. It hadn't been fun when Patrick had cleaned it, but it wasn't too bad either. "Just get this over with."

Violet's nails dug into the exam table when Dr. Penman started digging through the gashes to find whatever fibers had been left behind. The doc was not nearly as gentle as Patrick had been. Violet's muscles tensed and a silent cry pried her mouth open.

After easing her clenched fingers off the exam table, Patrick held her hands and pressed his forehead against hers. "I'm right here, Vi," he whispered, making tears build in her eyes.

"Looks like a piece of claw may have lodged itself in your back, Violet. It's tiny, but if I don't get it out, you won't heal properly." Dr. Penmann explained in a hushed tone. "I'll be as gentle as I can."

Eternity passed in a pain filled haze before the doc exclaimed she'd gotten all of the claw out. It had only been a peeling off the claw, but it broke every time Dr. Penmann tried to grab it, making the process much longer and more painful.

After having a pair of tweezers digging into her back and the sting of whatever the doc had used to clean each gash, Violet assured the doc she could get stitches without numbing the area... but Dr. Penmann snorted and told her she was pulling rank.

With the numbing agent taking away her pain, Violet's eyes began to drift shut while Dr. Penman sewed her back together. There was pressure and pulling, but no pain.

"Thank you for staying with me." Violet mumbled as Patrick's thumb drew lazy circles over her hand.

"You're welcome," Patrick answered. "How's she doing, Doc?"

"Two more and she will be all done," Dr. Penmann said. "Patrick, I wasn't joking. With the materials you had, you did an amazing job."

"I shouldn't have needed to."

Violet squeezed his hand, too tired to argue with him.

"I'm sorry, Vi."

Violet's eyes shot open. There was only one person who said her name like that, but she knew she hadn't heard Patrick's voice. She'd felt it... almost like the words had been planted in her thoughts... just like when she mind-linked with Jax.

"Did you just..."

Confusion filled Patrick's face as he blinked at her, "What?"

It had been a long day. She was probably imagining things. She'd never been able to link with another person before. Why would that change now?

"Nothing." Violet shook her head, "Never mind."

"Jax is on his way back," Patrick told her. "I'm going to go when he gets here. I need to talk with Alpha Draven."

Violet nodded, then buried her face again so he couldn't see her disappointment.

Chapter 23

Patrick

***EXHAUSTION SETTLED OVER PATRICK** as he made his way to his room after a long couple of days.* Meeting with Alpha Draven had been nearly as tiring as the trials he'd gone through. He wanted to know every detail, especially the parts involving Alistair. There was no way he was about to tell the alpha that his daughter had nearly made out with a bloodthirsty wolf just to save him. He only gave the details Mr. Draven needed to hear.

And no one needed to know exactly how much Patrick remembered.

He closed his apartment door and collapsed on the couch, too tired to make his way to the bedroom.

Running a hand down his face, Patrick groaned.

The silky-smooth feel of Violet's skin under his hands was something that would haunt his dreams for the rest of his life. He never imagined he'd get to hold her and be held by her the way they had been in that spelled circle. Remembering her breath mingling with his and feeling his fang tease her lip sent pleasant shivers down his spine that he despised.

Those were the actions of Alistair. His blood boiled thinking about that wolf touching Violet that way. He'd been there, too, clawing his way to the surface, too weak to do anything to stop his darker half.

Self-consciously, Patrick ran a tongue over his teeth, and a relieved sigh left him when he didn't feel any fangs. He'd already checked his ears, which were no longer slightly pointed. All signs of his wolfish self were thankfully suppressed once again.

A knock at his door pulled him out of his thoughts. "Come in."

Jax walked through the door and closed it behind him. He plopped onto the chair in the corner, but didn't say anything as he stared up at the ceiling… which made Patrick nervous. Not to mention the fact that he had knocked.

It was late. Jax should have been home, but he was here instead.

Patrick was about to ask if his friend was okay, when Jax's quiet voice slowly spilled into the air.

"I must be one of the stupidest people you know."

Confused, Patrick turned his head toward the defeated looking future alpha, "You're actually one of the smartest."

"How long?"

Patrick shook his head, "I don't under—"

"How long have you had feelings for my sister?"

Curling his hands into fists behind his head, Patrick tried to settle his nerves. When he didn't answer, Jax sat forward, resting his elbows on his knees, and stared at him.

"Answer me, Patrick."

Patrick swallowed the knot in his throat, then rolled onto his feet and headed for the kitchen.

"Patrick!" Jax quickly followed after him and waited with crossed arms while Patrick guzzled a glass of water.

How could he tell his best friend the truth? He'd kept his feelings a secret. Learned how to wear a mask and act like he didn't care. That mask had cracked the more and more Violet was around, and had shattered over the last forty-eight hours.

Patrick tried to leave the kitchen, but Jax stepped in his path. His eyes narrowed at the aggressive act, "What do you want me to say?"

Jax's eyebrows rose. "Just answer the question."

"I made you a promise shortly after I came here to never pursue her," Patrick quietly reminded him while his fingers curled and uncurled in fists at his sides. "I've kept that promise."

Jax shook his head, "That's not what I'm asking."

"I know what you're asking." Patrick grumbled and pushed past his friend. "I don't think you're ready to hear the answer."

"Days?" Jax followed him out of the kitchen. "Weeks?"

Patrick clenched his jaw and started pacing to try and avoid eye contact.

"It's longer than that, isn't it?"

"Stop."

Jax stopped behind Patrick. "You've always had feelings for her. Haven't you?"

Patrick froze. He couldn't lie to Jax. "Yes."

"How could you—"

"You can not ask me to control how I feel about her. You told me not to pursue her, so I didn't!" Patrick rounded on Jax, who actually took a step backward.

Jax glared, then yelled back, "If you had feelings for her then why did you agree to it?"

"Because I... Gah!" Patrick fisted his hair with both hands then let his arms fall back to his sides. "Your family was the first thing I had that was even close to a family since I killed those teenagers. My father disowned me, my clan banished me, and no one wanted a teen who struggled with a bloodthirsty wolf and whose life was destined to end the night of the trials. I was willing to do anything to protect that!"

Shaking his head, Jax sighed, "Even ignoring your own feelings."

"Yes." Patrick's tone gave no room for interpretation. "I would do anything for you and your family."

Jax stared at Patrick, unable to form words.

The conversation from years before replayed in Patrick's head. He remembered every word and the exact promise he'd made. Jax had been venting about some guy who was flirting with Violet—someone he knew was only interested in the alpha bloodline a mating with her could produce.

Even at fifteen, the politics ruled a lot of people's choices as they were influenced by their parents.

Jax had turned on Patrick and with wide, golden eyes, yelled at him. "You have to promise me you will never go after Violet. I can't fully trust you if I think you're going to try anything with her."

It had been a simple choice. It didn't matter that the moment his gaze collided with Violet's, he knew what she was to him. He'd do anything for her. He also cherished his friendship with Jax and the love and acceptance their parents had shown him.

"I promise," his younger self answered confidently believing it would be simple to ignore his feelings for her.

He'd been wrong. Over the next few months, Patrick had carefully crafted his new persona. He had watched over Violet from a distance, focused on Jax instead, reminding himself multiple times a day that he was doing all of this for her and her family.

The pain and disbelief that crossed over Violet's face the first time he rebuffed her, ignored her, and pretended like his heart didn't ache every time he forced his genuine reactions down, was a look that haunted his dreams… the shadows of it lived in her eyes every time she looked at him after that.

That same look broke him when she offered her help before his trial and he'd laughed at her.

When Jax had come to him and asked that he protect Violet and look after her, he was quick to answer. It gave Patrick an excuse to be close to her and make sure she was okay.

"You were there when I told your parents about my past. I knew I had to do anything to earn your trust, and once I had it, I knew I would do anything to keep it." Patrick quietly told Jax, as the memories slipped away. "Your order to protect her, and knowing she could do a thousand times better than me, made it easier."

He made his way back to the couch and took a seat.

Jax eventually followed, sinking into the chair he'd been in before, but he stayed quiet.

"Besides all of that, we've talked about the dangers a relationship with me would bring, and the secrets the person would have to keep."

Jax shook his head. "So, she knows everything?"

"No," Patrick buried his head in his hands. "But she knows about the red eyes and Alistair told her it was three teenagers."

Hearing Jax snort, Patrick lifted his head to find his friend shaking his head and... smiling? It was small, but the corners of his mouth were definitely curled toward the ceiling.

"Now what?" Jax asked, leaning back in his chair.

Patrick blinked at him. "What do you mean? Nothing. Everything goes back to the way it was."

"Are you blind, man?" Jax threw the pillow that was behind him at Patrick. It hit Patrick's shoulder then fell to the floor. "Violet knows and still held your hand. She helped you through the trial and defended you when questions about her back came up. My sister has been head over heels for you for years."

Hope burned in Patrick's chest, but he beat it back down into submission. "She doesn't know everything, and I made you a promise."

"The promise of a fifteen-year-old doesn't hold much value, and if I had known you better, I never would have asked you to make it." Jax gripped the chair arms. "I can't believe I'm about to say this..."

"Don't," Patrick warned him, but Jax shook his head.

"You know how protective I am over Violet. You've seen me and helped me chase guys away from her..."

Patrick groaned. He wasn't proud of those moments.

"I withdraw my promise and the order to protect her—"

"Jax."

"I won't stand in your way anymore—"

Patrick shook his head and tried to interrupt again, "Don't give me that privilege."

"Patr—"

"Don't!" Patrick held up a hand to stop Jax then lowered it back to his lap as he continued, "You were right to keep me away from her. Alistair is a danger to everyone, and the last people I want to hurt are your family."

"She helped you overcome Alistair!" Jax reminded him.

Patrick let out a huff of dry laughter, "And look where that got her?"

Jax flinched.

"Her back is torn to shreds; she had a piece of my claw embedded in her back..." He flexed his hand, producing the claws he'd hid for years. "*My* claw, Jax."

His friend eyed his claws, which were all intact. It had been years since Jax had shown any fear toward Patrick's wolfish features, but it still surprised Patrick.

"Alistair is gone," Jax said quietly. "You passed your trials."

Clenching his jaw, Patrick withdrew his claws. "He's not gone."

"I thought you said..."

"I told you I felt more in control. That is the truth. I never said he was gone." Patrick leaned back against the couch, feeling every ache in his body. The subtle, quiet presence of Alistair shifted within him. "He's still there. Waiting in the background. He's just too weak to do anything right now."

Jax scooted to the edge of his chair. "But you can control him."

Another dry laugh left Patrick, "Can I?" He bit his lip then leveled his friend with a tense look. "He likes her too, Jax. A lot."

Jax's throat bobbed. "She's a double-edged sword. Your kryptonite."

Closing his eyes, Patrick sighed, "Exactly."

"Geeze." Jax sank back into his seat and ran a hand down his face.

"I have more control." Patrick told him, "But that control has always been harder to maintain when Violet is around."

Chapter 24

Violet

HEALING SUCKED.

That's what Violet determined.

After three days, Dr. Penmann determined that the stitches would probably be there another three days before she felt comfortable removing them. Valentine's day had come and gone with little fanfare. Someone had left her favorite salted caramel cookies by her door with a single rose, and she'd had her suspicions that Patrick had been the giver... until she saw him walking down the road with Robin practically hanging off him.

The cookies turned to ash in her mouth, and she ended up throwing them and the half blossomed rose in the garbage.

Patrick hadn't come to check on her, and the couple times she'd purposefully run into him in the hallway he'd dodged around her and left Jax to talk to her. Surprisingly, her brother was being a lot nicer to her.

Thankfully, tomorrow she would have the stitches removed, and she'd be able to leave the house again! Her mom had placed her under house arrest because... well... she knew her daughter. That and she wasn't very happy Violet had tried to hide her injury.

Frustrated, Violet threw her pen across the desk and it bounced off the wall. She was supposed to be filling out college applications, but she couldn't focus.

Picking up her phone for the hundredth time, Violet went to send Lexie a message... but remembered her human friend was still in school and decided to wait.

Sighing, Violet put her phone back down. She pushed out of her chair and moved to the cushioned window seat that was tucked between two large bookshelves.

Yesterday, she'd thought Patrick was watching her from the street, but Jax appeared by his side a moment later, and they headed off with their gym bags to the training grounds. She didn't understand what had happened or why he was being so distant and cold.

A knock sounded, and Violet rested her head against the bookshelf she was leaning against while she stared down the road. "I'm not in the mood, Mom. Or Jax. Or whoever you are."

"Not even to see me?"

Elation sparked Violet back to life, "Lexie?"

Lexie burst through the door with a box in her arms, "Surprise!"

Joy filled Violet to the brim, nearly making her cry as her human friend stepped around a pile of books and over a small pile of clothes. "I was just thinking about you."

"Huh. Is that why my ears were burning?" Lexie winked at her then dropped the box onto the desk, sending a marker flying into the hamper. "I brought comfort food and a selection of three movies, and we are going to..."

Laughing, Violet interrupted her, "How did you get in here? I thought your banishment was still in effect."

Lexie shrugged, "I was told you could use some cheering up and that you hurt your back, but I didn't get any details. I ditched school and gathered all this stuff to come have a sleep over. I was fully prepared to beg your mom to let me come over, but she readily agreed and said you needed it, which made me even more worried and I grabbed an extra box of cookies."

Her eyes landed on the two-day old cookies in the garbage. "Unless you've recently given up your vice?"

Following her friend's gaze, Violet sighed. "No. I just lost my appetite for those ones."

Lexie investigated her trash can. "There's a rose, too."

"Never mind that." Violet waved her away from the trash.

Her friend frowned at her as she sank onto the bed, making her high, pale blond ponytail bounce. "Is it okay that I'm here?"

"Are you kidding? I'm so glad you're here," Lexie stood up, swiveled the desk chair over a bunch of clothes and closer to her bed, then sat facing Lexie.

"Before anything else, you have to tell me what happened."

Disappointment pulled Violet's shoulders down. "I'm sorry, Lex... for once I actually can't."

"What?" Lexie's eyes widened. "You haven't cared about the rules before!"

Violet shook her head, "This isn't my story to tell."

"But it happened to you." Lexie countered, as she straightened her spine and crossed her legs. "So, it is your story."

Bunching her lips to the side, Violet tugged the extra long sleeves of Patrick's shirt over her hands. She should have given it back, and definitely shouldn't have been wearing it, but the scent of chocolate peppermint still lingered... and she missed Patrick.

"All I can tell you is I was attacked by an out-of-control wolf," Violet looked toward the window. "He tore up my back and because I don't heal as fast as everyone else, I'm on lock down."

"Wow." Lexie was quiet for a minute. "You need more cheering up than I thought."

Violet turned her attention back to her. "What do you mean?"

"You've been hurt before, but you're acting like it was your heart that was torn through, not your back." Lexie fiddled with her shoe laces. "Who was it that scratched you?"

Shaking her head, Violet quickly answered, "Someone you've never met and believe me when I say I do not have feelings for him." Which was true... It was Patrick she had feelings for, not Alistair... even though you couldn't have one without the other.

Drawing in a deep breath, Lexie slapped the comforter. "What should we do first? Snacks? Movie? Snacks and movie? You look like you're already in pajamas, should I go change into mine?"

Violet glanced down at herself. Lexie was right, she was still in her pajamas. Bright pink, llama and rainbow pants complimented the light blue cami she wore under Patrick's shirts. "Uh, yeah. Why don't you change, and then we can dive into both a movie and snacks."

With a wink, Lexie gathered her pajamas and hurried to go change. "Oh, I almost forgot." She paused in the doorway and turned back. "Mya is going to join us later after her shift, but she won't be staying the night. Something about wanting to be with her boyfriend or whatever." She rolled her eyes playfully, making Violet chuckle then disappeared.

Violet felt her smile slipping and she moved back to the window, not really sure what she was hoping to see.

"Knock. Knock."

Violet snapped her attention to the door where Patrick leaned against the frame with his hands shoved into his pockets. "Patrick... um... hi."

His eyes traveled over her before settling on her face. "I see you're still wearing my shirt."

Embarrassed, Violet tucked some hair behind her ear. "Yeah... sorry. I should give it back..."

"No, don't." A ghost of a smile appeared on Patrick's face. "It looks good on you."

Violet dragged her bottom lip through her teeth as her cheeks warmed. "It's really comfortable." They were both awkwardly quiet until Patrick turned his head to look down the hallway. "Lexie's here," Violet explained, but wasn't sure why. "She's staying the night."

Patrick nodded as he looked back at her. "I'm glad you have some company. I'll leave you alone then."

"Wait." Violet stepped toward him. She tried not to think about the disaster her room was in, while also praying there wasn't a bra out somewhere. "I haven't talked to you since the doc's. How have you been?"

Shifting his weight, Patrick straightened to his full height. He looked nervous and wouldn't meet her eyes. His chin lowered before he spoke, "I'm good. Adjusting to the new norm. I laid Jax out on the mats yesterday."

He made a face, "I felt bad about that one."

Violet snorted. "He kinda deserved it after how terrible he's been lately."

Patrick's face fell. "You know he loves you, right? All he has ever done is look out for you."

Guilt spread through Violet and she looked at her dirty floor, "I know. But somethings are harder to let go of than others."

Patrick sighed, "Yeah."

They stood like that, awkwardly tolerating each others company. When Violet lifted her gaze again the words she had readied caught in her throat at the warm sadness staring back at her.

"I should catch up with Jax," Patrick said softly and backed away a step. "I just wanted to see how you were doing."

"Right, yeah, um..." Violet shrugged a shoulder, making Patrick's shirt—her shirt now—fall off said shoulder. "I should be back to training in a few days if everything goes well at my appointment tomorrow. I think Doc is being overly cautious, but who am I to tell her no." An awkward laugh left her and she folded her arms over her stomach.

A soft smile tilted Patrick's lips and he shook his head, "Right. Well, I'm glad you're healing." He backed away, lingering in her doorway a little longer, "Night."

"Patrick!" Lexie's voice pierced the weird moment as she hightailed it down the hallway and threw her arms around Patrick's neck. "It feels like I haven't seen you in forever!"

Patrick stumbled back a step and gave Violet a weird look, "Uh, hi Lexie? It's only been a few days."

"Yeah, but so much has happened since then!" Lexie let go of him and picked up the clothes she had dropped on the floor. She turned her head and winked at Violet who stared at her friend like she had multiple heads. "I hear you're an officially ranked member of the clan now. Congrats!"

Patrick shot Violet a tense look. "Thank you. I didn't know that was outsider information."

She chuckled before stepping into the room in her blue and white vertically striped pajama shorts and an over sized t-shirt. "Don't worry, Luna Momma downstairs told me, so I don't know any secrets I'm not supposed to."

Whether it was relief or disappointment that pulled Patrick's shoulders down, Violet couldn't tell, but he didn't pursue the conversation any further.

Lexie sat down in a criss cross position on Violet's bed. "How was Valentine's Day? Do anything nice for a special someone?"

Violet's eyes bugged, and she stared at her human friend.

After clearing his throat, Patrick ran a hand through his hair and rubbed the back of his neck. "Uh... it was pretty lonely, actually. I did give a small gift to someone, though."

"Oh?" Lexie trembled with excitement like a little chihuahua. "Who's the lucky girl?"

"Lexie, I'm sure Patrick doesn't want to go over all the details about his time with Robin right now."

Patrick's brows pulled together, "Robin?"

Dropping her gaze so she didn't have to look at him, Violet fiddled with the end of her sleeves. "Yeah, you know. I just figured that's who you were talking about since I saw you two walking down the road together."

"Violet, I was—"

"Hey, why don't you and Jax join us?" Lexie interrupted, drawing both of their attentions.

"No, Lexie, I'm sure..." Violet started at the same time Patrick said, "No, sorry, we can't..."

They looked at each other, frozen mid sentence, and frowned.

"Ooo-kay," Lexie chuckled. "Well, I guess I'll see you around then."

Patrick looked at Lexie briefly, then captured Violet's gaze again, "Yeah. Have a good time."

Violet closed the door after Patrick disappeared down the hallway and pressed her forehead against the wood.

"What was that about?" Lexie asked, sounding amazed. "It was like watching two kids who are terrified of each other because they actually secretly like each other." She whispered the last part before grabbing the box off the desk and bringing it to the bed.

"Well, we spent some time together a few days ago," Violet explained, pushing off the door. "And haven't talked to each other since. Apparently that makes for a really awkward conversation." She sat on the other side of the box on the bed and frowned. "Seeing him with Robin hurt. I thought..."

Lexie's hair flicked behind her when she lifted her head quickly to look at Violet, "What? That you had chemistry? Cause *that* you two have in spades." She rummaged through the box as she continued. "He just said he was lonely on Valentine's, do you really think he was with her? Where did you see them, anyway? I thought you've been locked up here in your tower?"

"I've been watching the clan pass by my window. Robin was all over him. I thought, maybe, the rose and cookies were from him, but there wasn't a note and then I saw that and—"

"Wow." Lexie's hands froze inside the box as she looked up, wide-eyed at Violet. "No wonder you were acting all broken-hearted earlier."

Violet pushed herself back on her bed until her back was supported by a pillow against the wall. "I've liked Patrick for so many years, and I finally made the connection between the stupid promise Jax gave me, and why, and I don't care anymore… but what if I'm wrong, and he doesn't like me back?"

After pulling out an Oreo package and handing it over, Lexie brushed back a few flyaway hairs from her face. "Maybe he's just acting like this because he realized he has feelings for you, too, and doesn't know how to act around you now."

Violet rolled the Oreo package around in her hands, "Maybe. Or maybe I was too friendly with him a few days ago, and it freaked him out."

"Why have you not ripped that thing open and eaten half of them already?" Lexie wondered with wide eyes. "This is even more serious than I thought!" She jumped up and grabbed the three movies she'd brought with her. "It's time to fall head over heels for one of these hotties!"

Violet eyed the video covers and shrugged, "Why not all of them?"

With an excited squeal, Lexie grabbed Violet's laptop bag and started setting everything up.

"Hey, Lex."

"Hmm?" Lexie fiddled with the laptop, only half listening to Violet.

"Who told you about my back?"

Lexie briefly looked up then shrugged a shoulder, "I actually don't know who it was."

Confused, Violet blinked a few times, "What?"

"Yeah, they sent me a text, but it was a number I didn't recognize."

"And you just believed them?" Violet asked sounding a bit hysterical.

Lexie snorted. "It's not like they were telling me to go find you down an abandoned road, Violet. They said you were basically under house arrest and needed some cheering up. So, I hightailed it over here and yelled at the gate guards to call your mom."

"You did?" Violet would have loved to have seen that.

"Yup. They looked a little lost having a whimpy human like me screaming at them."

Despite her depressing mood, Violet chuckled just as the movie started.

Mya joined them about halfway through and stayed for almost two hours before heading back to Aiden's. Violet was thankful for the company, but equally thankful for the movies so she didn't have to discuss her Patrick problems.

By eleven, Lexie was snoring, completely passed out with her hand in a bowl of popcorn on Violet's bed.

Violet finished the last movie alone... which was not a romance like Lexie had thought. Sure the main actor was hot, but he was fighting zombies the whole time, and it really lacked in the romance department.

Violet closed her eyes when a scary part came on screen, but when she opened them again her laptop had gone to sleep and her room was dark.

Sighing, she pushed off the bed to put everything away and try to clean up some of the spilled popcorn, cookie crumbs, Nerds, and Gobstoppers.

At least no soda had spilled.

Violet didn't mind clothes and books and papers being on the floor, but anything food wise drove her bonkers. And her bed was always clean—never made, but always clean.

That was something she beat Jax on. His bed was always covered in all sorts of stuff, she wondered how he ever slept there.

She sighed and set her laptop down on her desk before grabbing her curtains to close them.

Something shifted in the shadows down the road.

Staying her hand, Violet leaned toward the window as thick mist crawled its way toward Alpha House. The closer it came, the more Violet leaned in. She'd never seen mist like this before. Dread fell over her. Her chest rose and fell rapidly with the quickened pace of her breathing.

"Lexie." Violet breathed her friend's name when two figures emerged from the fog. A heavy weight clamped down on her chest, making it hard to breath. "Lexie!"

Oblivious to her cry, Lexie slept on, leaving Violet alone to stare wide-eyed as one of the figures looked her way and blood-red eyes glowed in the mist.

"NO!" Violet jerked awake, tossing a bowl of popcorn into the air and knocking a box of Nerds over the side of the bed.

Lexie stirred and opened her eyes halfway to mumble, "You okay?"

A few deep breaths and Violet had her breathing under control, but her heart still pounded away against her ribs. "Yeah... It was just a dream."

"M'kay," Lexie yawned. "Go back to sleep."

Violet waited until her friend's breathing evened out before sliding off her bed. A light sheen of sweat wet her forehead, and she grabbed a tissue off her desk to wipe it away. She peered out the window to find the base like it always was at night. The dirt roads were empty. Everything was quiet.

No mist.

No bloody-eyed wolven.

Sighing, Violet cleared off the bed. She tried to clean as much of the popcorn as she could, but the Nerds were a lost cause until she had some more light. Setting her laptop on the desk, Violet froze... she was doing the same thing she'd done in her dream.

She drew in a deep breath, held it, and turned toward the window.

The roads were still clear.

"Darn you, Lexie." Violet glared at her sleeping friend for bringing a scary movie to watch right before bed.

Needless to say, Violet did not sleep very well the rest of the night. Lexie kicked her legs a couple of times. Every noise the house made had Violet jumping out of her skin. Then, to top it off, someone started snoring ridiculously loudly down the hallway.

Morning came and Lexie lightly patted Violet's cheek. "Morning, gorgeous."

Violet smacked her hand away. "Get off me, you traitor."

"Traitor! What did I do?" Lexie sat up and stared at Violet with wide eyes.

"You turned on a scary movie then passed out and left me to freak out all by myself!" Violet rolled to her side, then pushed up with one hand to get herself into a sitting position. She tugged at Patrick's over sizedshirt, pulling it back into place.

Lexie stretched her arms over her head and said through a yawn, "Oh, yeah, I guess I did do that."

After glaring at her friend, Violet stood and gathered some clean clothes. "Lex, I was so freaked out that I had a nightmare! And it was real enough that I couldn't tell that I was sleeping!"

"Wow, was the movie really that bad?" Lexie asked as she pulled a brush through her long hair.

"In reality my nightmare had nothing to do with the movie and everything to do with Blood Moon pack," Violet admitted while she opened the door to go change in the bathroom. "The movie was good, just not at night all by yourself."

*****

Lexie opted to stay behind with Luna Draven while Violet had her stitches removed, which Violet was very grateful for.

"What's the verdict, Doc?" Violet asked while pulling her shirt back down.

Sighing, Dr. Penmann turned toward her patient and leveled her with a soft glare. "Can I trust you to take it easy for a few more days?"

Violet bit her lip and raised her shoulders. "Probably not."

Chuckling, the doc leaned back against the counter and crossed her arms. "Which is exactly why I left the stitches in a day or two longer than necessary."

Violet stared. "What? You mean I could have been free from my house two days ago?"

"I said a day or two. I'm not telling you which, and the extra healing was good for you." Dr. Penmann smiled. "I will still tell you not to be thrown into the mats for a couple more days, but mostly because it will not feel very good."

"I don't think that's supposed to feel good anyway," Violet mumbled.

Lifting a brow, the doc continued, "You aren't in any danger of your wounds splitting open. They've all completely healed, with the exception of the one that needed stitches. I'd imagine that one still has a little healing to do on the inside, but externally, it looks wonderful. Light pink scarring, which is what I was hoping for today."

Disappointment sank Violet's shoulders. "Scarring?"

A sympathetic smile softened the harsher lines of Dr. Penmann's face. "You'll have at least three, from what I can tell right now—maybe more. Scars are not the end of the world, though." She ran a gentle hand over the horizontal scars across her neck.

"I didn't mean..." Violet back peddled, feeling bad about having a couple scars along her back while the woman in front of her nearly lost her life and voice. "It just surprised me is all."

Dr. Penmann nodded. "The unfortunate part is, if your wolf was more connected with you, you may not have had any." Her lips bunched to the side as she thought about something. "Have you had any..."

"No." Violet interrupted. "I'm practically human at this point. I still don't know my wolf's name, and I've never felt her presence. I don't know what color of eyes I would have had and all I have to show for my wolven bloodline is a little extra speed and strength."

"Your senses, strength, and healing are heightened compared to a humans. Otherwise, you would have eight scars across your back. You are wolven."

Violet shook her head while she snorted. "Barely."

Dr. Penmann crossed the room and hopped up onto the exam table next to Violet. "You are not the only one to go without a wolf, Violet. There are others who didn't connect until their birthdays and some never did at all." She wrapped an arm around Violet's shoulders. "That doesn't mean you aren't wolven. You'll always be part of the clan."

"Without my wolf half, I will never have a rank. I'll be welcome here, but I won't hold a job within the clan. I won't be welcome on expeditions or scouting trips. I will always be a liability and have to have another to protect me."

"I can think of a few people who would gladly have that job."

"Maybe," Violet answered, feeling a little numb, and hopped off the exam table. "Thanks, Doc."

There was nothing left to say. Last year Violet had spent hundreds of hours in this office with Dr. Penmann running test after test. Everything came back the same. Violet was perfectly healthy. There was no physical reason why her wolf wouldn't connect with her.

Chapter 25

Violet

ON THE WAY BACK TO ALPHA HOUSE, *Violet stopped and stared at the wildflowers blooming in the fields.* They were every shape, size, and color. Around this time last year, she realized Jax could smell them from the road where she now stood, but Violet couldn't until she was halfway down the hill. It wasn't the first indicator that she was falling behind, but it was the one that made her start asking questions.

All of which had been met with little to no answers.

"Violet!" Jax's voice snapped her out of her depressing thoughts.

She turned to find him running up the road toward her. He was already dressed for the day in jeans, a dark navy shirt, and a coat, but his hair wasn't neatly placed like usual. A few dark chocolate tufts stuck up in funny directions, making Violet wonder what rushed him through his morning routine. "What's wrong?"

"You haven't seen Nicholas or Justin today, have you?" Jax asked as he slowed to a stop in front of her. "They didn't report for their morning duties and they aren't responding to clan-links."

"Justin… the playful guy who likes to jump in Patrick's truck bed? He's been helping Dad out a lot lately, right?"

Jax nodded.

She shrugged. "I don't know who Nicholas is, but I haven't heard from either of them." She pulled her phone from her pocket and looked at the time. "It's not even 8:30 yet. Are you really that worried?"

"Yes." Jax's answer surprised her. "A fissure was found in the fence line this morning. Dad's taking a headcount to see if anyone is missing."

Confusion pulled Violet's brows together. "If they wanted to leave, they could just walk out the gates."

Jax shook his head. "We're not worried about someone getting out. It's someone getting in."

The pit of Violet's stomach swirled into a tight knot. "Oh." She returned her phone to her pocket and looked in the direction of the commons, "Has anyone checked their apartments?"

"We're on our way to do that right now," Patrick's voice answered from behind her.

Lowering her chin, Violet drew in a deep breath to calm her heart, which had decided to try and leap from her chest.

When he reached her side, she greeted him with a facade of calm. "Hi, Patrick."

"Morning." He tossed a ring of keys to Jax then turned his hazel eyes to her. They appeared greener today, reflecting the forest green *Henley* shirt he was wearing. Even though it was chilly, his long sleeves were pushed up near his elbow and Violet had no idea why that was so dang attractive. "How'd your appointment go?"

Violet jerked her gawking stare away from him and shrugged as her cheeks lit up like a Christmas tree. "I'm—um—pretty much back to my normal activities. Doc recommended I don't get thrown against the mats or anything for a couple more days though."

"Good. I'm glad you're healing," Jax answered, stepping around her to stand beside Patrick. "We need to go."

"Mind if I come with you?" Violet blurted before she could stop herself. "Please?"

Both young men looked at each other briefly before Patrick asked, "Isn't Lexie waiting for you?"

Violet shook her head. "I left her with Mom. Lexie was showing her something with spreadsheets when I left. She's kind of obsessed with them. They'll be occupied for hours." She smirked. "Or at least until Mom says she's had enough."

Jax mulled this new information over for a moment, then shrugged. "I don't see why not."

Her excitement bubbled over and Violet let out a little squeal. Jax shook his head at her antics, but Patrick cracked a smile.

Patrick fell into step beside her, his long, black cargo-covered legs a stark contrast to her white, marble leggings. They'd made it about halfway up the hill when he started filling her in on the details, "Nicholas and Justin are my neighbors. They live on either side of my apartment. Both of them are pretty heavy sleepers, so I'm betting they just slept through the clan-link call."

Violet shot him an odd look. "Wouldn't talking through the link wake them up?"

Jax snorted. "Linking with someone who's asleep is a lot harder. Most people don't hear it. Some end up having it incorporated into a dream they're having."

"I guess that makes sense," Violet responded as a kid looking about twelve years old darted past them toward the parking lot.

Nothing looked out of the ordinary during the few minutes it took to cross the base. Younger kids darted off to the bus waiting for them in the parking lot. Older kids and teens passed them on their way to the study hall. Adults headed off to their jobs, whether that was inside the base or in their outer territory.

The sky was clear, the sun was shining brightly, and everyone was going about their usual lives.

Patrick lengthened his stride to reach the door of the commons first, then held it open for her and Jax. Once they were inside, he took the lead down the hallway to the left.

"This is Justin's room," he informed them, pointing to the door to the right of his own.

He raised his hand to knock, but his knuckles froze a few inches from the dark wood. Without taking his gaze away from the door, Patrick motioned for Jax and Violet to stand back.

"What's going on?" Violet asked Jax as he directed her to stand against the wall.

"The door is open," He answered quickly while returning his attention to the door.

Patrick pressed his back against the wall on the other side of the door. "Justin?" He called, then pushed the door open and stepped over the threshold.

Jax dropped into a defensive stance and followed immediately after Patrick. "Ugh, what is that smell?"

A cough sounded before Patrick spoke, "Witch."

Taking their casual banter as a safe sign, Violet joined them in the room and immediately flinched back. The overwhelming stench of sulfur made her eyes water. She choked back a cough while turning to take in the apartment.

It was the same layout as Patrick's—a small living room to the right, with the kitchen and dining on the left split by a bar countertop. There was one distinct difference though.

Patrick's apartment looked as if it had been staged without a single personal item in sight.

Someone definitely lived here.

A warm-looking, red plaid blanket laid haphazardly over the back of the gray loveseat, partially covering a few dark blue throw pillows that had been added. The loveseat itself still looked in good shape, minus the cushions sinking in the center from frequent use. In front of the loveseat sat a wooden coffee table with water rings marring the dark stain. A glass rested in the center of the rings accompanied by an empty plate and a gaming controller.

Violet turned to see a decent-sized TV covering the wall in front of the loveseat.

The other walls were simply decorated with a picture or poster of some sort here or there, but a nice ocean painting drew her into the small dining area where an equally small dining table, just big enough for an intimate dinner waited.

Violet noted a few dishes in the sink and smiled softly. Patrick's place was so perfectly put together that it was hard to believe someone lived there at all. This wasn't messy, but it was lived in.

"Do you hear anything?" Jax asked, relying on Patrick's better senses.

Patrick coughed again, drawing Violet's attention.

He rubbed his forehead, closed his eyes, and held very still. After a few seconds, he shook his head. "We're the only ones here."

Nodding, Jax scrunched his nose. "None of us would be able to stand being in here for long. We'll have to get a witch in here to clean this stench out. I let Dad know Justin is missing. Why would a witch be interested in him?"

A heavy weight clamped down on Violet's chest, making it even harder to breathe the sulfur-infused air.

Patrick shrugged.

With a sigh, Jax motioned to the door. "Let's see if Nicholas is home."

The young men headed for the door, but Violet's feet were frozen in place. Ringing filled her ears, followed by the slightest hiss of a whisper calling to her.

She looked down Justin's short hallway to the bedroom door. The whispers grew louder as her feet moved of their own accord, taking her closer to the nearly closed room.

Her pulse climbed to that of a runaway freight train when she stopped in front of the door.

Blood marred the white trim. A handprint, smeared beyond the threshold.

The indiscernible whispers grew louder as she reached for the handle… and stopped when she twisted the cold metal knob.

Breathing heavily, Violet pushed the door open.

Blood tainted everything. Even the sulfur saturated air had a hint of the sweet metallic life source. Red splatter painted every surface in sight; the bookshelf against the far wall laid in pieces—its contents gutted and scattered across the floor, the nightstand, dresser, and walls now mutilated with gouging claw marks, and the bed with the mattress dangling halfway off the box spring and the bedding torn to shreds.

There lay Justin's body. A tangled mess of bloody limbs.

Violet clamped a hand over her mouth to mute her scream as she ran from the room.

She never made it out the door.

Something hit her from the side, barreling her into the wall. Her back burned as she slid down the now fractured wall. A pained grunt left her when she hit the ground. She wasn't fast enough to react to the blurred movement on her right. The impact against her head made her relinquish whatever grip she managed to get on her attacker's leg.

Violet's vision blurred. Her back throbbed. Her lungs ached from the sulfur. That sweet, metallic scent was now in her mouth and she briefly worried she'd bit her tongue.

Taking advantage of whatever break she had from being hit, she launched herself through the door. Vice-like hands clamped around her leg and she dropped to the carpet with a loud thud. Rolling to her side, Violet drew her knee up and looked over her shoulder to target the person's face.

Terror-laced shock froze her in place as Vikter Stravek's sadistic, angry smile complimented his blood-red eyes.

"Hey, Snack," he growled.

It was enough to knock Violet out of her stupor. Her heel connected with his face, making him reel backward and drop her leg.

"Patrick!" Violet screamed, scrambling to her feet.

She gained traction and sprinted toward the door only to have Vikter tackle her to the ground. He sat atop her, twisting her arms behind her back as if he were simply tying a rope. Searing pain tore through her shoulders, but the cry that ripped from her throat only made him laugh.

"Scream all you want, little snack. I've got unfinished business with you." He leaned forward, pressing his weight onto her arms and back and increasing the pressure on her shoulders. Tears leaked from her eyes when his breath brushed across her ear. "No one can hear us."

Violet's stomach dropped.

The roar of an avenging angel filled the room.

Vikter's weight disappeared and the pressure on her shoulders, released. Jax knelt beside her as she tried to wrap her brain around what had happened. Her head throbbed, but it didn't feel the same as when she'd received a concussion.

"Are you okay?" Jax asked, slowly helping her to her knees.

She shook her head. The world didn't spin, so that was a good sign. Drawing in a deep breath, Violet turned to look at Patrick who had Vikter pinned against the wall with one hand to his throat. The snarl on Vikter's face, combined with the new red eyes, made him look like a rabid animal.

"Hello, reaper." Vikter snapped his teeth together as Patrick raised his fist.

Panic flooded Violet when she noticed Patrick's eyes were now a bright ruby. "Patrick!"

His fist knocked across Vikter's face, and the crazed teen crumpled unconscious to the floor.

Slowly, Patrick turned his head to gaze at her and Jax. "It's okay." His voice was calm and devoid of any hint of Alistair. "I'm in control."

Without thinking, Violet launched herself from the floor toward Patrick. Warm, protective arms readily wrapped around her, squeezing her against his chest before he let out a relieved breath. His lips grazed the top of her head while one of his hands wound its way into her hair.

Jax cleared his throat and Patrick gently pushed her to arms length. His firm grip on her shoulders held her in place while he looked her over.

Seeming satisfied that she didn't need immediate care, Patrick released her to nudge Vikter with the toe of his converse. "What happened?"

"You both left, but I thought I heard whispering. I followed it to Justin's bedroom..." Violet clamped a hand over her mouth. Tears flooded her eyes and she shook her head. "Oh gosh."

Jax hurried around her to the bedroom. His face was pale when he returned. "I informed Dad. Guards are on their way to take Vikter to Lockup." Shaking his head, he quietly closed the bedroom door. "We should get you to Doc's."

"I'm fine," Violet insisted, but her voice was weak.

Patrick brushed a hand across her back. "It's better to be safe." He looked at Jax, his expression serious. "I can take her. You don't need me here to wait for guards."

Nodding, Jax moved to stand over Vikter's unconscious form and ran a hand down his face. "I can't believe he would do this."

"Really?" Violet asked, but the sarcasm in her voice was lost. Truthfully, she couldn't believe it either. "He thought you were out for his clan, you beat him publicly multiple times, he thought I embarrassed him. He was out for revenge… but this…" She looked down at the teen near her feet. "He completely snapped, didn't he?"

Four guards stormed through the door, interrupting whatever response she would have received. Jax gave a last order to Patrick to make sure she actually went to Doc's before directing his attention to the guards.

Sliding one arm around her waist, Patrick led her out of the commons and down the road. They were both quiet for a while before Violet's weak voice broke the silence.

"Sulfur is the smell of witchcraft. He had a witch with him."

The silence that followed could have been cut with a knife.

"Yes," Patrick finally answered after a few steps. "A powerful one, too. I only came back because Nick's room smelled the same, but his body was on the couch. I couldn't hear you."

"Oh."

He groaned and added, "Alistair also insisted I check on you. We both had a really bad feeling."

"Alistair was worried about me?"

Patrick pulled her to a stop then lowered his head toward hers. His eyes swirled ruby and she sucked in a quick breath. "You are the one thing Alistair and I have in common. It's both a great asset and an incredible hindrance."

Ever so slowly Patrick's eyes returned to the gorgeous golden-flecked hazel she loved.

She placed her palm against his cheek, and he surprised her by leaning into her touch. "Thank you for coming back."

"Always."

His eyes were normal, but there was a hint of a growl in that one word. A promise made by both young man and wolf. A cascade of delightful shivers ran down her spine.

Clearing her throat, Violet took a much-needed step back. It would have been too easy to grab him and kiss him in that moment.

"Can witches create fog?" Violet blurted, loudly.

A hint of warmth touched Patrick's cheeks as he rubbed the back of his neck. "Some witches have the ability to manipulate weather. Which would include fog or mist."

She stared at Patrick with wide, terrified eyes and whispered, "I think I saw them last night."

Confusion passed over his face. "What do you mean you saw them?"

Violet shook her head. "I didn't actually see them."

"What?"

Taking a deep breath, she prepared herself for being called crazy. "It was a nightmare." Violet swallowed the lump in her throat and nodded. "I saw two figures walking toward Alpha House out of this creepy mist. One of them looked up at me through the window, and his eyes were red. I woke up right after that and looked out the window. There wasn't anything there."

Patrick's features softened. "Have you told anyone else this?"

"No. Lexie knows I had a nightmare, but that's it."

He nodded and began leading the way to the medical office again. "Let's keep it that way for now. We can tell Jax and Alpha Draven later."

"Why?"

"Because premonitions are a witch ability. There is enough going on without them worrying what you might be capable of."

Violet's eyes bugged. "I'm not a witch." She shook her head. "That's impossible."

Patrick's warm eyes found hers. "Nothing is impossible."

*****

The visit to Doc's would go down in history as Violet's shortest appointment. Her wounds hadn't reopened, but Doc did warn her away from anymore fighting—not like she'd planned this one in the first place. With that, Doc released them and it wasn't long after that when Alpha Draven summoned Violet and Patrick to Lockup.

Violet flinched away from the grabby hands pawing at her from the barred cells of Lockup. She'd never been inside before, and now she knew why.

Very few of the inmates had silver, bronze, or muted gold eyes.

Crimson gazes followed them down the walk and catcalls rang into the air. The slurs and foul language were abhorrent, but it didn't compare to the disturbing threats thrown their way.

Someone with abnormally long arms snagged her sweater sleeve, making her yelp and jump into the wall on the other side.

Patrick stepped between her and the inmate, drove his elbow into the guy's exposed appendage, then hauled her forward as the guy howled in rage and pain.

"Stay beside me," he told her softly. "I won't let them touch you."

Violet nodded and kept between Patrick and the far wall. The second floor was much quieter and had fewer inmates. Most of which stayed far away from the bars and only cast them casual glances from their cots.

Dismay filled her as she looked over their arrangements. She knew they were in here for good reasons, but their living situations were terrible. Some had torn clothing or were missing a shirt completely. None of them had socks or shoes. The cots looked like they were maybe an inch thick with no pillow or blankets or even sheets in sight.

Not even a Blood Moon pack member deserved to be treated this way. Sadly, most of them had killed someone on accident and succumbed to the rage of blood lust their wolves fell under. For most Blood Moon members, they never wanted to be killers.

Violet chewed on her lower lip and cast a worried look at Patrick. What would happen to him as time went on? Would Alistair eventually win?

They rounded a corner and Violet slowed as a familiar face came into view.

"Scar Face?" Violet wondered out loud.

The man who had partnered up with Ponytail Guy and attacked her and Lexie during the tourney looked up from the book he was reading with a raised brow.

His brown eyes swirled red as he looked her over. A sinister half-smirk exposed one of his fangs before he spoke. "Hello, little miracle."

The scar she'd noticed in the dimming light of sunset looked even more jagged in the bright white lights of Lockup. It ran the length of his face and neck, disappearing under the low V-neck collar of his gray shirt.

"Can I ask you a question?" He set his book down and looked over her thoughtfully.

"We should go," Patrick whispered, but Violet didn't move.

"What would you like to know?"

Delighted she was playing along, Scar Face shifted his seated position on his cot so he was facing her. "How did a wolfless little thing like you manage to knock me out?"

With a shrug, Violet looked at Patrick. "I had a good teacher." She tipped her head to the side in thought as she looked back at Scar Face. "Getting a knee in where the sun don't shine helped as well."

Scar Face's… face… scrunched at the memory. "Yes. That was a cheap shot."

His gaze slipped to Patrick and while they eyed each other Violet looked over the inmate.

Other than a change of clothing, the location and his very short cut hair—which drew attention to his pointy tipped ears—the guy looked the same. She thought the light of a new day would expose something, but her nightmares of that night had kept his image perfectly intact.

"To answer your question," Scar Face dragged his attention off Patrick so he could look at her again. "Yes, I am lycan."

Her brows pulled together. She remembered Patrick saying some lycan possessed special abilities… "Can you read my thoughts?"

Scar Face's brows rose toward the ceiling before he tipped his chin back and let out a hearty laugh. His mirth gave way to a dark chuckle and he gazed at her with amusement, "No, you silly little thing, it's written all over your face." His smarmy eyes looked her up and down, "The real question is… what are *you*?"

"We should catch up to Alpha Draven."

"Hush, Patrick," the lycan snapped, glaring at her companion.

Violet startled at the use of his name. She looked up to find Patrick staring the inmate down; the muscle in his jaw somersaulted, but his face had paled ever so slightly.

They hadn't said his name… had they? How did this lycan—this Blood Moon member—know who Patrick was?

"I have questions," Scar Face smirked and returned his attention to her.

"Be a dear and answer me."

Her face scrunched at his wording. She crossed her arms over her chest and shrugged. "I'm nothing. I have no wolf. No special abilities. I'm basically just a souped-up human."

He clicked his tongue. "I don't believe that for an instant." Ever so slowly, the lycan behind the bars rose to his feet and stalked toward them. "There is something inside of you, Violet Draven. I can feel it."

Knowing *her* name wasn't surprising. If he knew she was the miracle twin, he would know her name. It was still disturbing coming from his mouth though.

"Enough!" Alpha Draven shouted, startling her into taking a step back as he stormed down the walkway.

Violet ran into Patrick who stabilized her when she lost her balance.

Turning to glare at Scar Face, Alpha Draven paused. "How did you get a book?"

Scar Face sneered, "I asked nicely."

A loud snort left her father, which was a sound she wasn't sure she'd ever heard him make, before his bruising grip dragged her away. "Let's move. We aren't here to talk with this traitor."

"Traitor?" Violet wondered out loud, looking back at the lycan who watched her with hungry eyes as they hurried back the way the alpha had come.

Alpha Draven finally released her just outside another hallway, and she rubbed the spot where his fingers and dug into her flesh.

"Vikter's cell is halfway down the walk." He explained, ignoring his daughter and looking at Patrick instead. "If he sees or hears anyone other than the three of you, he will stop talking. Which is asinine because you're going to tell me everything he says the moment you are done speaking to him, do I make myself clear?"

Jax stepped out of the hallway and sighed. "Yes, Dad, we get it."

The alpha's eyes swirled molten gold which reflected in Jax's gaze. "Speak to me like that again, son, and you'll regret it."

Swallowing the lump in his throat, Jax nodded. "Understood."

With Alpha Draven's dismissal, the three of them made their way down the walk.

"Did you like my surprise, Draven?" Vikter's voice reached them before they had made it to his cell, followed by a low, creepy laugh.

There wasn't another inmate in this hallway which was curious, but part of Violet was grateful as well.

"You've really lost it if you would stoop so low as to kill others to get back at me." Jax turned to stare into the cell when they reached it.

Vikter's sadistic, angry smile contorted his face as he looked over the three of them. "Killing them was only the pre-game."

With the speed of events earlier, Violet hadn't been able to get a good image of Vikter, but now she almost wished she hadn't.

Unlike Scar Face, Vikter looked very different than the last time they'd spoken.

Old Vikter had a haughty air about him and a nasty tendency to be paranoid. His blond hair was always kept short and styled and his clothing reeked of money.

Tourney attack Vikter was slumped, disheveled, and dirty.

Blood Moon Vikter looked flat-out crazy with red eyes that never faded and were nearly luminescent in the bright lighting. His hair laid haphazardly in every direction, a few inches longer than she'd ever seen it. Heavy, dark circles hung around his eyes, and he'd lost weight—looking like he hadn't been eating nearly enough since the tourney attack.

"Are their deaths what turned your eyes red?" Violet asked. "How could you do something like that just because you were mad at Jax?"

Vikter chuckled darkly while his blood-red eyes roamed freely over her. Patrick shifted so he stood slightly in front of her and Vikter's grin grew. "Oh no, my little snack. I've been killing since the tourney attack." One corner of his mouth pulled up into a nasty grin. "You see, I found others that were happy to join my cause—" His head dipped to the side, "perhaps for their own reasons, but the outcome will be the same."

Tension rippled across Patrick's shoulders. "And what outcome is that?"

Vikter looked at him with an expression of boredom, but didn't respond. His gaze slipped to Jax. "You should never have threatened to take Stanislaus from me."

Anger curled Jax's lips back in a snarl as he stepped forward. "I never said that! I told you, you weren't fit to be an alpha, and that your clan would be better off with a different one. Clearly, your clan agreed with me seeing as you were demoted due to your paranoia."

"Lies," Vikter hissed, his face contorted with rage into a deranged beast.

Jax clenched his jaw, then shook his head. "I never wanted your clan, Vikter. I still don't."

"LIES!" Vikter lurched forward, slamming into the bars.

A loud snap echoed through the cells, making Violet jump. Vikter collapsed to the ground breathing heavily as the last of the electricity sizzled off the bars.

Crazed laughter rose into the air from Vikter's prone position.

Violet stared in horror. He'd gone mad. His paranoia had eaten away at him, and being demoted made him snap. That was the only explanation for this.

"You will be hurt, Draven." Vikter rose onto an elbow and shook his head. "So much worse than I've been. You will lose everyone you love." Crimson eyes lifted to Violet and he scowled. "Starting with my snack."

"Why?" Violet asked, cutting off whatever Patrick was about to say and he gave her an uncertain look. "Why me?"

Slowly, Vikter rolled to his feet. He approached the bars, but didn't touch them again. "You'll hurt them the most."

Low growls echoed in the hallway coming from the young men protecting her. She placed a hand on Patrick's arm and tried to step around him, but he wrapped his arm around her waist to keep her from venturing too close.

"Did you choose this?" Violet asked. It mattered, even if he was crazy now. "Were you so desperate for revenge that you took another's life?"

Vikter laughed, "I've been working with Blood Moon since my title was revoked. I signaled the tourney attack. I drew first blood—my initiation into the pack."

Disgust rippled through Violet and she shook her head. "What's the name of the witch who helped you attack our clan mates?"

Vikter snorted. "Even if I had her name, I wouldn't tell you. Witches like to keep their identities a secret." He eyed his bloody hands while he spoke, "She was fantastic, though; taking out the guards along the fence, calling an incredible mist that engulfed us and hid our movement in case anyone was watching…"

Violet's mouth went dry. He was describing her dream.

"…and creating a soundproof barrier while I tore your two little friends into pieces. When we finished, she told me I had one more job to do. I knew it would be the perfect moment to kill you."

"You failed."

"Maybe." Vikter shrugged as he replied to her. "But this is just the beginning. I'll get another chance."

"I've heard enough," Patrick growled and led her toward the exit. "Enjoy your time behind bars, Stravek."

"I have a message for you, Cowen!" Vikter called. "Blood Moon is eager for you to hear it."

Patrick stopped to look at the crazed wolven.

Vikter's sadistic grin shot goosebumps across Violet's arms, and she barely suppressed the shiver that rolled down her spine.

"We know what you are. We know where you are. We know what you did…" Vikter's deranged sneer spread, and he whispered, "We're coming for you."

The story continues in

Moon & Ruin

Book 2 of the Sentinel Rising series

Acknowledgments

How do you put a heart full of love and gratitude on paper? Honestly, you can't! This book has only been in the making for a couple of years, but my desire to be an author has been lifelong. I have so many stories and worlds to share! I'm just getting started! And even just starting out, I have so many people who have helped make this dream a reality. I know that number will continue to grow and I'm excited to share this journey with you!

Richard—love of my life and eternal companion—thank you for your unwavering love and support. You fill my life with love and laughter and geekiness! You helped me see that I was good enough. You helped me realize that I am smart enough. I know you're not a reader, but you are a fantastic sounding board and problem solver and are always ready to hear the newest story idea that has flown into my head. I love you with all of my heart.

Mom, you are the best cheerleader and supporter a daughter could ask for. Even when I know something needs a lot of work, you're always there to remind me of the good in it. Thank you for always asking for updates and sharing your love of me and this book with the world!

Dad, without you the fight scenes I write would be empty. Watching your katas was always inspiring and relaxing. Your love and practice of Shoto-kan are always in the back of my mind when I write any training, sparring, or fighting sequence.

To my siblings, thanks for waiting for me to open up and show my true colors. Thank you for never giving up on me. I love that we are friends by choice! Thank you for your love, support, and excitement of this process and this book!

Tony, thank you for telling me to trust my own voice. I can't adequately thank you for the time you took to read and edit for me. Thank you for your love, for the best bear hugs, and for being my big brother.

To the best alpha reader in the world, Erin. I love you, girl, and miss your face. Thank you for being excited about this story even when it was barebones! You made the Moaning Cavern come alive! Thank you for sharing your experience with me and allowing me to use it in this book. I truly wouldn't be the writer I am today without you. Time and space will never dull our friendship.

To the outlaws! I love you. I'm so happy you are part of my family. Thank you for your friendship, love of books, Cupbop, and Sodalicious.

To the Dust Jackets, may we always enjoy talking about books and geeking over new ideas! I'm not sure I would have ever become an author without you showing me the way. Thank you for all of your help, there is too much to list here, but thank you. I can't wait for that book signing.

A special thanks to my beta readers! Denise Nelson, Debby Barry, Angel Call, Tony Newell, Peaches, Heather Frost, Kimberly Frost, Julie Mortensen, Erin Kasper, Kim Campbell Thank you for reading, making notes, edits, texts, visits, and making time in your busy schedules to read this book. It wouldn't have become what it is today without you. You're amazing!!!

Thank you to my early readers for surprising me and exceeding my expectations. You helped encourage me to keep going.

A huge shoutout to Irlen Institute for helping me and my family. Thank you for opening the doors of possibility and helping me realize a love for reading and storytelling.

And finally, thank YOU! Thank you for giving this book a chance, reading it, and leaving reviews. Thank you for sharing this story and your excitement.

*** If you enjoyed Sun & Blood, please consider leaving a review! It helps more than you know. Thank you!***

About the Author

Crystal Frost is excited to kick off her writing career with her debut novel Sun & Blood and the Sentinel Rising series. She is a sucker for action packed fiction (mostly fantasy), complex characters, and breathtaking slow burn romances. She hopes to write exactly that and leave imprints on her reader's hearts. As a dyslexic author, she is thrilled to be beating the odds and living her dream.

Although she was raised in California, Crystal is a transplant, and current resident, to the snow-capped mountains of Utah. She spends most of her non-writing time being a mom to three rambunctious kids, a fur mom to Merlin the Poodle, and geeking out with her husband. Obsessing over Harry Potter and Zelda may play a part in her life as well.

Learn more about Crystal at frostcrystal.com

www.ingramcontent.com/pod-product-compliance
Lightning Source LLC
Chambersburg PA
CBHW030547310726
48979CB00010B/2070/J

* 9 7 8 1 9 5 7 0 5 1 0 1 7 *